'Samara' is a novel I wrote 10 years ago at a dark period in my life. Creating these characters created such a release of emotions for me. I will forever be grateful for the journey writing this novel has taken me on and the joy it has brought me. I hope you guys enjoy reading it as much as I enjoyed writing it.

Domonique Martin

PROLOGUE

Brooklyn, New York 1992

"Baby he's just a co-worker I swear to you," she begged him to believe her, knowing that his temper was quick to surface. She was running out of lies to explain the bruises.

"You were on the phone pretty fucking late last night, bitch!" He screamed at her. He used his two-hundred and ninety pound frame against her, pinning her to the wall. She saw in his eyes that there was no talking him down. He was going to hit her. He didn't believe that she and Herman were working on a project that was approaching its deadline. He wouldn't even listen to her explain that Herman was gay. Herman had no interest in her and she had none in him. He didn't care. No man was allowed to see her or talk to her unless he approved. He never approved. The TV blared reruns of 'The Jefferson's'. She could still smell the pepperoni pizza they had ordered. One minute they were eating as a family and the next, she was begging for mercy. More and more frequently, nights seemed to end up like this. She gulped down her fear and tried one more time to get through to him.

"He just wanted to go over some numbers, that's all baby! Please believe me! I would never do anything to jeopardize our relationship." She tried unsuccessfully to convince him. His skin on her was hot with anger. She saw his nostrils flare. That's how she knew what was coming next.

"Lying bitch!" He slapped her across the face. She didn't scream. She was used to this. She choked it back and shook off the dizziness it brought on. The slaps didn't bother her as much anymore. It was the punches and the kicks that came next that always got the best of her. She lay cowered on the floor in a ball clutching her stomach, shielding her head as he continued his assault. She could feel the pain spread throughout her body. Punch after punch, kick after kick. The pain intensified. She was close to passing out. She prayed his energy would run out.

"Mommy!" Their daughter screamed through tears and ran into the hallway. She looked up and saw the fearlessness on her five-year-old daughters' face.

"Don't hurt mommy!" She ran towards her father and used all the strength a five-year-old fist could muster, and punched him on his arm. He stood up in surprise. Everything stopped. She looked at her baby girl. So strong and unafraid. She turned her swollen face to him and saw something dark come across his face. He wasn't looking at their daughter like she was his princess anymore. She was now the enemy. She had challenged him. Reprimanded him. Turned on him. He turned towards his baby girl and pushed her away. Her pigtails bounced as she flew backwards into the living room, hitting the lamp off the coffee table. Her daughter's body lay still and unmoving.

Every ounce of fear she previously had disappeared. Seeing her daughter's motionless body broke something inside her. Cradling her stomach, she pushed herself up with one arm from the floor and lunged at him. "DON'T TOUCH MY BABY!" She screamed, veins bulging, spit flying out of her mouth. All the rage she had felt the last six years came rushing out of her as she reached for his throat. She was going to kill him. He could hit her all he wanted, but no one would hurt her child. She dug the fingernails on her left hand into his throat and raked the nails of her right hand across his face. She wanted to claw his eyes out.

"SHIT!" He groaned before grabbing a hold of both her wrists. She ground her teeth and tried to kick him in the balls. He gripped her wrists tighter, then he head butt her and pushed her backwards into the darkened hallway. He heard her body make impact with something solid. She made a gurgling sound, then went completely silent. He touched his neck and felt where she had broken the skin. Blood was on his fingers. "Crazy bitch," he mumbled to himself. He slowly walked over to the wall and flipped the light switch up. Her body lay sideways facing the opposing wall. He couldn't see her face. But he could see a thin line splitting the back of her head in two. Blood steadily streamed out and stained the carpet. He looked at her chest, it wasn't moving so he knew she wasn't breathing. Blood and brain matter were on the end table that was in the hallway. He watched the blood flow, pooling around her head for a few minutes trying to decide if he could get rid of both bodies by himself. The voices inside his head told him he had done a good job. She was a lying slut that deserved to die! Yeah, she did, he told himself.

"MOOOOOOMMMMMMYYYYYYY!" His daughter's screams pierced through his haze. He watched his daughter run to her mother's dead body. He hated the anguished cries coming from her mouth. The voices told him to get rid of her too. He walked towards her, his steps faltering as he saw his hand reach out to grab the back of his daughter's neck. He didn't have control of himself. He panicked. His shirt was soaked in sweat. It was too late for this family to work. He had another family in another city. He could go there and hide out until he figured out what to do next. He looked back at his daughter's face, twisted in pain and sadness. She lay down over her mother's dead body. He felt nothing. Fuck her, she wasn't worth getting caught. He took off, running out of the house, down the steps and through the streets until he got to the nearest train station.

Present Day

SAMARA

I was bored, lonely, and horny. That was the only reason I was sitting in this café on a Sunday night. I knew ninety percent of the crowd would be male. The café was packed with diners and the music level was low. But men were on the prowl, as always. I crossed and uncrossed my legs. The friction from the rubbing was making me even hornier. I sipped my iced tea and scanned the room for prospects. There were your usual types there. The 'gangstas' whose pants sagged so low you could see the back of their damn kneecaps. The cocky types that made women come to them. And last but not least, the fine ass brothas who stared at you from across the room, calculating when to make the first move. I wasn't one for playing games but I couldn't lie, sometimes it was very tantalizing. This café may have been known for its waffles and industrial loft-style setting, but to me it was a singles haven. A goldmine. Usually I would be here with my girls Anna, Tatyana, and Sandra. But tonight I was on a mission. I needed to get laid. It wasn't to the point where I would do anyone, but it was getting close to it. The last time I met a guy at this café was about two months ago. I should have known it was a mistake to go back to his apartment because he was the 'gangsta' type. He talked a lot of shit and promised that he would have me screaming his name all night long. Of course I knew that was bullshit, but I was horny and wanted to believe anything that came out of his mouth. The only thing on my mind was cumming. We walked into his apartment complex and the hallway was full of guys scattered around like roaches. Graffiti was sprayed all over the walls and the smell of weed was the only scent in the air. I almost turned back when I saw a baby crawling around in the hallway unattended. I took a deep breath and told myself I wouldn't be here long if he knew what he was doing. I ignored all of that and walked into his apartment. He flipped the light switch but no lights came on.

"Oh shit!" He cursed under his breath. His name was Deondre'. Deondre' apparently hadn't paid his light bill. That was cool though, because I wouldn't have been able to cum looking at his face anyway. He was in his early twenties and still had acne. It wasn't your run of the mill acne either. There were big bumps, three shades darker than his skin tone. It was like a Nestle crunch bar had exploded on his face. I was only attracted to his muscular body. He was a little taller than me, and in the café I had seen a big bulge in his pants, so I overlooked his shortcomings. He wore a du rag over old braids, like the du rag would magically make them look fresh again. I ignored that as well. I was so horny that day that I was willing to overlook a lot to cum. It was pathetic. I didn't have a steady boyfriend, so I had to stoop to low levels to get off when I needed to. It wasn't that I couldn't get a man. I just seemed to lose interest quickly with them. A man had to bring more than a banging body and a handsome face to the table, so a one night stand had seemed like a better idea at the time just to get some release.

"Watch your step," he said. *He had better be the bomb or I was blowing this whole building up!*

"Just guide me to your room." I told him impatiently wanting to get started. It was pitch black in the apartment. His hand grabbed mine and I walked slowly behind him. I sat down on something hard and heard a loud creaky noise that sounded like bed springs. I unbuttoned the four buttons holding my blazer closed and exposed my naked breasts underneath. It was warm that night so I'd just decided to not wear a shirt. I shimmied out of my black shorts and slid them down my legs while waiting for him to get undressed. I kicked my heels off and sat leaning back on my elbows looking at him, my legs open. There was a sliver of light coming through the window in his room and I could see him staring down in awe at my body. Most men did that the first time I got naked in front of them. I am not happy about it, but I am a member of the itty bitty titty committee. I'm not an A cup but I'm a small C, a very small C. But what I lacked in the breast department, I more than made up for in the hips, legs, and ass department. When I was younger my dad was constantly cursing somebody out over my ass. Men both young and old. My ass wasn't abnormally large, but you had to have big hands to palm it. I was proud of it and did a lot of lunges and squats to keep it toned. It paid off.

"Well? What are you waiting for?" I asked, annoyed. This wasn't a date so I didn't see why he was prolonging this moment. We both knew what we were there for.

"I'm just savoring the moment," he said trying to make his voice deeper. I almost laughed but didn't want to spoil the mood.

"Well take a picture. Now come over here and show me what you've been bragging about all night." He took his clothes off and dropped his pants. I instantly sat up and looked at him dumbfounded. At the café there had been a huge bulge in his pants, but looking at him now I was trying to figure out where the hell it went. He couldn't have been holding anything over four inches down there, and that was with it fully erect.

I kept staring at his crotch in confusion. He looked self-conscious, which I hated in men, and bent down to pick up his pants.

I looked down and saw a pair of socks balled up inside his jeans. Apparently he had been faking his bulge. What a waste!

"You jackass!" I said in irritation and put my clothes back on. I pushed him out of my way and felt my way out of his dark apartment.

"Sorry!" He yelled as I opened his apartment door. I ignored him and kept going.

"Damn you got a fat ass! You doin' the walk of shame?" One of the roaches yelled out at me from down the hallway when I walked out the apartment. I looked at the group of them gathered in the corner smoking weed. I thought about walking over there and trying my luck with one of them. But I heard that when a man was high he did not perform well in the bedroom. Plus, I wasn't in the mood to smell like an ashtray or a skunk. So I gave him the finger and walked out to my car. I punched the dashboard and drove home. That night I had to rely on my fingers for pleasure. It was so frustrating. I'd just wanted a good lay, just one.

That was two months ago and I still hadn't gotten any yet. It wasn't like I couldn't call one of my exes or past flames, but I needed some fresh and new dick. Plus, I didn't want the drama of calling an ex. They always thought the hook-up meant something more. There was jazz playing and a bunch of thirsty women walking back and forth past the tables. They were so obvious. I just sipped my drink and waited. Three men had already tried and failed at getting my attention. This time I was being a little pickier. I looked at my watch and told myself if I didn't get a decent offer in ten minutes, I would go home and use my middle finger like I'd never used it before. Ten minutes passed and I had had enough. I stood up to motion for the waitress to get the check.

"You're leaving already? The night is still young." I turned and saw two tall sexy ass men walking towards my table. I smiled at them and smiled inwardly. Their timing was impeccable. I sat back down slowly.

"I was getting bored sitting here by myself so I decided to call it a night," I said. I wasn't going anywhere now. They were so good looking I didn't know who to focus on. There was a resemblance between them that was evident. One was light skinned, the color of an ice cream cone, with hair so short he was almost bald. His skin looked soft and probably tasted like heaven. He had a strong jaw line and long eye lashes. His perfect teeth were bright white as he smiled down at me. I could tell that he lived in the gym. I could see that his nails were cut short and clean. I didn't know his name yet so I nicknamed him Cream. The other one I called Cocoa. His skin was a mix between the color of brandy and almonds. He was taller than his friend and a little slimmer. I pegged him as a runner or basketball player maybe. He had his hair cut short, but had a wavy curl pattern running through his hair. His eyes were hazel. They were what I called bedroom eyes. Every time you looked into them, you wanted to head straight to the bedroom. His face was round and when he smiled his whole face lit up. It was hard to keep my eyes off of his full lips. He was holding a glass of lemonade and an iced tea, which I assumed was for me.

"Do you want some company?" Cocoa asked me. I looked at both of them and thought, *this could get interesting.*

"Sure, why not." I looked at Cocoa as he sat to my right, and then at Cream who sat to my left. They smelled so masculine.

"What's your name beautiful?" Cream asked me.

"Samara." I replied, appraising both men.

"Is that for me?" I asked Cocoa, pointing to the drink he set down on the table.

"Yes it is. That's what you're drinking right?" He was so damn fine. He smiled at me and I felt heat in between my legs.

"Yeah it is. So what are your names?" I didn't have time for idle chit chat. I wasn't playing games tonight. I was more than ready for some action. Cocoa spoke up first.

"I'm Ryson and that's my brother Dwayne," he said pointing at Cream. I pulled my head back in confusion and looked from one to the other.

"We have the same dad," Dwayne chimed in.

"Oh okay. So what's up? Are you here alone tonight?" I sipped the drink slowly. Dwayne leaned in and whispered in my ear.

"We came with somebody, but you caught our attention." His voice in my ear was deep and sexy. I wanted him.

"Oh really? So what makes me so special?" I looked at Ryson, who had gone quiet. He downed the rest of his drink and licked his bottom lip. Now I wanted him. I was so confused and turned on at the same time. I knew at some point I was going to have to choose, but for now I wanted to keep this flirtatious game going. I loved the attention.

"It could be these thick thighs." Ryson looked down at my crossed legs. I wore a little black dress. It was strapless, tight, and stopped just below my thigh. It hugged my body and accentuated my ass just the way men liked. When I sat down it rose about two more inches, exposing more thigh.

"Or it could be all of this pretty hair." Dwayne took a tendril in his hand and twirled it around his finger. I was half black and half Cuban. I wore my hair out wild and curly most of the time not wanting to tend to the crazy mane. Men seemed to like it like that.

"Or it could be that wagon you're sitting on." Ryson laughed when I blushed. They were both coming on real strong. I had to make a decision quick. Maybe they could make the decision easier for me.

"So now that you have my attention, what are you going to do with it?" I asked boldly. I was never known for being shy. The brothers looked at each other and then Dwayne nodded to Ryson. Ryson leaned into me and kissed me softly on the neck. His soft lips pressed onto my skin and then his tongue slowly slid up my neck and inside my ear. That was my spot. My body quivered. I bit my lip and put my hand on his cheek. I was turning my body towards Ryson, when Dwayne put his hand under my chin and pulled my face towards his, breaking my contact with Ryson. He roughly shoved his tongue into my mouth, causing my pussy to throb in excitement. I loved his aggression. His tongue was all over the place, in my mouth, licking my tongue, and running along my lips. I tried to keep up, but he was devouring my mouth. He grabbed my thigh and uncrossed my legs. I knew people were watching but I didn't care. Dwayne slid his hand underneath my dress. He stopped kissing me when he realized I didn't have on any panties. My head was fuzzy with lust and I wanted both of them. I was ready to make my decision.

"I guess you both forgot about me sitting over at that table by my damn self!" An irate female stalked up to the table. She looked at the brothers pissed, but she cut her eyes at me. Her hair was cut into a shoulder-length bob with a blunt bang. She had a pointy nose and slim frame. She was holding in the breast department, but had no hips and not a lot of ass. Her fake lashes almost completely covered her actual eyes. But she was pretty. She put her hands on her hips and sucked her teeth. Her dark blue jeans looked like they were painted on. Her black sequined top did not cover her stomach. Looking at her stilettos, I could tell she was high maintenance.

"Shar, nobody made a commitment to you," Dwayne said to her, never taking his hand from underneath my dress. It felt kind of naughty to be sitting in a public place fooling around with two brothers, one of whom was using his middle finger to circle around my clit. I tried not to react to the spasms going through my body.

"You came here with me. You can't just leave me over there by myself!" She sat down at the table then. I didn't say anything because this wasn't my battle. I didn't come here with her, and I damn sure didn't force them to sit with me at my table. Ryson got up and sighed heavily, like he had the weight of the world on his shoulders.

"Can I talk to you for a second?" he asked Shar, sounding disappointed. I guess my decision was made for me. As hot and bothered as I was from what Dwayne was doing, I was going to choose Ryson. From the way he kissed me, I could tell he would be a tender lover. Plus, there was just something about him that was very alluring. But nothing was wrong with a good old fashioned fuck. Dwayne pulled on my hair to get my attention when he noticed me watching Ryson walk away.

"Let's go. You're going home with me tonight," he said. He was so sure of himself. Just like me. We got up to leave and I snuck a glance back at Ryson and Shar talking by the bar. He was talking to her and watching me. Oh well, it wasn't meant to be I guess. I paid my bill and walked with Dwayne outside into the cool spring air. Dwayne said he came with Ryson.

"I drove." I said pointing to my white Mercedes-Benz SLR McLaren across the parking lot. His eyes went wide for a split second in appreciation of the car, then we walked towards it. I got behind the wheel and started the car up.

"Where to?" I was ready to get this show on the road, literally.

"Your place?" he suggested, purring. I smiled and tried to persuade him otherwise.

"How about we go to your place?" I asked. I wasn't comfortable with people I barely knew in my home. He shrugged, letting me know it didn't matter. Then he gave me his address in a nicer section of town that wasn't that far from the café. But with all of the sexual tension in the car, I didn't think we would make it without pulling over.

I pulled out of the parking lot. At the first light, Dwayne put his hand in between my legs again.

"Ah… I don't think you should do… that while I'm driving." I moaned, but didn't stop him. I gripped the steering wheel and inhaled as pleasure sparked inside me. These were the first touches I'd had from a man in months. I didn't realize how much I'd missed it. I felt his middle finger go inside me and I gasped. I tried to concentrate on driving. I had to remind myself that red meant stop and green meant go. His thumb played with my clit and I felt another finger enter me. I thought I would swerve off of the road. If this was any indication of the night ahead, I was glad I ended up with him. He now had two thick fingers inside me and was pulling them in and out, in and out. I looked down at the speedometer and saw I was only going fifteen miles an hour. I opened my legs wider. I couldn't concentrate on driving anymore when he leaned over and bit me on the neck. The burst of pain and pleasure was almost unbearable.

"Oh god!" I whimpered as I pulled up to his house. I parallel parked with the butt of my car in the street, but I didn't care. As soon as the ignition was off, I took off my seat belt, and threw my body on Dwayne. I moaned and kissed him deeply. He put his hands in my hair and grabbed a handful. If I had to compare all the men that I'd been with to Dwayne, there would be no comparison. None of them excited me like Dwayne. He pulled my head back.

"Let's take this inside." He growled on my lips and pulled me out the passenger side door with him. He held my wrist tight and dragged me up the few steps to the front door and inside his house. It looked spacious. Probably a three bedroom bungalow. Most homes in this section of town were. I didn't have time to really take it in. Dwayne was dragging me behind him and had picked up his pace. I did see a plush tan carpet throughout the first floor and a spacious open kitchen. We were up the stairs and in his bedroom thirty seconds after getting out of the car. He pushed me into the dark room and turned on the light. I backed up slowly and lowered my eyelids in lust. I threw my keys on his dresser. My stomach was doing somersaults in anticipation. I knew he was going to fuck the shit out of me and I was ready. His eyes raged with desire and I could see his bulge growing inside his jeans. He looked ferocious as a lion as he rushed towards me, crossing the room in three strides before pushing me onto his bed.

"Oh shit," I whispered. He grabbed me by the neck and pulled my face to his.

"You ever been choked during sex?" he asked me, running his tongue over my lips. His body was on top of mine pinning me down. My legs were spread wide and my hands were wrapped around his wrists. He tightened his grip on my neck and I suddenly got nervous. I shook my head no to his question and he smiled. He let my neck go and I caught my breath. He got back up and undressed. I sat up and pulled my dress over my head. My nipples were hard as hell. There was a wet puddle on his bed where I was sitting from my juices. I was excited about what he was about to do to me. He seemed sexually dangerous and I wanted to see how far he would go. I looked at his dick and held my breath, he was blessed down there. He got back on top of me and started kissing me again. His cologne permeated his bedroom. I ran my hands up and down his smooth, muscular back and hooked my legs around his waist. Our warm bodies became entangled. My heart raced at the thought of being with him. I was long overdue for an orgasm, and I could hardly contain myself. He was so hard, it felt like a hammer was poking me in the stomach. I ached so much for him to enter me but I didn't want to be the aggressor. This was my night and he was going to take care of me, not the other way around. He stopped kissing me and put his hands around my throat again. This time he squeezed tight and I gagged. I grabbed his wrists and looked at him in shock. His face was stone cold as he constricted my airway. I felt my clit pulsating as I struggled to breathe. He smiled devilishly, then pushed his hard dick inside of me fast and hard. My eyes went wild and I felt a rush of pleasure gush through me. I couldn't breathe, but I was getting hornier as the seconds ticked by. He lifted me up in the air and pinned me against his headboard. My legs were wide open. He pounded into me and started screaming in my face.

"Cum! You know you want to cum!" And I did want to so bad. My head hit the headboard repeatedly as he went faster and harder. He was so big, it was a mixture of pleasure and pain. I didn't want him to stop. My pussy was so wet I was dripping. I started to get lightheaded from not having air. One of my hands let go of his wrists. I was getting so wet it was scary. No one had ever choked me during sex before, and it was electrifying. I felt myself about to cum just as my eyelids started to get heavy.

"Don't pass out girl, that nut is going to feel so good." He grunted, pumping into me harder and deeper. He put his mouth on mine. I felt the orgasm coming but didn't think I could hold on. He loosened his grip around my throat a little and I was able to steal a few small breaths. That was all I needed to hang on. I grabbed his hips, helping him pump into me. I wondered how it would feel to choke him, so I did. His eyes opened wide in shock. I didn't know how much pressure to apply so I didn't squeeze his throat tight.

"You like that don't you? You like choking me you fucking freak!" His voice was raspy from the lack of oxygen. I started to cum after that. I loved dirty talk, it just drove me crazy.

"That's right, cum on this dick girl!" He yelled in my face. He tightened his grip around my neck and I did the same to him. He grunted and grabbed one of my breasts. I wanted to scream "Oh god, oh god, oh my fucking god!" at the top of my lungs, but I couldn't. Instead I came hard all over his dick. My whole body began to spasm and a tingling sensation ran up and down my back. My eyes nearly bugged out of my head when the orgasm took over my body. We let go of each other's necks and he pulled out of me.

"FUUCCKKK!" I screamed out when I was able to breathe again. He laughed and flipped me over onto my stomach.

"Give me a second Dwayne." I panted as I tried to regain my composure. I got on my knees and crawled away from him. I didn't think I could go again so soon, but I knew he wasn't done with me. He grabbed my thighs and roughly pulled me back to him.

"Nope. You don't get any breaks in my bed." He reached into his drawer and pulled out a pair of handcuffs. I was too spent to fight him, as he cuffed my hands behind my back. He pulled my hips back towards him.

"At least let me catch my breath then." I begged, feeling horny all over again at his assertiveness. He grabbed me by the hair and pulled me backwards.

"OUCH!" I screamed as he gripped my hair tight. The next thing I knew he was inside me again, ramming his dick deeper than the first time.

"AHHH I CAN'T TAKE IT!" The mix of pleasure and pain was killing me. I couldn't believe I was getting fucked so hard. I wasn't as ready for him as I thought I would be. He kept going, ignoring my pleas and in a weird way that turned me on too. He grabbed my hair tighter and pushed my face down hard onto the pillow. I felt him smack my ass.

"Look at that fat ass bounce!" He grunted and smacked it again even harder.

"PLEASE I CAN'T TAKE IT!" I tried again to get him to slack up a bit, to no avail.

"You want me to slow down?" He was panting now. I felt his sweat dripping on my back.

"YES!" I screamed out in pleasure.

"Okay." He stopped completely. He took his dick out of me painstakingly slow, then slammed it back into me with so much force I choked on the saliva that was in my mouth.

"DWAYNE!" I whined as I started to cum again. The pain was telling me to make him stop, but the satisfaction was telling me to let him keep going. I didn't know which one to listen to. He took his dick out slow again and smashed it back inside me. I couldn't take it anymore.

"DWAYNE STOP!" I screamed and bit the pillow.

"You're going to regret it if I do, trust me," he said in a low voice. He didn't stop. He pulled out slow and rammed into me three more times. I started to whimper because it felt so damn lovely. The more of him he gave me, the harder I came. He drove into me again then started fucking me fast and hard. I lifted my head up in surprise as I came again. This time I was able to scream out.

"OOOOO GGGODDDDDDD!" I screamed so loud my head hurt.

"WHAT THE FUCK DWAYNE!" I screamed at him as he continued to pound into me.

"Ha-ha, you know you love it!" He taunted me. My pussy was throbbing with pain but it was dripping with cum. I was in for a long night.

SHAR

That flat-chested, mixed blood, big stank booty bitch! Just when Ryson and Dwayne were starting to really pay me some attention tonight, they had to see her ass. They were waiting for the right time to approach her after seeing her turn down three other losers. I was having a good time with Dwayne and Ryson. I secretly hoped they wouldn't notice when she came in. With her fucking long curly hair, she looked like a fake ass Puerto Rican. She just had to have those almond-shaped eyes and those fucking plump lips didn't she? I hated her at first glance. When Ryson's eyes went to her, I knew it was over. Ryson ordered an iced tea then they just got up and left. Next thing I know they're walking over to her table just as she was about to leave. She was such a whore. What type of woman would openly flirt with two men at the same time? And with brothers at that? I mean, I was doing the same thing but it was different for us. We had a connection. I saw Ryson look down at her thighs under the table. I wasn't what you would call thick, but I was working with a little something-something. I didn't see the big fucking deal about her anyway. I fumed inside when Dwayne twisted one of her little nappy curls around his finger. Whenever I thought that it would just be us against the world, they wanted to add another person to the mix. I met Ryson and Dwayne about four years ago. We'd realized how much we had in common. We all instantly hit it off and were inseparable until they found another female they wanted to play with, that is. I had slept with both of them over the years but neither really committed to me like I wanted them to. There would be times when I thought Ryson would ask me to be his girlfriend. Then there were times when I felt really close to Dwayne. But when they set their minds to something there was no arguing with them. They knew what they wanted and how to play the game to get it. Dwayne nodded to Ryson, then Ryson leaned over and kissed that bitch on the neck. I nearly fell out of my seat. I knew if I went over there tripping, they would probably curse me out. So I sat and watched heatedly. When Dwayne turned her towards him I lost all my control. He was kissing her like he kissed me and I wasn't about to have that. I got up and stalked over to her little table.

"Hello! Did you forget that I was over there?" I asked irritated and a bit jealous of the attention she was getting. She eyed me up and down, trying to size me up. I knew what I was working with so it didn't bother me. Dwayne had the nerve to tell me some bullshit about not being committed to me. Like for real? Both of them came there with me! What was more of a commitment than that? I sat down, trying to spoil their little party. Ryson got up and asked could he talk to me for a second. I could tell he didn't want to. Obviously he wanted her for himself, and by walking off with me he was forfeiting his chance to be with her. Oh well, he could suck it the fuck up. Somebody was going to pay me some attention! We walked over to the bar and he paid his tab.

"We can stay and just chill together if you want." I whispered in his ear. He wasn't paying me any mind. His eyes were locked on her ass sashaying out of the door with Dwayne. What a hoe! I felt pity for her though. She was in for a big surprise with Dwayne. Dwayne liked to fuck you hard, real hard. One time Dwayne fucked me so hard, I couldn't walk straight for days. But that was how Dwayne expressed his love to me. Ryson looked at his watch like he had somewhere to go. I got the hint.

"Can you take me home?" I asked and tried to give him a sexy pose.

"Can't." He dashed my hopes quick. I pouted my lips in frustration and walked back over to our table. That was the most attention Ryson had paid me in a long time. It was kind of nice, even if it was just a front. I was surprised they even agreed to let me tag along tonight. They acted like they didn't want anyone to know I existed. Maybe one of these men would take me home tonight. Maybe I should go home with two of them, that way I could pretend one was Ryson and the other was Dwayne. Yes, that's what I would do. Ryson left the café without looking back at me. How could he leave me here with no ride home? They had picked me up, so how the fuck did they expect me to get home without them? A cab? Did they even care? I swear sometimes if we weren't so connected I would have left both of their asses. But they knew just what to say to pull me back in every time. I walked over to a table where two guys were seated and cleared my throat. It was time to hitch a ride home.

SAMARA

I stared up at the ceiling fan and watched it spin in circles over and over. I exhaled. It was four-thirty in the morning and Dwayne was knocked out. My body felt like it had been hit by a truck. Dwayne made me cum three more times, before he had finally bust his nut in the crack of my ass. He had put me on his lap and I rode his dick while I was still handcuffed. He bent me over the edge of the bed with one leg on the bed and one leg on the floor. Then Dwayne sat me on his face and overwhelmed my clit with his tongue. It was long and thick just like his dick, and he knew exactly how to use it. I was close to my sixth orgasm when he stuck his finger in my ass. He moved his finger in and out as he continued to suck on my clit. I let the orgasm that I was holding in spill out of me. I'd been properly fucked. I was exhausted and I had to pee. I didn't think I could walk, but I had been holding it for almost an hour. I took a deep breath and put one leg over the edge of the bed.

"Shit!" It hurt to open my legs. I ached with a vengeance. It felt like my pussy had run a dick-a-thon. Dwayne had shown me no mercy. I had pleaded, begged, cried, and screamed for him to slow down or stop, but of course he didn't. When it was all over, I felt so relieved. I couldn't lie, I had at least six orgasms, but I was paying for them now. I could honestly say

Dwayne was the freakiest and roughest lover I'd ever had. I didn't know where this thing with him would go, but I knew I couldn't take being fucked like that on a daily basis. I couldn't find my dress, so I picked up a t-shirt that was lying on the floor and put it over my head. My hair was even wilder now that Dwayne had pulled and yanked it in every direction possible. I tiptoed slowly out of the room, I didn't want to wake up Dwayne. He would probably be ready to go again and that was the *last* thing I needed right now. I opened the door and peered down the hallway, looking left and right for the bathroom. Dwayne never gave me a tour so I didn't know where the bathroom was. I walked out into the darkness towards an open door at the end of the hallway on my right. I pushed the door open and it was the bathroom.

"Thank you." I whispered in relief as I closed the door behind me. I turned the light on and waited for my eyes to adjust to the light before I ventured over to the toilet seat. I gingerly sat down on it and let out a sigh.

"Ouch. Shit!" The pee stung as it came out and I had to squeeze my eyes closed tight to brace for the burn. I emptied my bladder, gently wiped, and got up to wash my face and hands. I looked my body over from head to toe. There were dark handprints starting to emerge on my left ass cheek where Dwayne had spanked me. Dark handprints were forming around my neck too. I shook my head. I had a feeling I was getting in way over my head. Maybe I should have just picked Ryson instead and let Dwayne go with Shar. I tried unsuccessfully to run my fingers through my hair and stretched out.

"Time to go home." I said aloud. I decided not to stay the night. I didn't want the whole awkward scene to play out in the morning. The one where the girl would ask the guy if she would see him again. He would say "I'll call you" knowing that he wouldn't. I wasn't clingy so I knew when to exit. I've had quite a few one night stands over the years, and if anything, the men would ask me if they would see *me* again. Men were funny that way. When you acted clingy, they couldn't wait to kick your ass out. But when you acted icy towards them, they would be drooling after you. Humping your leg like a little puppy dog. That was fine with me. That just meant I always had a stash of dick anytime I wanted it. But I had drained that well dry and wanted some new dick, hence the reason I was at that café. I turned off the light and walked out into the dark hallway again. I stopped in my tracks. I sensed something right in front of me. I told myself to stop being so paranoid and to go get my things from Dwayne's room. As I walked along the wall down the hallway, I felt something hard rub up against my body. I jerked back.

"Dwayne?" I asked on alert.

"No, it's Ryson." His deep voice filtered through the quiet house.

"Ryson? What are you doing here? You scared the shit out of me!" I couldn't see his face, but I could smell that it was him.

"I live here." He reached past me and turned on the hallway light.

"You live here? With Dwayne?" I tried to wrap my head around that as my eyes adjusted to yet another light. Could this be more awkward?

"Well, he lives here with me, but yeah. My room is right next door to his." He looked at what I had on. When he said that, I thought about all of the screaming I did when Dwayne and I were fucking. I was instantly embarrassed.

"When did you get home?" I asked warily. *Please say you just got home.*

"I got here in time to hear Dwayne's headboard banging against my bedroom wall," he said with a little attitude in his voice. I resented his tone. If he wanted me, he should have asked me to come home with him instead of walking off with Shar. It wasn't my fault Dwayne had taken charge of the situation. At first I was embarrassed that he'd heard me getting fucked by Dwayne, but then it kind of aroused me. I pictured him with his ear to his bedroom wall, listening to my screams of agony and pleasure. Wishing I was in his room instead.

"What are you doing up? The way you and Dwayne went at it, I assumed both of you would be knocked the hell out," Ryson said, crossing his arms. Did I hear envy in his voice?

"I couldn't sleep," I admitted.

"In too much pain?" Ryson asked and lifted his eyebrow. I let out a small laugh. I didn't want to admit to that. My body was still reeling from the sex, but I didn't want to talk about that with him.

"No, I'm cool. What are you doing up?" I switched subjects and leaned on the wall.

"I never went to sleep. I figured when you two finished I could get some sleep. I just didn't think you would go until three-thirty," Ryson said with a strained smile. I suddenly felt like I had dissed him in some way. At the café I was fair game for him and Dwayne. But now I felt that by picking one, I had played the other. I stood up straight and looked Ryson in the eyes, trying to think of something to say. He smiled at me then and eased the tension in the hallway.

"You better get back in there before he wakes up and comes looking for you." Ryson walked past me towards the bathroom. I watched him close the bathroom door. I walked back into Dwayne's room and sat down on the bed, deciding to stay the night after all.

I woke up to Dwayne's hard dick poking me in the back.

"Mmmmm." I moaned and turned around. I nudged him awake. He moaned and stretched his naked, muscular body.

"Stand up in front of me," I ordered him. He looked surprised, then came around to the side of the bed I was on. He did what I told him to do. I sat up and took him deep in my mouth.

"Shit, yeah!" He groaned and started grinding his hips. I sat up on my knees on the bed and tried to better take him in my mouth. He was thick and it gagged me to take him deep, but that didn't stop me from trying. He loved it. His breathing sped up and sweat started to form on his forehead.

"I'm about to cum!" He grunted and grabbed my hair, pulling my mouth down deeper onto his dick. He pumped his dick into my mouth, forcing it down my throat. I held my breath and kept him in my throat as long as I could. I put my hands on his hips, gasping for air as thick saliva rolled down my neck.

"Keep doing that!" His voice rose an octave as he begged me not to stop. I grabbed the base of his dick and jerked it, while I tried my best to keep from gagging. I breathed through my nose and took him a little deeper. His body started to shudder, then I felt warm liquid filling my mouth. I gulped it all down and licked my top lip. I softly ran my tongue over the head of his dick and then kissed it. He shuddered again, then stepped back.

"I can't believe you just swallowed my cum! You are a fucking freak girl!" He laughed and put on a pair of underwear. I usually didn't drink the nectar of men that I just met, but he tasted so good I couldn't resist. His skin was so velvety smooth, I just couldn't take him out of my mouth. I got up and looked around the room for my dress. I used his shirt to wipe the saliva off my neck and mouth and threw it on the floor. I put my dress back on and adjusted myself.

"Give me your number." Dwayne demanded as I put my heels on. I smiled at him and rolled my eyes.

"How polite of you," I commented sarcastically. I recited my cell phone number and he saved it in his phone. As I got up and turned to leave, he grabbed my arm, pulling me back.

"What, no goodbye? What's up with later on tonight?" He asked me, looking at my ass. I wanted to be clear about where this was going.

"What do you mean?" I asked.

"You know what I mean. Come by tonight and give me some more pussy." He grabbed my ass.

"Then what?" I wanted to know what he thought this thing with us was. He scrunched up his eyebrows and shrugged.

"Then nothing. I'm not looking for a girlfriend if that's what you're asking me." He let me go and stepped back a few feet.

"We're just having fun right?" He looked at me hoping I would agree. I thought about it, and realized it could be a good idea to have him as my new stash of dick.

"Yeah, we're just having fun. I'm not looking for a man either," I lied. I actually *was* looking for a man. I wanted and needed someone steady in my life. These one night stands were just for sex, but secretly I hoped one would turn into something more. But judging by his reaction to my question, he wasn't looking for a girl anyway. He smiled happily.

"Good girl. As long as neither of us gets too serious everything will be cool." He held out his hand for me to shake. I shook it.

"And no strings or complications," I added, arching my eyebrow. Men seemed to have a problem with that part. If we were going to be casual then I wanted to be able to continue my search for a steady man in my life. I didn't need his male ego getting in the way.

"I like how you think. Yes, no strings attached. We can both fuck with whoever we want. So now that we got that out the way, what's up with tonight?" I stood on my tiptoes and kissed him lightly on the lips.

"Tonight and tomorrow, I recoup from the hurting you put on me last night. But the day after that give me a holler." I winked at him and left his room. After freshening up in the bathroom, I walked downstairs and stopped when I heard water running in the kitchen. I walked over and peeked inside and saw Ryson washing dishes. There was an island in the middle of the room with pots and pans dangling on hooks just above it. On the island was a built-in grill and Ryson had slices of bacon sizzling on it. The stainless steel appliances gave the room a modern look.

"That smells good," I said, bringing his attention to me. He looked at me and smiled. I didn't know if it was a polite smile or a genuine one, so I walked into the kitchen to feel him out. Now that the boundaries had been set with me and Dwayne, I could spend a little more time getting acquainted with Ryson without feeling guilty. There was just something about him that pulled me to him.

"You must be hungry after burning all that energy last night." Ryson's voice was full of sarcasm. I had to nip that in the bud.

"Okay, okay enough with the jokes. How are we going to become friends if you keep trying to play me like that?" We both laughed.

"You want to be my friend huh?" He gave me the cutest little smile. I blushed of course.

"I just don't want there to be a strain between us because of last night. I know we don't know each other. But you seem really cool and I wouldn't mind getting to know you better." I said it sincerely. He nodded his head and turned the water off.

"Why wouldn't there be a strain? I saw you first." I saw a small glint in his eyes and knew he was trying to play around with me. I relaxed.

"What about Dwayne?" He turned his beautiful eyes to me. For a second I couldn't speak. He stopped what he was doing and gave me the same look that must have been on my face. Damn he was fine. I snapped out of my trance and slightly shook my head.

"We're just keeping it casual with no strings. I don't expect anything from him and he doesn't expect anything from me. We're both free to pursue other interests." He thought about what I said and flipped his bacon over.

"Okay good. Now I won't feel guilty about inviting you to my party." He put his bacon on a plate and cracked a few eggs into a bowl.

"A party? I haven't been to one of those in a long time." I walked over and stood next to him, wanting to be closer to him all of a sudden. He looked down at me and then his eyes went to my lips.

"You were talking about the party? What's the occasion?" I broke him out of his daze. He smelled so damn manly. Like freshly cut wood.

"Oh, yeah the party. It's no occasion besides a good time. I have them every now and again. I'm inviting some friends over. We drink, dance, and eat. It's fun. You should come." I took the bowl of eggs out of his hands and beat the eggs for him. He opened his mouth to say something but decided against it. I looked down at his pants and saw that he was hard. I loved having that effect on men.

"Do you want me to *come*?" I put emphasis on the last word and eyed him sideways. He knew I was flirting with him. He came behind me and put his hands on the counter on my right and left, boxing me in. I could feel his erection on my ass. I was grateful for the thin fabric of the dress.

"I most definitely want you to come," he said into my ear. The hairs on the back of my neck stood up.

"Well, I will be there then." I put the bowl down on the island and ducked underneath his arm.

"Get my number from your brother and text me." I sashayed out of the house.

SHAR

"Ugh! How come she's invited to the fucking party, but *I'm* banned?" I wanted to hear his explanation. I was sitting between Dwayne and Ryson on the couch in their living room, watching Dwayne flip through the channels.

"Because it's my party Shar, and I don't have to explain anything to you," Ryson said simply. He was too damn stupid for his own good. Samara had fucked his brother in the room right next to his, but he still wanted her to come? They always let their dicks do their thinking for them. Dwayne stopped flipping through the channels and looked over at Ryson. It was the morning after and they were still talking about that bitch. That was a first. I was still shocked she got to spend the night. They usually kicked every girl out afterwards, even if it was the middle of the night. But not Samara. I had an uneasy feeling that Samara was going to be trouble.

"Invited who?" Dwayne chose that moment to tune in to the conversation.

"Samara." Ryson smirked.

"When did you talk to Samara?" Dwayne asked suspiciously. He scooted to the edge of the couch, looking a little surprised. Good. He needed to curse Ryson out for that shit and tell him not to invite that whore to the party. If I wasn't allowed, she shouldn't be either. They never invited girls they were fucking to parties. The game they were playing was dangerous and neither of them cared. If Samara knew that Ryson and Dwayne frequently tried to go after the same girl just to see who could get her, she wouldn't go to the fucking party. I should just tell her, but that could end up causing more trouble for me than her. But if history had taught me anything, it was that whenever they found a plaything, they would get bored of her quickly then toss her aside. They would always come back to me, well Dwayne would at least.

"This morning she came into the kitchen and we talked for a few minutes. I invited her to the party. Oh yeah, give me her number so I can call her. As a matter of fact, where does she live? I could just go over to her place before I go to work." Ryson dug into his pocket for his phone and looked at Dwayne expectantly for the number.

"She's not going to invite you over to her place man. What did y'all talk about?" Dwayne asked, looking Ryson up and down. They were so competitive it was irritating.

"Not you. Now give me her number." Ryson leaned over and picked up Dwayne's phone off the table.

"You think she's busy tonight?" Ryson teased Dwayne.

"She busy recovering from all that dick I gave her last night," Dwayne said proudly. Ryson cracked up at that. They were so juvenile sometimes.

"So that means no! I'm going to give her a call right now to see what's up." Dwayne got up and snatched his phone out of Ryson's hands.

"Stop playing man. That shit ain't funny!" Dwayne was fuming. Ryson laughed even harder.

"I'm only playing with you. Damn, you act like she's your wife or something. Since when did you start to care about females? She told me y'all are just fucking. So I guess that makes you a booty call." Ryson took Dwayne's phone from him again and got that bitch's number. Samara was already causing friction between the brothers. Dwayne clenched his fists at his sides.

"It doesn't matter anyway because she's not your girl either Ryson. Now why don't you stop talking about her and pay me some attention for once. Every time you chase after some hoe I get put on the back burner!" I was tired of this shit! Ryson could care less about how I felt and that was the fucking problem.

I hated the fact that Samara was still a topic of discussion. Why? Because of her huge lard ass? Because she had curly hair running down her fucking back? I wished they weren't so obsessed with these fucking women. Each woman presented another challenge for them. Each woman had something they wanted to conquer. Why can't they pursue me the way they pursued these women? They made me the jealous lunatic that I am today.

"Shut up Shar, you're just jealous." Ryson snickered at me. Why was he always so mean to me? What did I ever do to him?

"What are you doing over here anyway? You know the rules about being over here. Only nighttime hours," Ryson said with irritation in his voice. I wasn't allowed to come over unless the sun was down. How fucked up was that?

"Don't be mean to Shar. She just forgot that's all," Dwayne said softly. I smiled at him and stood up to be closer to him. I didn't forget about their stupid ass rule. I'd just felt like I needed to make my presence known now more than ever. He put his arm around my shoulder, and pulled me into his chest. I could see in his eyes he was still a little pissed off at Ryson, but he would never admit it.

"Since you here, make yourself useful and make me a sandwich. Then take your ass home until the sun goes down." Dwayne pushed me off of him.

"I HATE Y'ALL!" I screamed at both of them. I stomped into the kitchen to make his sandwich. Sometimes I wish I had never met them four years ago. I wiped tears from my face and plated the sandwich.

"Here! You fucking bastard!" I slammed the plate down on the coffee table. Dwayne laughed at me. I hated that. Dwayne picked up a throw pillow and threw it at me.

"Stop being a cry baby girl. You know I'm only playing with you. You can suck my dick before you go home." Dwayne unzipped his jeans. Oh, now he wanted me huh? I walked back over to him and got on my knees in front of him.

"Say sorry first," I demanded.

"Sorry Shar. Cry baby," he mocked me. He was such a fucking jerk. I put him in my mouth and watched as Ryson left out the front door. I closed my eyes and focused on the task at hand.

RYSON

Shar was so fucking cheap. She got down on her knees to give Dwayne head like it was nothing. Like I wasn't even standing there. She had no shame and no dignity. I had to get out of there. It was fun at first to joke around with Dwayne, but after a certain point that shit was starting to get old. We went through this game over and over again. We would pick up a girl, see who got to fuck her first, then the other one would try to hit. Sometimes we would see who she would choose when we both came at her. After that we moved on to the next. We had done that with every female except Shar, but that was a whole different story. It was fun for a long time, but it just seemed like lately the game was getting old. Don't get me wrong, I'm not settling down any time soon. It just gets tiring doing the same shit over and over. I was debating whether I wanted to try to go after Samara or not. She seemed like a cool girl. In the kitchen she had seemed so lighthearted and bold. She was definitely my type. Sexy, funny, and thick as hell. I would think it over later. I don't even know why I invited her to the party. I never invite women I know to parties, it was only fresh meat allowed. I put Samara on the outskirts of my mind as I made my way to go get some ass. I met this chick a few weeks back but she was with another guy at the time. She was interested though, and still gave me her number. I called her and got her address. I needed to bust a nut. I planned on being with Samara last night, but Shar had to fuck that up. Now I had to make up for what I had lost. I pulled up to her house, which was only a few blocks away, and beeped the horn. She opened the door and I got out of my Jeep. She was short and thick, just my type. I walked onto her porch and looked her up and down. She had on a pair of black leggings and a black wife beater. She was braless and her double D's had me drooling.

"Are you going to invite me in?" I asked her and leaned against the doorframe. She licked her lips and moved aside to let me in. Her walnut complexion was smooth and blemish free. She walked ahead of me and up a flight of steps. Her ass was just the right size for her five-foot four frame. I followed her, pulling my shirt over my head as I walked up the steps. I had to be at work in an hour and a half, so this was going to have to be a quickie. I realized that I didn't even remember what her name was. I had saved her number in my phone under *"new ass"*. Oh well, it wasn't like I would see her again after this anyway if the sex wasn't good. She climbed on her bed and opened her legs. I climbed in after her and pulled off her leggings, then slid her panties down her legs. She leaned up to kiss me. I turned my head to the side so she could kiss my cheek instead. I pulled her hips up to mine forcing her to lie down. I only kissed when it was necessary. That was too personal to be doing to every girl I fucked. For me, when it came to casual sex, the less kissing the better. I didn't even really enjoy kissing these females. They seemed to want it so I complied most of the time, but not this time. I pulled one of her breasts out of her shirt and popped the nipple in my mouth. She moaned and squirmed under me. I made my way to her other breast while she unbuckled my pants and pulled my dick out. It wasn't at full attention yet.

"What's wrong?" she asked with an attitude. Like that was going to help matters.

"He needs some motivation that's all." I took off the rest of my clothes. I switched places with her and guided her mouth to my dick. This was turning into a chore. I wanted to get in and come out, literally. Her mouth was warm as she took as much as she could into her mouth. I closed my eyes and tried to enjoy the head I was getting. As soon as I felt my dick get harder, I jumped up and bent her over.

"I want to see you fuck me," she said seductively. The problem was I didn't. I could only nut if I was fucking doggy style. I couldn't look into the faces of the women I was fucking and have an orgasm. I knew there was something wrong with that, but until I figured it out I had to do what I knew best.

"Don't worry about that. Just worry about this dick." I slid my dick in her wet pussy.

"Ow!" She groaned and buried her face in a pillow. I edged my dick in slow and steady until I was almost all the way in her pussy. She whimpered when I started to pump my dick inside her. After a few seconds I stopped thinking about anything but the tight pussy I was in.

"Go slower, it kinda hurts," she said into the pillow. I slowed down some and gave her a little more.

"Don't give me all of it yet!" She practically screamed at me. What the fuck? I looked up at the ceiling and shook my head, I deflated immediately. I pulled out of her. What a fucking waste of time! As quickly as it had started, it was over. I wasn't even going to trip on it though. I got up and put my shit back on. She pulled the covers over her naked body and ran her hands through her short hair.

"Maybe we can try again some other time," she offered. Like that was going to happen.

"Yeah… I'll call you." I tossed the lie over my shoulder on my way out of her house. Now I had to go back home, shower, and make my way to work. This shit was getting tiresome, and now I was hornier than ever. I was tired of this shit! It was times like these that made me long for one girl to go home to, to fuck. Casual sex was fun when you wanted a quick hook-up, but when you had to search for your next piece of ass, the fun got sucked right out of it. I slapped myself and came back to reality. I wasn't a one-woman man, so I was stuck with these sometimes unsatisfying hook-ups. I got in my Jeep and made my way back home.

SAMARA

"Why don't you come over to my place instead?" I tried to convince Dwayne. Four days after our first hook-up, he was on my phone at midnight begging me to come over. Of course I jumped up at the chance to be with him again. But first I had a request.

"I want to fuck you in my bed that's why. Why are we even having this conversation? Bring that fat ass over here now!" he ordered. Just thinking about what he would do to me tonight made my pussy wet. I just couldn't sleep with him knowing his brother was in the next room. I was serious when I told Ryson that we should try to get to know each other.

Hearing me screaming his brother's name at the top of my lungs would definitely put a damper on that.

"Why didn't you tell me you lived with your brother, or that his room was right next door to yours?" I wanted to know. He blew air out of his mouth in frustration on the other end of the phone.

"If you want my dick to stay hard, I suggest you stop talking about my brother. What difference does it make? He probably had his ear glued to the wall trying to listen in anyway." What I got from that sentence was that he purposely fucked me like that so Ryson could hear us.

"Come on now girl. Why are you teasing me like this? He's not going to be home tonight anyway!" Dwayne's voice raised a notch higher. He was getting edgy.

"Where will he be?" I was being nosy.

"WHY?" Dwayne yelled at me. I could see this conversation wasn't going anywhere.

"No reason. I'll be there in half an hour," I said.

"Hurry up!" Dwayne hung up on me.

The front door was unlocked when I got there, so I let myself in. I jogged up the stairs, anxious to meet with Dwayne. As soon as I got to the second-floor landing, I could hear loud screams and moans. I walked over to Ryson's bedroom door and didn't hear anything. They could only be coming from Dwayne's room.

"Dwayne! OH DWAYNE!" A female voice screamed out. I leaned against the wall in the hallway and smirked. Dwayne knew that I was on my way over here. For someone who did not want strings attached, he sure seemed to be going out of his way to make me jealous. Little did he know, I was not a jealous person. Especially if I knew that the man wasn't mines. The screams stopped and I heard the bed creak. The door swung open a few minutes later and Dwayne had the nerve to look shocked.

"Oh, damn. I didn't know you would be here so fast." He smiled that sexy smile of his and fixed his underwear. I grinned at the show he was putting on. The bedroom door opened wider and a naked, frazzled Shar limped out. She looked satisfied. I knew the feeling of satisfaction after being with Dwayne.

She actually did look surprised to see me.

"What the fuck is she doing here Dwayne?" Shar yelled at him, quickly trying to cover her body.

I ignored her. "Is it my turn yet?" I asked Dwayne, biting my bottom lip. I would not let him think I was jealous. His ego deflated quickly and he looked upset that his plan had not worked.

"Uh… just let me take a shower real quick." He walked towards the bathroom. Shar huffed in annoyance.

"Wait! You said tonight was our night! You didn't tell me she was coming over!" Shar yelled at him but kept her eyes on me. The look of despise on her face almost made me laugh. She hated me because Dwayne wanted me. How petty. She needed to direct that anger towards Dwayne, not me. I lifted my eyebrows at Shar in amusement. Dwayne stopped in his tracks and looked back at Shar.

"Get your stuff and go home Shar," was all he said before he continued towards the bathroom. She went back into the room and grabbed her stuff. Watching me intently as she hurriedly got dressed. She was seething by the time her shoes were on. Lifting her head up with pride, she rushed down the stairs and out the door. I walked into the bedroom and pulled the wet, rumpled sheets off of the bed. I threw them in the hamper in the corner. I wasn't fucking on stale or used sheets. The room smelled like ass and cologne. I cracked the window to air the room out, then walked out to the hallway closet and pulled out a fresh set of sheets. I picked his cologne up from his dresser and sprayed it in each corner of the room. I remade the bed and stood in the middle of the bedroom until Dwayne got out of the shower. He walked in naked and dripping wet. My jaw almost dropped. He was erect already and his skin glistened. I wanted to slurp all of the water off his sexy hard body.

"Sorry you had to see that, but I don't let a hard dick go to waste." Dwayne was studying me. He was trying so hard to get a reaction out of me. It wouldn't be that easy. For one, I could never be jealous of Shar, because I was better looking than her. Second, when I told him I wanted no strings or complications, I meant that. And lastly, I was starting to gain an interest in Ryson. So the only thing about Dwayne that concerned me was his dick. As long as that was functional and ready to be inserted into me whenever I wanted, I didn't care who went before or after me.

"That's okay. You're free to do your thing just like I am. Now is it my turn yet?" I asked and pouted my lips.

"Oh, it's your turn alright. What took you so long to get here huh?" Dwayne walked over to me with his dick standing at attention. When he was within arm's length of me he pushed me backwards into the wall.

"I'm sorry." I apologized and stared him down. He grabbed my arms tightly and pinned them above my head against the wall.

"When I call, you come," he said and bit me on the neck.

"I came as fast as I could." I whispered sticking my tongue out for him to suck. He took my tongue in his mouth and pressed his dick against my stomach. I knew it was going to be on tonight. I had on a thigh-length navy blue trench coat and six inch stilettos. He pulled the coat open, exposing my naked body.

"Damn Samara." He bent down and put my nipple in his mouth. I shrugged out of the trench coat.

"Oooh… it's easy access." I moaned and closed my eyes. Dwayne bit down on my nipple hard, causing me to scream out in pain.

"You like that?" Dwayne asked me. I wanted to say no it hurt like hell, but I didn't move my lips.

"I said, do you like that?" he asked me through clenched teeth. If it was possible, I swear I saw his dick get harder. I ignored him again. He pulled me off the wall, and then pushed me backwards, sending me across the room onto the bed. The amount of force he used scared me a little, but it made me tingle inside. Excitement rose inside of me. I looked up at him, ready to get to business.

"Open your legs," he ordered. I did as I was told, already extremely wet. He got down on all fours and crawled over to me. I licked my lips ready for whatever he was going to throw at me. He got on his knees in front of me.

"Shit." I said to myself, anticipating the touch of his tongue to my waiting pussy. He pulled my lips open wide and slid his tongue inside my wet pussy.

"Oooh Dwayne, that shit feels good!" I panted. His tongue was thick. I squirmed on his mouth. He grabbed my hips and smashed his face into my pussy.

I sighed and let my head fall back onto the bed. I pulled at my hair, closed my eyes, and enjoyed the ripples of pleasure flowing through me. When I felt myself about to cum, I started to grind my pussy on his tongue.

"Fuck my face you little freak!" Dwayne demanded, his voice muffled by my pussy. So I did. I ground my clit on his tongue like there was no tomorrow.

"Oh!... oh!... oh!" I tried to hold onto my orgasm, to prolong the feeling. I almost succeeded- until Dwayne put his middle finger in my ass.

"SHIIIIIITTTTTTT!" I cried out in passion. That felt so damn good.

"CUM!" Dwayne yelled at me and sucked hard on my clit. He didn't have to tell me twice.

"YEEEEESSSSSS! AAAAHHHHH!" I grabbed a pillow and put it over my face to muffle my screams. The orgasm was almost too much to take, and Dwayne wouldn't stop sucking on my clit. I begged him for mercy but he ignored me as usual.

"Dwayne please!" I whimpered into the pillow.

"You get no mercy in my bed," he said in a husky tone. I was so turned on I couldn't think straight. Dwayne moved away from between my legs and reached into his drawer. He pulled out a pair of handcuffs. I broke out of my haze and sat up, quickly putting my hands up in defense. I couldn't handle a repeat of the last time.

"I don't want you to tie me up," I protested. He violently grabbed my wrists and cuffed them together. He pushed me down onto the bed. I lay still, fearful and excited. I knew he wouldn't listen. He reached into his drawer of goodies and pulled out two long, black, silk scarves. He sat on the edge of the bed and grabbed my ankle.

"Wait! Not my ankles," I pleaded with him, but it fell on deaf ears. He tied the scarf around my ankle and stretched my leg backwards.

"Oh shit!" I exclaimed when I realized he was tying my ankles to the bedposts. He had my legs open so wide, they were spread into the shape of a wide V. Dwayne slid his dick into my wet pussy slow and easy.

"Are you ready for this dick?" He asked me, doing a slow grind inside my pussy. I couldn't respond. My eyes rolled to the back of my head in ecstasy.

"OOOOO." I moaned. He kept a slow pace, which surprised me. I was expecting to get my brains fucked out, but this was good too. It didn't last long though.

"Enough of this slow shit!" He grunted and began to pump his hard dick into me. This was what I was looking forward too.

"You want this dick?" he asked me, pumping harder.

"YES! GIVE ME THAT DICK!" I screamed out. He put his hands around my ankles and started to bang into me so hard I bit my tongue.

"FUCK!" He grabbed my face and dug his nails into my cheeks. I closed my eyes and let him fuck me into submission. My legs were open so wide I could feel every inch of his dick in my pussy. I could feel him in my stomach, hard as a rock. I felt myself about to cum, but I didn't scream out. I ignored the pain from his nails in my skin.

"YOU WANT IT HARDER?" Dwayne screamed and thrust into me with all of his strength.

"AAAAAAHHHHHHHH!" I pulled at the cuffs trying to free myself. It was no use. I put my cuffed wrists on his chest hoping to slow him down. My legs and hands were bound and I was his prisoner. He was banging me so hard my legs started to throb.

"I'M CUMMING!" I cried and unleashed what I was holding back. He began to pump faster and I got dizzy. The pain mixed with my orgasm had my head spinning. I'd never been with anyone who fucked me so hard.

"I can't take anymore, for real." I was out of breath. He slowed down, but didn't stop.

"You don't have a choice. I didn't cum yet." He panted and leaned down to put his tongue in my mouth. I opened my mouth wide and let his tongue run rampant in my mouth. I was getting aroused again. He took his tongue out of my mouth and his dick out of my pussy.

"Don't stop!" I panicked. I hoped he didn't take me seriously when I said I couldn't take it. I would endure a lot more pain just to have another orgasm. He untied my ankles and uncuffed me. I rubbed my wrists and tried to get up, but he pushed me back down onto the bed, and flipped my body over so that I was lying on my stomach.

"Where do you think you're going?" He asked me and grabbed my wrist again.

"Um... nowhere apparently." I answered truly confused. He cuffed my wrists behind my back.

"I want to fuck that ass," he whispered in my ear. I didn't say anything. Anal sex was not my favorite thing to do. The two times that I let a man put his dick in my ass had been disastrous. The first one rushed into it and hurt me. The second one didn't know what to do once he got in there. Dwayne moved away the hair at the nape of my neck. I felt his tongue slide down the back of my neck all the way down my spine.

"Mmmmm." I moaned. His tongue ran down my back and kept going until his tongue was circling my asshole.

"Aaahhh!" I lifted my head off the bed at the sensation. He spread my ass cheeks and inserted the tip of his tongue into my hole.

"Dwayne," I whined as he pushed his tongue in and out of my ass. I wiggled my ass from side to side trying to get more of his tongue.

"Aaahhh!...Oh god!... Don't stop please!" I cried out hoping he would go forever. I licked my lips and arched my back.

"OH SHIT I'M ABOUT TO CUM!" I was shocked at how quick I was cumming tonight. I guess I was backed up on orgasms. They kept coming like they were going out of style. I bounced my ass back on his face while he licked and sucked my ass hole rapidly.

"FUCK FUCK FUCK! DWAYYYYNNNEEE!" I screamed his name repeatedly. I started to shudder as I continued to cum.

"YES!... OH YES!" Nothing could top that orgasm, or so I thought. Dwayne took his tongue out of my ass and sat up on his knees behind me. He slid his finger in my ass. I held my breath as he slowly inserted two more fingers, one at a time. So far so good.

"How does that feel?" he asked me, his voice deep with lust. I nodded my head up and down telling him it felt okay. I turned my head to the side and laid it flat on the bed. I enjoyed the feeling of his fingers moving inside me. He took his fingers out of me and I felt the head of his dick rubbing against my asshole. My heart started to beat faster. I tried to calm down, but I was nervous. I didn't want him to hurt me. I heard him open his drawer again, then I felt a warm liquid gliding down the crack of my ass. It was lubricant. He rubbed the lube all around my asshole.

"Prepare yourself for this dick," he warned me.

"I can't. You're too big, it's going to hurt," I bitched.

"Don't you trust me Samara?" he asked me in a serious tone. I turned my head and looked into his eyes. They burned with intensity, waiting for my answer. Did I trust him with the most sensitive part of my body? So far he hadn't hurt me beyond having rough kinky sex with me. The pain was mostly because he had a big dick. Not his fault. He knew enough about the pain associated with anal to use lubricant, and to stretch me with his fingers first. Yeah, I did trust him. I smiled at him. He smiled back. He was so sexy.

"Yes Dwayne, I trust you." I lay my head back onto the bed and closed my eyes.

"I won't hurt you." He said softly. Again, surprising me with how tender he was being. He slowly slipped the head of his dick inside me, crossing that sensitive threshold. The hardest part was getting the head in.

"OH!" I cried out more in surprise at the feeling than at the pain. I felt him put in more and more, inch by inch. I held my breath and pulled at the handcuffs until my palms were sore.

"Ouch!... Ouch!... Ouch!... Ouch!" I muttered into the bed as my ass tried to adjust to his large dick.

"I'm almost all the way in. Relax," he said in a soothing voice. He was breathing heavier now. I took four deep breaths, slowly letting each of them out. I relaxed my body as much as I could. All twelve inches of his dick were now inside me. He kept his dick still inside me for a few minutes. He bent down and laid soft kisses on my back, which relaxed me even more. The pain started to lessen as my hole expanded to handle his bulk.

"Yeah. Like that." Dwayne purred as he leisurely took his dick out of my ass.

"Mmmmm." I moaned. He was back inside me seconds later.

"Your ass is TIGHT!" Dwayne screamed out in delight. Dwayne did a slow grind in my ass, but didn't give me all of him. My ass started to pulsate.

"Dwayne, put it all in!" I demanded of him. He seemed to be getting harder as he pumped his dick inside me. I didn't think I could handle it all, but I didn't care.

"You want all this dick?" He asked me in surprise.

"You brave girl," he said under his breath. Dwayne started to thrust deeper into my ass.

"OH GOD! DON'T STOP!" I pleaded. The pain increased as he began to fuck me a little faster. It was a sweet agony. I whined into the bed sheets as he continued to fuck me. As the pain started to build inside me, so did an orgasm. I felt Dwayne's dick gliding in and out of my ass with ease. That wasn't from the lubricant. My ass was cumming.

"I'M CUMMING!" I heard Dwayne choke out.

"You better cum in my ass Dwayne!" I ordered him. I arched my back and got on my knees to get the full effect of his dick in my ass. With Dwayne, there was no pleasure without the pain. I strained my muscles and took his dick until I felt him start to fuck me even harder.

"YOU WANT THIS CUM IN YOUR ASS?" He yelled out yanking my hair.

"YESSSSSS! I WANT ALL THAT HOT CUM IN MY ASS!" I yelled back at him. His hand slid across my stomach and went down to my clit.

"DWAYNE OH GOD!" I was ready to cum now.

"OH!...OH!...OH!...SHIIITTT!" Dwayne's screams drowned out mine. We both came at the same time. His warm nut burst into my ass as mines ran down his hand. Dwayne pounded his dick in my ass one last time, then fell backwards on the bed exhausted. I lay face flat with my ass tingling and clit throbbing. A lock of my hair was in my eyes. I was beat.

"Dwayne, un-cuff me," I said breathlessly. To my surprise, he got up and did what I asked. I guessed that he was spent too. I delicately turned onto my back, sighed, and enjoyed the aftershocks of my orgasm.

Dwayne rolled over onto his side. He put his arm around me, pulling me into his body. I froze and looked at his arm. Cuddling definitely wasn't a part of casual sex. He grabbed my chin and turned my face towards him. He looked at my lips, then leaned down and kissed me. Soft and sensual. Completely unlike how he'd ever kissed me. It was such a turn on. I moaned on his lips and let him kiss me for the next few minutes. When he broke the kiss, he ran his thumb over my bottom lip. I looked into his eyes and realized he was watching me intently. I was so caught off guard. I just stared back, not knowing what to say or do. He let my face go and laid down behind me, holding me even tighter against him. Dwayne's whole demeanor tonight was different. From the moment he realized I wasn't jealous of him having Shar here, he'd changed. I let him hold me until he fell asleep less than ten minutes later. I had to pee and I wasn't going to hold it like I did last time. I gently moved his arm and got out of the bed. I put on one of Dwayne's shirts and walked down the hallway to the bathroom. I grabbed the side of the sink for leverage when I sat down. My pussy wasn't sore, but I felt like there was a big gaping hole where my ass hole was supposed to be. I finished and turned on the sink tap. I glanced up at the mirror.

"What the hell?" There were three scratches on my left cheek. I forgot Dwayne had dug his nails into my face. Now I had skin missing as a reminder. The next time I was setting some ground rules. No hits or scratches to the face or neck. The bruises around my neck were still there from the other day, and were even darker now. People were going to think I was getting my ass beat. I opened the bathroom cabinet looking for something to clean my face with. I took out a few cotton balls and a small bottle of alcohol, then closed the cabinet and put the items on the sink.

"GEEZ!" I jumped out of my skin when I saw Ryson's reflection in the bathroom mirror behind me. I put my hand on my heart to still my breathing.

"You have to start wearing a bell or something." I laughed, trying to calm my nerves. I wondered how long he had been standing there. He stood stoically at the door watching me.

"What are you doing here?"

"Are you going to ask me that every time I find you in my bathroom in the middle of the night?" His voice lacked humor. Ouch. I decided not to let that comment get to me. It was obvious he was angry or envious or both.

"Were you here all night?" I asked, hoping he would say no.

"Yup." His eyebrows shot up and he shook his head in dismay. My heart sank. Dwayne told me he wouldn't be home. I should have known better. Why hadn't Ryson made his presence known when I got there? He had to have heard the commotion in the hallway between me, Shar, and Dwayne. I couldn't blame him though, it was no one's fault but mine.

"I don't know what to say. I'm so sorry. Dwayne told me you wouldn't be home tonight. I really did not know you would be here. If I did, I wouldn't have come." My words ran out of my mouth like diarrhea. Ryson smirked and rubbed the stubble on his chin.

"Why wouldn't you have come over here if you knew I was here?" He looked at me and his eyes demanded an answer.

"Because I don't want you to hear me with Dwayne. I like you and I don't want you to get the wrong idea about me." The words sounded so stupid to me. I had fucked his brother with him in the next room. I had flirted with him in his kitchen the next day, and then fucked his brother again days later. There was only one thing he could think that I was. A hoe.

"I don't have the wrong idea about you. I know that you and Dwayne are just fucking. The problem I have is that you think that we could be anything more than whatever we are, if you're fucking my brother." He stepped into the bathroom and closed the door behind him. I looked at the tiles on the bathroom floor and ran my tongue over the top row of my teeth as I weighed my options.

"Okay, I'll stop sleeping with Dwayne. How about that? There's something here with us that I want to explore further. I don't know exactly what it is. But I do want to get to know you better." I said honestly. He tilted his head slightly and looked into my eyes. For a moment we just stayed that way. Eyes locked. Something electric moving between us. He walked over to me and took the cotton ball out of my hand.

"Dwayne did this to you?" he asked, referring to the scratches on my face and the scars on my neck. For some reason I got embarrassed. My face flushed red. I looked down at the floor again and nodded my head yes. His voice took on a stern tone.

"Don't ever let him bruise your beautiful skin again." I looked into his eyes and saw what I thought was anger, but I couldn't be sure. I bit my lip and nodded my head in agreement. I was at a loss for words. He stepped closer to me.

"You shouldn't use alcohol on open skin. Peroxide is much better and it doesn't sting." He opened the cabinet and took out the peroxide, then saturated the cotton ball with it. He still hadn't responded to what I said. I didn't push. He gently ran the cotton ball along the scratches on my face, staring at me fiercely the whole time. He finished and threw the cotton ball in the trash. He opened the cabinet again and took out the Vaseline. In a circular motion, he applied a little on each scratch. It was kind of erotic in a way. We stood in the bathroom in silence. I played with my hair nervously awaiting his response. He stepped closer to me and leaned down towards my face. Ryson didn't have on anything besides a pair of black briefs. His body was perfect. I snuck a glance down at his navel and the hair descending into his briefs. His skin was hot on mine as he bent down further towards me. I blinked and waited. He laid his lips on top of mines and applied pressure. I shuddered as his tongue separated my lips and went inside my mouth. I kissed him back gently. He pressed his body into mines, pinning me against the sink. I felt his hard dick on my upper thigh. He broke the kiss first and put his forehead on mines.

"So what now?" I said breathless, not sure what to make of the kiss. It was wonderful, but he still hadn't commented on what I had said.

"We'll see," he said and kissed me on the nose.

"Okay." I smiled like a teenager and watched him walk out of the bathroom. I was giddy with excitement, almost forgetting that I came over here to be with Dwayne. Thinking of Dwayne took the smile off my face. He lied to me about Ryson and I didn't appreciate that. I was going to spend the night again, we had to talk in the morning.

SHAR

WHAT THE FUCK? How dare Dwayne fuck me and kick me out like some hooker! I was so mad! I wanted to peel my skin off. I slammed his front door and ran down the steps to my beat-up twenty-year old Chevy Impala. I was already suspicious when he texted me saying to come over there as fast as I could. It was almost midnight. Then he rushed through sex and didn't even make sure I had an orgasm. He'd never done that before. Then, seeing Samara standing in his hallway waiting for him was just too much to take! He rushed me so he could hurry up and be with that bitch?

"That fucking bastard!" I lay my head on the steering wheel and cried. How long would I take this shit from Dwayne and Ryson? I deserved so much better than what I was getting. I'd been there for them since the day I met them. Doing everything they wanted me to do. I moved out here to be with them! I sacrificed everything and tried so fucking hard to impress and please them! I was driving around in a car that left a trail of smoke behind it, but breaking my neck to buy designer clothes. Who the fuck was I fooling? I had only known them a short amount of time before I started sleeping with them. The first time I was with Ryson it was like heaven. After a while, I started to mess around with Dwayne. At one point I was with both of them at the same time. They fulfilled all of my sexual desires and fantasies, but never the emptiness in my heart. I wanted to please them so bad. I was so ashamed of myself. I could barely look in the mirror anymore. Why couldn't they see that I was devoting my whole life to them? Samara was going to be the last woman to take their attention away from me. It was time for me to take matters into my own hands.

RYSON

"We'll see," I said and kissed Samara on the nose. Why did I break my rule and kiss her? For some reason when I saw her lips I was compelled to kiss them. They were so soft and moist. She smiled like she had a school-girl crush on me. She was so fucking cute. Lying in my bed and hearing her screaming Dwayne's name had sent me over the edge. I don't know why I stayed home that night. Maybe I secretly hoped she would come back over. But that had backfired as her screams of passion came through my walls. I put my pillow over my face and pressed it down hard. Why had that shit bothered me so much? Dwayne fucked so many women on the other side of that wall, it was ridiculous. Not once had it bothered me like it did tonight. She told me that she was just fucking Dwayne. I wanted that to stop. I wasn't sure why though. Whenever I was around her I felt... different. I wasn't catching feelings or anything like that, but I had to admit I did like her. I liked her a little more than I should. She was just another girl that we picked up, but I couldn't bring myself to toss her aside.

   I hadn't hit it yet, so that probably was why I was tripping like this. If I got some pussy from her I could get her out of my system. She wanted to know where we stood and I couldn't answer her. I didn't even know what this thing was. There was a spark there though. I felt it in the bathroom. Some invisible force making me want to be near her. Crazy. I would have to call her up and see where things go from there. When I get to her place, I'll fuck her and then I'll be able to move on. That was the only solution I could think of. She wasn't special or different from all the other women who have been in my bed, so why should I treat her differently?

SAMARA

I sat on the bed closing up my trench coat, watching Dwayne sleep. His mouth was open and he was snoring lightly. I thought about my decision to stop sleeping with him to focus my time on Ryson. Was it a good decision? Was I a whore for jumping from one brother to another? Some people might feel like I was, but I didn't think so. It was a tricky situation though. I wasn't shy about my sexual openness. I loved to have sex and that wasn't a crime. They both knew that I was single and had no reservations about being with either of them. Men did it all the time, so why not me? There was nothing wrong with getting good dick. Maybe good dick could lead to a good man. I was single by choice because I was very picky. I had about three serious relationships in my life and they had all ended badly. I had casual sex here and there, but I was still searching for that special someone. I wanted someone who was kind-hearted and honest. I wanted the whole package and I had yet to find him. I had hoped maybe Dwayne or Ryson would turn out to be that. Dwayne's lies and disgust at having a girlfriend had crossed him off the list of prospects. I was on to the next. It would be pretty awkward between the three of us from now on though, no matter what happened. Dwayne snorted, then coughed. His eyes opened and he looked up at me.

"Why did you lie to me?" I asked him before he was fully awake. He sat up and rubbed his eyes. His hands went over his head as he stretched his body. I admired his spectacular body, knowing it was the last time I would see it.

"Why did you lie?" I asked again, this time pushing him awake. He slapped my hand away and got out of bed, ignoring me. He was getting good at that. I stood up and cut him off, blocking him from leaving the room.

"Hey! Wait. Why did you say Ryson wouldn't be here last night?" I asked him, feeling myself getting agitated. Dwayne looked at me impatiently.

"Move," he ordered. Was he serious? Was he really going to ignore my question? I was starting to see a new side of Dwayne that I did not like.

"I will move when you tell me why you lied." I stood my ground.

"Why the fuck do you care if he was here or not? You came over here to be with me!" He yelled, getting closer to my face. His anger surprised me. The look in his eyes confused me. I didn't say anything right away. He looked like an angry bull ready to attack me with his horns. I pushed away the urge to kick him in the nuts and focused.

"You didn't have to lie to me. That wasn't cool Dwayne," I said softly, not wanting to anger him anymore than he already was. He shrugged in indifference. I moved out of the way. I watched him walk to the bathroom and knew I had made the right decision to leave him alone.

RYSON

"You look pissed." I watched Dwayne yank open the freezer door and slam it shut. His beige skin looked flushed and his jaw was set.

"Mind your business!" he spat at me and brushed past me.

"Dwayne, what's wrong with you?" I asked, following him into the living room. He plopped down on the couch and picked up his phone. He looked at the screen like he was waiting for something.

"I'm not calling her again." Dwayne said to nobody in particular. I couldn't help but laugh at his sullen expression.

"Who are you not going to call? What girl got your panties all bunched up?" I nudged his shoulder playfully.

"That bitch Samara!" He tossed his phone on the table. Now she was a bitch? I wanted to be nosy.

"What did she do?" I asked innocently. It had been a week since I kissed Samara in the bathroom, but I couldn't stop thinking about her.

"She's not answering my fucking calls or texts. All week I've been blowing her up and she just keeps ignoring me and shit!"

"Why is she ignoring your calls? I thought y'all were cool." I picked his phone up and went through it. He had called Samara over fifty times and sent her over a hundred texts. Damn.

"Because of you!" He pointed at me. He got off the couch and paced back and forth. I didn't have the slightest idea what he was talking about.

"How is it because of me? I'm not messing with Samara. I mean I wouldn't turn her down either but," I started jokingly.

"For real man! She's mad because the last time I asked her to come over here I lied to her."

"About what?"

"She was asking me all these questions about you. Like, why I didn't tell her you lived here. I got mad and lied and told her you wouldn't be home." He folded his arms and rocked back on his heels. Dwayne was really upset. And here I was thinking *I* was tripping over Samara. She asked about me? I didn't want to acknowledge that hearing that perked me up a little bit. Just a little.

"Well why did you lie to her in the first place?" I asked him and started to read some of the texts he had sent her.

"Because she shouldn't have been asking about you! She was coming over here to see me. What the fuck! Then she wakes me up the next day asking me why I lied and shit like that. I told her ass she shouldn't be worried about you. Then she said something like, 'that wasn't cool', or something. Now she won't answer my phone calls or text messages. I can have any bitch I want! I hope she don't think she's the only female in this city!" Dwayne rambled on like that for another couple of minutes. I tuned him out. I read the messages he sent to Samara.

I want to eat your pussy

You know you miss dis dick

Please come over I miss u

Why u ignoring me?

Fuck you then!

Dwayne's text messages ranged from explicit, to whiny, to disrespectful. I never saw him this angry over a female before. Ever since I could remember, Dwayne had been the man when it came to women. He never got turned down or dumped. He even stole a couple of chicks I brought home. Now Samara was giving him a taste of his own medicine. He couldn't handle it.

Shaking my head, I put his phone down and went upstairs to my room leaving Dwayne and his emotions behind. Why had it mattered to Samara so much that I not be here when she got here? She told me she didn't want me to get the wrong idea about her, and now I didn't know what to think. I convinced myself that if I fucked her I could just leave her alone. But that was getting harder to believe. Could I just fuck Samara knowing she cared enough about my feelings to make sure I wasn't home when she came over here to be with Dwayne?

Could I just fuck her knowing she cared period? I was being pulled in two different directions. On the one hand, I knew I should just hit it and quit it. I was good at that and I could probably get some damn peace of mind from it. But on the other hand, the more I thought about her the more I wanted to be around her. She was such a free spirit that she made me feel like a horny teenager when I was around her. She made me want to chase her. It touched me to know that she stopped fucking with Dwayne altogether for me. She'd suggested that in the bathroom, but I didn't really think she would. How was I supposed to react to that?

Should I just invite her over? But what then? I had never been so confused by and attracted to someone that I hadn't slept with. I didn't really date. I maybe had four actual girlfriends my whole life and they never lasted longer than the next full moon. Whatever would happen between us would have to be on my terms. I just needed to see her. Maybe then I could determine what to do next.

SAMARA

Two weeks after Ryson kissed me, I finally got the call I was waiting for. Dwayne called me almost every night since the last time we were together. I ignored every call and deleted every text before reading it. I was no longer interested in being with him sexually or socially, so what was the point of responding? A number showed up on my screen and I couldn't help but smile when I heard Ryson's voice.

"Hello?" I answered pulling at my bottom lip. I hadn't seen or heard anything from him and I was beginning to get worried. I was avoiding one brother's call and desperately awaiting a call from the other. So crazy.

"Hey Samara! I hope you didn't forget about my party tonight." Ryson's cheerful voice filtered through the phone. I had totally forgotten about his party. I was more concerned about him.

"Oh... no, of course not. How are you?" I changed the subject. I wanted to talk about us.

"I'm good! I can't wait to see you tonight. I've been so busy trying to plan this party and get some things together. I wanted to call you sooner but I got tied up. You know how it goes. Anyway, I'm all done and I'm all yours tonight." I blushed and touched my lips, remembering our kiss.

"You're all mines tonight huh?" I asked coyly. "What should I do with you?" I giggled over the phone.

"Anything you want to do. It starts at seven. Don't be late." His sexy voice floated through the line and then he hung up.

I couldn't decide what to wear. I wanted to wear something flirty and girly. Something that accentuated my assets, but didn't look trashy. I finally decided on a midi dress. It was black with small white polka dots. The back was cut out in the shape of a 'U' leaving my back bare. I wanted to stand out, so I wore a pair of skin-tight knee-length boots. They were leather with a stiletto heel. I put some moisturizer in my hair and twisted my curls around my finger to give them definition. The charm bracelet my father had given me as a child was around my wrist. I felt good. I looked in my bedroom mirror and gave myself a once over. I didn't want to leave anything to chance. I had to be on my A game. I was very attracted to Ryson even though I didn't know that much about him. There was something in his eyes that pulled me in whenever I looked at him. I wanted to see what my fascination with him was all about. If he turned out not to be what I expected, I would just cut my losses. I would just have to start from scratch and re-enter the dating pool. I wasn't getting any younger. I wanted to get married and start a family. The clock was ticking. I looked at the scratches on my cheek. They were almost completely gone. That made me think of the person who had put them there. Dwayne would be furious at me tonight. I had ignored him for weeks and I knew he would be all over me when I stepped into his house. I decided to avoid him at all costs until I knew what was up with Ryson. Hopefully he would just ignore me. I drove to the house with butterflies in my stomach. The party was in full swing when I pulled up. There were people hanging out in front of the house with drinks in their hands. Music was blaring from inside the house. I could see Ryson standing in the middle of the living room talking. I got out of the car and walked past a group of guys in front of the house. I felt all of their eyes burning a hole in my ass as I walked by to get into the house. A few of them tried to get my attention, but I kept walking. Ryson spotted me instantly and stopped talking mid-sentence.

He smiled at me and walked over. He was dressed casually with a pair of brown cargo shorts, and a chocolate brown V neck t-shirt. The shirt showed off his biceps and chiseled chest. I couldn't help but check out his muscular calves. Looks-wise, Ryson was the cream of the crop.

"Wow! You look good enough to eat." Ryson hugged me and kissed me softly on the neck.

"Want a nibble?" I challenged, looking into his eyes. He smiled at me and shook his head.

"You're going to get me in trouble at this party." Ryson joked and put his arm around my shoulder as we walked around the living room. He introduced me to people when they came up to him to say hi. They all gave me a once over. I had yet to see Dwayne and was secretly relieved. The only thing that kind of ticked me off was how he introduced me. He just said, "This is Samara." That was it. He didn't say I was his friend, associate, or anything. I knew that I technically wasn't anything to him, but it still made me feel a little bit invisible. It was like he wasn't trying to make anyone remember me. Like he knew this thing with us wouldn't last long.

"I want to talk to you about something Samara. It's loud down here. Let's go upstairs." Ryson whispered in my ear. I nodded and followed him up the stairs. We walked to his bedroom and sat down on his king-sized bed. It felt weird coming up the stairs and walking into his bedroom instead of Dwayne's.

"Look, I want you to know up front that we can kick it and chill, but I want to keep it casual." My face dropped. That's what he brought me up here for?

"So you want us to have the same arrangement that Dwayne and I had? No thank you." I got up, heated and ready to leave. Did he not understand that I wanted to date him, not just screw him? If I was only looking for a frequent fuck, I would still be messing around with Dwayne.

"Wait, wait, wait." He gently grabbed my hand and pulled me back down onto the bed. I crossed my arms and looked down at the carpet. I was so disappointed.

"No of course not. But we don't know that much about each other, so right now we're just feeling things out. Let's just see where it goes. Don't put too much emphasis on labeling what this is. This is all new to me, to be honest. Samara, you understand right?" He asked me and his eyes softened. I couldn't be annoyed with him. He was too damn sexy. I twisted my lips and shrugged as if to say 'whatever'. He bent down and kissed me on the cheek. I closed my eyes and smiled. I couldn't ask for more than that right now especially taking into consideration our unique situation. After all, I had slept with his brother right on the other side of this wall not too long ago. So I could understand Ryson being hesitant to commit to me fully.

"Are we exclusive?" I put the question that was on my mind out there. He sighed heavily and rubbed the bottom of his chin.

"It's only day one. Let's cross that bridge when we get there." That was a yes and a no. I would just roll with the punches. He bent down to kiss my cheek again, but I turned my face towards him and snuck a kiss to his lips. He put his hand behind my ear and pulled my face closer to his, kissing me deeper. His tongue darted into my mouth and swirled around my tongue. I started to get hot and my body started to tremble. Ryson's lips were so soft I didn't want to stop. He broke the kiss first and looked at me then at his door.

"You think they would miss us?" He asked me, his breathing heavy. I looked into his eyes and knew he wanted me. I wasn't expecting to be with him tonight, I just wanted to learn more about him. I actually wanted to take it slow with Ryson. I had made a disastrous mistake by sleeping with Dwayne so quickly and didn't want history to repeat itself. I went with the flow nonetheless.

"Probably not. You bought enough drinks to keep them occupied right?" I joked and uncrossed my legs. Ryson looked down at my boots and ran his hand from my knee up my dress. I held my breath as he leaned over and ran his tongue up and down my neck.

"Oh shit!" I gasped for air when his hand slid further up my leg. I looked up at the ceiling and hissed in pleasure. His tongue traveled down from my neck to my shoulders. His hand stopped mid-thigh as he continued to kiss and lick my body. Ryson climbed onto me, forcing me to lie back on his bed. He stopped kissing my shoulder and glided down my body. I watched as his face went underneath my dress.

"I like these boots." He whispered and kissed my knee cap. I didn't say anything as I took pleasure in his exploration of my body. He planted hot wet kisses on my knee and made his way up my thighs. Every kiss made me pant for breath. I grabbed onto one of his pillows. My clit started to tingle as he got closer and closer to her. His face was in between my legs and I could feel his warm breath on my panties. I heaved a sigh of disappointment when he abruptly stopped.

"Come on," he said, standing up and holding out his hand to me.

"Huh? Wha… what?" I couldn't even talk. I was so confused and caught off guard. I grabbed his hand and stood up, not sure how to feel. I fixed my dress and adjusted my wet panties.

"You didn't think it was going down tonight, did you? What, do you think I'm easy or something?" Ryson started to laugh. I was off-kilter at what just happened, but I laughed with him.

"Don't tease me like that," I whined and pushed him softly.

"Samara, did you really think I was going to try to hook up with you at this crowded loud ass party? Oh no baby. I don't roll like that. Trust me, you won't be disappointed when the time comes." He kissed me on the lips and tenderly palmed my ass.

"Okay." I wrapped my arms around his waist.

"Let's get back." We walked out of his room and back to the party.

I was having so much fun! Ryson made me dance with him to almost every song. His friends were dancing too and the females actually stopped giving me the evil eye. A few guys asked me to dance with them. Ryson spoke up each time with a firm 'no'. It was too cute.

"One more song Samara. Don't tell me you can't hang." Ryson taunted me when I started walking back over to the couch. I could hang, I just didn't know how long I could dance with these shoes on. But I never backed down from a challenge and I wasn't about to start today. When Sinead O'Connor's 'Downpressor Man' started to play I strolled back over to him.

"Oh I can hang. Just you wait and see." I gently pushed him back so that he was against his living room wall, then I turned around and started to slowly wind my hips.

'If you run to the sea, the sea will be boiling. If you run to the sea, the sea will be boiling. If you run to the sea, the sea will be boiling. Oooh on that day...'

I put my hands above my head and rotated my wrists.

'If you run to the rocks, the rocks will be melting. If you run to the rocks, the rocks will be melting. If you run to the rocks, the rocks will be melting. Oooh on that day...'

I licked my lips and bent over. I started to grind my ass onto him. He put his hands on my hips and squeezed. I slowly came back up and started to grind my ass back on him, slow and rhythmic. My head lay back on his shoulder. I took his hand off my hip and put it on my thigh.

'And if you make your bed in hell, I will be dere. Make your bed in hell, I will be dere, I say make your bed in hell, I will be dere, on that day...'

I took his hand and slid it farther up my thigh until his index finger was touching my lace panties.

'Downpressor man, where you gonna run to? Downpressor man, where you gonna run to? Downpressor man, where you gonna run to? Oh on that day. Where you gonna fucking run to?'

I turned around and put my hands around his waist. His dick was hard, poking me through his cargos.

"I guess you can hang." Ryson laughed and pulled me closer to him. I stood on my tiptoes and poked my lips out for a kiss. Ryson obliged me. I felt his hand slide down my waist and underneath my dress.

"Be careful." I warned him, talking on his lips. He laughed, put his hand inside my panties and pinched my ass cheek.

"Ouch!" I laughed and grabbed his hand.

"Wassup Dwayne!" I heard someone call out across the room. I turned towards the voice in time to see Dwayne set his eyes on me. Shar was attached to his hip and also looking at me.

"What's up Devon." Dwayne spoke to his friend half-heartedly. His eyes were targeted on me. I turned my attention back to Ryson. I let him go and cleared my throat.

"I don't want this to get uncomfortable. I should just leave before any drama pops off." I suggested.

"It's still early Samara. You're going to let Dwayne run you out of my party?" Ryson asked me. I didn't want to leave, I just had a feeling that something bad would happen if I stayed there. Ryson could see the indecision on my face.

"How about this. Let's go to your place. We can chill and talk there." Ryson got off the wall and began walking towards the front door. It wasn't a bad idea. I followed him. I smelled Dwayne's cologne as I walked past, ignoring him. I had a nervous feeling in my stomach that made me wring my wrists.

"My bracelet!" It wasn't on my wrist anymore. I looked over to where I'd been dancing and didn't see it.

"It must have come off when we were upstairs. I'll be right back." I told Ryson and ran up the steps to his room.

"I'll be at your car." I heard him yell behind me.

SHAR

Of course that bitch was here. Kissing Ryson while he had his hand on her ass. How trifling could she get? She didn't care that there was a living room full of people. She was so scandalous. Dwayne didn't want to come to the party and I wasn't even invited, but I had a plan and I needed him. After work he came straight to my apartment intent on staying there. It was his house too and I wasn't letting Samara make him feel unwelcome in his own home. I didn't tell him what my plan was but I knew he would do it. Dwayne was easily manipulated if you challenged his manhood or his ego. So I used the only ammunition I had to get Dwayne mad. Mad enough to hurt somebody. Mad enough to hurt Samara. After I finally convinced him he should go to the party, the first thing he saw was that bitch with her ass all on Ryson.

"That's crazy how she just hopped from you to Ryson so quick," I said, trying to sound casual. Which was hard to do given that I was trying to talk over the music. Dwayne's eyebrows twitched slightly. I was getting through.

"I don't give a fuck about that bitch!" Dwayne yelled with a lack of concern. I knew he was lying. If he didn't care, why did he let her get under his skin like that?

"Yeah, but you used to until she stopped answering your calls. She just used you to bust a nut." I shook my head in sympathy. He cut his eyes at me. If looks could kill, I would be dead. But I knew he was seeing Samara's face instead of mine. All I had to do was add a little more fuel to the fire to get him really riled up.

"She didn't use me. I used her ass and let her loose when I got bored. She's the one missing out, not me." Dwayne tried to save face. I knew that Samara had kicked him to the curb when she set her sights on Ryson. She was a whore so I expected as much from her. I wasn't letting Dwayne justify her actions.

"Even if you did cut her loose, she's at a party in *your* house, with *your* brother. That's the most disrespectful thing somebody could do to you. Are you going to let her get away with playing you in front of all your friends?" I put the nail in the coffin. Dwayne's muscles flexed in his arms as Samara walked past. His eyes were cold as ice as he watched her run up the steps.

"If I was you, I would set her ass straight." I goaded him. He was moving a little too slow for my liking. I needed him to react sooner rather than later. Samara needed to get her trick ass out of our lives. If Dwayne didn't do it, then I would have to go to plan B. Samara did not want me to go to plan B.

"Naw. Fuck her man. I'm not trying to start no shit with Ryson over her. She ain't worth it." Dwayne closed his eyes and took a deep breath. His anger was just below the surface, he was trying to push it back.

"Don't worry about Ryson. I'll handle him. You go ahead and handle your business." I assured him that it was okay. I nudged him a little. He looked at me and nodded. Dwayne's lips curled into a snarl as he ran up the steps. I waited until he was at the top of the stairs to go over and turn the radio up a few notches. I leisurely walked out of the house over to Ryson, who was standing at what I assume was Samara's car.

"What's up Ryson?" I asked him, leaning onto the car.

SAMARA

"Where the hell did that thing go?" I looked under the bed and all around the room and still couldn't find my bracelet. I scanned the dresser and the floor by the door and still didn't see it.

"Okay focus. I came in, sat on the bed, and then...voila!" The bracelet was tucked underneath one of Ryson's pillows. I walked over to the window and saw Ryson standing at my car talking to Shar. He looked up at me and smiled. Shar was trying so hard to get his attention. I don't think I've ever met someone so desperate in my life. Whenever I turned my back, she was in one of their faces. I still didn't understand their relationship with her. Was she an old flame of one of theirs that just wouldn't go away? Was she a sideline hoe who didn't know her place? I would have to do a little digging into that. I didn't really like it when she was in Ryson's presence. I knew I was being territorial, but a woman knew when another woman was pushing up on her man. Not to say that Ryson was my man, but he had the potential to be. Only time and god knew how this thing between us would go. I didn't need Shar interfering. I put my bracelet back on my wrist, closed the clasp, and headed for the door. I turned around and Dwayne was standing inches away from me. He did not look happy. *Shit.* My heart skipped a beat. I knew this would happen, but I was not in the mood to argue or to go back and forth with him. I had to face the music though. I couldn't hide from him forever. The only way to get out of this without getting into a confrontation with him was for me to be a woman and just tell him the truth.

"Hey." I smiled weakly. I was instantly uncomfortable. It didn't help that he was looking at me with such contempt.

"What the fuck are you doing here?" There was nothing friendly about his tone. I realized that he had come up here to argue. I held back the remarks I wanted to say and calmly responded to him. One of us had to keep a cool head. From the looks of things, that was going to be me.

"Ryson invited me to the party Dwayne, that's why I came." I played with one of the charms on my bracelet nervously. The tension in the room was so thick. I could feel the anger seeping through Dwayne's pores.

"You knew I would be here. You didn't think that shit would be fucked up? I mean, you weren't answering any of my calls or texts. Did you think you were going to come to the party and I was just going to act like shit was cool?" The conversation was turning quickly. I had to do something to diffuse the situation fast. I stilled my shaking hands and looked him square in the eyes. He was beyond angry.

"No. I didn't think it would be cool, but I thought we would be adults about this. I haven't returned any of your calls beca---,"

"Because you're fucking Ryson! I'm not fucking stupid!" He yelled and stepped closer to my face. He balled up his fists and narrowed his eyes. His outburst caused me to pause before reacting. Where was all of this coming from?

"What? No! I didn't fuck Ryson! We're just hanging out!" My voice squeaked as it rose an octave. Dwayne seemed to be getting angrier by the second. Why was he so full of rage? "You were the one who said you weren't looking for anything serious. Why are you so upset?" I asked and his expression hardened.

"Dwayne trust me, I didn't do anything with your brother." I tried to sound as convincing as possible.

"Why the fuck are you up here in his room then?" His voice got low. Damn. He had me.

"Listen Dwayne, it's not what you think. We were up here earlier talking and then my bracelet---," He grabbed me by my upper arms before I could finish my sentence. He yanked me closer to him, tightening his grip. The force of him grabbing me temporarily knocked the wind out of me. It took me a few seconds to catch my breath. His hands felt hot on my arms. No the fuck he didn't! I looked up at him in shock.

"Look, I know you're mad but you need to ease up Dwayne, for real!" I said through clenched teeth. He tightened his grip on my arms. I forced my face to stay neutral, even though it felt as if he was crushing every bone in my arms.

"SHIT! Dwayne what the fuck is wrong with you?" I yelled at him and tried to break free from his grasp.

"You think you can just disrespect me in front of my boys?" He squeezed my arms harder, lifting me slightly off the floor. His anger rose.

"OWW! DWAYNE! I'm not trying to disrespect you! YOU'RE HURTING ME!" I screamed in his face. I wriggled my body, trying to gain some leverage to loosen his grip. He was starting to piss me off. I was trying to be level-headed, but he was pushing my fucking buttons. I knew self-defense, but he was so much stronger than me. It wouldn't be easy for me to take him down. I could try using what I knew, but I didn't want to have to hurt him. I was hoping it wouldn't escalate to that. I didn't think he would really hurt me anyway. He was just angry and venting.

"I was just another dick to you wasn't I?" He violently shook me, making my head spin.

"If you don't get the fuck off me Dwayne, I swear to god!" I tried again to pull myself free.

"WHAT ARE YOU GOING TO DO?" He screamed back at me. His eyes blazed, and I saw for the first time that he really did want to hurt me. I wasn't going out without a fight, but I didn't want to hurt him too bad. I pulled my right leg back and with the toe of my heel I kicked his shin as hard as I could.

"AAAHHHHH! FUCK!" He loosened his grip on my arms and stumbled back. I fell to the floor. I got up and tried to get my bearings and re-evaluate the situation. I looked down at my arms. Dark bruises were starting to form, which made me even madder. I looked at him and he shot daggers at me with his eyes. I was ready for anything at this point and I knew I had to protect myself at all costs. I wasn't going to be tossed around. Anger boiled inside me, but I really just wanted to get the hell out of that room.

Pushing past him, I ran towards the door and made it to the doorknob. He grabbed my arms and aggressively pulled me backwards like I was a rag doll.

"GET OFF OF ME!" I screamed and pulled one arm free from his grasp. He yanked the arm he still had and grabbed a chunk of my hair.

"AAHHH! DWAYNE LET ME GO!" I yelled and tried to take my hair out of his grasp. I hated to admit it, but I was getting scared. He dragged me back towards the bed.

"No! You not leaving without apologizing!" He said angrily and pushed me down roughly onto the bed. My head jerked backwards. At this point I was beyond mad. If he wanted a fight, he had one. How dare he manhandle me! Here I was, trying to hold back when he was trying to beat the shit out of me! I bounced right back up like a jack-rabbit, and pushed him away from me with as much strength as I could muster. He grabbed my wrists and pulled me close to his face.

"I'm waiting for my apology." His eyes were blazing with anger.

"Let me go RIGHT NOW! I'm trying to be nice, but you're HURTING ME! I don't want to hurt you Dwayne," I warned him.

"You don't want to hurt me? You're cute." He pushed his lips roughly onto mines. His tongue was in my mouth before I could blink. The violation I felt at that moment enraged me. I felt his erection against my stomach. He was actually enjoying this. I took one of my wrists from his grasp and pushed his head back from my face. When his head was a few inches away from my face, I used the space I created and slapped him hard across the face. The sound of the slap took us both by surprise. He let me go completely. I stood in front of him scared, taking gulps of air, not sure of what to do next. My hands slowly came up and covered my mouth. I was shocked at myself. I didn't really mean to hit him, I was just so upset that he had roughed me up. He touched his cheek where I hit him and then closed his eyes. He took a deep breath and I knew then that I had made a huge mistake.

"I...I... I'm sorry for hitting you, but you were hurting me. You shouldn't have put your hands on me! I was just defending myself!" I said quickly. I moved farther away from him, closer to the window. If my intention was to diffuse the situation, I had failed miserably. If anything, I made it worse. I should have called Ryson to handle this. It wasn't the best idea to get into a fight with someone twice your size. Especially someone with a short fuse. He stared at me in silence, his eyes sparkling in the light. It was time for me to go.

"I'm sorry okay. I'm just going to go home and leave you alone. Just calm down okay?"

I took a few small steps forward. The vein in his neck flexed. I stopped walking. Panic coursed through my body as I stood frozen where I stood. It was almost surreal. I saw his hand coming, but I couldn't move.

"DON'T!" I pleaded. The sound of the back of his hand making contact with my face was deafening. I fell hard against the wall, losing my footing, and fell into the corner.

"DWAYNE!" I cried out in pain and pressed my hand to my cheek. It burned like hell! My whole head throbbed painfully. He bent over me and I saw his hand raise to hit me again on the same cheek. I was already so dizzy, I had no time to block. The second hit almost knocked me out. It hurt worse than the first hit. I couldn't scream. I curled myself into a ball. My bottom lip felt like it was torn in half. My face felt as if it was on fire. Something sharp felt like it had cut into my lip and I bit the inside of my cheek. They both started to bleed. I touched my lip and looked at the blood on my fingers, still not believing that he had just hit me. I was too light-headed to react.

"Shit." I muttered as blood continued to drip from my lip and mouth.

"WHAT THE FUCK ARE YOU DOING DWAYNE?" I heard Ryson yell.

SHAR

"What do you want Shar? I *specifically* remember telling you not to come." Ryson said to me, rolling his eyes like I was getting on his nerves or something. I leaned closer to him so that he could get a good glimpse of my black bra showing through my black fishnet shirt.

"It's a free country. I just came out here to see what's up with you. I haven't talked to you in like two weeks. What's up?" That was actually the truth. After Samara had stopped fucking with Dwayne, it was clear to see that she had moved on to Ryson with her dirty ass. Ryson hadn't answered any of my calls or texts either since then. I was mad as shit. I didn't tell him that. His nose was so wide open I could have parked my car in his nostrils. He and Dwayne always did this shit, but this time it seemed different somehow. Now Dwayne was sweating Samara and Ryson was trying to make her his girl? Even though he would never admit it, I could tell Ryson was feeling Samara. He never brought a date to his parties, he always met new women there. It had been a few weeks and Ryson was still fucking with Samara. I wasn't going to give him the opportunity to take that shit any further. That shit wasn't happening on my watch. I have invested too much of my time, my heart, and my damn money, to be replaced by some skank. With every fiber in my body, I hated Samara. I wanted to see her suffer the way she was making me suffer. Hopefully Dwayne had her upstairs in a choke hold or was on the verge of pushing her out the window. How funny would it be to see her fat ass go splat on the concrete?

"I'm cool Shar. I haven't seen you on purpose. I'm not trying to be around you right now. I see you enough as it is." Ryson stood up straighter and looked up at his bedroom window. Samara came into view and for a second she and Ryson looked at each other. I looked at Ryson and almost flipped my lid. He was falling for that bitch! I could see it all over his fine ass face.

"What do you mean you're not trying to be around me? What did I do to you?" I asked pulling his attention back to me. It was bad enough that this bitch came out of nowhere and had a hold on the two men in my life. But for them to like her back was something completely different. Ryson and Dwayne had played the I fuck her you fuck her next game dozens of times since I'd met them. Rarely had either one of them given the girl a second glance when the night was over. Now they were both drooling after Samara like she was Cleopatra or something.

"I don't want you telling Samara shit she doesn't need to know." Ryson looked at me for the first time since I walked over to the car. He looked serious. I crinkled my brows. What the fuck was he talking about?

"Like what?" I asked him, oblivious. He tilted and shook his head.

"You know what the fuck I'm talking about Shar. I don't want her to know how we met, what we did, or anything else that's not any of her business." Oh? That was it. He was ashamed about fucking me? Did he really just tell me that shit?

"First off, I'm grown and I can tell anyone anything I fucking want to! Second, how can you say that to me? Nobody forced you or Dwayne to fuck me! If you didn't want her to know then you shouldn't have done it!" I couldn't keep my anger under control. I loved Ryson, but he was disrespecting me in the worst way.

"That was an error on my part and I regret it every day." He looked me straight in the eyes as he said that. If it was possible for a heart to literally break, I think mine would have at that moment.

"But I thought you loved me! You can't stop me from trying to get back what's mines!" I practically screamed at him. How could he say that to me?

"I'm not playing with you Shar. I don't want you telling Samara shit! When I'm ready to tell her, I will. I don't need your jealous, scheming ass telling her shit out of spite. You understand me?" Ryson was talking to me like I was a little girl. Looking down on me and bossing me around like I was a baby or something.

"I am not jealous of Samara! Please!" I said, fidgeting with my shirt. How dare he say that to me! Yes I was jealous, but guess whose fault that was? Theirs! Ryson laughed then and looked at me like I was the most pitiful girl in the world. I hated it when he looked at me like that. He was making it harder and harder for me to keep from doing what I really wanted to do to Samara. My plan B.

"Shar, you've been jealous of Samara since you walked over to her fucking table and interrupted me and Dwayne. You can't really be that dumb to think we didn't notice that. That doesn't matter anyway. Just don't talk to her, period." He stood all the way up and looked up towards his bedroom window again. How was he going to tell me not to talk to her? She wasn't the fucking Pope! I picked my face up off the ground and stood in front of him.

"Okay, I will make a deal with you. If you spend some 'quality' time with me then I won't tell Samara anything." I laid my cards on the table. He scrunched up his face and sucked his teeth.

"Are you trying to threaten me Shar?" He looked like he wanted to push me into traffic. Shit, what else could I do?

"No! I'm just saying I will do what you want, if you do what I want." I whined. Why couldn't he see how much I wanted him? Most men would love to have a woman fawning all over them. I haven't been with Ryson intimately for almost a year. He just stopped wanting me and it was killing me. Dwayne took any piece of ass that was thrown at him, so it was already a given that we would still be fucking. Ryson just seemed to have distanced himself from me out of nowhere.

"That sounds like a threat to me Shar. It's cool though. Trust me, if you tell Samara anything about how we met or anything that went on between us in the last four years, you will regret it. Just because you're miserable, doesn't mean you need to make everybody else miserable too. Heed my warning Shar." He left me standing at the car with tears falling from my eyes. I wiped them away and took pleasure in the fact that Dwayne was probably upstairs beating the shit out of Samara. I walked behind Ryson back into the house.

"What's taking her so long?" I heard Ryson say to himself before he started to climb the steps. I ran up the stairs after him with a smile on my face. It was show time.

DWAYNE

She was going to be at the party. I just knew it. She ignored the shit out of me for weeks, but I bet she would be there with Ryson. I should go and curse her the fuck out in front of everyone, and dare her to say something back. I was so mad! I didn't know what to do with myself.

"Would you stop pacing back and forth? You're making me dizzy." Shar was laying on the bed. I needed to blow off some steam, so I had decided to let Shar suck some stress out of me. I was naked in her bedroom trying to decide if I should go home or not.

"I'm just going to stay here and calm down because if I go to that party..." My voice trailed off as I got angry again. I balled up my fists then released them. Why did Samara have me so damn worked up? Why was she even still on my mind? If this had been any other female, I would have said fuck it, and moved on to the next. Shar sat up quickly, her breasts bouncing from the sudden movement.

"Fuck that! That's YOUR house! What are you talking about you staying here? You have every right to be mad! She fucking rejected all your calls and texts for weeks. Who the fuck does she think she is?" Shar's angry outburst caused me to stop pacing.

"You're right! That bitch disrespected me! Why should I try to be the bigger person? Get dressed Shar. We heading out." I hurried into the bathroom to shower. Samara wasn't going to get away with treating me like dirt. I was going to demand an apology. And if she played her cards right, I might let her have the privilege of having this dick again.

I parked down the street from the house. I could hear the music blaring. I took a few breaths to try to calm myself down. The whole drive over here, Shar kept saying shit, making me angrier and angrier.

"If she wanted to be with Ryson, why would she waste your time by going home with you that night? Nobody put a gun to her head and made her choose you." Shar said while she applied lipstick.

"Yeah, but I don't know if she chose me or not. When you came over all jealous, Ryson kind of like, forfeited his chance. So it's like she got me by default. I actually told *her* she was going home with me." Who's to say she would have chosen me? I thought about that during the last few days. If Shar hadn't come over to the table, what would have happened? Maybe she wanted Ryson all along and I was just her consolation prize. That thought was fucking me up in the head. I mean I could tell she was attracted to me, her dripping pussy said it all, but was she just settling?

"No, no, that's bullshit! First off, I wasn't jealous. Y'all fucking ditched me, so I had every right to come over there." She was offended. I rolled my eyes at her.

"Shar, you lucky you was even invited. Even though I don't remember inviting you at all. I remember you saying you needed a ride somewhere, then conveniently ending up having to go to the same place as us." I watched her face register guilt. She was so obvious.

"*Anyway!* All I'm saying is whether I came over there or not, she could have chosen whoever. She went with you and then tried to play you like a dummy. She could have at least answered one text and said 'it's over' or something like that. She looked at *all* your texts, and saw your number pop up for weeks and hit ignore *each* time. That's some disrespectful shit. I wouldn't do that to my worst enemy." Shar was right. I grabbed the steering wheel and cracked my neck. I was going to set Samara straight tonight, whether she liked it or not.

"Alright, get out." I motioned for her to hurry up. I put the car back in drive. She blew air out her lips and got out of the car.

"You really making me get out a block away?" She sounded hurt. Oh well. She knew the drill. I didn't want anybody thinking Shar was with me.

"Yes, and when you get there don't try to be all up under my ass either." I sped off before she could say anything else. I parked outside the house and got out of my truck. I scanned the street and saw Samara's sports car. *I knew it.* I walked up to the house and started greeting everybody. That gave me a few minutes to gather myself before I stepped into the house. Shar made her way up the steps, looking furious, but wisely didn't look my way. She trailed behind me a few feet as I stepped into the living room. I quickly scanned the room and my eyes landed on Samara. Or more accurately, my eyes found her ass. Ryson's hand slid underneath her dress and grabbed her cheek. The room seemed like it was spinning. Everything slowed down. I suddenly felt this hot fury building up inside me. Calm down. Breathe.

"Wassup Dwayne!" I heard my name but all I could see was Samara. She turned towards me and we locked eyes. God, she's beautiful.

"That's crazy how she just hopped from you to Ryson so quick," Shar's voice yelled into my ear over the music.

"I don't give a fuck about that bitch!" I yelled back. Samara turned to Ryson. They both looked at me and exchanged words.

"Yeah, but you used to until she stopped answering your calls. She just used you to bust a nut." I turned angry eyes on Shar. Why the fuck would she say that? That wasn't true. Was it?

"She didn't use me. I used her ass and let her loose when I got bored. She's the one missing out, not me," I said, trying to save face. Samara and Ryson started walking towards us. *She better be coming over to apologize.*

What was that voice? I closed my eyes and tried to clear my mind.

"Even if you did cut her loose, she's at a party in *your* house, with *your* brother. That's the most disrespectful thing somebody could do to you. Are you going to let her get away with playing you in front of all your friends?" I tried to rein in my temper, but all I could think about were all those texts and calls Samara blatantly ignored. She was within arm's length of me. I held my breath and waited for her to stop and acknowledge me. She kept walking past without even looking at me. What the fuck! I felt so much rage. I felt a headache coming on. I started to get overheated. I needed to get out of here before I did something I regretted. She stopped and said something to Ryson. *Here comes the apology.*

That voice again! Was I going crazy? Again she ignored me and ran upstairs. I watched her ass bounce as she made her way up the steps. I remembered the last time she was up there with me and it made my dick hard. I was the angriest I had ever been, but I couldn't help thinking about being with her again.

"If I was you, I would set her ass straight." Shar's voice broke me out of my trance. I took one step forward then stopped myself, What the fuck was I doing here? Was I really tripping over a two night stand? Was it worth causing drama at this party? Ryson would definitely have an issue with me stepping to Samara like this. I was surprised he even invited her to the party. Something more was going on than they were letting on.

"Naw. Fuck her man. I'm not trying to start no shit with Ryson over her. She ain't worth it." I closed my eyes and took a deep breath.

"Don't worry about Ryson. I'll handle him. You go ahead and handle your business." I knew I shouldn't be listening to Shar. I was so caught up in those crazy emotions I was having towards Samara. I was so confused. Shar gave me a little push towards the stairs. Fuck it! I'm going up. I ran up the steps after Samara. I walked towards my bedroom but realized Ryson's door was open. I peered in and saw Samara looking out the window. What was she doing in Ryson's bedroom? SHE FUCKED HIM!

The voice boomed in my ears. I looked at the bed and saw that the pillows were messed up. It was true. She had fucked Ryson. She treated me like shit just to get with my brother! I wasn't going to let that shit go! I walked in and quietly closed the door behind me. Her perfume smelled delicious. She turned around and jumped in surprise at seeing me. She licked her lips nervously. Images of that tongue circling the head of my dick popped into my head.

"Hey." She gave me a hesitant smile. Her body looked so fucking good in that dress. I wanted to rip it off her. I tried to stay focused.

"What the fuck are you doing here?" I cut right to the chase. She played me. Fucked me over. Treated me like I was nothing. I had to remember that.

"Ryson invited me to the party Dwayne, that's why I came." She started playing with her bracelet. So she could keep in touch with Ryson all this time, but not me? Not even a fucking text saying she was done with me? Nothing? I could feel the tension in the room. My skin was lava hot. I felt like smoke was emitting from my skin.

"You knew I would be here. You didn't think that shit would be fucked up? I mean, you weren't answering any of my calls or texts. Did you think you were going to come to the party and I was just going to act like shit was cool?"

Was she that heartless to not even care that I would be here? Why would she come, knowing what she'd done to me? Was she deliberately trying to make me angry? My hands started shaking. I was so angry I wanted to break something. She looked me in the eyes and I almost forgot about being angry.

"No I didn't think it would be cool, but I thought we would be adults about this. I haven't returned any of your calls beca---,"

"Because you're fucking Ryson! I'm not fucking stupid!" I yelled and got in her face. I wanted to punch her. I got dizzy all of a sudden and I started seeing red. Her eyes got huge and she took a step back.

"What? No! I didn't fuck Ryson! We're just hanging out," she squeaked.

"You were the one who said you weren't looking for anything serious. Why are you so upset?" That gave her the right to act like I didn't exist? My muscles were so tight, I felt like they would snap at any second.

"Dwayne, trust me. I didn't do anything with your brother." She tried to sound innocent. She was anything but.

"Why the fuck are you up here in his room then?" I didn't recognize my voice then. It was like it hadn't come from my mouth. She stopped talking. She couldn't answer the question. My vision got redder and redder. She started rambling.

"Listen Dwayne, it's not what you think. We were up here earlier talking and then my bracelet---," Hands reached out and grabbed Samara. She was yanked closer to me. I looked down and realized those were my hands. I didn't remember doing that! She looked up at me with fear in her eyes. My hands pulled her even closer. I felt my grip on her arms tightening. What the fuck was happening? It was like I was outside of my body watching myself. I had no control over my own body.

"Look, I know you're mad, but you need to ease up Dwayne for real," she said through clenched teeth. I tightened my grip on her arm. I felt her bones and knew I was applying way too much pressure. I couldn't make my hands stop.

"SHIT! Dwayne what the fuck is wrong with you?" She yelled at me and tried to break free from my grasp. I tried to let her go, but I couldn't.

"It's not me!" I yelled but nothing came out.

"You think you can just disrespect me in front of my boys?" I heard myself say. I started getting scared. What the hell was happening to me? I squeezed her even harder almost breaking her arm. I looked down and saw that her feet were no longer on the ground.

"STOP! PUT HER DOWN!" I screamed as loud as I could at no one in particular.

"OWW! DWAYNE! I'm not trying to disrespect you! YOU'RE HURTING ME!" She started screaming. I was hurting her. Her eyes darted around the room like a frightened animal. She started trying to wiggle herself free. Suddenly, I stopped being scared. I had no control over what was happening, but why should I care? She deserved this didn't she?

"I was just another dick to you wasn't I?" This time the voice was mines. I shook her hard, jerking her head back and forth. I felt sensation in my fingers again. I was starting to regain control of myself.

"If you don't get the fuck off me Dwayne, I swear to god!" She tried again unsuccessfully to break free. I wasn't done with her yet. She needed to know I was serious.

"WHAT ARE YOU GOING TO DO?" I screamed at her. Her hair was so wild. She never looked sexier. I wanted to kiss her. I felt a sharp pain in my shin and realized she'd kicked me.

"AAAAHHHHH! FUCK!" I loosened my grip and let her go. She wanted to fight back? This was going to be fun. She fell to the floor, then quickly got up. She examined her arms and looked at me in anger. We stared each other down. She had yet to apologize, so I wasn't letting her leave until I got it from her. She ran towards the door and made it to the doorknob. I grabbed both of her arms and pulled her backwards. HELL NO! She wasn't getting off that easy!

"GET OFF OF ME!" She screamed and got one arm free. I reached out and grabbed a big chunk of her curly hair and dragged her towards the bed.

"AAHHH! DWAYNE LET ME GO!" She scratched at me and tried to take my hands out of her hair. She failed.

"No! You not leaving without apologizing!" I said and pushed her down hard on the bed. The things I wanted to do with her in this position ran through my mind. She still had a chance to make it up to me. She bounced back up and pushed me away from her. I grabbed her tiny wrists and pulled her close to me.

"I'm waiting for my apology." I was so angry yet so turned on.

"Let me go RIGHT NOW! I'm trying to be nice, but you're HURTING ME! I don't want to hurt you Dwayne," she said with a serious look on her face. She was breathing heavily now.

"You don't want to hurt me? You're cute." I saw my opportunity and bent down to kiss her. Nice and rough just like she liked it. She tried to fight it, but I managed to get my tongue in her mouth. She tasted so fucking good. I moaned on her lips. My hard dick was pressed against her stomach. We were definitely going to fuck when this was all over. She pulled one of her wrists free and pushed my face away. Why was she acting like she wasn't enjoying this? I moved my head out of her reach and went to grab her wrist. The sting of her slapping me in the face was like cold water being thrown in my face. I let her go completely. Did she just fucking hit me?

I closed my eyes and tried to rationalize not hitting her back. My hands itched in anticipation. I heard her breathing erratically.

"I...I... I'm sorry for hitting you, but you were hurting me. You shouldn't have put your hands on me! I was just defending myself!" I ignored her. I looked up and saw her back up towards the window.

"I'm sorry okay. I'm just going to go home and leave you alone. Just calm down okay?"

She timidly walked towards me. My hand retracted before I could stop myself.

"DON'T!" she pleaded. It was too late. The sound of the back of my hand making contact with her face was like a shotgun blast on a quiet street. She fell against the wall and slid down onto the floor.

"DWAYNE!" She started crying and put her hand on her cheek.

I didn't care. I felt that red haze come over me again. I felt myself bending down. She looked up at me in shock and sadness. She moved her hand and exposed her cheek. This time I put some force behind it as I hit her again. I think she whimpered. I couldn't be sure. The next thing I knew I was being flung across the room.

"WHAT THE FUCK ARE YOU DOING DWAYNE?" Ryson yelled. I looked at Samara curled up into a ball and picked myself up off the floor. I made eye contact with Shar, who gave me a thumbs up. I got to my feet and walked in a daze over to Shar.

RYSON

I will admit that I'm ashamed of my relationship with Shar. It shouldn't have happened in the first place. When Dwayne and I met her she was a totally different person. We were all friends in the beginning, then she came onto me. I resisted at first, but in the end I gave in. I was weak when it came to the female flesh. She was sexy and innocent looking. I wanted to be inside her even though I knew it was wrong. Looking at her now with her see-through shirt and short shorts, I don't know why I ever touched her. She was so clingy and desperate. It was revolting to even be in the same room as her. She was trying so hard to get my attention, I couldn't stand it anymore.

"What do you want Shar?" She was the last person I wanted to see. I didn't want her to be here when Samara finally came out of the house. She had the nerve to look hurt. Dwayne had probably called her every type of bitch in the book and she never gave him that look. I sensed that she had deeper feelings for me than she did for Dwayne, but they were one-sided. Some people would think it was wrong for me and Dwayne to have fucked Shar. She loved every minute of it. She would jump from one bed to the next. She loved all of the attention that we showed her. Now that she wasn't getting that attention, she was furious. Dwayne was still fucking her, but I had to stop. Not only did she become physically unappealing to me, but it was wrong. In the back of my mind I knew it was wrong from the beginning, but I listened to my dick instead of my brain.

"It's a free country. I just came out here to see what's up with you. I haven't talked to you in like two weeks. What's up?" Yeah right, like I was going to believe that shit. Shar always had an ulterior motive for what she did. Everything had to benefit her and hurt somebody she didn't like in the process. There was no other way with Shar. I caught onto the fact that she was trying to push up on me, but I blocked her advances like a boxer and cut her off.

"If you tell Samara anything about how we met or anything that went on between us in the last four years, you will regret it. Just because you're miserable, doesn't mean you need to make everybody else miserable too. Heed my warning Shar." I left her standing by the car looking like a wounded bird. She was so frustrating. I didn't even feel guilty anymore when I had to curse her out. The music was louder than I remembered it being. Samara was taking too long looking for that damn bracelet. If she didn't have it by now, then she would have to come back to get it tomorrow. I was ready to go. I took the steps two at a time and walked towards my room. I turned around and saw Shar on my heels smiling from ear to ear like a Cheshire cat. Something wasn't right.

"DON'T!" I heard Samara shriek, followed by a loud thud.

"What the hell was that?" I heard myself ask. My bedroom door was closed. I opened it and saw Dwayne to my left.

"*Dwayne!*" I heard her muffled voice say.

I walked into the room further and saw Samara curled into a ball on the floor shuddering like a scared animal. I stood in shock as Dwayne bent down and slapped Samara across the face. She grunted in pain.

"WHAT THE FUCK ARE YOU DOING DWAYNE?" I grabbed him and roughly tossed him to the side. I bent down over Samara and gently pulled her up off the floor. This couldn't be real.

"You okay?" Tears were streaming down her face. Her complexion was pink. She started to hyperventilate. Her bottom lip was split in the middle and blood was trickling down her chin.

"Shit." I slowly walked with her over to the bed and sat her down.

"He attacked me!" She mumbled in shock. Her hands were shaking. Her mouth was almost full of blood. I looked around the bed and pulled a pillow out of the pillowcase. I balled it up and put it up to her lip. She winced in pain. I picked up her hand and pressed it against the pillowcase.

"Hold this to your face." I instructed her before I straightened up. I could see dark hand prints on her arms and a dark bruise was forming on her left cheek. She spit a mouthful of blood into the pillowcase. She started softly crying. I turned towards Dwayne. He looked like he had been caught with his hand in the cookie jar.

"What the fuck is your problem Dwayne? What did you do?"

"You don't even know what happened!" He had the audacity to get loud. He must have been out of his fucking mind! I walked over to him and pushed him against my dresser. He fell back hard and looked at me like I was crazy. I was incensed with anger. At that moment he was less than a man. At times, I played around with Dwayne, but right now I needed to be his brother, not his friend.

"What? You can hit a female but you can't hit me back? Hit me back Dwayne since you're so fucking tough!"

I swung a punch and caught him square in the jaw.

"SHIT MAN!" Dwayne yelled out and fell like a deck of cards on his hands and knees.

"OH MY GOD! RYSON STOP!" Shar screamed and knelt down to where Dwayne was crouched.

"MOVE SHAR!" She looked up at me and slowly moved away. She knew better than to interfere.

"Get your ass up Dwayne and hit me back. Get your PUNK ASS UP!" I kicked him in the stomach.

"FUCK RYSON! CHILL OUT!" Dwayne groaned as he fell to the floor while holding his side. He closed his eyes tight and tried to stand up.

"Keep your bitch ass on the floor." I kicked him again in the side. He was my brother, but he was also a man. If I saw a man on the street violating a woman like he just did to Samara, I would have done the same thing. Dwayne needed to learn his lesson. Our mother did not raise us like that. She would slap the sensation out of Dwayne's mouth if she ever saw him put his hands on a female. What the fuck was his problem? I listened to him grumble and groan on the floor. He took short breaths and looked up at the ceiling.

"Get out." I growled at him as he lay on the floor. Shar and now Dwayne were becoming my least favorite people.

"What?" He scooted away from me and grabbed onto the doorknob. I decided to let him get up. He grimaced and pulled himself up. He stood up straight and put his arm around his stomach.

"You heard me. Get out. Get your shit and get the fuck out! You better be lucky I don't call the police and have Samara press charges on your ass." I threatened him.

"You're kicking me out because I slapped Samara? She hit me first!" Dwayne complained. I was about to explode.

"SHE'S A FEMALE! And you're twice her FUCKING SIZE! What the fuck do you mean she hit you first? You sound like a little ass kid! And what did you do for her to hit you in the first place?" I couldn't believe he was really acting like this. This was not the Dwayne I grew up with. This was a whole new Dwayne.

"She... she was trying to play me in front of everybody! Shar told me that she was---," Dwayne stopped talking immediately when he saw my expression. As soon as Shar's name left his mouth, she averted her gaze from me.

"Shar told you what?" I stepped closer to him but my attention was on Shar. She was such a fucking troublemaker! I knew she had to have something to do with this shit. It dawned on me that she had been trying to distract me outside.

"You're always running your fucking mouth and starting shit Shar! Both of y'all get the fuck out NOW!" Shar cut her eyes at Samara and grabbed Dwayne's arm.

"Come on Dwayne, you can stay with me." Shar offered, but he wasn't listening to her. He looked over at Samara, who was sitting on the bed staring at us intently. Dwayne pulled his arm from Shar and started to walk over to Samara. She stood up and moved back towards the window in fear. I stepped in his way, incredulous.

"You're really pressing your fucking luck. Get out right now, that's the last time I'm saying it." I said through clenched teeth. He looked at me, hurt, and turned towards the door to leave. I saw Shar throw a smirk Samara's way. Looking at Shar, I understood the urge to want to hit a female. They left and I closed the door behind them.

"Samara, what happened?" She closed her eyes and took a quivering breath.

"Tell me. What the hell happened up here?" I asked, leaning over and kissing her on the forehead. The pillowcase was soaked with blood. The cut looked deep, she would probably need stitches. Dwayne wore a ring, so I assumed it cut the shit out of her. I suppressed the urge to go after Dwayne again. She sat back down on the bed.

"We got into an argument. He accused me of sleeping with you and then he grabbed me. He tried to break my arms it seemed. It turned ugly real fast after that. I tried to run out of the room, but he wouldn't let me. He grabbed my arms and my hair then threw me on the bed. I pushed him away from me, then he gripped me up and he… he stuck his tongue in my mouth." She closed her eyes in disgust. I felt my fingernails digging into my palms from the pressure of my balled-up fist.

"I didn't know what to do next, so I slapped him to get him off of me. Then he hit me back. I fell into the wall. Then he… he hit me again after I fell," she whimpered. "I really didn't want to hit him, I just wanted him to get off me! I thought he was going to really hurt me. What other choice did I have? Ouch!" She moaned and put her head down. My temperature rose immediately. The whole time I was outside, Dwayne was up here tossing her around and trying to violate her. I felt so fucking stupid and even madder than before.

"You did the right thing." I reassured her. "I'm so sorry he hurt you. I shouldn't have left you alone." I felt like such a dumbass for being distracted by Shar. She looked pale now. I took Samara's elbow and lifted her up. I could only imagine what would have happened if I had stayed outside talking to Shar. Now I wish I hadn't held back with Dwayne.

"Come on, walk with me. I'm going to take you to get that cut looked at okay?"

"Okay," she whispered. We walked slowly down the steps and I noticed the music had been turned off. Two dozen pairs of eyes watched us coming down the steps in surprise.

"Um… sorry but the party is over." I said with enough authority in my voice for everyone to realize they had to go home. They scrambled out of the house, each taking a glimpse of Samara before leaving. She was probably beyond embarrassed. I tried to get her to her car as quickly as I could without drawing any further attention. Once she was situated in the passenger side seat, I got behind the wheel and started her car up.

"You can't kick him out." I jumped at Samara's voice. She turned towards me and put the pillowcase down. Blood had dried up on her lips. It left a thick line of dark crimson on her lip, even as more blood seeped out. The bruises on her arms and face were now turning purple.

"What are you saying Samara? I just beat my brother up defending you and you want me to go and find his ass?" She sounded crazy. How could I ever look at Dwayne the same after what he did? Whether or not Samara and I became anything more than we were, I still could not take Dwayne's side over hers.

"That's exactly why you need to go find him, because you beat him up." She tried not to move her lips too much. I turned off the car and shifted my body so that we were facing each other.

"You're not yourself right now Samara. You just got attacked so you're saying crazy shit that you don't mean." I hoped that was the case. She took a deep breath and her eyes pleaded with me to understand.

"He's your *brother*. You're going to make up eventually. And when you do, where does that leave me? I don't want to come in between you and your brother more than I already have. So please just go find him."

"You don't think what he did to you was wrong?" I couldn't comprehend where her mind was at right now.

"Yes! But he's still your brother Ryson," she said, looking me in the eyes. I didn't know what to do. She was right. Me and Dwayne would eventually make up and talk again. Where would that leave me and Samara? Don't get me wrong, Dwayne was wrong on all accounts, but where did I go from here? This shit was frustrating. I turned back around and started the car up again.

"For right now, let's just worry about getting you to the hospital." I ended the conversation. We drove in silence to the hospital. Maybe I had overreacted with Dwayne. I was more than just disturbed by the situation. I felt… protective. Samara was a spitfire and had one of the most outgoing personalities that I'd ever encountered in a woman. There was something about her that made me want to protect her. It was her eyes. They were so innocent and bright. They reminded me of my mother's eyes. What was happening to me? I didn't care for females. I picked them up and fucked them until I got bored. Then I kicked them to the curb, never contacting them again. But Samara was like a gust of wind. When she was around, she was the center of attention. It wasn't just her looks that kept your eyes glued to her, it was her aura. I loved being around her and on more than one occasion found myself randomly thinking about her. As much as I hated the way my father had treated my mother by dogging her out, I couldn't help but follow in his footsteps.

He casually slept with women and never fell in love. To some, never falling in love would seem like a bad thing. It really wasn't. If you never fell in love, you never got your heart broken. Watching my mother cry herself to sleep over my father made me realize that your heart was a fragile thing. I didn't plan on getting mine broken anytime soon, so I had to keep Samara at arm's length from here on in. I wanted so badly to be with her in my room, but I knew if I gave in so quickly it would turn out catastrophic. Look what had happened with

Shar. Thankfully, she only needed five stitches and we were out of the hospital four hours after walking through the doors.

"I'm going to drop you and your car off. I can call one of my homies to come get me from your house." I turned onto her street, parked in her garage, and got out of the car. I walked around and opened her door, but she didn't get out. She turned sad eyes on me and I felt a tug in my heart. Shit. This was the last thing I needed. What did I look like falling for Samara? *Get a fucking grip man*, I scolded myself.

"Don't leave me alone tonight please." She whimpered and started sobbing. I stood there, not sure how to react. I wasn't good with criers.

"Don't cry. I'll stay with you tonight. Come on." I reached for her hand and she took mine. We walked into her living room and she sat down on the couch. There were trophies on her mantle along with pictures of her family. There was a framed picture of her parents hanging on the wall next to the steps. Navy blue and brown was the color scheme in the living room. A mahogany coffee table sat in front of the navy blue, linen covered couch. Chocolate brown throw pillows littered the couch. Her home was cozy. She leaned forward and tried to unzip her boots. I sat on the coffee table to face her and unzipped her boots for her. She smiled at me and leaned her head to the side, sizing me up. Oh god. It was going to take every ounce of self-restraint I had not to sleep with her tonight. Even with a busted lip and a dark bruise on her face, she was beautiful. Worst of all, she was so damn sexy. She knew it too, which made her even more dangerous.

SAMARA

I couldn't believe that motherfucker hit me! I was not expecting the night to turn out like this. I was mad as shit! He actually hit me! Twice! No man had ever put their hands on me in my life! If I had known all of this would have happened, I would have kicked his ass as soon as he walked into the room!

To be honest, deep down I knew I was wrong for what I did. That was why I held back so much and tried so hard not to retaliate when he started attacking me. I could have at least answered one of his calls and told him it was over. Maybe I shouldn't have come to a party at his house with his brother, and then pretend he wasn't there. It wasn't my proudest moment. Despite that, I still felt Dwayne deserved to get his ass beat for putting his hands on me. It still surprised me that Ryson had done it.

Sitting there in that room, I couldn't stop thinking about Shar. My face throbbed, my lips ached, and my feelings were hurt. Still, all I could think about was Shar. I had to do something about that bitch. At first I was going to overlook her obvious dislike for me, but I couldn't anymore. If I had heard correctly, Shar had hyped Dwayne up to confront me. What if Dwayne had seriously hurt me? I knew in my heart that that was her intention. I sat there on the bed, contemplating my next move. The thing that hurt the most was my feelings. Yes, it probably wasn't the best idea to sleep with one brother and then try to date the other. And it didn't help matters that I came to the party. I had no doubt that when he cleared his head, Dwayne would be remorseful. I didn't know what I would do if he came to me looking for forgiveness. It hurt me more than I thought it would that Dwayne had attacked me like that. I thought he had a little more reverence for me than that. A man's pride was not something to mess with, but you dealt with it like a normal person by talking.

Knowing that it was so easy for Dwayne to hurt me, made me realize that I had pegged him all wrong. I'd watched in silent satisfaction as Ryson kicked and stomped his boot into Dwayne's ribs. Shar had released all types of madness by running her damn mouth. She made a big mistake. It also surprised me when Ryson kicked Dwayne out. I thought that was a little extreme, I mean, they were brothers. Walking to my car with Ryson, I realized that if he actually kicked Dwayne out, the blame would be put on me. He would come to resent me for coming between him and his brother. I couldn't do that. As wrong as it was, Dwayne and Ryson would make up at some point. If I wanted to further my relationship with Ryson, I couldn't let him do that.

"You can't kick him out." I put the pillowcase down. I touched my lip and felt dried blood. Ryson was livid.

"What are you saying Samara? I just beat my brother up defending you and you want me to go and find his ass?" I must have sounded crazy to him, but I was far from it. I couldn't let their relationship suffer on my behalf. Whatever rift they would have because of this incident was between them now. I was over it. I didn't forgive Dwayne for what he did, but I didn't plan on dwelling on it forever. He was irate and he took it out on me. I was angry and I retaliated. It was tit for tat and we were both wrong. I didn't plan on ever seeing Dwayne again or dealing with him in any capacity. Ryson didn't agree with me, but he left the topic open for discussion later. We pulled into the parking lot of the hospital a short while later. I told the doctor I had been attacked, but I wasn't pressing charges. He gave Ryson the evil eye, but he didn't push it. I gave Ryson directions to my house, but I was mostly quiet on the ride there. All I could think about was Shar. Shar had set this whole thing into motion. She was jealous of the attention I was getting from Dwayne and Ryson. Instead of coming to me like a woman, she would rather connive and plot a way for someone to hurt me. She was going to be very sorry for that.

"I'm going to drop you and your car off. I can call one of my homies to come get me from your house."

I looked out the window and realized I was home. I really didn't want to sleep alone tonight. I wanted some company. Some intimacy. I was still a little shaken up about what happened. I pressed the button on my key ring to open my garage door for him to park. When Ryson opened my door, I tried so hard not to let my emotions get the best of me, but I failed. I wanted him near me tonight. There was no way I was letting him leave.

"Don't leave me alone tonight please." I begged him, my voice choking. He sighed and touched my chin.

"I'll stay with you tonight." He helped me out of my car. I lived on a relatively quiet street. We walked towards my house. It was a detached two-story bungalow that had three bedrooms. I'd recently remodeled, so there were all new cashmere ceramic tile floors throughout the dining room and kitchen. Granite countertops and brand new appliances were also a new addition. I punched in the code on my security alarm and sat down on my sofa. Ryson helped me take my shoes off. There was something different about him. Maybe it was the drama or maybe it was something else. Ryson had been angrier than I thought he would be at his brother. Of course I knew he would be furious, I just thought he would give Dwayne a piece of his mind and then take me home. I didn't want to jump the gun, but I was getting the sense that Ryson was feeling me more than he wanted to admit. I tried to catch a glimpse of his eyes. The eyes never lied. He looked up and smiled awkwardly. He looked nervous. He was so cute. If I wasn't so out of sorts about what just happened, I might have been turned on. But tonight, I just wanted a warm body to lie on. I stood up and held out my hand to him and led him upstairs. He seemed hesitant, but followed me anyway. I didn't say anything for fear of ruining this moment. I opened the door to my bedroom, walked over to the lamp by the bed, and cut on the lights.

"It smells good in here." I heard Ryson say as I pulled the comforter back. He stood by the door looking unsure of what to do next.

"Come on, I won't bite I promise." I smiled and a twinge of pain pierced my lip. I put out my hand to him and watched as he slowly came to me. I felt flutters in my stomach as he approached me. He was so handsome. He stood before me, holding my hand and looking down at me. I slid into the bed, never taking my eyes off of him and never releasing his hand. He followed suit and climbed in after me, boots on and all. I watched as he lay on his back and got comfortable. I lay my head on his shoulder and wrapped my arm around his abdomen.

"Can you hit the lights?" I asked him sleepily. He stretched out and turned off the lamp. I sighed heavily as I listened to his breathing quicken. I wondered what was going on in his head. I closed my eyes and tried to go to sleep. I breathed in his scent and snuggled closer to him, draping my leg over his. He hooked his arm around my body and placed his hand on my side. I smiled because I could tell he was trying to feel me out. Trying to see if I wanted to go a little further tonight. He was letting me take the lead. I decided to ease his mind. I inched up and kissed him behind his ear.

"Goodnight." I whispered in his ear and rested my head back on his shoulder.

"Goodnight." His deep voice resonated throughout the quiet room. I promptly fell asleep.

SHAR

"You can stay with me as long as you need to." I was trying to talk to Dwayne, but he was somewhere else altogether. I was still in shock. Ryson really kicked Dwayne, his baby brother, out of their house over Samara. He was further gone than I thought. Maybe trying to get to him was futile, but I didn't come this far to give up. Last night Dwayne stopped talking completely when we got in his car. He was in a trance it seemed. Once we got inside the apartment, he went to the couch and sat down. That's where he was when I went to sleep, and where he was when I got up in the morning. I got up from the blue and white checkered sofa that I'd found at a garage sale, and walked into the kitchen. I opened the refrigerator and ignored the fact that the only thing edible inside it was Chinese food half-eaten from last week. My stomach growled but I ignored it. I wasn't wasting the money I had saved up on something as stupid as food. I had better things to do with that money. I gave up on looking for food and walked back into the living room. Dwayne was staring at the thirty inch TV screen. It was off.

"Dwayne, can I have some money to get some food?" I asked, seeing if he would break out of his daze. He dug in his pants pocket, took out a wad of money, and held his hand out. He still didn't look my way. I took the money, but held onto his hand. He looked at me then.

"It's okay Dwayne. Ryson will come to his senses in a few days." I tried to comfort him. My best guess was that he was extremely pissed off at Ryson, I was wrong.

"I'm not worried about Ryson," he said, breaking his silence. I let go of his hand and sat down next to him. If he wasn't worried about Ryson, then what could he be worried about? He better not say what the fuck I thought he was about to say.

"I'm worried about Samara. I attacked her! I put my hands on a female. I could have really hurt her. I'm still trying to figure out why the fuck I did that shit!" He shook his head and lay his head back onto the couch. He looked up at the ceiling and shook his head from side to side. Inside, I was smoldering. He was worried about Samara? Samara? Samara? What the fuck? Did she have gold in her pussy or something? I wasn't trying to go to plan B, but fuck that! I was making that call today. I will be damned if she causes an even greater divide than she already had between me, Ryson, and Dwayne.

"Well she pushed you to it. Shit, she's not innocent in this either!" I said bitterly. Dwayne sat up and made a steeple with his fingers.

"Even if I felt some type of way about her being there, I should have just talked to her. You just don't know how shitty I feel right now. I have never put my hands on a woman like that before." So what? She deserved much more. Dwayne should have taken her head off and strung it up on a flagpole for the world to see in my opinion. He put his hands on his forehead. He was getting a headache. I didn't understand why he was getting so worked up over her. Ugh. I was so done with her. Hearing about her. Seeing her. I wanted her gone completely. That would happen sooner rather than later.

"But she shouldn't have tried to play you like that. I mean, why would she come to that party knowing you would be there and then ignore you? She was trying to play games and mess with your head!" How hard was it to comprehend? Sometimes I just wanted to shake the shit out of him. He turned towards me and smirked.

"She didn't play me Shar. If anything, I tried to play her, that's what's so fucking crazy about this whole situation." He stood up and turned towards me.

"From the beginning, I told her I wasn't looking for anything serious. That we could fuck with whoever we wanted to. I fucked you that day because I knew she was coming over there. I just wanted her to see you and get jealous, but she didn't. I lied and told her Ryson wasn't home when she came over, knowing he was. I wanted him to hear me fucking her like it was a fucking game!" He was getting upset again. His face was flushed and he started moving his hands erratically, emphasizing every word. I was trying to digest the fact that he only fucked me that day to make Samara jealous. *Don't react*, I told myself. I would have my revenge in due time.

"She was up front with me about our arrangement. I'm the one that tried to fuck it up." He started pacing back and forth.

"I believed her when she told me she didn't fuck Ryson, but I tried to hurt her anyway. Man the look on her face after I hit her again and again makes me feel like the fucking scum of the earth. I need to go talk to her." Dwayne walked towards the bathroom. I didn't know how this whole thing had gotten so out of hand so fast. I should have taken care of Samara when I found out Ryson had invited her to the party. I heard the shower going and knew Dwayne would be leaving soon. She was the cause of all of the problems in my life. It was time for me to solve those problems. I went through the contact list in my phone, found the number I was looking for, and hit the call button.

DWAYNE

The hot water felt so good on my head and back. I leaned my body onto the wall in the shower, letting the hard water beat down on me. I didn't know who I was anymore. How many women had I fucked and never gave a damn about afterwards? Around five dozen, so why was Samara so different? I wasn't used to getting rejected or told no. I guess that was what was really ticking me the fuck off. She got me so riled up that I hit her, twice! I completely and utterly lost my fucking mind last night. I must have snapped. That was the only explanation I could come up with for me having an out of body experience like that. That had never happened to me before. It freaked me out a little to think about it, but I had bigger issues I needed to worry about. I needed to apologize for what I'd done. But she needed to apologize for playing me too. She wasn't my girl or anything like that, but I had pride. Walking into my own house and seeing her kissing and grinding on Ryson was total disrespect. Then she had the nerve to walk right past me like she didn't know me. She didn't answer my calls or text messages, and then she didn't acknowledge me in my own house. She had some explaining to do herself. She by no means deserved what I did, but she did need to be told about herself.

I didn't know why I really gave a fuck though. She was just another piece of ass who decided to fuck with my brother. That had happened at least three times before, and I had never given it a second thought. I mean, she was okay I guess. She was sexy, you couldn't deny that shit. Her body was fucking perfect from head to toe. It didn't hurt that she was gorgeous. She carried herself like she knew she was the shit, but she wasn't obsessed with it. She had confidence that made her stand out and made me want to keep seeing her. Usually when I fucked a girl, I fucked until I got bored and that was it. If the sex was okay, then I answered the girl's text for the next hook up. If not, I went to the next one in line. But for some reason, I couldn't do that with Samara. I was the one texting *her* ass! That first time we fucked, I thought I was going to turn her out and have her begging to see me again. But she had the fucking stamina of a stallion. She put my ass to sleep. That never happened to me before. I usually cum, then kick the girl out. But I didn't even care that she stayed the night. Again, something I never let females do. She wasn't even concerned about hooking up again. She was ready to bounce without even saying goodbye the next morning. Her nonchalance turned me on. It was like she made me chase her. I couldn't stop thinking about her. This shit was unnerving! I was getting worked up over her like we were dating or something. After I apologized to her, and she said sorry to me, I was cutting all ties with her.

The water was going cold, which told me it was time to get out.

"Shit!" I cursed under my breath when I realized I was at Shar's fucked up apartment. I didn't have any clean clothes to put on because she never fucking did the laundry. I left clothes over here all the time, just to come back to the same funky smell. Her apartment wasn't anything to write home about either. There were holes in almost every wall, and no room had the same paint color. Her furniture smelled old and there was a layer of dust on every surface. She spent all her money on clothes and shoes and shit. I was getting a little tired of Shar too. If she hadn't taunted me with all that shit about Samara playing me, I wouldn't have gotten so mad. I mean, I couldn't blame her for the fact that I hit Samara, but she instigated that shit. I guess she was just trying to look out for me. Shar was always there when I needed her no matter how bad I treated her. She was harmless, but she was irritating too. I stepped out of the shower and wrapped the only towel Shar had around my waist. I opened the door to Shar leaning against the door frame.

"Where do you think you're going?" She purred and batted her lashes at me. What was she up to?

"I told you I had to go talk to Samara." I walked around her and headed to her bedroom.

"Can't you worry about that later?" Shar wrapped her arms around my waist from behind. I felt her tongue glide up my back. Usually when she did that, I couldn't help but tear her clothes off and fuck the shit out of her. But it didn't work this time. All I kept seeing was Samara's face looking up at me in fear. I turned around towards Shar and untangled her from my waist.

"I'm not in the mood Shar. Where are those shirts I left here last week?" She was taken aback at my rejection, but I didn't care. I just told her how shitty I felt. Why would she think I was in the damn mood? She was just trying to prevent me from going to Samara's house, she wasn't fucking slick.

"In the closet," she said, sounding disappointed. I pulled a shirt over my head. I walked back into the bathroom and put my underwear and pants back on. I needed to go home to get more clothes too.

"I'll be back later." I left before she could protest.

The sky was a dark shade of gray, and rain clouds hovered over the city. Today was going to be one of those days. I got behind the wheel of my truck and turned on the radio. I turned to an easy listening station to calm my nerves as I drove to Samara's house. I'm a little ashamed to admit this, but I paid some sleazy website to find her address that first week she wouldn't return my calls. I had planned on just dropping by unannounced and demanding an apology, but chickened out each time. I slowed down on her street. Almost all of the homes on Samara's block were identical, but her backyard was fenced in. I parked across the street from her house.

"Now that I'm here I don't know what the fuck to say," I said to myself. My hands started to feel clammy and for some reason, I was nervous. I was just here to give an apology and get one back, that was all. Nothing to be nervous about. I took a deep breath and turned off the ignition. I looked over at Samara's window just in time to see the curtain open.

"Shit!" I didn't want her to see me parked over here. She would think I was crazy or something. I wasn't ready yet. Shit! Shit! Shit! Man up. I put my hand on the door handle then stopped in my tracks. The living room curtain swung open wider and Ryson's face came into view.

"What the fuck? Don't tell me he spent the night!" He disappeared from sight then his hand reached through the mail slot and picked up the paper. My chest burned. I looked down at my white knuckles and released my grip on the door handle. I needed to calm down. He probably stayed with her just to make sure she was okay, that's all. Knowing Ryson, he probably fucked her last night. No, Ryson wouldn't do that. I was sure of it. I think. I don't know. What the fuck man? I started the truck back up and pulled off. Since Ryson was over there, I made my way home to get clothes and toiletries. I would do what I needed to do another time. When Ryson wasn't at her house. When we could be alone.

SHAR

"Five thousand dollars? I don't even have half of that!" He was bonkers to ask for so much money to do such a simple thing. I was expecting him to say a thousand dollars, or at least something in that range. Maybe this wasn't such a good idea. No! This shit had to happen no matter how much it costs. I paced back and forth in my living room, mindful to listen out for Dwayne. He was still in the shower.

"It's a two person job, lady. Plus the way you want it done, we could easily get caught. We putting our necks out there not you. It's five thousand or you call somebody else." The male voice on the other line threatened. Fuck! I didn't have that kind of money! I had to figure out a way to make some extra money. My plan B was happening if I had to sell my fucking body to do it.

"What if I paid you another way?" I suggested flirtatiously. I was stooping to a new low, but it was worth it. I heard him snort on the other end of the phone.

"Call me back when you get the money." *Click*. Fuck! I only had a few hundred saved up and that was including my rent for next month. I could flip that but it wouldn't come close to five grand. How was I supposed to get the rest? I walked over to my window and looked out at the gray sky. Why did everything have to be so difficult? Why couldn't Samara just fucking leave us alone? I looked down at my Impala and knew I had to sell it. I hated taking the bus, but it was my only option. The water stopped in the shower. I ran to the bathroom door just as Dwayne was coming out.

"Where do you think you're going?" I licked my lips. He seemed uninterested. I wasn't letting him leave here without fucking me. He needed to redeem himself for fucking me to make Samara jealous. That wasn't sitting right with me. I was going to fuck him so good he would forget all about Samara. I might even let him in my ass. I thought that was disgusting, so I always told him no, but desperate times called for desperate measures. He walked past me into my bedroom. He was rushing to leave. Fuck that shit! I grabbed his waist and ran my tongue up his spine. That was his spot. I always got him with that one. He turned around and pulled my arms from around his waist. Huh? What the fuck was going on? That shit never failed before! Did Samara really have Ryson and Dwayne sprung like that? That bitch had to go! I told him where his shirts were and he left. I stood at the door for a few seconds thinking of a way to get the money. My car was busted so I would only get around fifteen hundred if I was lucky. I had to make some sacrifices. Like I said, desperate times called for desperate measures.

SAMARA

I opened my eyes. Immediately, pain shot through my face and bottom lip.

"Ouch!" I touched the stitches in my lip and sat all the way up. I looked around my room and didn't see Ryson. I would bet anything that he'd left after I fell asleep. I couldn't blame him. All of this damn drama was annoying. I got out of bed and undressed. I still had on the blood-stained dress from last night. I put on a pair of sweats and a black t-shirt. I could still taste blood in my mouth. I made a beeline for the bathroom where I delicately brushed my teeth and washed my face and neck. I put my hair back and did the best I could to get it into a ponytail. I didn't dare look at my face. It had to be turning all shades of purple by now. I touched it gently and realized it was swelling up. My scalp was sore from Dwayne trying to yank a chunk of my hair out. I made my way downstairs. I smelled coffee brewing and I heard the TV on. I smiled as hard as I could without hurting my lip. Ryson had stayed! I walked into the kitchen and saw him sitting on a stool sipping coffee. He was deeply engrossed in the paper.

"Morning." I said and walked over to him. He looked up and smiled. His whole face lit up.

"I made some coffee. I didn't know if you were hungry or not." He put the paper down and gave me all of his attention. He looked at my lip and tilted my head to the side to examine it further.

"It doesn't look that bad. I give it two weeks, three tops. You won't even be able to tell you had stitches. And that bruising on your cheek will be gone too."

"You think so?" I asked, hoping that was true. I wasn't obsessed with my looks, but I didn't want to walk around looking like a battered woman.

"Yeah I do. You didn't say whether you were hungry or not."

"Oh... I'm not that hungry. I'll cut up an apple or something." I got as close to him as I could without actually touching him.

"Thank you for staying with me last night." I said gazing into his eyes. I meant that sincerely. It touched my heart that he'd stayed all night. Again I was getting the feeling he was digging me more than he let on. He shrugged in indifference.

"It was the right thing to do." He said with detachment like it was no big deal. Okay. He was acting different. One minute he was hot, then one minute he was cold. I cleared my throat and an uncomfortable silence settled over the kitchen.

"I should be out of here in like five minutes. I called somebody to pick me up while you were asleep. I have to get to work." He stood up and put his cup in the sink. If I hadn't woken up, would he have left without saying goodbye? Was I missing something?

"Is something wrong?" I asked out of confusion. He was practically all over me yesterday, and now he was acting like I was a stranger.

"No. Why?" He asked, still facing the sink. He wouldn't look at me.

"Nothing, just asking." I took a knife out of the chopping block and busied myself with slicing an apple. I didn't know what kind of game he was playing. Was he feeling me or not? Why did men do shit like that? They could never just put their feelings out on the table. Would it kill him to show some emotion? I put an apple slice in my mouth and closed my eyes. I wasn't about to make a fool of myself and demand that he tell me why he was acting differently. When he was ready he would tell me, hopefully. I looked up to find him staring at me. He looked away as soon as our eyes met, surprised that I had caught him. What the hell? I shook my head at him, not sure what to make of this situation. His cell phone vibrated on the counter. He picked it up.

"Yeah... okay... I'll be right out... thanks man I really appreciate it... alright." Ryson ended his call and walked past me to the front door. Damn, was it like that? Maybe I had done something wrong that I didn't know of. He was up before me, so he had time to think things over. He must have figured I wasn't worth all of the trouble. Whatever it was, I didn't like it. I stayed in the kitchen until I heard the front door open and close. I put my hands on the counter and looked up at the ceiling. Why did things have to be so complicated? I tossed the knife in the sink and left the kitchen. My alarm would be going off soon, it was still set. Ryson stood in the middle of my living room. I stopped and stared at him not sure what was going on. He swiftly walked over to me and pulled me into his arms.

"I want to kiss you, but I don't want to hurt you," he whispered to me. Now I was all the way confused. *Just go with it*, I told myself. What other choice did I have? It was either tell him to get the hell off, or enjoy the feeling of his warm body wrapped around mine. He kissed the corners of my mouth slowly. I closed my eyes and held him tighter. I felt his lips brush across my top lip. His breathing was labored and I could feel his heart beating quickly through his chest. His lips trailed down to my chin then my neck. A car horn honked outside interrupting the moment, making me jump in surprise. Ryson told me to open my eyes. He took my hand in his and kissed my index finger then my palm.

I crinkled my eyebrows. He was such a mystery. I could never tell what he was thinking.

"I'll call you later." He let me go and was out of the door seconds later. I couldn't move. I stood in my living room looking down at my hand where he'd kissed it.

RYSON

What the fuck was I thinking? I should have just left like I had originally planned. Fuck. I couldn't just leave though. Trust me, I tried. But when I opened the door, a little voice inside my head started screaming "kiss her you dumbass!" Careful not to kiss her bottom lip, I couldn't resist getting a taste. I wanted so badly to do more, but I knew I was getting in way over my head. I dashed out of her house before I did anything stupid and jumped in Devon's car.

"What's up man? I heard what Dwayne did to Samara, that's really fucked up!" Devon said shaking his head. I knew that was coming. His tall broad frame could barely fit into his Nissan. Devon was a good friend and had been since high school. I was debating whether or not to tell him about this tug of war going on inside of me over Samara. No, I couldn't. I didn't even know how to describe it to myself yet, how could I tell it to him?

"Yeah I know. She's cool though, that's all that matters." I wondered if he knew I had kicked Dwayne's ass too. If he did, he didn't show it.

"So why did he do it in the first place? I didn't know she was messing with Dwayne. I assumed she was with you when I saw y'all at the party." Devon was digging. I had to be careful what I told him, because that would be what everyone else at the party would know. There was no doubt in my mind they had asked Devon to fish for the details from last night.

"He got jealous that's all. We both met Samara at the same time and we both tried to get at her. She chose me, he didn't like it. End of story." I hoped that was good enough. It was partially the truth. The only part I left out was the part about Samara sleeping with Dwayne.

"Damn, that's crazy! So where is Dwayne now? Is she pressing charges?" Devon turned onto my street. I was tired of talking about last night's events.

"More than likely he's at a hotel or something cooling off. And no, she's not pressing charges. Thanks for the ride man. I'll hit you up later alright?" I got out of the car before he could fire anymore questions at me. I walked into the house to cups and plates scattered everywhere from the party. I was exhausted and decided to handle the mess later. I couldn't really sleep last night holding Samara. She wanted me to stay with her just to keep her company. I thought she would try something but she didn't. For some reason, I was thinking that all Samara wanted from me was sex. That was probably because she flirted with me so hard. That had been at the back of my mind since she stopped fucking with Dwayne and started hanging with me. At least, if all she wanted was sex, it would be easier to give in and then let go. Laying in her bed holding her made me change my mind about her. But it didn't change how I felt. Which was what exactly? I still couldn't put it into words. Was I in love with Samara? Hell no. Was I starting to like her? Yes. But how did that turn into me fighting my feelings for her whenever I was around her? I tried to be cold as ice this morning, but she saw right through me. It would have been easier if she had called me out on it, but she let it go. She was the total opposite of the women I usually fucked with. She wasn't willing to sacrifice her dignity for a man. I liked that about her. All of this fighting against myself was getting tiring. Maybe I should just face the truth and admit that I was falling for Samara. No! I was... *infatuated* with her. That's what it was, infatuation and lust. It couldn't hurt to spend a little more time getting to know her better. But the first rule of business was to call Dwayne and talk to him about what he did last night. I would let him cool off for a few more days, then it was time to talk.

DWAYNE

"Hello?" I picked up my cell, surprised to see Ryson's number flash across the screen. I didn't expect to hear from him anytime soon. I wasn't mad at him for what he did at the party. I snapped, and as my older brother it was his job to keep me in check and put me in my place. Growing up I couldn't count the amount of ass whippings I got from Ryson for my bad behavior, so I knew now was no different. I wasn't even hurt that he had kicked me out.

"Where you staying?" Ryson asked me. He sounded like he was being forced to talk to me. His voice was strained.

"I'm sleeping on Shar's dirty ass couch, ha-ha. Why?" I asked out of curiosity.

"Bring your ass home Dwayne." Ryson hung up. Damn, that was it? I wasn't going to argue. I was tired of staying at Shar's apartment anyway. She kept trying to get me to fuck her. So I stayed on the couch and out of her bedroom. There was a time when turning Shar down was like an alcoholic turning down a drink. But she was acting too clingy and desperate. That was a big turn off for me. Plus I was getting the feeling that Shar was up to something, and I didn't need sex clouding my judgment. She was always jumpy and on edge. She was starting to look bad too. Shar was always on the thinner side, but she had lost at least five pounds in the last week. I know I should have cared more, but it was Shar. If it was important, she would have told me or Ryson. She was such a drama queen that when something happened she was quick to bring us into the mix. I wasn't concerned.

"Shar!" I called out to her. She came running into the kitchen, full of energy. Her eyes were bloodshot red and she had strands of hair on the collar of her shirt.

"What's up with you?" She shrugged like she didn't know. I could hear her stomach growling. What was she trying to do?

"I don't remember you eating anything the last few days. I hope you're not trying to lose weight or nothing because you're already skinny as shit as it is." She was unusually quiet.

"I need money," she said quickly.

"Money for what?" I eyed her skeptically. There it was. Shar was always asking for money for bills and food, then turning around and spending it on clothes and shit.

"My rent is backed up."

"How backed up?"

"Four months." She averted her eyes.

"WHAT? Why did you wait so long to ask for the money? Damn Shar, you lucky they didn't kick your ass out yet!" She got on my damn nerves! Now even if I didn't want to give her the money, I had to so she would have a place to stay. She damn sure wasn't staying with me and Ryson.

"You told me not to ask you for any more money, and you know Ryson don't even like me like that anymore." Her voice was depressing. She looked like she was ready to cry. I never saw Shar like this, looking pitiful and beat down.

"How much do you need Shar?" I walked over to the table and picked up my wallet. I wasn't rolling in dough, but I had some money put away for a rainy day thanks to Ryson. It was eighty degrees outside today, but it would end up being a rainy day after all. I had a couple hundred in my wallet I could give her.

"Three thousand." She was right behind me, salivating over my wallet.

"DAMN! How much is your rent?" Three thousand dollars was a little bit steep. Her back rent couldn't possibly be that much. There had to be something else. She put her hands up in surrender.

"Wait, listen before you say no. My rent is six hundred a month, but they added on a hundred dollar late fee every month I was late. And I need to go food shopping and get some other stuff. Please, I'll pay you back I promise." She put her hands together in prayer begging me for the money. I was going to give it to her, but this would be the last time.

"You never pay me back, but I'll give it to you anyway. From now on you better learn how to budget your fucking money better! I'm not bailing you out any more Shar. You're too grown for this shit!" I picked up my phone and called my bank. I transferred the money from my account to Shar's.

"Thank you sooo much! Trust me, it will go to good use." She smiled and walked out of the room.

"It better," I said to her back. I shook my head at her recklessness. I sat on the couch and my mind wandered back to Samara. After I rode past her house that day, I couldn't gather up the courage to go back. Say I did apologize, then what? I wouldn't feel any better. And if she didn't apologize back would I get mad? I would, and I didn't trust myself not to hurt her again. Samara was taking up too much space in my head. I wanted and needed to see her again, but I couldn't predict what would happen when that time came. I was grateful that she didn't press charges against me. I secretly fantasized that she didn't press charges because she wanted to get back with me. To our little arrangement. It was stupid, but I couldn't help but think that. Samara was my perfect match in the bedroom. I'd never experienced that before. I was always known for seducing and turning girls out. I had a book full of numbers that I could call and have a female at my beck and call at any time. I slayed the pussy and even created stalkers. Samara, on the other hand, could hold her own in the bedroom. I fucked the shit out of her and she begged for more. She sucked my dick like her life depended on it. She rode my dick like she was a champion rodeo clown. My dick was getting hard just thinking about that last night we spent together. I did miss her though. I couldn't deny that. I could deny how I really felt about her all day and night, but I couldn't lie about me missing her. She was funny, sarcastic, and a crazy flirt. It was like she couldn't be tamed. I wanted to tame her. *You will.*

"What the fuck?" I heard the voice in my head again. I hadn't heard it since the night of the party. It just came out of nowhere that night. I don't know why, but I wasn't as worried about it as I probably should be. I shook my head to clear it and packed my bag.

"SHAR! I'M GOING HOME!" I yelled down the hallway. I didn't get a response, so I walked out the door and down the hall to the elevator. I felt like a kid being called to the principal's office the whole drive home. My stomach was in knots. I knew Ryson would have words for me. I pulled up to the house and parked. Ryson was standing outside leaning on his Jeep. I approached him slowly with my head held high. I would take this curse out like a man. His face was stern as he crossed his arms over his chest. Here comes the lecture, I thought. I'd expected it. I was nervous about seeing him after what happened that night.

"What's up?" I asked, standing a few feet away.

"Before we go any further, I just want to say one thing. After that I'm going to leave it alone," Ryson started. I nodded and waited for him to speak his mind. I cleared my throat. He stood up straight and looked me in the eyes, but somehow looked down on me at the same time. Only a big brother could do that shit.

"If you ever put your hands on or try to force yourself on another female, I don't care who it is, I'm going to fuck you up! Momma didn't raise you like that and neither did I. No brother of mine is going to be a damn predator! I'll kill you before I let you go down that road. You hear me?" His finger was in my face as he talked. My heart fell down to my gut. I swallowed hard. Ryson never talked to me like this. He must have been so disappointed in me. I was disappointed in myself too.

"Yes, I hear you. I feel real bad Ryson. I need to make peace with Samara too."

"NO! You're not going near her again. EVER! I'll tell her you said sorry. From now on you don't need to have any contact with her." Ryson walked around the Jeep and walked towards the house. I stood near the Jeep deciding if I should say something or not. I mean, I got what he was trying to do. But he couldn't stop me from saying sorry to Samara in person. I followed him into the house and decided to keep my thoughts to myself. I knew where Samara lived, so I could go see her at any time. I just needed to make sure Ryson didn't find out. I tried to get comfortable on the couch. He said he would tell her that I was sorry, which meant he was still going to be dealing with her. Was that what this was all about? Did he really threaten me because of what I did or was he trying to protect his woman? Ryson didn't have girlfriends, so I was confused why he would still be messing with Samara. The first few days after what happened I could see why he would keep in touch. He wanted to make sure she was okay, but now I didn't see why. If I wasn't supposed to go near her, what gave him the right? I snuck a quick glance over at Ryson in the kitchen and noticed him looking straight ahead. His fists were clenching and unclenching.

"So, how is she anyway?" I asked in a low voice. I couldn't help it, I had to know. Ryson turned and looked me straight in the eyes.

"Your ring cut her lip and it split down the middle. She had to get five stitches. The bruises on her arms and face are purple, swollen, and getting darker and darker." I didn't even ask him all of that! Why the fuck would he tell me that shit? I was already feeling like shit, now I felt like the shit at the bottom of a pile of shit. Fuck! I felt my hands balling into fists. I had to calm down. Why was he trying to make me feel worse than I already did? Now I really had to see her. I couldn't believe she had to get stitches. I saw the blood that night, but I just thought my ring had cut her lip or something. What did I do? Aww man, I had to make this shit right. Samara had a caramel complexion and the bruises on her would stick out like a sore thumb. I really didn't mean to hurt her like that.

"I just meant, how is she mentally?" I said to Ryson in a small voice.

"I knew what you meant." His voice was cold. I could see that he hadn't forgiven me yet. So why was he letting me come back home?

"Oh, and there's something you need to take care of." Ryson started heading upstairs. I got up and followed him. He walked into his bedroom. I stopped at the threshold and took a breath.

"You need to clean that up." He walked into the middle of the room and pointed to the corner. I couldn't look at what he was referring to.

"That's to remind you of the damage and pain you inflicted on a defenseless human being." Ryson's cold voice lingered even after he walked out. I stood there as still as a statue getting angrier and angrier at myself. I glanced over at the blood splatter on the walls and carpet. Samara's blood. Ryson was making me clean it up as a punishment. It had turned a dark maroon color. FUCK! What kind of monster was I? I walked out into the hallway and got cleaning supplies from the closet. I filled a bucket with warm water from the bathroom. I slowly made my way back to the bedroom. I stood in front of the blood stains on the wall. I raised my hand and sprayed the solution. The blood slowly ran down the walls. Like blood tears. I wanted to cry. I'd done this. To Samara. Someone who was defenseless against me and my strength. I could have killed her! I scrubbed the blood from the walls and got on my knees to clean the blood out of the carpet. I shouldn't have hurt her like that. I had to figure out what to do about Samara. Knowing that I hurt her made me feel like less of a man, but knowing that I scarred her made me hate myself. I would never want anyone to treat my mother that way. I could only imagine what I would do if the tables were turned and I was in Ryson's shoes. My anger had gotten the best of me and I had to pay for that mistake. *She deserved it.*

What the fuck? There was that voice again. Was that my subconscious or some shit? If it was, it was wrong. No one deserved that, especially not Samara. I looked at the water in the bucket and watched as it turned from clear to red. Hopefully Samara could find it in her heart to forgive me. When Ryson left for work tomorrow morning I would go see her. I had to.

SHAR

It technically wasn't a lie because my rent *was* backed up. But only by one month. I wasn't stupid enough to not pay my bills. I let Dwayne believe that because I knew he had the money I needed. I sold my car for thirteen hundred and Dwayne had just given me three thousand. Only seven hundred more to go. That wouldn't be hard though. I had a friend who could take this money and flip it for me. I didn't think I could work another double shift at that damn restaurant so this money had to stretch. I couldn't eat and I couldn't think of anything but getting this money. It wasn't until I went through Dwayne's wallet and saw a wad of money, that I got the idea to ask him. Dwayne was an electrician and I knew he made good money. But I knew he had money saved too. Ryson must have been looking over his money for him. I wanted to be greedy and ask him for the whole amount I needed, but he would be on to me if I did. Once he put that money in my account I ran to my room to call RC. I met RC when Ryson and Dwayne left me stranded at the café that night we met Samara. RC and his friend Greg went home with me that night and you can guess how the story ends. As we lay in bed afterwards, RC lit up a joint. We passed it back and forth as I contemplated going another round with them.

"I saw those two dudes you were sitting with. Why they leave you?" Greg had asked me and took a long drag on the joint. I took it from him and inhaled as much as I could take.

"They ditched me for some hoe they met." I blew smoke out through my nose and passed it to RC.

"I saw her. Shit, I would have left you too, ha-ha. Did you see that ass?" RC laughed and finished the joint without passing it back. She wasn't all that. The only thing she had going for her was that ass. That's all. That bitch didn't look better than me. Men were only interested in the physical appearance of a woman's body anyway, so I should have known they would take Ryson and Dwayne's side.

"I don't care if she had the biggest ass in the world, they came there with me so they shouldn't have ditched me! I knew that bitch was trouble when I first saw her. I didn't appreciate that shit at all!" I was so fucking mad.

"I guess you don't like her then, ha-ha." Greg put his hands underneath the covers trying to play with my pussy. I didn't stop him.

"I hate her. The only thing that's keeping me from fucking her up is knowing they're going to be done with her by tomorrow." I opened my legs wider. Greg wasn't the best looking guy but he took care of his business in bed. Neither of them could hold a candle to Ryson or Dwayne, but they got the job done.

"What if they don't? She was fine as shit. I wouldn't just hit it and quit it. I would be trying to get in that ass every chance I got," RC said. I thought about that for a second. That wouldn't happen. Ryson and Dwayne did this dance so many times before. I already knew that by the time the sun came up, she would be getting kicked to the curb. *Or so I had thought.*

"They will, and if not I'll worry about it then."

"What are you going to do, beat her up?" Greg joked with me and stuck his finger in my pussy. I grabbed his hand and looked him dead in the eyes.

"I will do more than that if I have to. They belong to me and nobody is taking them away from me."

"Damn girl, you sound serious." He laughed nervously and removed his hand.

"I am serious. Nobody is taking them from me. I don't care what I have to do," I said, meaning it.

"I know a couple of people who could help you with your problem." RC started to roll another blunt.

"It's not a problem yet. Plus I can handle it myself if it does become one." I wondered what he meant by that. How could anyone solve my problem?

"But if I did need somebody, what could they do to solve my problem?" I asked nonchalantly. I wasn't actually considering it. I just wanted to know.

"Whatever you wanted them to do. If the price is right, you can get them to do anything." RC lit the blunt, took a hit from it, and passed it to me.

"Well, what price are you talking about? My funds are limited. Not that I need help, I'm just asking." I inhaled slowly.

"If you need help with the money I can help you with that. Give me a couple grand and I can flip it for you." RC said, taking the joint from me. I could guess how.

"Well like I said, it's not going to come to that. If it does, I can handle it, If I can't I'll call you. You can be my plan B." I climbed on top of RC.

"Enough talk. I'm still mad at Ryson and Dwayne. Take my mind off of them." I stuck my tongue in RC's mouth. He grabbed my hips and kissed me back. Greg put the blunt in the ashtray and got in the mix.

Now that I had some real money, it was time to call RC and see if he came through for me.

"Hey RC, its Shar. Can you still help me?"

"That depends on what you need my help with." RC replied in a hushed tone.

"I need monetary help." I whispered into the phone.

"I think I can help you with that. Did you talk to my friend about the price already?"

"Yes, I talked to him a few days ago."

"Okay good."

"SHAR! I'M GOING HOME!" I heard Dwayne yell down the hallway.

"That's why I need your help. What time can you get here?"

"Around eight."

"Okay, see you then." I hung up on RC. I walked out into the living room expecting to say goodbye to Dwayne. He had already left. He couldn't wait for me to come out of my room huh? Fuck it, it didn't matter anyway. I got what I needed and now Samara would get what was coming to her. Ryson and Dwayne could ignore me all they wanted, but once Samara was out of the picture they would come crawling back to me. And I would have open arms.

DWAYNE

I heard Ryson's Jeep start up and then pull off. I overheard him yesterday telling somebody he was doing overtime today, so I knew he was going in early. I jumped up out the bed fully dressed. I didn't know if this was a good idea or not but I had to try. I hopped in my work truck and drove over to her house. It was five-thirty in the morning and it was still dark outside. I parked and sat in my truck watching her house. I looked up at the second-floor windows and wondered which room was hers. I got out and closed the door of my truck slowly, not wanting to wake anybody up. I took a deep breath and walked across the street and onto Samara's porch. I put my finger on her bell but I didn't push it. She had to be asleep. All of the lights in her house were off. I didn't want to wake her up and have her disoriented while I tried to apologize to her.

"I should just come back later," I said to myself. *No! Go in now!*
The voice whispered to me. I was hearing it more often now, but only when I thought of Samara it seemed. In a way it was comforting. It was like I had a voice of reason in my head. I

studied her doorknob. Maybe I could leave her a note to call me. I'd write it and leave it in her mail slot. Yeah, I could do that. That would eliminate the embarrassment of me catching her off guard. I would ask her to meet me somewhere public where we could talk face to face. I suddenly had another idea. I turned towards her lawn to see if she had the logo of whatever security system she was using on it. She did. It was a company I was subcontracted to do electrical work for. Could my luck have been any better? I frequently visited the homes of their customers to re-wire their systems when they went haywire. I could disarm her alarm if I wanted to. She had one of the newer model systems, which was even easier to disarm for me. All I had to do was punch in the override code after I entered the house, assuming she didn't have it set to motion detection mode. That was a risk I was going to have to take. It wasn't really breaking and entering because I wasn't going to break anything to get in. I just wanted to write her a note then leave.

I walked around to the back of her house and vaulted over her fence. I looked around at the surrounding homes to make sure there were no prying eyes. It was clear. I picked the lock on her back door, which was surprisingly easy. Whenever we got back on speaking terms, I would have to let her know about her weak ass locks. I slowly turned the knob and put a little pressure on the door. It squeaked open and I slid in as fast as I could. I closed the door slowly and quietly. I stood in the kitchen as my eyes adjusted to the darkness. This was my first time inside Samara's house, so I didn't know where anything was. It would be hard to find a pen and paper in the dark. I didn't want to be fumbling around in her house and wake her up. That would be a whole different problem I didn't need. I needed to find her alarm systems' central control panel. I hung close to the walls and crept through the kitchen and dining room. I heard a beeping sound, notifying me that the door had been opened. I followed the sound and found myself in her living room. I was facing a mantle and a coffee table. I walked over to her door and punched in the override code. It instantly shut her alarm off with two quick notification beeps. I lightly trod over to the table, picked up a piece of paper, and found a pen next to an issue of '*Shape*' magazine. I tapped the pen on my chin, not sure exactly what to write. Shit. I was at a loss for words. I did all of this, just to come up speechless? I put the pen and paper back on the table. Fuck this man. I would just call her or something. This was too much. I turned around prepared to leave. *She's right up those stairs.*

I looked up at her staircase. It couldn't hurt to see her. I mean, just to make sure she was okay. I know what Ryson said about the stitches and the bruises on her arms, but I wanted to see them for myself. If I actually saw the damage that I'd caused, maybe I would realize how my anger had spiraled out of control. Seeing her could help me the next time I felt myself slipping. My heart beat a little faster in fear as I climbed the stairs. When I made it to the second floor, I noticed multiple bedrooms. I walked to each one, listening for any noise coming from behind the door. When I got to the last door, I heard her breathing. The house was dead quiet. I put my hand on the knob and turned. I couldn't turn back now.

RYSON

I was spending too much time with Samara. I knew that I liked her, but damn if I wasn't falling for her ass. Damn! This was the shit I was trying to prevent from happening in the first place. I came back to her house that same day I left her standing in her living room. I told myself it was because I was still concerned about her. It wasn't like she called me or asked me to come over, I just wanted to. When she opened the door wearing a pair of black spandex shorts and a hot pink sports bra, I was flabbergasted. My legs couldn't move and my dick instantly woke up. She was sweaty and breathing hard.

"Hey! I didn't know you were coming over. Come in." She smiled widely and moved sideways to let me in. I tried to keep my breathing under control as I walked cool as a cucumber into her house. Inside, my stomach was doing karate kicks. I was breaking out into a sweat like I was the one working out.

"Let me turn the video off." Samara toweled off her face and neck. She craned her neck and closed her eyes. She had worked up a sweat and her breasts were moving up and down. I swallowed and closed my mouth. I looked at her abs and her toned legs. Fuck! Her body was definitely eye candy.

"Uh… no don't let me stop you. Continue. I'll just chill out until you finish." I suggested, sitting down on the couch.

"You sure?" She licked sweat off her top lip. *Oh. My. God.* I needed to get some air, but if I stood up I couldn't hide what was dying to rip through my pants.

"Yeah I'm sure, go ahead." She had moved all the furniture to the left side of the room so there was nothing but open space. She stood in the middle of the living room facing her TV. *Don't look, please don't look.* I begged my eyes not to look at her ass, but they wouldn't listen. My eyes rested on the curve in her back, just above her ass. It trailed down to the back of her thick thighs. Her ass was taunting me, begging me to touch it. Her ass was like two round basketballs sitting in her spandex. Her ass was perfect and firm. I remember pinching it the night of the party. I covered my face and pretended to cough when she turned the volume up on the TV. She pushed resume on her video and started throwing jabs. I looked at the screen and realized she was doing some type of Tae Bo or boxing workout. I watched in fascination as she executed her round kicks and her combinations. She was pretty good. I was doing okay until I heard the instructor say, "Let's do some lunges and squats!" Samara's face was set with concentration as she put her hands on her hips and did a forward lunge. She came back up and let out a breath. She did the other leg and the muscles in her upper thigh flexed. I had to think about something else besides her body right now. I picked up the newspaper off the table and read the same article four times. Don't ask me if I remembered anything from it. I heard the TV go off and the remote control hit the table. *Thank goodness.* I didn't know how much longer I could stand it. The sexual attraction was killing me.

"I'll be back in ten minutes. Help yourself to anything." She sprinted up the steps. *I want to help myself to that ass.* It bounced up and down with every step. I shook my head to snap out of it, then got up and walked into the kitchen. I got a bottle of water and went back into the living room. I decided to help her out and move the furniture back into place. Who was I kidding? I was trying to do any and everything to keep my mind off how good she looked standing there in front of me in spandex. I sat back down and drummed a beat on my knee nervously. What was I so nervous about? I got up and stretched out. I still didn't know what I was doing here. I'd had a long day at work and was supposed to meet Devon and some of the fellas for a drink. I was at the light thinking that Samara's house was only four blocks from where I was, and the next thing I knew I was ringing her bell. She came back down the steps wearing a pair of black drawstring pants and a white t-shirt. Her hair was pulled back into a ponytail and she was bare foot. Even in sweats and a t-shirt, she was sexy as hell. She smiled at me and went into the kitchen. I followed behind her.

"I wasn't expecting to see you again so soon. If at all honestly." She pulled out a bottle of water and took a swig.

"I was in the neighborhood, so I said what the hell?" I drank my water, trying to play it cool.

"Oh yeah?" She knew what it was. I came there to see her.

"So how are you feeling?" I asked, breaking the ice. She just stared at me like she was trying to decipher some ancient text.

"I'm trying to figure you out." She zeroed her eyes in on me.

"What do you mean?" My voice was a little shaky.

"I mean I don't know what's going on in that handsome head of yours. Like, why are you really here?" She finished her water and sat the empty bottle on the counter. She crossed her arms and waited for an answer. Did my face give me away? What did she know? Her eyes burned a hole in my face.

"Like I said, I was in the neighborhood. I just wanted to check on you. As a friend." I added quickly. She wasn't getting me to admit shit. She chuckled lightly when I said that.

"As my 'friend'?" She put up quotation marks with her fingers when she said that. She exhaled and walked up to me.

"Let's talk Ryson." She walked back into the living room and sat on the couch. I walked behind her, not sure what to say. We both knew damn well I didn't look at her like she was a friend. It was the only thing that I could think of that wouldn't have me putting myself out there. I sat down next to her and smelled whatever soap she had used.

"Ryson, I'm not going to bullshit you. I like you, a lot. I know that you like me too. You don't really look at me and see a friend. You don't kiss your friends the way you kiss me. You don't touch your friends the way you touch me. Even if you can't admit it Ryson, I already know." She smirked because she knew she had me. I sat quiet for a minute before saying anything. She played with her hair and dared me to tell her different.

"I'm not admitting anything," I said finally. Shit! I felt like I was being backed into a corner.

"But you're here, so that tells me everything." She leaned in and kissed me. Damn her lips were soft. I could feel the stitches in her bottom lip. I took hold of her swollen face and looked her in the eyes with concern.

"It doesn't hurt?" I asked, looking down at her lip. She did a half-smile and shook her head no. She held on to my wrists and kissed me again, this time sliding her tongue into my mouth. I could honestly say I never did this with any of my friends. I put my hands on her shoulders and tried to push her down onto her back. She stopped kissing me and put her hand on my chest, stopping me.

"If my head hits the couch then we'll be leaving 'friend' territory." She looked up at me in amusement. I tried not to smile, but I couldn't help it.

"So you're a smartass now huh?" I laughed and pulled her back up.

"That's one of my many talents, ha-ha." She sat up and put one of the throw pillows on her lap.

"That's real funny." I smiled at her. She was so damn cute. I did like her a lot. I just couldn't tell her yet. After I knew a little more about her, I might feel a little more comfortable telling her how I felt. I barely knew anything about Samara. I knew she was single, sexy, and funny. She was a flirt and had the brightest smile. She was fun to be around, but I didn't really know any real details about her. It was getting harder for me to deny the attraction was purely sexual. I needed a distraction because if she kissed me again there was going to be a problem.

"What's your last name?" I asked suddenly. She jerked her head back in surprise and blinked.

"Um... it's Cipriano." She looked stunned that I would care enough to ask.

"What's your middle name?" I threw out another question. If it would take my mind off her body, I was prepared to interview her like I was Oprah. The more I talked, the less I thought about how much I wanted to jump on her. Kind of. She got comfortable in the chair and turned to face me.

"Laida. It was my grandmother Adelaida's nickname," she said and smiled at a memory she was having. I studied her bruised face. She was so beautiful.

"That's pretty." I slid closer to her on the couch. Not too close though. I wasn't stupid.

"Since we're getting to know each other, what's your last name, middle name, and how old are you?" She fired the questions at me back to back.

"Ha-ha okay. Well my last name is Turner. I don't have a middle name and I'm thirty-three. How old are you?" I asked. With her youthful appearance, she could pass for twenty-two. But I knew she was older than that. She had an air about her that didn't belong to someone in their early twenties.

"I'm twenty-eight. How many kids ya got?" I almost choked. What the hell? She started cracking up at my reaction.

"I don't have any kids! If I did they would probably be running around my house tearing it up as we speak." I wasn't ready for kids yet. I was still raising Dwayne.

"What do you do for a living?" I watched her lips move.

"I'm an accountant." I was happy the conversation had turned.

"Oh, so you're a nerd then?" She laughed at me.

"Yes, I am a nerd." I laughed with her.

"What do you do?"

"I was a coordinator for a Human Resources firm but it was temporary. I'm looking for something else. I'm just living off an inheritance right now." She tilted her head to the side. She was trying to read me. I redirected my eyes to the pillow in her lap.

"Cipriano? That name sounds so familiar." I couldn't remember where I had heard that name before, but it definitely sounded familiar. She looked at the wall behind my head then back at me. Whatever she was about to tell me it seemed like she didn't want to.

"If you lived in this city in the nineties the name would sound familiar. My father was Andy Cipriano. He was the mayor for two terms." Something in her eyes changed. They were clouded.

"Andy Cipriano is your father? Wow!... that's crazy. But the resemblance is there now that I really look at you. What's wrong?" She looked like she would cry at any moment. It then hit me that Andy Cipriano had died years ago from cancer.

"Nothing, it's just hard talking about him that's all."

"I'm sorry." I said, truly meaning it. The conversation was meant for me to get to know a little bit more about her, but it had taken an emotional turn. I didn't know what to do or say. I wasn't too good with emotions.

"Uh... well tell me what he was like. I heard a lot about him. The first Cuban mayor in this city. It was a big deal in the ghetto. He was the Obama of the nineties." I tried to make her laugh. It worked. I saw a small smile creep across her face and then she looked at me. Her eyes were glistening like she was on the verge of tears. She cleared her throat and took her hair out of the ponytail. I liked it better that way.

"Let's see, where to start. My father was a celebrity in our neighborhood. People respected him and looked up to him. He was into politics for as long as I can remember. I remember painting him a campaign sign when I was in kindergarten, ha-ha. He was always at a debate or making an appearance at this place or that. There were times when I didn't see or hear from him for days. There was always something that needed his attention or some cause that he was involved in." She stopped talking for a second.

"I have a younger brother, Julio. He wants to follow in my father's footsteps after graduating law school. He called me the other day to tell me that he was thinking about running for mayor in Philadelphia in a few years. I wished him good luck, but I don't want that life for him. He has a wife and my four-year old niece Sofia. I remember those days when me, Julio, and my mom would be home alone. Every day we would wait for my father to call or to come home. It wasn't a good feeling. We knew what he was doing was important to the community, but I just wanted my daddy. He missed a lot of things in my life and I don't want that for Julio and his family, you know?" I nodded my understanding. She talked with such passion, I was wrapped up into her story. I liked this. Just sitting here talking. It wasn't bad. It didn't compare to being entangled in her body, but it was nice.

"He bought us material things all the time. Things we didn't want or need. I think it was his way of trying to make up for not being there. When he told us we were moving from our small two bedroom apartment in the hood, to a three story house in the suburbs, I thought he was joking. I mean, come on, the suburbs?" She laughed and reminisced.

"My father saved up a lot of money and purchased the house on their wedding anniversary. It was a gift to his family. It was beautiful and spacious but it was empty. When he became mayor, I saw even less of him. As I got older I started to act out. I was a real bitch to my mom, ha-ha. My teenage years were crazy. I just did those things for my father's attention though. I would sneak out the house at night, get into fights at school, you name it, I did it. I was the class clown, the life of the party. Anything I could do to get attention, I did it. My mom would always call my father. He would stop by the house to scold me and give me a lecture about life. He told me that I shouldn't waste my life doing insignificant things. He told me that I had to grow up and take responsibility for my actions. Those talks always made me feel like crap, but they were the only times I had him to myself. I think he sensed that I was doing all those things for attention. When we found out he had cancer everything changed." She put the pillow on my lap, laid her head on it, and stretched out on the couch. I moved robotically to put my right arm on the couch arm and my left on the back of it. Her head was in my lap. I swallowed hard and tried to focus on what she was saying. She was looking up at me now. She played with her hair as she continued to talk. I willed my dick not to get hard, hoping my will was stronger than my longing.

"He started to work from home then. I got my act together fast so I could be there for him. He had the best doctors money could buy. He convinced us that he would beat this 'imposter'. That's how he referred to his cancer, as an imposter inside his body. As the years passed and he was still with us, I began to believe it. We lost him the day of my high school graduation. I had told my mother to stay home with my dad because he was too weak to come. I made Julio promise to take a million pictures of me so I could show them to my dad afterwards. I was standing in line waiting to receive my diploma, when this strange feeling came over me. Almost like I felt nauseous. I chalked it up to nervousness and continued up to the stage. When I turned towards the crowd for Julio to take a picture of me holding my diploma, he was on his cell phone. I was so angry at him! I stormed off the stage and walked over to him ready to curse him out. When I walked up to him I knew my father had passed. His face said it all. We rushed home and found my mother on the living room floor shaking. I stuck around long enough to take care of the funeral arrangements and to make sure my mother was okay. But I could no longer stay inside that house. It was empty again and it had too many memories. On top of the money from his life insurance policy, my father also left us money in his will. Both combined were enough for my mother to live comfortably. The amount he left me and Julio was enough for us to buy homes and pay for college. I didn't go to college, instead, I bought a car and a house. I haven't really done anything with the rest of the money since then outside of living expenses." She shrugged her shoulders and looked down at her nails.

"Can I tell you something?" Her voice was barely above a whisper.

"Sure," I said delicately. She was baring a lot of her soul to me right now. I didn't know how to feel about that.

"Did you wonder why I didn't press charges on Dwayne?" She looked up at me again. I had wondered about that, but I just thought she wanted it to be over with and decided against it.

"Why?" I wanted to hear this. Talking to her made me feel closer to her. She was so open and vulnerable. This was a side of Samara I wasn't used to. I was used to the outgoing, self-assured Samara.

"If my father were alive, he wouldn't want me to punish Dwayne by pressing charges. He would want me to get him help with his anger. He thought the prison system was the worst place to send someone who needed therapy. He didn't raise me to turn my back on someone when they needed help." Her father sounded like he lived up to his reputation of being a leader.

"I know what he did to you was wrong, but I'm glad you didn't press charges." I reached down and wiped away a tear that fell from her eyes. She closed her eyes and let more fall. I felt guilty sitting there with her. She just told me something deeply personal and I couldn't do the same. There was so much I couldn't tell Samara that went beyond my feelings for her. I stroked her hair and watched her. I felt a tug in my heart and panicked.

"Uh... what time is it?" I asked even though I had a watch on my wrist. She sat up and wiped her eyes.

"It's almost seven I think." She sniffed and ran her hand through her curly hair.

"Damn! I was supposed to be meeting some of my boys for drinks. I lost track of time. Shit. I'll call you okay?" I got up and grabbed my keys off the table.

"Okay." I felt bad leaving her in the state she was in. But I couldn't continue to sit there and not say or do something I was going to regret. I walked to the door and looked at the back of her head. Fuck.

"Samara?" I called her name. She turned towards me.

"Come here." I watched as she slowly walked over to me. I didn't like playing games like this, but what else could I do? I was scared. I tilted her chin up and kissed her softly on her lips. She got on her tiptoes and kissed me back with passion. Damn. Why couldn't I just leave out the fucking door? I kissed her back just as passionately. I really got pleasure from kissing Samara. Her lips kept me stimulated. I pulled her closer to me and got the courage to touch her ass. I was itching to lay my hands on it since I walked through her door. I grabbed as much of it as I could, squeezed, and kneaded it in my palms. I plunged my tongue deep in her mouth and walked forward, forcing her to walk backwards. She moaned and opened her mouth wider for me. With my tongue in her mouth and my hands on her ass, I was gone. I couldn't stop. I had to have her right then and there. My phone vibrated.

"Aaaaahhhhh!" I let out an exasperated sigh. I put my forehead on hers and she giggled. I smiled at her and regrettably took my hands off her ass.

"It's a text from Devon asking me where I am. I'm like an hour late." I sighed and put my phone back in my pocket. I didn't want to leave, but I had to. If my phone hadn't vibrated, I would have done something I might have regretted. I had a feeling that once I slept with Samara, I wouldn't be able to just walk away, even if I wanted to. I needed to keep her at arm's length. I told myself that when I first met her and look where it got me. I just had to get out of her space and breathe in some air. Reality would set in and I would realize I was tripping for nothing.

"I gotta go. I'll call you." I thought about kissing her again but I made my legs walk away from her.

"All right then." She eye fucked me. Damn. Damn. Damn. I damn near tripped trying to get out of her house. I speed walked to my Jeep and jumped in. I turned on the ignition and peeled off before I convinced myself to go back. I told myself to be careful. I was swimming in uncharted waters. But the next day I was back at her house again. And then the day after that and the day after that. I was at her house more than I was home. I kept telling myself to just drive home, but my hands guided the steering wheel to her house almost every day. I had to give myself props though. I hadn't slept with her yet and that was a big achievement. It wasn't like I didn't want to, but there was something different about Samara. I was noticing it the more time that I spent with her. She was more than just a body and a face. I actually wanted to be around her, to talk to her. We would talk for hours about nothing and everything. She would have me laughing to the point of tears and vice versa. But she never made a pass at me. She didn't flirt with me or try to make a move, we just chilled. And surprisingly, that was enough for me. I felt like we were getting closer, becoming friends. I'd never been friends with a female and it was strange. She would call me in the middle of the day to tell me the most random things, and I actually looked forward to hearing her voice. I would call her late at night and ask her what she was doing, knowing that she was trying to sleep. She told me she didn't mind though. We would talk all night. That feeling in my chest was getting stronger as the days went by. I couldn't pretend it was just heartburn anymore. I was starting to fall for Samara. That was the dilemma I was in. How could I possibly be falling in love? I'd avoided going through that my whole life, but I couldn't fight it any longer. Samara never hid how much she liked me, so I already knew the feeling was mutual. But I couldn't tell her. If I told her how I felt, I had to tell her everything about me. All of my dirty little secrets. If I told her, I was sure I would lose her. So I had to continue to pretend that all of this time we spent together was no big deal to me. I hoped Samara was willing to be patient with me. I was nowhere near ready to tell her the truth that I'd been trying to hide all of these years.

DWAYNE

The fucking bedroom door squeaked. I held my breath and prayed she didn't wake up. She didn't. I let out the breath I was holding and inched further into her bedroom. It was dark but the sun was starting to rise, so light shined in through the window. I could make out her silhouette on the bed. She was asleep on her stomach with her ass up in the air. Goddamn! I remembered being in that. *Focus! You came here to check on her so just walk over to the fucking bed and check!* Her whole room smelled like lavender. I took a whiff and closed my eyes. Damn. I walked over to her bed and stood over her. She snored lightly and her hair was strewn across the bed. She looked so fucking sexy lying there in only her bra and panties. Her white lacy panties barely covered her ass cheeks. Her bra strap had slipped down her shoulder, leaving it bare. I got on my knees so I could be eye level with her. I looked at her arm and saw the bruise I created. They weren't as dark as I thought they would be. But her cheek was swollen and a dark shade of purple, the only blemish on her perfect face. I reached out and touched a strand of her hair. Timidly, I twirled it around my finger. I kept my eyes locked on hers just in case she woke up. She looked so peaceful. I wanted to touch her. I wanted to touch her so fucking bad. I wanted to be inside her even more. I got up and told myself to leave before I did something stupid. I took a few steps towards the door and stopped. If I was careful, she would never know if I touched her or not. As long as I didn't wake her up, I could basically do whatever I wanted to do. There wasn't anything wrong with that right? *Not at all.*

I got back down on my knees, but this time I was eye level with her ass. I hesitantly stuck my hand out and let it hover over her ass like a spaceship. I closed my eyes and slowly lowered it until I felt flesh.

"Shit!" I whispered. Her ass was soft and warm. My dick got hard as soon as I made contact.

"Mmmmm." I moaned, gently squeezing her ass. My heart was beating loudly in my ear. I glanced at her face. She was still asleep. My hand slid over her ass crack over to the other cheek. Damn her ass felt so good in my hand. My dick was throbbing to be inside her. I decided to do the next best thing. I unzipped my pants and put my dick in my hand. A nervous excitement ran through my body as I got harder. I was actually in Samara's room rubbing on her ass. I squeezed her ass and stroked my dick up and down. A vision of her riding my dick handcuffed popped into my head. Her ass bouncing up and down on my balls. Her erect nipples poking out and begging me to bite them. I felt myself about to cum. I spit on my hand and yanked my dick harder. That night her pussy had been so wet and gushy. I wanted to cum in her so bad, but I had to hold on. I couldn't let her make me cum first. I remember how she took my entire dick in her ass. I slid a finger in between her ass cheeks. I slowly felt my way to the front of her panties and made circles on her clit. I bit my lip and looked at her again. She didn't stir.

"Yeah, you like that don't you?" I asked her. She wasn't a light sleeper. The veins in my dick were throbbing. Sweat ran down the side of my face as I jerked harder. I picked up my momentum. I wanted to put a finger inside her, but I didn't want to push my luck. She moaned. I froze. I grabbed my dick firmer and continued stroking. *She's enjoying it!*

 She had to be, why else would she be moaning in her sleep? I couldn't hold my nut any longer. I searched her room for something to cum on or in, but I didn't see shit. Fuck it. I touched her clit. I wanted to plunge my dick in her so bad. Was it worth the risk? Hell yes, but she would definitely wake up if I did that. I chanced it and slid my finger into her panties, feeling her pussy lips. I put my finger in my mouth and tasted her juices.

"Oooh shit!" I missed that taste. I started cumming immediately.

"FUCK!" I whispered through clenched teeth. I stood up and jerked my hot nut onto her back.

"Damn!" I caught my breath and wiped the sweat from my forehead. She was still asleep. That was good. I zipped my pants up and looked around the room for something to wipe her back off with. I picked up a black shirt, gently wiped her back off, and put the shirt in my back pocket. I couldn't leave any evidence that I had been there. I bent down and kissed her softly on the lips. My knee hit something under her bed. It was a black shoebox. I quietly pulled it from under the bed and took the lid off. There were dozens of pictures of Samara and what I assumed was her family. I picked out a picture of her from high school in a track outfit. Her big curly hair was out wild as usual. Her hands were on her hips and she looked like she was trying to catch her breath. She was sexy even back then. I stuffed the picture in my pocket.

"I'll be back." I promised and crept out of her room. I ran down the steps worry-free. She wouldn't wake up. I opened the front door, reset her alarm, then made my way back to my work truck. I couldn't help but whistle. I couldn't believe that shit had just happened. Now that I knew I could get in and get out, there was nothing in my way.

RYSON

Once again I was at Samara's house chilling. She sat on her counter while I cooked dinner. It felt foreign to do these couple type things. It also felt very natural.

"What are you making? I don't like surprises." Samara asked me, peering into the frying pan.

"Nunya! That's what I'm cooking." I joked with her and covered her face with my right hand. She laughed and swatted my hand away.

"Just feel lucky I'm cooking for you at all." I said and added some olive oil to the pan so I could sauté the vegetables.

"You're the lucky one because I can't cook. If it was up to me we'd be ordering a pizza ha-ha." She laughed and crossed her legs. I really loved being around her. It was getting to a point where seeing her was already on my agenda before I even got out of bed in the morning.

"Do me a favor and see what's on ESPN?"

"Hmmm let me guess... sports?" Her voice was dripping with sarcasm as she opened her eyes wide in innocence.

"Just go check smart ass!" I took the dish towel and slapped her on the leg with it. She hopped down off the counter and walked into the living room. The food was almost finished. I was just waiting for the chicken to brown a little bit more.

"They're talking about something called Fantasy football, whatever that means," she yelled from the living room. I smiled and shook my head.

"What are they saying?"

"That people are going to be mad at some guy if they thought he was going to put up big numbers this week. Again, whatever that means."

"That means that if somebody picked him for their Fantasy football team, and figured he would rush a certain amount of yards, they're fucked. He probably didn't do shit this week."

"That sounds interesting." Her voice lacked excitement.

"You always have to be a smart ass don't you?"

"It's part of my charm," she giggled from the living room.

"The food is done."

"You want to eat in the living room?" She came back into the kitchen and stood inches away from me. I snuck a look her way and nodded my head yes. She was dressed plain, but I couldn't help imagining myself in between her legs. She had on a pair of tight blue jeans, a white t-shirt and a fitted leather jacket. She took her heels off when I got there.

"I know you want to see the highlights from SportsCenter." She smiled and winked at me. She knew a little more about sports than she let on.

"Go get comfortable and I'll bring the food out." I brought the baked chicken, brown rice, gravy, and mixed vegetables out and sat the plates on her coffee table. We put pillows down and sat Indian style facing the TV.

"This looks good." Her eyes got huge as I sat a steaming plate in front of her. *Not as good as you.*

I had to get my mind out of the gutter. But it was difficult being around her without wanting to sleep with her. Breathing in her scent was torture. Watching her walk and sway her hips was torment. Everything was going good. I didn't want to mess it up by trying to push up on her. Even though that was exactly what I wanted to do. She took off her jacket and dug in.

"Why aren't you eating?" She turned towards me while sucking gravy off of her index finger. I opened my mouth to talk but nothing came out. I watched her lick and suck her finger until there was nothing left on it. I stared as her lips came together then opened back up. My dick pushed at the fabric of my jeans.

"Hot," was all that came out of my mouth. She burst out into laughter and almost choked on her food.

"Hot? What's hot? The food?" She looked at me and laughed again. I must have looked like an idiot with my lips drooping open. I snapped out of it and shook my head.

"Yeah, the food is hot. I'm going to let it cool down some," I explained quickly. I turned my attention to the TV, mindful that she was still looking at me with a grin on her face.

"You're funny." She continued to eat. For the next twenty minutes we ate and watched ESPN. I was grateful for the distraction. I got up to collect the dishes but she stopped me.

"You cooked, I'll clean. Sit back down." I did as she said and leaned back against the couch. She picked up the plates and went into the kitchen.

"Thirsty?" She called out from the kitchen.

"Yes!" Among other things, I wanted to say. She walked in with two glasses filled halfway with red wine. I took the glasses from her as she sat down.

"The food was delicious. The last time I attempted a home cooked meal, I was six and tried to make a grilled cheese sandwich in the microwave, ha-ha." She laughed, but I laughed harder. There was nowhere else I wanted to be at that moment.

"Where did you learn how to cook like that?" She put her elbow on the table and laid her cheek in her open palm.

"I learned the hard way. Trial and error, ha-ha. When I was growing up my mom worked two jobs, so Dwayne and I were home alone a lot. As the older brother, it was my responsibility to make sure we ate, that the house was clean, and that the homework was done. My father was never really around. I kind of had to fill those shoes." I don't know why I was telling her this. I never told anyone about my childhood. I guess I felt at ease with her. She sipped her wine and looked contemplative.

"I thought you and Dwayne had different mothers." She remembered.

"We do, but Dwayne's mother I think abandoned him. I never got the full story behind it. When I was around nine years old, my dad dropped him off at the house. That's where he stayed. I was excited to have a little brother, but he was a pain in my ass, ha-ha."

"That's really sad about his mother. Did he help out around the house?" She asked and laughed.

"Hell no! My mom spoiled Dwayne rotten because of his situation, so he ran amuck. She did the best she could, trying to raise two boys by herself. It was, and still is, tough trying to raise boys into men in today's society. I mean, we knew who our dad was, and he came to see us from time to time. But as I got older it became evident that he was only coming over to see one person and for one reason only." She crawled closer to me and took my hand in hers. Was that my voice sounding wobbly?

"My mom always let him back in, and he was gone as soon as he got what he came for. I always hated that about him. I would hear my mom crying at night in her room after once again being pulled into my father's trap. My father was a player. It got so bad that he had other kids by other women, hence Dwayne, while he was with my mom. It was hard, but it just made me grow up faster and take responsibility for my family." I linked my fingers with hers.

"So when Dwayne was bad, did you have to spank him?" She smiled and tried to lighten the mood. It didn't go unnoticed.

"No, I wouldn't spank him. I would kick his little ass. Dwayne was bad as shit!" She smiled hard and her eyes sparkled.

"I want you so bad." It escaped my lips before I had a chance to stop it. Her smile faded. She took her hand from mine and looked down at the carpet. Shit, I knew I should have kept my fucking mouth shut. Damn!

"I want you too." She looked at me and I could see the lust in her eyes. Well if we both wanted each other, what was the problem?

"If I walked upstairs to your bedroom right now, would you follow me?" I wanted to know what was standing in our way. I didn't want to mess anything up, but if she wanted me as badly as I wanted her, I didn't see what the issue was. I was scared to cross that line though because I honestly don't think there was any coming back afterwards. I think I was willing to take that risk with her.

"No, I wouldn't." Disappointment rang throughout my body.

"Why not?" Who was playing games now? I didn't want to sound desperate, but shit, I was horny.

"Because the timing is all wrong," she said hesitantly. I tried to bite my tongue, but I couldn't.

"Was the timing wrong when you slept with Dwayne? You knew him for all of twenty minutes before you slept with him." I regretted the words as soon as they left my mouth. She looked hurt and offended. She flinched.

"What are you trying to say?" Her expression was severe waiting for my response. Shit.

"I didn't mean it like that. I'm just saying we got a good vibe going on. I know you're feeling me more than you were feeling Dwayne. Why was it the right time for you to be with him, but you're making me wait?" She pursed her lips and wiped her hands up and down on her legs like she was cold.

"Let's just address the elephant in the room." She looked me dead in the eyes and talked frankly.

"Okay, let's." I got off the floor and sat on the couch. She followed.

"I slept with your brother." I flinched inwardly. That shit was still bothering me. I didn't want to admit it, but it hurt knowing that Dwayne had fucked her. I lay in the room right next door, forced to listen to him bang and fuck the shit out of her. And she enjoyed every minute of it. I was jealous. I wanted to be with her because I was so fucking attracted to her. But I also wanted to be with her so I could show her that I was the better lover. That probably didn't matter to her, but it did to me. As a man, knowing that the woman I was falling for had slept with my little brother, was crushing to my ego and my pride. I tried not to let that shit get to me, but I couldn't control it. I wasn't saying she was a hoe or anything, but if she could fuck him on the first night, what was wrong with me?

"And you were in the next room when all of that went down, so I can only imagine what you heard. It was a spur of the moment decision and I do regret it. If I had known all of this pandemonium would come out of it, I would never have done it. If I had known I would develop feelings for you, I wouldn't have done it. But I did do it and now it's biting me in the ass." She took another sip of her wine and closed her eyes. No one knew any of this shit would happen, so I knew where she was coming from. But it still hurt.

"The only thing that I can say in defense of myself is, I slept with Dwayne out of loneliness and boredom. It was purely sexual and it didn't mean anything to me. I don't want Dwayne. I don't have feelings for Dwayne. But I have feelings for you, and I am interested in you in ways that go beyond sex. I don't want to be with you out of lust or boredom. I want our first time together to be special. I want it to mean something for the both of us. I care too much about you to have casual meaningless sex with you." Wow. What could I say to that? At that moment I realized that I loved her. I truly and deeply loved her. There was no way I was rushing into sex with her now. I wanted our first time to be special too. She watched me with uncertainty, unsure of how I would react. I grabbed her hand and pulled her to me.

"This situation was jacked up from the start. But I can't let how we began, determine how we go about things now. I understand where you're coming from and I agree with you. I want our first time to be special too, so you don't have to worry about having this conversation again. What happened in the past is in the past." I kissed the tip of her nose and enveloped her in my arms. Dwayne might have fucked her, but he would never be able to make love to her. He would never have her heart or her respect. I had those things and I intended to keep them.

SHAR

I have the money.

I texted the number that RC had given me. It was the only way I could contact the guy I hired to carry out my plan B. I stood at the bus stop contemplating whether I should call a cab or not. I was hot, tired, and traffic was a mess. I knew I wasn't going to be home anytime soon. I worked a double shift for the fifth time in the last two weeks. It was all worth it though. The feeling of jubilation that coursed through my veins was making me high. I finally had the money! All my troubles would be over soon. As soon as I got a response back that is. What the fuck was taking so long?

When and where do you want to make the drop?

I suddenly thought about what I was doing. My happiness deflated and common sense kicked in. Could I really go through with paying somebody to do bodily harm to Samara? I hated her, that was a fact, but I had a conscience too. Hyping Dwayne up to rough her up was different from hiring some goons to do god knows what to her. I looked down at my phone, unsure.

I'm having second thoughts, I typed and pressed send. Maybe the situation would get better. Maybe Ryson and Dwayne will come to their senses and see Samara for what she was. A whore. An attention loving, big butt slut. My phone vibrated.

Contact me when you're serious.

I saved the number in my phone and searched for the bus. I would try again on my own to deal with Samara. If that failed, then I would re-examine my options.

SAMARA

I put my iPod on the iPod deck and turned to my favorite playlist. It was a mix of classic love songs and a few recent ones. Anita Baker, Ledisi, Maxwell, Al Green, Marvin Gaye, Toni Braxton, and Musiq Soulchild, were just a few of the artists on my list. I talked to Ryson earlier when he was at work. I knew he was coming over tonight. I wanted to set a relaxing mood for him. After our talk a few weeks ago, I couldn't help but see a change in him. He was less on edge and more comfortable around me. I knew he wanted me, any blind man could see that. From the longing looks, to the constant hard-ons that he sported every time we were together, I wasn't oblivious to his attraction to me. But I meant what I said about our first time. I rushed into sex with Dwayne and it did not turn out well. I wasn't making the same mistake with Ryson.

That was why I had taken my time planning tonight. I was ready. I sprayed the bedroom with my perfume. I had two glasses of wine and a bottle of warm Jojoba oil waiting next to the bed. Ryson was unaware of all of this, which would make it all the more special. I wanted to start off slow and gradually start ripping his clothes off. Ryson would see the set up in the bedroom and realize that it was on. I was so ready for him. I planned on giving Ryson the royal treatment tonight. Starting off with a back rub. I heard the doorbell. I pulled the door open, and fought to contain myself as Ryson stepped into the living room.

"You look... uh... really good." He smiled and slanted his head at me suspiciously.

"Thank you." I blushed uncontrollably. I was trying to keep it together, but I was so excited.

"What are you up to?" Ryson pecked me on the lips and put his hands on my hips.

"Nothing. Take off your coat." I'd searched my closet for something special to wear, but I couldn't find anything that suited the occasion. After hours of searching and shopping, I finally found the perfect dress. It was a cherry colored strapless bandage dress. The sweetheart top gave my breasts a nice lift. The spandex material drew attention to my ass, like it needed any more attention drawn to it.

"I know that you had a long week at work. I just wanted to help you relax." I set my alarm and put my hand out for him to grab. Déjà vu of the first time I led him up my steps flashed in my head. He took it and we walked up the stairs.

RYSON

My eyes were burning. I'd been doing audits all week. If I had to look at another number, I was going to fucking scream! I headed to Samara's house to take a load off and to let her cheer me up. She had a knack for that. I loosened my charcoal gray silk tie, and unbuttoned the top three buttons on my black dress shirt. I regretted not bringing a pair of sneakers with me. I slid my foot out of my black dress shoes and cracked my toes. I parked on the street and rang the bell. When she came into view, I forgot everything I had been complaining about. She had on a red skin-tight dress. Her hip to waist ratio was ridiculous. She was so fucking thick. I could have bust a nut just by looking at her. She never dressed this sexy around me. Something was going on.

"What are you up to?" I pulled her to me so I could get a better view of her breasts.

"I just wanted to help you relax." She put her hand out. I blinked three times to make sure this wasn't a dream. Was she really taking me upstairs? Wearing that dress? Something was going down tonight. I wasn't going to say shit. She opened her bedroom door and her scent sailed through my nostrils. She had two glasses of wine on the dresser. Since Samara and I started seeing each other, I ignored every hard dick I had. Every time I would get aroused, I convinced myself to think of something else to take my mind off her. Not tonight. I wasn't stopping shit or talking my dick out of anything. I was letting go. I realized that she set all of this up for me. She was ready for me. I was a little nervous. I really felt like it was my first time all over again.

"Come over to the bed," she instructed me. I sat on the edge of the bed ready for whatever. It was her show, so I was letting her do her thing, for now. She got on the bed behind me and put her breasts on my back. I felt her lips on the back of my neck. Soft and hot she kissed me from the back of my ear down to the side of my throat. I instantly got goose bumps. Her hands came around and took my tie off. Her fingers then worked their way down my shirt unbuttoning it. I shrugged out of it. She brought her head around and put her lips on mine. Her hair fell over her shoulders and onto my bare chest. My dick was so hard it started to ache. She started off kissing me slow, which I liked. Samara was the only woman that I wanted to kiss, and could kiss for hours. She moaned on my mouth making the head of my dick jump. She turned me on so much.

SAMARA

I moaned on his lips. They were so soft. My body was so prepared for him. I thought I would cum right then and there. But I paced myself. I wanted to take my time with him. I had a lot that I wanted to do to him, and I could only imagine what he had in store for me. I decided to turn it up a notch and slide my tongue into his mouth. At first I searched his tongue with mine. Then I made slow circles around the tip of his tongue with the tip of my tongue. It was his turn to moan. He put his hand in my hair and massaged my scalp, while my tongue danced with his. I took my tongue from him and ran it across his lips. I pulled away from him.

"Lay flat on your stomach, I have a surprise for you." His eyes were half closed. He was in the zone and so was I. He got on the bed and lay down on his stomach. He got comfortable and sighed. I slid my leg over his back and sat on his lower back. I reached over to my dresser, took the oil, and poured a few warm drops onto his back.

"You're giving me a massage?" He asked in surprise.

"Among other things." I whispered in his ear. He moaned and closed his eyes. I ran my palms down his back and applied pressure with my thumbs. I brought them back up his strong back. I spread the oil over his shoulder blades and rubbed the oil into his sides.

"I definitely needed this baby," he mumbled. I smiled because I knew I had him right where I wanted him. I wanted him to be totally relaxed during our lovemaking. I kneaded my fingers into his back and ran my hands over his shoulders and arms. He sighed and moaned the whole time. The oil had seeped into his skin. My hands ran over his skin like silk. I bent down and kissed him at the nape of his neck. Slowly I kissed down his back, making sure to use my tongue.

RYSON

Her tongue sent chills down my back. I wasn't used to this level of foreplay. I usually attempted to do a little to the women I slept with to get them in the mood, but I rarely got anything besides head in return. This was a nice change and a surprise. Her thighs were hot on my back, and I could feel her pussy on my lower back. She didn't have on any underwear. The massage was feeling so fucking good I caught myself dozing off. I snapped my eyes open and rolled over onto my back.

"I wasn't done baby," Samara said as she straddled my lap. She was so beautiful looking down at me. Her eyes twinkled and her smile was easy. Her curly hair framed her face as she bent down. Once again she was kissing me, making me want to bust. This time I couldn't help but add a sense of urgency to the kiss. She put her hands on my wrists and pushed them down onto the bed, pinning me down. I surrendered and let her hold me down. I put my head back and reveled in her kiss. She kissed me on the chin and made her way down my neck. She kissed my shoulder then trailed her tongue down my chest. My eyes popped open when her tongue glided over my nipple.

"Ooooo!" I gasped and looked down at her. Her back was arched and her ass was in the air. Her tongue circled my nipple, then she put it in her mouth. She gently sucked it and then repeated the process. I tried to take the pleasure, but I'm not going to lie, she had me squirming in her bed. She let go of my wrists and used her hands to unbuckle my pants. Her mouth was still on my nipple. She sucked on it until it hardened, then she moved on to the next one.

"Damn," was all I could say. My dick was about to rip through my dress pants. She slid my pants down my legs and came back up to claim my mouth. I couldn't take her tongue anymore. I took hold of her arms and sat up, pulling her arms behind me in an embrace. She wrapped her legs around me. The hairs on her pussy tickled my navel. I grabbed her ass and rammed my tongue in her mouth. I was loving the foreplay, but it was driving me mad. She started a slow grind on my lap, wetting my briefs with her juices. She moaned and dug her nails into my back.

SAMARA

He stopped kissing me and put his lips on my neck. I bit my lips and leaned my neck to the right, giving him easier access to my spot.

"Aaaaahhhhh!" At that moment, I couldn't help but compare the two brothers. Dwayne was fun and dangerous, and it was always a given that you would cum with him. But Dwayne was only focused on the satisfaction of a nut, not on the pleasure that came before it. With Dwayne the sex was always rough. Ryson liked to gently touch, taste, and lick all over my body. He was making love to my entire body. He would probably be the better lover. I was so anxious to see if my prediction was right. I felt his hands on the zipper to my dress. He got the zipper down then looked at me. I returned his gaze. I could read exactly what was on his mind. It was the same thing that was running through mine. *Finally.*

His hands cupped my breasts then he pulled the dress down to my waist. I shivered with anticipation. My strapless push up bra was the same color as my dress.

"You're so beautiful baby," Ryson whispered before burying his face in my cleavage. He pecked the top of my breasts and ran his thumb down my stomach. It was time to let him take control.

"SCCCCRRRRRRREEEEEECCCCCCCCHHHHHHH!" A blaring noise roared throughout my house. My heart rate spiked. My hands instinctively went to my ears. I fell onto my side off of Ryson's lap.

"OH MY GOD!" I screamed. The noise drummed through my head.

"WHAT IS THAT?" Ryson yelled, covering his ears also. What the hell was going on? I never heard that sound before.

"I DON'T KNOW! IT MUST BE MY SECURITY ALARM!" I screamed out to him. The noise penetrated my head, making me dizzy. Ryson buckled his pants back up and dashed out of the room. A minute later the noise stopped. I zipped my dress back up and rubbed my temples. I had an instant headache. Ryson walked back into the room in disbelief.

"Your security alarm is broken Samara. When I entered the code it went off but it said, *'Invalid key entry. Please contact customer service'*. How long have you had that system?" Ryson cracked his neck in frustration. That was the last thing on my mind. The mood was totally ruined! A whole week's worth of planning was down the drain. I sighed in resignation and took off my shoes. I walked over to Ryson and put my arms around his waist.

"That was fun." I tried to make light of the situation. Ryson scoffed and put his hands in my hair.

"It would happen right at that moment wouldn't it? That shit was crazy! Well I guess it wasn't meant for us to go there tonight." I heard the disappointment in his voice, and wished I could do something to make it up to him. I was disappointed too, sexually. I worked myself up and thought I would be making love to Ryson tonight. I was so let down I wanted to cry. What were the odds of that happening at that precise moment?

DWAYNE

I couldn't take it anymore. I saw Ryson's Jeep pull up and park outside her house. I'd been watching the house for three hours waiting to catch a glimpse of her walking past her window. I could see her moving about the house, up and down the steps. What was she doing? When she opened the door with that red dress on, I just about bolted across the street. Why was she dressed so fucking sexy? For Ryson? Maybe she was going out with her girlfriends or something. But then why would Ryson be over there? I waited to see where her shape would turn up next. When I saw them enter the bedroom, I knew. She was trying to fuck Ryson. I couldn't have that shit. Why should he get to be with Samara over me? I saw her first and I fucked her first. That made her mines! I sounded irrational, but seeing Samara with Ryson was killing me.

I watched her house almost every night, waiting to see her silhouette through her curtains. Of course I had to keep parking further and further down the street so Ryson wouldn't recognize my damn truck. Good thing I had binoculars. I couldn't sleep unless I saw her. I wasn't crazy. I wasn't stalking her. I wasn't obsessed. I just wanted to make sure she was okay. Every day that Ryson showed up I kicked another dent into my work truck. I was up to twenty dents on the driver's side. Ryson was my brother, but he was also my competition.

There was no doubt in my mind anymore that after I apologized to Samara, she would be willing to go back to the way things used to be between us. How the fuck could I apologize if Ryson was always over there? I couldn't stop images of Samara from flashing into my mind. When I woke up all I could see was her face. I heard her voice when I ate breakfast. I could feel her skin whenever I was sitting outside her house. I couldn't count how many cum stains were on the black shirt I stole from her room. I masturbated with it every day.

That's what I was doing, when Ryson's Jeep pulled up and fucked up my flow. Ryson never spent the night or went into her bedroom, so when they entered her room I was alarmed. What were they doing up there? I wasn't naïve, so I knew they had to be fucking or at least trying to fuck. I got some tools and got out of my truck. I walked across the street on a mission. I jumped Samara's fence and let myself into her back door. I had a key made last week. I was doing my usual routine of watching her sleep, and saw her keys on the dresser. I took them and made a copy at the late night hardware store. That way I could come and go in any time I wanted, without worrying about picking the lock. I tiptoed into the living room and put in an override code that would set her alarm to go off when motion was detected. Once I put the code in, it would start blaring due to my movement. I knew I would have to haul ass out the back door so I wouldn't be caught once she or Ryson came downstairs to check the alarm. When the noise started to screech I smiled. My job here was done. There was no way they were getting into anything tonight. That noise was enough to turn off the horniest of motherfuckers. Before I dashed out the back door, I punched in a disable code so she couldn't reset it. My workplace would call her about the alarm and then call me to come out to look at it. And I would clear my schedule of every appointment, just to make sure I took care of Samara. It was the perfect set-up. I could finally talk to her face to face! I bent down low and jogged my way back to my truck and waited for the inevitable. As if on cue, Ryson emerged from the house twenty minutes later and got in his Jeep. Good riddance.

SHAR

They were both ignoring me now. Dwayne and Ryson totally forgot about me. Samara was such a fucking bitch! Why did I back out on my plan B? That bitch obviously deserved it. How fucking dare she steal the only two people that I had in my life! I wasn't letting that shit fly anymore! I was tired of Samara making Ryson and Dwayne jump through hoops just to be in her presence, while I had to break my back just to make them glance my way. What the fuck! I looked down at my phone pondering whether or not to text the guy again. It would be so easy for me to text him that I changed my mind back. What was holding me back? Was it my conscience? At first I wanted to believe that, but it was something else. If Ryson or Dwayne found out what I was planning, they would stop fucking with me altogether. Especially Dwayne, since he was the one funding this endeavor. I looked down the street to hail a cab, I wasn't taking the bus today. Fuck that. Then I was sent the sign I was looking for. It was such a small world. Samara was across the street leaning on her car talking to some guy. I couldn't make out who she was talking to. It definitely wasn't Ryson or Dwayne, I was sure of that. She laughed and playfully slapped the mystery man on the arm. I put my phone up to try to take a picture, but she was too far away. Even after I zoomed in as far as I could with my cheap ass phone.

"Shit!" I muttered and tried to think of a way to catch her in the act. I dialed Ryson's number, and as usual it went straight to voicemail. Usually I didn't leave one, but this was just too juicy not to share.

"This is Shar, Ryson, like you didn't know. You might not want to talk to me, but you might want to talk to your new friend Samara. She looks *real* cozy talking and laughing with some random guy at the library. If you don't believe me, she has on a long pink dress and she has her hair up in a bun. Just thought you should know." I hung up and smiled. Maybe I didn't need to go to plan B after all. Samara might bring about her own downfall.

RYSON

I didn't want to leave Samara's house that night, but I had to. If I had stayed I would have taken my sour attitude out on her. What were the fucking odds that her alarm would go haywire at the exact moment we were about to make love? That shit couldn't have been a coincidence could it? Of course it had to be. I was just tripping because I was going through withdrawal. I had never gone this long without sex before since I'd lost my virginity at fourteen. It was starting to get to me. I promised Samara and myself that I would wait until the time was right for us to make love, but I didn't think I could hold out any longer. It's been exactly two and a half months since Samara walked into my life. That might not seem like a long time, but ask any of the other women I dated how long those relationships lasted. They had all been extremely short. Sunday I could be fucking with someone, and by the next Sunday I would be reading the paper as a single man. This was the longest time I'd let a woman stay in my life before. That had to mean something. I loved Samara, I really did. I knew that if I pushed too much about the sex thing, it would blow up in my face. The next time I saw her I was just going to put my tongue in her mouth and throw her down on the floor. Yeah right, I knew that shit wasn't going to happen. Like she said, when the timing was right it would happen. Problem was, neither of us knew when the timing was going to be right again. Could I really go another two and a half months without sex? My phone rang. It was Shar. I pressed ignore like I did all of her other calls. Shar tried to reach out to me numerous times since the night Dwayne attacked Samara to apologize. I wasn't trying to hear that shit. She wasn't sorry. She just didn't want me to be mad at her. Plus I had some work to catch up on and I wasn't in the mood for Shar. My phone vibrated, notifying me that I had a voicemail.

"Oh god." I rolled my eyes and took off my reading glasses. I punched in my pass code to see what Shar left me on my voicemail. I half paid attention to the message until I heard Samara's name.

"She looks real cozy talking and laughing with some random guy at the library. If you don't believe me, she has on a long pink dress and she has her hair up in a bun. Just thought you should know." The message ended. I held the phone tight in my hands and replayed the message again.

"She looks real cozy talking and laughing with some random guy at the library. If you don't believe me, she has on a long pink dress and she has her hair up in a bun. Just thought you should know." I listened to the message five more times before I put my phone down. *Calm down Ryson. This is Shar we're talking about. Since when did you start putting stock in anything she said?* Yeah, she had to be lying. It was Shar. All she did was lie. I blew air through my nostrils, trying not to let the hurt that I was feeling surface. Samara wouldn't do that to me. She was crazy about me. She never let me forget that shit. Samara couldn't have done that. It wasn't like her. I picked up my keys from my desk and hopped in my Jeep. I raced through the streets ignoring stop signs on my way to the library. It couldn't be true. Shar was just starting trouble. That's what she was good at. She just wanted to stir up some shit. I pulled up to the library and no one was outside. Fuck! I did a U-turn and drove to Samara's house. I haphazardly parked and ran up the steps to ring the bell. No answer. That was odd. I spoke to her earlier and she didn't tell me she was going anywhere today. I paced back and forth on her porch until I heard her garage door open. She pulled into the garage and then she emerged.

"Oh hell no!" I gulped down the lump in my throat as I watched Samara come up her steps. She was wearing a long pink dress, holding a box with a bakery logo written on it. Her hair was up in a bun.

"Hey baby! What are you doing here?" She smiled happily and hugged me with one arm. I stood as still as a statue not returning her hug. She looked up at me perplexed.

"Why aren't you hugging me back? What's up?" She looked at me strangely. I couldn't believe Shar was right. She probably just saw Samara out and about and made up that whole story about her flirting with another guy.

"Ryson? Cat got your tongue?" Samara smiled at me and shook me slightly, bringing me back to the present.

"Where are you coming from?" I asked, my throat dry.

"I was at the library. Oh and guess who I ran into?" She smiled enthusiastically.

"Who was the guy you were talking to?" I couldn't hold it in any longer. I couldn't believe this shit! Was she really going to smile in my face like she didn't just come from flirting with some other dude? This was some bullshit!

"Excuse me?" Her eyes got huge and she stepped back. She looked at me like I had lost my damn mind.

"You heard me Samara. Who the fuck was he?" She recoiled from my tone. I could see her lips forming into a smile. She was amused.

"You think this shit is funny?" I asked incredulously. This was our first fight. She started giggling. Was she the fuck crazy? She scratched her cheek and looked at me with a huge smile on her face.

"Who told you I was with another guy?" She seemed to know something I didn't. I didn't see what was so fucking funny about the situation.

"That doesn't matter! So you don't deny that you were with another guy today?"

"Nope! I sure don't." She smirked and put one hand on her hip. Was I in the twilight zone?

"What the fuck Samara? You're really going to stand there and tell me some shit like that? That's fucked up girl!" I sounded like a little bitch. I was so fucking stupid to fall for her ass! This is exactly why I didn't have girlfriends. I thought Samara was different from the usual women I messed with, but looking at her standing there giggling in my face made me realize she wasn't. She didn't even care enough to lie about it. I shook my head and ran down her steps. I wasn't going to stand there and let her play me. I wasted all this fucking time trying to get with her ass when I should have stayed true to what I knew.

"It was your friend Devon. You know? The one you introduced me to at your party?" I stopped on the third step. I swiveled around and looked up at her. She tipped her head to the side and leaned against her railing.

"You can call and ask him if you don't believe me. I was just about to tell you that when you started throwing accusations at me. Now back to *my* question. How did you know I was talking to Devon?" Shit. She was talking to Devon? I instantly felt like a dumbass. Fucking Shar was always stirring up trouble! I was really ready to just walk away from Samara just like that. What the fuck was I thinking? How could I think she would betray me like that? I should have known better. I walked back up to her porch, embarrassed. She shook her head and smiled at me.

"Shar left me a voicemail saying she saw you flirting with some guy." Her smile disappeared immediately.

"Shar? Now you're listening to Shar too?" She was angry.

"Well Samara, she described what you had on and everything, what was I supposed to think?" I said trying to defend myself. I mean, it was common sense. What would you think?

"You could have thought, hmmm if Shar is telling me this it must be a lie!" Well damn she had me on that one.

"Or better yet you could have thought that I would never do something like that to you. It was funny at first that you thought I would do something like that, but now it's insulting. I thought you knew me better than that!" She walked away from me and unlocked her front door. She walked straight to the kitchen. How had all this shit happened? I came over here to catch her in a lie, now I was on trial.

"Samara, you have to see it from my point of view. If somebody called you and said they saw me flirting with some female, and described what I had on, you would be suspicious too!" It wasn't that farfetched. She hopped onto her counter and took the bun out of her hair. Even though we were arguing, I couldn't believe how pretty she looked in that pink dress with her hair pinned up. I snapped out of it.

"The difference is, I would have asked you about it. My first instinct wouldn't be to accuse you. Don't you trust me?" Her eyes closed as she tried to rein in her temper.

"Of course I trust you baby." I said, walking closer to her.

"Why would you believe anything that woman says anyway?" She asked annoyed.

"I don't know, honestly." I felt like a dumbass.

"What is it with you and Shar?" She asked me, narrowing her eyes. My heart stopped for a second. What did she know? I tried to think of a quick lie, but one wasn't forthcoming.

"What do you mean?" I stalled. I knew she would ask sooner or later. I didn't have an answer that she would like though.

"I mean, is she one of your exes? I know she slept with Dwayne, so that's a yes for him. But what about you? Why is she so interested in you? Did you date or something?" Her questions flew at me like knives. Each one pointed directly at my head.

"Neither me nor Dwayne 'dated' Shar. Dwayne slept with Shar and I... I crossed the line with Shar too." I chose my words carefully.

"Crossed the line? You slept with her."

She wouldn't let the shit go. I was trapped between lying and telling the truth. Both would have dire consequences.

"Ryson, if you slept with Shar just tell me. Geez! It's not that serious! We both had lives and partners before we got together." She seemed to think it was so easy. I slept with Shar but that wasn't the problem. The problem was why I slept with Shar and how wrong it was. I knew I had to tell her one day, but I just couldn't right now.

"Dwayne and I met Shar, and I started to sleep with her. Then she started sleeping with Dwayne. At one point we were both sleeping with her. I knew it was wrong so I stopped. I haven't been with Shar in almost a year I think, or close to it. Shar can't wrap her head around that shit. That's why she's causing problems for me and Dwayne." I told her the half-truth. I took a breath and hoped she would leave it at that. She watched me intently, trying to dissect my story.

"Where does Shar live?" she asked me, completely catching me off guard. I hesitantly recited Shar's address.

Samara jumped down off the counter and ran upstairs. I waited in the living room confused as hell. What did she need Shar's address for? She came back downstairs in a white jogging suit and her hair was back up in a bun.

"Are you going for a run?" I asked, trying to comprehend what was going on.

"No. I'm going to pay a visit to Shar." She got her keys from the kitchen counter and headed to the door. This couldn't be good. If Samara showed up at Shar's door, all hell would break loose. Shar would have no problem opening up her blabber mouth and telling Samara everything. I couldn't let that happen. I grabbed her elbow just as she was stepping over her threshold.

"It's not that serious Samara. Just ignore Shar. She's unhappy in her pathetic life so she's trying to fuck with ours. She's not worth it. I promise you this will never happen again." I tried to reason with her. She looked at me and then down at her elbow which I was still holding. Her eyes slowly came up to land on mine. The look in her eyes scared me and I let her elbow go quick like it was hot to the touch.

"The last time Shar took it upon herself to fuck with you and Dwayne, I ended up being assaulted with five stitches in my lip." She had a point. I gulped and nodded my head. She ran down the steps. The shit was about to hit the fan. Just great.

SAMARA

I had a fierce headache. I had been on the computer for hours and my eyes were aching. I needed some fresh air. I decided to head down to the library and see if there were any interesting reads I could check out. I was probably the only adult in America who still went to the library and checked out books. I could have downloaded an e-reader, but I didn't have a tablet and didn't see the need for it. And I wasn't a big fan of reading a novel on my computer. I just really loved the smell of actual books. I looked over a few titles that seemed intriguing and checked them out. I finished up and walked outside to my car.

"Samara?" I turned around at the sound of my name. The voice was vaguely familiar.

"Darren? Hey!" He leaned in and gave me a hug. I hadn't seen him since Ryson's party. He was about six and a half feet tall and weighed around two eighty. He was not a small man by any means. His big arms enveloped me as he bent down to hug me. But he looked like a big teddy bear so his size didn't intimidate me.

"It's Devon ha-ha! And how have you been? I heard what happened. You okay?" He asked concerned. I knew he was referring to the incident with Dwayne. Ugh, that was the last thing I wanted to think about.

"Oh snap! Sorry. I'm better with faces than names, ha-ha. And um... I'm okay. You know, as good as can be expected at least."

"I hear that. So what have you been up to?" He put his hands in his pocket and leaned against the meter.

"Nothing much. I wanted to check out some books at the library so..."

"As in actually check books out? Like with a library card? Don't you have a tablet or something? Is it broken? I bet I can fix it." He was talking so fast I had to laugh.

"Yes with a library card silly. And that's very nice of you to offer, but I don't have a tablet." He looked stunned.

"Hold up, wait. There must be a hidden camera around here somewhere. That's a joke right?" He looked inside the back seat of my car and then behind him. I laughed lightly and slapped him playfully on the arm.

"I don't really need one okay. Don't make fun of me." He shook his head at me playfully.

"You better step into the new millennium girl, ha-ha. So you just read books the old-fashioned way huh? I couldn't live a day without my tablet."

"And that's the problem with people today, too dependent on technology. Back in the day you had to send telegrams to get a message to someone. Now all you have to do is text. It's so lazy and impersonal," I joked.

"Back in the day? Girl you can't be a day over twenty talking about back in the day." We both laughed at that. Devon seemed nice. I wondered if he would tell Ryson he saw me and what Ryson would say. We hadn't come into contact with any of his friends since the party, so I didn't know what he was telling people about me.

"I'm going to let you go. It was nice seeing you again. Have a good one!" Devon said as he walked in the opposite direction. I waved bye and got in my car. It was a little warm outside so I rolled the window down and let the air hit me. I was feeling really good and decided to stop at the bakery I liked. Having one of their baked goods was the ultimate indulgence for me. I didn't do it too often, but I was craving something sweet so I bought a dozen donuts. I spotted Ryson pacing back and forth on my porch as I was pulling into my garage. What was he doing here? It was Saturday, so I definitely wasn't expecting to see him so early in the day. Ryson liked to catch up on his work on the weekends, so I didn't see him until late in the evenings, if at all. I ran up the steps with a smile on my face, happy to see him anyway.

"Hey baby! What are you doing here?" I squeezed him tight with one arm and smiled as his scent filled my nose. I realized he wasn't squeezing me back. I looked up at him and noticed the look on his face. He was angry about something. I'd only seen that look on Ryson's face two times. The night of the incident with Dwayne and the night we attempted to make love. He asked me where I was coming from. I answered him, not sure where this line of questioning was leading. I had almost forgotten that I ran into Devon. Just as I was about to tell him, he asked me a question that put me on high alert.

"Who was the guy you were talking to?" How the hell did he know I had talked to Devon? Was he following me? I didn't like the accusatory tone in his voice. I looked at him and decided to mess with him a bit. I smiled at him, throwing him off balance.

"Who told you I was with another guy?" I had to hear this. Ryson was going to feel like a complete idiot. He told me it didn't matter who told him, which meant it was somebody he didn't want to mention. Was it Dwayne? It couldn't have been him.

"So you don't deny that you were with another guy today?" Ryson asked me, his anger escalating. It surprised me how little faith he had in me. If I was going to sneak around behind his back, it wouldn't be at a fucking PUBLIC library! Men did stupid things like that, not women.

"Nope! I sure don't." I smirked and balanced my donuts with one arm and put the other arm on my hip.

"What the fuck Samara? You're really going to stand there and tell me some shit like that? That's fucked up girl!" I put my hand over my mouth and laughed. I really couldn't believe he was acting like this. If only he could see how ridiculous he looked standing there having a temper tantrum. He turned away and began to descend the steps. I called him back.

"It was Devon, Ryson." He stopped and turned towards me.

"You can call and ask him if you don't believe me. I was just about to tell you that when you started throwing accusations at me. Now back to *my* question. How did you know I was talking to Devon?" He was embarrassed, as he should be.

 "Shar left me a voicemail saying she saw you flirting with some guy." I was no longer amused.

"Shar? Now you're listening to Shar too?" This bitch never gave up did she? Why the fuck would he listen to anything she said anyway? I guess he didn't learn his lesson the last time when he had to beat up his own brother. I opened my door and went into the kitchen. I dropped the box of donuts on the counter, uninterested in them now. I needed to calm down. It was time for me to get some answers.

"Why is Shar so interested in you?" His eyes shifted. He was either about to lie or stall.

"What do you mean?" He chose to stall. He knew exactly what I meant. I still didn't get it. Shar was fucking Dwayne so why did she give a fuck what Ryson did?

"I... I crossed the line with Shar," he said slowly. He was trying to admit to fucking Shar without actually saying it. I didn't care about the women he was with before me. I had men in my past too, so I couldn't judge. I just didn't understand that whole connection between the three of them. It was weird. Ryson told me that he and Dwayne had fucked Shar but he stopped close to a year ago. I believed him. So that was Shar's problem then? She was envious of me because Ryson didn't want her anymore? It wasn't enough for her to have Dwayne, she had to have Ryson too? It was time I handled Shar.

"Where does Shar live?" He looked surprised, but he gave me the address and apartment number anyway. I ran upstairs to my room and quickly changed clothes. I wasn't putting anything past Shar, so I needed to be prepared. Ryson tried to stop me on the way out the door. There was no way I was letting him rationalize why I shouldn't confront Shar. Obviously he and Dwayne didn't know how to handle her. I did though.

"The last time Shar took it upon herself to fuck with you and Dwayne, I ended up assaulted with five stitches in my lip." He looked taken aback. He wasn't expecting me to say that. It was the truth though. If the last time was any indication, Shar wasn't going to stop until she had Ryson back. Who knew what other types of sinister shit she had up her sleeve?

I rang every bell in her building until somebody buzzed me in. Shar lived on the fifth floor, so I had time to think of a strategy while I rode the elevator up. Should I just punch her in the face when she opened the door? Maybe I should try to stoop to her level and throw insults at her. I got off and walked down to her apartment. I put my hand over the peephole and knocked on her door hard.

"Who is it?" I heard her call out. I ignored her and knocked on her door harder.

"Who the fuck is it?" She yelled out, irritated. Again, I ignored her and continued to bang on her door. She ripped the door open, ready to jump on whoever was knocking at her door.

"Who the fuck... Samara?" She was surprised to see me. Her whole facial expression changed. I could tell she despised me. The feeling was mutual.

"Can I come in?" I asked her politely. She snickered and moved to the side. Shar's apartment was small and dingy. Her furniture needed dusting and her carpet needed cleaning. I could smell something stale as I took a breath. I told myself to try to resolve this matter amicably. I didn't want a repeat of what happened at the party.

"What do you want?" she asked with an attitude. I was tempted to give her one back, but I kept my composure.

"I want you to stay out of my business." I said, getting straight to the point. That's all I wanted her to do. If she did that, I wouldn't have a problem with Shar. Of course it wasn't that easy. She was dressed in a form-fitting yellow spandex dress. Half of her hair was curled and the other half was straight. I had interrupted her primping.

"Ryson and Dwayne *are* my business, so as far as I'm concerned, you need to stay out of OUR business bitch!" She got in my face and pointed her finger an inch away from my nose. Alright, this wasn't working. I came here to talk to her on a mature level, but she was trying to take it somewhere else. If she wanted it, I would give it to her. I smiled at her, grabbed her skinny finger and quickly bent it backwards until I heard a snap.

"OWWW! WHAT THE FUCK!" She shrieked and clutched her finger. Her eyes watered as she bent over in pain. I really didn't want to take it there, but she left me no choice. She would be okay, nothing a splint couldn't fix.

"Don't call me out of my name, and don't ever put your finger in my face again Shar. I'm trying to be nice here okay? After what you did at the party, you're lucky I'm not in your ass right now." I meant that. Doing that would make me feel better, but I didn't think it would solve anything. I just wanted her to realize that Ryson wasn't her man. She needed to back off. She stood up and cut her teary eyes at me. Her breathing was quick, which meant she was upset. I smiled at her again.

"Like I was saying, you need to stay out of my business. Ryson does not want you anymore. He's with me now, so you need to get it out of your hard head that he's your man. Now, usually I would NEVER step to a woman over a man, but after what you did at the party, I feel like these are extenuating circumstances. Stop spying on me. Stop 'snitching' on me or whatever the hell you think you were doing. I'm not going to tell you again." I stood waiting for her to respond to what I said. She looked at me and then her eyes danced around the room. She was looking for something to hit me with. She was so predictable. I was ready for that. I was also ready for her to take a swing on me, which she did. I grabbed her arm in mid-air and twisted it behind her back.

"GET THE FUCK OFF ME YOU FUCKING WHORE!" Shar screamed at me. Damn, she really hated me. She tried to reach behind and hit me but I had the upper hand.

"You don't even know me well enough to call me that Shar. It's sad how quick you are to judge me. If you got to know me you might even like me." I slid my hand down to her wrist and twisted it back. She struggled to get free.

"FUUUCCCKKKK! I WOULD NEVER BE FRIENDS WITH A SKANK LIKE YOU! I HATE YOU!" Oh well, I tried. I put my knee in her back and slammed her face down onto the glass table in the middle of the living room. I pulled her arm up higher and applied pressure to my knee until she screamed out in pain. I didn't like inflicting pain, but she was asking for it.

"HEELLLLPPPP!" Shar screamed at the top of her lungs. She tried to squirm free but I had a firm grip on her. Shar was no challenge.

"Just tell me that you're going to keep your nose out of my affairs and I will leave." I promised her, my voice sugary sweet. I bent down close to her face so I could hear her response.

"OKAY! YOU CRAZY BITCH! I'LL MIND MY BUSINESS! JUST LET ME GO!" She was lying, but that was okay. I let her go and stood back up. She got the message.

"GET OUT!" She cradled her arm and started to cry. Pathetic.

"Don't make me come back Shar. I won't be in as good a mood as I was today. Have a great day!" I waved at her and left.

SHAR

I was never so happy to be at my little dingy apartment than I was today. I jumped in the shower then looked through the closet for something to wear. I knew Ryson was home today. On Saturdays he would be cooped up in his room catching up on work. It was the perfect time for me to go over there. I was going to break that stupid ass *only come over at night* rule Ryson and Dwayne put on me. It was one of the few times he wouldn't be attached to Samara's hip, so I was going to jumped at the chance to catch him alone. If he had listened to my voicemail, which I would bet a million dollars that he had, then they would have argued. He would be vulnerable, maybe enough to let me back into his bed. I took the yellow party dress off the hanger. Ryson used to love it when I wore that dress. One time he actually tried to rip it off me before fucking me. My pussy tingled. I missed Ryson so much. I missed how he used to bend me over any and every surface available. I missed his tongue on my body. I missed everything about him. Dwayne was only useful if you wanted to get your brains fucked out, but he couldn't go the distance. Because Dwayne was so rough, I could only go one or two rounds with him before the sex wasn't even enjoyable anymore. There were plenty of times when all I felt was pain, but I didn't stop him because I wanted him to continue to want me. With Ryson there was never pain. He always waited until I was nice and wet before he would slide his juicy dick inside me. The last time we were together, I didn't know it would be our last. Ryson had me bent over while I sucked Dwayne's dick. I kept feeling his dick getting softer and softer inside me. That wasn't good. I took Dwayne out of my mouth and asked Ryson what was wrong. He stopped fucking me and said, "All of this shit is wrong!" He got up off the bed and put his clothes back on. He wouldn't even look at me before he ran out the room.

I knew it was wrong to be fucking Dwayne and Ryson. But it felt so good to be wanted by the both of them, I just took advantage of it. Ryson left that day and never returned to my bed. My heart broke a little that day. Since then I'd been trying to win Ryson back. It hadn't turned out like I had hoped it would. Between the countless hoes he took home and now Samara, shit kept getting in the way. Not today though. Today he would come around.

I plugged in my curlers and started to do my hair. Halfway through, someone started banging on my door. I looked through the peephole, but couldn't see anything. Whoever it was had their hand over the peephole. I kept asking who it was, but I didn't get an answer. They were interrupting my fucking beauty time! I opened the door annoyed, ready to curse out whoever it was. Except if it was Ryson of course.

"Who the fuck… Samara?" This bitch couldn't possibly be at my door. I looked her up and down, wondering what the fuck she was doing here. How did she get my address? I saw that she'd changed her clothes, so she must have talked to Ryson already. She probably tried to deny that I saw her, but the proof was in the pudding.

"Can I come in?" She tried to act nice like I would fall for that shit. She knew she was busted. I let her and her fat ass in. I smelled whatever cheap perfume she was wearing as she walked past me. She turned her nose up when she walked into the living room like the stuck up bitch that she was.

"What do you want?" I couldn't stand to look at her another minute.

"I want you to stay out of my business." She smiled at me. Who the fuck did she think she was talking to? Stay out of *her* business? Please! First off, she just met Ryson and Dwayne a few months ago. I didn't know why she thought anything that had to do with them was her business. I was here first. If anything, she was in *my* fucking business! I stuck my finger in her face and told the bitch as much. Samara just looked at me. I knew she was a punk. Then that sneaky bitch grabbed my finger and twisted it backwards. The shock of what she did overrode the pain at first.

"OWWW! WHAT THE FUCK!" She was fucking crazy! Her smile never faltered. I swung at her, trying to wipe that smug look off her face. She grabbed my arm before I could hit her, and banged my head down on my glass table. Now this bitch had gone overboard! I tried to get free but she was strong as shit! I had underestimated Samara. I screamed for her to let me go.

"I HATE YOU!" I yelled and tried to hit her. If she would just let me up, maybe I could throw a punch or something. She started to bend my arm even farther. My arm had to be broken.

"HHHEEEELLLLLPPPP!" This slut was trying to kill me! I was afraid for my life!

"Just tell me that you're going to keep your nose out of my affairs and I will leave." She tried to sound sweet and innocent. She was anything but. I agreed and she let me go. I grabbed my arm and rubbed it up and down. It wasn't broken, but any more pressure and it would have been. Who the fuck was this chick?

"GET OUT!" I kicked her crazy ass out before she tried something else. She threatened me before she left. It sent a chill right through me. She was going to pay for this shit. I looked down at my finger and sobbed. It was bent backwards and there was no doubt it was broken. I ran into my room and picked up my cell. I searched my contacts and sent out a text.

I changed my mind. Come get the money NOW!!!

DWAYNE

I called Shar to see what was up with her rent situation. I hadn't heard anything from her about it since I transferred that money. I was starting to feel like I had been duped.

"Is your rent up to date now?" I asked her when she answered her phone.

"YES! Why wouldn't it be?" She yelled loudly. I pulled my ear away from the phone.

"Why are you screaming into the fucking phone?"

"SORRY! I'm mad as shit!" She yelled again. She was such a drama queen. She was probably upset because she broke a nail or something stupid like that.

"What's wrong Shar?" I asked, not really caring. I just wanted to make sure my money was used for what she said it would be used for. I wasn't trying to talk to her. I had other things to do. I was waiting for a call from work at any minute.

"That crazy bitch tried to kill me!" She was even more hyped up as her voice rose a notch.

"What are you talking about girl? What crazy bitch?" I was confused.

"SAMARA! She came over to my apartment a couple days ago and BEAT ME UP!" She was huffing on the phone. She sounded upset. I laughed so hard I started choking.

"It's not funny Dwayne! She broke my finger!" Shar was screaming. I put the phone down and tried to calm down. That shit was too funny. I couldn't imagine Samara doing that but it served Shar right. She deserved whatever Samara did to her.

"Are you cool now?" I choked out before I burst into laughter again. I couldn't take Shar seriously even if I wanted to. I wiped tears from my eyes and cleared my throat.

"I knew you wouldn't fucking care! She got you and Ryson so pussy whipped you can't see straight!" Shar hung up on me. I wasn't pussy whipped by any means. Just because I spent most of my free time parked on Samara's block watching her house, and my nights in her bedroom watching her sleep, didn't mean I was sprung. Ryson was the one who was at her house every fucking day wasting her time. He was the whipped one, not me. It didn't matter though, because today was a new day. I was getting Samara back. I picked up my cell and called my boss. I couldn't wait any longer for the call.

"Any calls come in today?" I asked him anxiously. I heard paper shuffling, then he was back on the line.

"Yeah, just one call. A faulty alarm system. Not far from your neighborhood actually. I'm sending Pete since he's out already."

"NO! I just finished up a job. I have time. I'll do it." I tried not to sound too desperate.

"I don't care as long as it gets done. I'll call Pete and tell him never mind. Let me give you the address." When he started reciting Samara's address, I cut him off. "I have it already." I hung up and jumped out of my work truck. I walked across the street, for the first time not worrying if anyone could see me or not. I straightened my work shirt and wiped imaginary dust off my pants. I took a few breaths through my nose to calm my nerves. My feet tapped nervously on her welcome mat. I knocked lightly on the door and waited for her to open it. I saw Samara come onto her porch early that morning to pick up the paper. Before she closed her door, I saw her fiddling with her alarm system. I was wondering when she would make the call to get it fixed. That incident was over a month ago. But when I saw her messing with the system, I knew today was the day. I just had to sit back and wait for my boss to call me and ask me to come out. He was taking too long, so I took the initiative. Hopefully it would pay off. The door opened slowly. I forgot she had a peephole. She could see me before she opened the door. I could only imagine what was going through her head when she saw me standing on the other side of her door. When she came into view, my breath got caught in my throat. She had on a pair of white khaki shorts that stopped mid-thigh. Her breasts stood at attention in the thin material of her white t-shirt. She wasn't wearing a bra. Her small, beautiful, breasts were mesmerizing. I already knew my dick was hard. I didn't try to hide it either. She smiled uneasily and played with her hair nervously. She was anxious.

"Uh... what are you doing here Dwayne?" she asked softly. I didn't want her walking on eggshells around me. It wasn't right that I made her afraid of me.

"You called about your alarm? I'm here to fix it." I said, smiling trying to reassure her I meant her no harm. She looked like she wanted to say something, but she didn't. She moved to the side and let me in. She smelled so good.

"I'll be out of your hair in thirty minutes I promise." I told her and set my tool bag down. She nodded and crossed her arms across her chest. I snuck a peek at her legs. I remembered prying them apart to lick on her pussy. I shook my head and focused on why I was there. I didn't want to fuck anything up. I went to work opening up the panel and pretending to move wires and shit around. All I needed to do was enter a reset code and it would be fixed. But I pretended to move wires around and punch in random numbers on the keypad. The only thing I was going to change was her alarm response time. I set it so that I had a longer window of time to open the door and punch in the code, before the panel sent out a signal to the company and the police. That would work perfectly for me. I was finished in about forty-five seconds, but I made myself look busy for an additional fifteen minutes. Samara had gone into the kitchen as soon as I got to work. I walked into the kitchen ready to put my plan in motion. She was sitting on her counter drinking a bottle of water. She didn't seem surprised to see me walk in. I calmed my jitters and took a deep breath.

"Can I use your bathroom? I have this weird residue on my hands from those old wires." I lied and smiled. She watched me for at least a minute before responding. My heart stopped. What was taking her so long to answer me? I told myself not to get angry. That would mess everything up. She jumped down from the counter and walked over to me. My pulse quickened.

"You can use the hose outside," she said harshly and started to walk past me.

"Samara?" I called her name softly. She stopped and turned to look at me. She was inches away from me.

"I'm so sorry," I started. She tilted her head down then looked away. She wasn't trying to hear it.

"I shouldn't have attacked you and put my hands on you. I've been trying to work up the courage to tell you how sorry I am for weeks. When Ryson told me to stay away from you, I didn't think I would have a chance to tell you." I threw in what Ryson told me for good measure. That didn't sit well with her.

"Ryson told you to stay away from me? When?" She seemed to relax a little. That's exactly what I wanted her to do.

"A few days after. I told him I wanted to apologize to you and see how you were doing. He told me to stay away from you and that he would tell you I was sorry. I just assumed he did. But I still felt that I had to tell you to your face. Samara please believe me, I did not mean to hurt you. I don't know what the fuck was wrong with me! I lost my damn mind that night. I've been beating myself up over this since it happened. I know you won't forgive me, but I am truly, truly sorry for ever hurting you. I'm not that type of man. I'm so ashamed." I said sincerely and walked towards the front door.

"Dwayne?" She softly called my name. I smiled inwardly. I had her. I turned around with a blank expression on my face. I couldn't let her see how happy I was.

"I...forgive you." She took a breath and bit her bottom lip. I wanted nothing more than to throw her on the floor and fuck the shit out of her.

"You do?" I asked, pretending to be shocked. I knew she would accept my apology. How could she not?

"Yes I do. I was to blame too for what happened that night and I'm sorry for the way I treated you. I mean, nothing gave you the right to assault me, let's make that clear." She looked me square in the eyes. I swallowed hard and nodded my head in agreement. "Your apology seems to be sincere, so I forgive you." She gave me a small smile. My knees almost turned to jelly. I got my apology after all.

"You can use the bathroom. It's the first door on the left." *I know.*

She moved to the side to let me pass. I quickly ran up the steps. I closed and locked her bathroom door. I smelled her soap and looked down at my pants. My dick was itching to come out so I let him loose. I picked up her shampoo bottle and squeezed some of the shampoo onto my dick.

"Yeah that's good." I moaned and put my dick over the sink. I splashed some water on my dick. I let the shampoo lather up on my dick as I stroked it up and down.

"Mmmmm." I moaned low so she wouldn't hear me. I grabbed the side of the sink and jerked my dick faster and harder. The smell of her shampoo filled the bathroom. My body started to shake. I clenched my teeth and put a firmer hold on my dick. I was starting to cum. I picked up her shampoo bottle and twisted the top off. I put the head of my dick over the opening and yanked on my dick until my nut was flowing into the shampoo bottle. I couldn't scream out so I grunted and bit my lip. When my entire nut was inside the bottle, I put the top back on it and cleaned up my mess. I washed my dick, face, and hands then dried off with her towel. I opened the cabinet in her bathroom. She had lip gloss, floss, tampons, and some pain pills. I picked the lip gloss up and put it up to my nose. The scent was familiar. She was wearing it now. I pulled out the stick that was inside the lip gloss and ran it over my tongue. This stick had been on her lips, so now her lips were on my tongue. I was getting hard again. I couldn't masturbate again or she would wonder what was taking me so long. I put the lip gloss in my pocket to save for later. I felt great walking back down her steps. She was sitting on the arm of her couch swinging a leg back and forth. It was only a matter of time before I was in between them again.

I was beyond happy. I chanced it, and opened my arms for a hug and approached her. Her eyes got huge and she put her hands up to shield her face. I stopped instantly. Shocked.

"Oh god! I'm… I'm sorry Samara. I was just trying to get a hug. I wasn't going to… I would never…" I couldn't stop stuttering. She thought I was going to hit her? She was that afraid of me? I felt sick to my stomach. I panicked. I felt myself overheating. I looked over at her and felt ashamed. She put her hands down and looked embarrassed.

She got up and sat on the couch.

"I'm sorry." I heard her whisper, looking at her hands.

"You don't have *anything* to be sorry for. I should be saying that to you! This is all my fault. I'm so sorry Samara." The feeling of devastation I felt at that moment was heartbreaking. How was I supposed to get her back when she feared for her life around me? I really fucked this all up. How could I fix this? I tried to think quickly. Every second that passed she was slipping further and further away from me. I heard a whimpering noise and realized she was sobbing. I timidly walked over to her, but didn't sit down or touch her.

"Please forgive me Samara. I never in a million years set out to make you fear me. I can't bear it knowing you think I'm going to hurt you." I choked out the last few words. She looked up with a tear-soaked face and shook her head.

"Why did you hurt me like that? Was ignoring your texts that serious?" My heart broke. Tears slid down her cheeks and fell onto her thighs. I didn't have an answer. *You're losing her.*

"No it wasn't. I was… I was fucked up that day. How can I make this up to you? I don't want you scared of me." I felt my own eyes tearing up. She wiped her face and stared at the ceiling.

"I don't know Dwayne." She wrapped her arms around herself and started to rock back and forth on the couch. The walls suddenly seemed like they were closing in on me. I was going to lose everything! Terror seized me. I felt my hands start shaking. THINK DAMMIT!

"Hit me!" I blurted out grasping at straws. She looked at me in confusion.

"What?" She asked incredulously.

"Hit me." I repeated it. This time with more authority in my voice. She looked at me sideways then rolled her eyes.

"Yeah okay. Very funny Dwayne." She stood up then and glared at me.

"This isn't a joke! I am literally terrified of you right now! Don't you get that?" She screamed at me. Her face turned pink with anger. Her eyes raged with fire. She was so beautiful angry.

"I'm serious. You're angry. You're scared. Right now I have all the power. I'm going to give it back to you." I tried to talk in a soothing tone. She didn't trust me, that much was clear. I put my hands up in surrender and slid onto the couch and sat down.

"I'm going to sit right here. I want you to come over here and hit me. As hard as you want to. Get all the anger and fear out of your system." She half laughed, then bit her lip. She was considering it.

"This is crazy you know that?" She scanned my face. I tried to look as genuine as I could.

"So is what I did to you." I held my hand out to her. She looked at it like it was kryptonite.

"Come here." I said softly. She took a deep breath and closed her eyes.

"Come on, take my hand." I wiggled my fingers. She looked me in the eyes and slowly walked towards me. I was nervous and turned on. She clasped my hand. We both held tight. Both of our hands shaking for different reasons. I led her by the hand to stand her in front of me.

"Now, when you're ready. Just let it out. I won't block, I won't stop you I promise." She nodded that she understood. My heart was beating a mile a minute. What was I doing? If it would bring her back to me, I'd do anything. I closed my eyes and waited. I relaxed and took a deep breath. I braced myself. Ten seconds passed. Twenty. Thirty seconds. I kept my eyes closed and waited. Forty seconds passed. I felt sweat forming on my lower back. What was she doing? I started to crack open my left eye.

SLAP!

FUCK! The sound of her petite hand making contact with my hard jaw bounced off the walls. It seemed to make an echo in my head. I felt kind of dizzy. The sting started to settle as I breathed through the pain.

SLAP!

SHIT! I wasn't prepared for the second slap. I almost cried out in pain. I held it in and clenched my fists. I opened my eyes and looked up at her. She was in a daze. Her hand was frozen in mid-air.

"Are you ok---" SLAP!

"GODDAMN IT!" I screamed out and covered my face. That was the hardest slap yet. I felt anger starting to boil inside me. The room started turning red. I moved my hand from my face and went to get up. Her fist came so hard and fast I had no time to move. She started pummeling me with punches at lightning speed.

"OOWW FUCK!" I covered my face, but I didn't stop her. I let her punch me over and over again. At least twenty punches landed on my head, arms, and rib cage. I held my breath as the pain spread throughout my body. I heard her grunting as each blow landed. Her punches were swift and hard. I winced in pain and groaned until the punches started slowing down. She stopped using so much force behind her hits. I heard her ragged breathing. The last two punches barely made contact. I looked up from underneath my arm. She stopped completely and collapsed on the floor. I let a few minutes of silence go by. She was sweating and trying to catch her breath. My face and body were throbbing with pain. She just basically beat my ass. It was almost funny in a way. Her little thick frame slapping and punching the shit out of me, while I cowered on her couch. I licked my chapped lips. I could taste blood in my mouth. My face was definitely going to be bruised. She really did a number on me. I deserved it.

"Are you still afraid of me?" I asked quietly. She shook her head no and looked at me sadly. She started crying. Hard, body shaking sobs. I got on the floor with her and pulled her into my arms. She didn't flinch. She didn't push me away. I gently put my hands in her hair and laid her head on my shoulder.

"Sshhhhh... it's okay. I'm sorry I hurt you." I whispered into her hair. I felt her arms go around me and hug me. My eyes almost flew out of my head. I gulped and hugged her tighter.

"That was intense," she said and started to calm down.

"Look at me Samara." I said softly, letting her go. She pulled away and looked up at me with a tear-stained face.

"I will never *ever* hurt you again. Okay?" She nodded her head yes. I had her back! I slowly bent my head down and kissed her cheek, catching one of her tears. She smiled, then laughed. I laughed too. It eased the seriousness of the situation. She took a deep breath and stood up. She put her hand out for me to help me up. Well if that wasn't progress, I didn't know what was.

"We don't ever have to bring this up again." I said, still holding her hand. She looked around her living room.

"Thank you Dwayne. You didn't have to do that." She hugged me again. My heart almost burst with love for her. She let me go and wiped her face. She walked away towards the kitchen.

"All this crying is making me thirsty, ha-ha," she joked.

"Let me take you out for a drink as a peace offering." I offered eagerly. She shook her head no.

"Ummm... I don't think that's a good idea. This was good enough. Ryson wouldn't want me to do that." My face fell. I tried to hide my disappointment. I hadn't expected her to say that. After everything I just put myself through, she had the nerve to turn me down?

"You're right. I don't want to cause any more problems. I just wanted to take you out and show you that I appreciate your forgiveness. It's very big of you to accept an apology from me. I don't deserve it and I definitely wasn't expecting it. I'm just happy that you did. I'm all finished so I'll just get my stuff and go. It was nice seeing you Samara." I got my shit and walked towards the door. I was so fucking angry I wanted to pull the door off the hinges. I reached for the doorknob. She was still worrying about Ryson? That shit had to stop! I needed another plan because I was *not* throwing in the towel!

"Dwayne wait! How about Friday night?" She asked and half-smiled. I suppressed my urge to jump for joy.

"Friday is good. I'll see you then." I walked out of Samara's house feeling light as a feather. Bloody and swollen, but still.

SAMARA

I looked again at the person standing on my doorstep. All I could think about was his eyes blazing with anger, and his hands coming towards me to hurt me. But now his eyes were soft. I was stunned to see him. I didn't know what he was doing there. To be honest, I was a little scared. I slowly opened the door.

"Uh... what are you doing here Dwayne?" I asked him cautiously.

"You called about your alarm? I'm here to fix it." That took me by surprise, until I remembered Ryson saying Dwayne was an electrician. I moved to the side and let him in. I was nervous as hell. I stood off to the side for a few minutes, then walked into the kitchen. I got a bottle of water and sat on the counter to think. He was going to apologize. I could feel it. I didn't know how I would react. On the one hand, my father would want me to accept his apology, but on the other hand, I was still so upset over what happened. The Dwayne in my living room couldn't have looked more harmless. I was contemplating what to do when I heard his footsteps coming towards the kitchen.

"Can I use your bathroom? I have this weird residue on my hands from those old wires." He smiled at me politely. He was breathing heavy. He looked on edge. I sipped my water and waited. I was trying to wait for his apology. But after a minute of silence, he didn't offer one. I got off the counter and told him to use the hose outside. I was so annoyed. After all this time, that should have been the first thing out of his mouth! He called my name, stopping me. I didn't want to turn around, but I did.

"I'm so sorry." There it was.

"I shouldn't have put my hands on you. I've been trying to work up the courage to tell you how sorry I am for weeks. When Ryson told me to stay away from you, I didn't think I would have a chance to tell you." I leaned my head to the side, trying to understand why Ryson told him to stay away from me. Why would he do that? Well I *know* why he did it, but I didn't really like it. I wasn't a child that needed protecting, and he of all people should have known doing something like that would make me furious. I would ask him about it when he came over tonight. Dwayne seemed to really mean what he was saying. He looked sorry, and that was all I could ask for. I softened my gaze and realized I couldn't stay mad at him. He had taken a big leap of faith coming to my house in the first place. He could have told one of his co-workers to handle it, but he took a chance. He didn't know if I would slam the door in his face or not. I had to acknowledge him for his courage at least. I forgave him and gave him an apology for my role in the whole situation.

"You can use the bathroom." I told him and laughed inside at my pettiness. I was really going to make him use the hose outside to clean up. He ran up the steps. He seemed pleased at my acceptance of his apology. Maybe we could start over as friends and put all of this drama behind us. Ryson and I were really starting to get serious, and it would be nice to be on speaking terms with Dwayne, or at least not have all this tension. I didn't want us to have an uncomfortable relationship. He was Ryson's brother after all. He came back down the steps with a huge smile on his face. When he got to the last step, he opened his arms like he was coming in for a hug. He started walking towards me. Fear instantly ran through my body. I flashed back to the night of the party. He was bent over me with his hand raised ready to hit me. I shrieked in fear and shielded my face.

"Oh god! I'm... I'm sorry Samara. I was just trying to get a hug. I wasn't going to... I would never..." I heard him stuttering. After a few seconds, I put my hands down. I was instantly embarrassed and angry. I didn't know I would have such a knee jerk reaction to him getting close to me. I sat down on the couch and looked at my hands. I couldn't look at him.

"I'm sorry." I whispered. This situation couldn't get any worse. All that fear and terror I felt that night, was resurfacing. I felt it building its way up from deep in my belly.

"You don't have *anything* to be sorry for. I should be saying that to you! This is all my fault. I'm so sorry Samara." He sounded so sad and sincere, it made me feel sorry for him. That was crazy to me. How could I hate him for what he did, but feel sorry that he was sad about it? I was so conflicted. I whimpered and tried to stop the crying I knew was about to happen. Ugh! I hated this!

"Please forgive me Samara. I never in a million years set out to make you fear me. I can't bear it knowing you think I'm going to hurt you again." He choked out the last few words. I looked up at him and saw he was starting to cry. I shook my head in confusion.

"Why did you hurt me like that? Was ignoring your texts that serious?" I still didn't understand how he got so angry that night. People got ignored all the time. It wasn't so horrible that I deserved to be beaten like that. Was it? I felt hot tears slide down my cheeks.

"No it wasn't. I was... I was fucked up that day. How can I make this up to you? I don't want you scared of me." Was there a way he could make up for what he'd done? I didn't think there was. I sniffed and cleared my nose. Tears kept falling no matter how I tried to get my emotions under control. I angrily wiped my face and stared at the ceiling.

"I don't know Dwayne." I wrapped my arms around myself. I felt myself rocking back and forth. I used to do that a lot after my dad passed away. It calmed my nerves then. Hopefully it would do the same for me now.

"Hit me!" Dwayne blurted out. I looked at him in disbelief. Was he serious? He couldn't be. I must have heard him wrong.

"What?" I asked him incredulously.

"Hit me," he repeated it again. He was serious. I rolled my eyes in annoyance. He wasn't taking this seriously if he thought that was the solution to all of this.

"Yeah okay. Very funny Dwayne." I stood up, ready to curse him out.

"This isn't a joke! I am literally terrified of you right now! Don't you get that?" I screamed at him. What part of that didn't he understand?

"I'm serious. You're angry. You're scared. Right now, I have all the power. I'm going to give it back to you." His voice was calm. Oh, was it that easy? He was delusional. I looked at him like he'd lost his damn mind. I honestly think he did. Then he put his hands up in surrender, and slid onto the couch and sat down.

"I'm going to sit right here. I want you to come over here and hit me. As hard as you want to. Get all the anger and fear out of your system." It was so ridiculous I had to laugh. But was it really that crazy? I *was* angry enough to hit him, but violence didn't solve anything. I looked at him trying to show me he was willing to be vulnerable for me. I felt my hand tingle in anticipation. Should I do this?

"This is crazy you know that?" I scanned his face to see if there was any hint of deception. There wasn't. Was I going to do this?

"So is what I did to you." He had a point there. I let that sentence sink in as I made my decision. He held his hand out.

"Come here," he said softly. I took a deep breath and closed my eyes.

"Come on, take my hand." He wiggled his fingers beckoning me. I looked him in the eyes and slowly walked towards him. I clasped his hand. We both held tight. My hand started shaking. I think his was too. Was he actually nervous? Oddly, that made me feel a little bit better about this. He led me by the hand to stand in front of him.

"Now, when you're ready. Just let it out. I won't block, I won't stop you I promise." I nodded okay. He closed his eyes and took a deep breath. I regarded his face for a minute. I hated to leave a mark on his unblemished skin, but...

SLAP!

I hit him hard enough for my hand to sting. Wow. It felt really good doing that. I looked down at him and noticed his nostrils flaring.

SLAP!

Whew! I don't think I was supposed to hit him twice, but dammit if it didn't feel great! I hit him a little harder that time, really testing my strength. I was feeling like a third slap would really make me feel good. I brought my hand up just as he opened his eyes and looked up at me. There was an actual handprint on his cheek. I felt no remorse for putting it there either.

"Are you ok---" SLAP!

"GODDAMN IT!" He screamed out and covered his face. That was the hardest slap yet. I didn't hold back at all that time and it felt fucking awesome! He moved his hand from his face and went to get up. I wasn't done with him yet. I remembered how he grabbed my hair, almost yanking it out of my scalp. My fist made contact with his ear hard and fast. I left him no time to block. I thought about how he grabbed my arms so tight it felt like he was crushing my bones. My fists took on a life of their own. I started raining punches down on him.

"OOWW FUCK!" He yelled out and covered his face. He bent his body to try to shield himself, but he didn't try to stop me. I thought about how he forced his tongue into my mouth and I got even angrier. I unleashed all the fury I had inside, as I punched him over and over again. I was switching my fists from my right to my left, trying to punch everywhere he wasn't blocking. If I could have punched him in the dick, I would have. I felt sweat start to roll down my face. I was running out of steam.

I lost count of how many times I'd punched him. The last couple punches barely made contact with him. I stopped and tried to catch my breath. I felt euphoric and spent. I collapsed on the floor with a thump.

Besides the sound of my ragged breathing, it was dead silent. He slowly sat up, his face twisted in pain. Again, I felt no remorse for inflicting that onto him. This was a good idea. It felt so good getting all that anger and aggression I had towards him out. I needed this release more than I knew I did.

"Are you still afraid of me?" He asked me in a quiet voice. I definitely wasn't anymore. I shook my head no. I was so pumped up with adrenaline. All of a sudden this deep sadness settled over me. I was happy that I was finally free of the hold the fear had on me. But I felt miserable that it had to come at this price. I started crying. Hard. Body shaking sobs. My nose started running. I felt Dwayne's arm wrap around me. I didn't even flinch. That quickly, the fear had disappeared. I found comfort in his hug. He put his hands in my hair and laid my head on his shoulder.

"Sshhhhh...it's okay. I'm sorry I hurt you," he whispered. I believed him. I put my arms around him. I heard him take a breath. I was guessing he was sore from where I'd punched him. He rocked me softly for a few minutes, letting me cry and get tears and snot all over his shirt.

"That was intense." I took a calming breath.

"Look at me Samara," he said softly and let me go. I stared up at him. The whole left side of his face was dark, almost red, and looked like it was starting to swell. I did that to him. Just like he'd done to me. Things had come full circle.

"I will never ever hurt you again. Okay?" He sounded so regretful, I had no reason not to believe him. I watched him slowly bend down towards me. I didn't feel any apprehension. He kissed my cheek, just as another tear fell. I smiled despite everything and couldn't help but laugh. All of this time, all I had to do was punch Dwayne in the face to resolve our issues? I took a deep breath and stood up. I put my hand out to help him up. I never thought I'd see the day that I would be helping him do anything.

"We don't ever have to bring this up again." He said, still holding on to my hand. That was such a relief. I didn't know how I was going to begin to tell Ryson about this.

"Thank you Dwayne. You didn't have to do that." I hugged him.

"All this crying is making me thirsty, ha-ha." I joked, wiping my face and walking towards the kitchen.

Before I could make it there, Dwayne offered to take me out for a drink. A red flag went up in my head, because I knew Ryson would not like that. But what harm could it do? After the release he'd just given me, I could see no harm in letting him do that. He just wanted to show me how sorry he was. I couldn't deny him that.

"How about Friday night?" I asked him as he walked towards the door. He smiled wide and nodded his head in agreement. I watched him walk out of the house, and I felt no fear.

"I'll cook." Ryson offered when I opened the door to him. After Dwayne had left, I had taken a long hot bath. I needed to get myself together emotionally and mentally before I saw Ryson tonight.

"We always stay in. I want to go out." I whined, only half serious. We did seem to spend all of our time together in my living room. I didn't really want to go over to his place, too many awkward and bad memories.

"I don't want to share you with the world okay," he joked and kissed me on the lips.

"That could be it. Or you could be trying to hide me from the world." I joked. He didn't laugh.

"I was only playing, Ryson."

"I knew that." He laughed nervously and walked into the kitchen.

"Hey babe I… uh got my alarm fixed today."

"I almost forgot it was broken. Did you call the company today?" Ryson opened the refrigerator and took out the ingredients for dinner.

"Yeah. I called them this morning and they sent someone out to fix it. It was Dwayne." He stopped what he was doing and looked at me. His eyebrows came together in a scowl and he walked over to me.

"What happened? Did he hurt you? I'll kick his fucking ass!" Ryson took hold of my arms and searched me like he was expecting to find bruises. I brushed him off.

"Nothing happened. He just fixed the alarm. Calm down Ryson. I'm okay, really."

"Are you sure?" He didn't believe me. I mean, I couldn't blame him for being worried.

"Yes I'm sure. He actually apologized to me." I waited to see his reaction. He narrowed his eyes.

"Did he sound sincere?"

"Yes, very. We actually kind of made up you could say. It was weird, but I think we came to an understanding about what happened that night. We're both going to move forward and put it behind us." That was the best explanation I could give without having to go into details about what really happened. I hated holding things back from Ryson. But what happened earlier was too bizarre for even me to understand, let alone try to get Ryson to.

"He even offered to take me out for a drink as a friend. To show me how sorry he is." Ryson's eyes damn near flew out of their sockets.

"Hell no! I don't want you going anywhere with him unless I'm there!" He turned away from me and busied himself with the food. It wasn't up to him to make that decision for me. Plus, I already told Dwayne yes. I was going.

"I already told him yes Ryson." I waited for the argument that was about to ensue. He slowly turned towards me and looked at me like I had a third eye.

"What? Why would you tell him yes? What's wrong with you?" His voice rose as he walked towards me. Why was he so upset? It wasn't like I said we were going on a fucking date! How dare he give me an attitude!

"Nothing is wrong with me. It's a peace offering Ryson." I put my hands up in surrender. "He's trying to reconcile and I'm going to let him. I thought you of all people would be happy that he's trying to clean up his mess." I gave him an attitude right back.

"He said sorry already, he doesn't need to buy you a fucking drink to reiterate that! He's just trying to get back on your good side, so he can get you back in his fucking bed!" Ryson screamed in my face. I gasped in shock. I couldn't believe he just said that to me. I took a step back and swallowed.

"Damn. That's what you think huh? You don't think I thought of that? Why would I go if I thought that was his motive? I would *never* hurt you like that," I said softly. Ryson looked at me, closed his eyes, and put his head down. He knew he had crossed the line. I walked into the living room and sat down on the couch. I sat back and played with my hair. I didn't want to be having this conversation with him. He was extremely angry. It wasn't that big of a deal was it? It was just a drink. Why did men always think everything was connected to sex? Why couldn't he believe that Dwayne was genuinely sorry? He had to turn his offer into a fucking negative. He didn't see the look in Dwayne's eyes today. He didn't see how he responded when I told him I forgave him. He didn't feel and understand the magnitude of what we shared, crying together. Dwayne was sincere. I didn't care if Ryson believed him or not. I did. And on the off chance that Dwayne did try something, I would shoot him down immediately and put him in his place. Ryson sat down next to me on the couch, but didn't say anything.

"He's really sorry Ryson. I thought it would be a good show of faith if I accepted his offer. It's an iced tea. It's not a date. It's not dinner. It's one beverage. It needs to happen to ease all of this tension between us. You can't even imagine how much fear I felt today when I saw his face through my peephole. Do you think I enjoyed being afraid around him? This is for my benefit, just as much as it is for him. I'm going whether it sits right with you or not." He didn't say anything. I still had beef with him for telling Dwayne to stay away from me. I chose to leave it alone, because ultimately he had my best interests at heart.

"I don't want you to go," he said gently.

"You don't trust me." It was a statement not a question. I knew from the start that Ryson would never trust me around Dwayne again. I just thought that by now he would see that I only had eyes for him. I couldn't make him trust me when it came to his brother. I slept with Dwayne on numerous occasions, and I hadn't even slept with him yet. So I knew he was feeling some type of way about me spending any alone time with Dwayne. But like I said, it was a gesture, and I was going to take Dwayne up on it. It was the right thing to do.

"I do trust you." He looked at me, but I could see the indecision in his eyes. I sat up and took his face in my hands.

"You don't have anything to worry about. At the end of the night, I'll be coming back to you. Only you baby." I kissed him on the lips. He wrapped his hands around my wrist and kissed me back softer than usual. I slowed down my kiss and let my lips linger on his. I felt my panties start to moisten. How the hell did I go from being furious to being horny? I put Dwayne in the back of my mind and thought about Ryson's lips. All of this sexual tension was not helping anything. I forgot about our argument and had an idea.

"I'll be back." I ran up the steps to the bathroom and ran some bath water. I waited for the water to reach the middle of the tub, then turned the water off. I went back downstairs and found Ryson in the kitchen chopping up some lettuce.

"Take a break from that real quick and follow me." He said okay and followed me. I walked over to my alarm system and made sure it was set. I didn't want any interruptions this time. We walked upstairs to the bathroom. When he saw the bath, a small smile crept up on his face.

RYSON

I didn't like that shit one bit. I didn't trust Dwayne. He was my brother, but he was sneaky. He had Samara believing his little bullshit apology, but I didn't. There had to be a motive. If not, why wait so long? It's not like he was afraid of me. If he really wanted to apologize, he could have done it by now, whether I told him to stay away or not. She was so stubborn. I knew I couldn't convince her not to go. I was a little bit worried about them spending time together again though. They had a sexual history and I knew Dwayne might try something. But as they say, it takes two to tango. I had to trust that Samara wouldn't cheat on me.

"He's really sorry Ryson. I thought it would be a good show of faith if I accepted his offer. It's an iced tea. It's not a date. It's not dinner. It's one beverage. It needs to happen to ease all of this tension between us. You can't even imagine how much fear I felt today when I saw his face through my peephole. Do you think I enjoyed being afraid around him? This is for my benefit, just as much as it is for him. I'm going whether it sits right with you or not." Her mind was made up. I never thought about the fact that she would be afraid of Dwayne. I never realized how traumatic that situation must have been for her. That made me feel like a jackass. She was right. She had to face her demons too. I did trust her. I think. She couldn't still be attracted to Dwayne after what he did to her. It was just too complicated of a situation to fully trust either of them. She kissed me and tried to reassure me that she would be coming home to me no matter what. I grabbed her wrists and let my lips sit on hers. I was trying to capture the feeling of kissing her. I didn't want to lose her to Dwayne. But if I did, at least I would have my memories. She excused herself and went upstairs. I sighed and walked back in the kitchen to start cooking. I had to do something to keep my mind off of this shit.

"Take a break from that real quick and follow me." Samara came back in the kitchen and grabbed my hand. She made sure her security system was on. I followed her upstairs absentmindedly. I couldn't stop thinking about this Dwayne shit. She walked into the bathroom and turned towards me. I looked over and saw that she had run a bath.

"Uh... what's going on?" I asked, smiling a little.

"Take your clothes off," she ordered me in a seductive voice. My dick got beyond hard hearing her speak in that tone. I pulled my yellow polo shirt over my head and unzipped my black cargo shorts with the speed of a track star. I let them fall, and slipped out of my sneakers. I went to pull down my briefs.

"Not yet," Samara whispered. She took my hand and brought it to the buttons on her dress. It was a gray, V-neck, button-up dress, that hit her at mid-thigh. She was bare foot and her hair was pinned up. She was the epitome of sexy. She made me unbutton her dress and push it off her body.

"Damn." I saw her nipples poking through her lacy see-through bra. They were pointing right at me, begging me to put them in my mouth, so I did. I bent down and made small wet circles around her erect nipples with my tongue. She arched her back and poked her chest out for me. Samara had small, pretty breasts. Just enough to fill my mouth. She threw her head back and moaned. I looked up at her and saw her face twisted in pleasure. Her body was firm, but soft in all the right places. I took another taste of her nipples, then stood up. She looked up at me and I could see she wanted me as much as I wanted her. Long months of lusting and longing were about to pay off. I still couldn't believe it was actually going down like this. I grabbed her waist, picked her up, and put her up on the sink.

"Oh!" She exclaimed in surprise and pulled me closer. I put my tongue in her mouth and opened her legs wider. She wrapped her hands around my head and kissed me slowly and passionately. I felt so connected to her. I was in love with her and I wanted to show her how much. I planned on taking my time, and showing her that I could take care of her every need. I could hear my heart racing in my ears. I never thought I would be making love instead of fucking a woman. The women I messed with didn't get the effort or time it took to make love. I used to think it was a bitch move to make love to a woman, but Samara changed all of that. She was everything I didn't know I was looking for, and everything I wanted. I was going to make sure to show her that tonight. My hands glided down her soft body and slid her panties down over her wide hips. She lifted her body up to help me. My finger was on her clit before her panties hit the floor.

"Oh shit!" I looked down at my finger and saw her juices. They were thick and creamy like syrup. She was past being wet, she was soaked.

"I get soaked whenever you touch me," she admitted huskily. I put my finger in my mouth and tasted her for the first time.

"Mmmmm sweet." I reached behind her back and unhooked her bra. She cupped her breasts in her hands and squeezed.

"Let me do that." I replaced her hands with mine. We stared at each other keenly, as I massaged her breasts.

"Perfect timing right?" she asked me with a smile.

"Hell yeah," I said and she giggled. I leaned forward and put my tongue in her ear. She stopped giggling then. She grabbed my shoulders and whimpered. I knew that was her spot. I slipped my finger in her wet pussy and continued to lick and suck on her ear and neck.

"Oh god!" She licked her lips and panted. I had Samara naked on her bathroom sink, squirming with my finger in her juicy pussy. Yeah, it was definitely perfect timing. She grabbed my hand and took my finger out of her. She looked me in the eyes as she put my finger with her juices on it in her mouth. Goddamn. She hopped down off the sink. I pressed my body onto hers, pushing her against the sink. She took a shuddered breath and put her hand on my chest. Her hand trailed down my chest, my stomach, and down past my navel. Her hand was so warm. She bent forward and kissed me in the middle of my chest and continued down until she was on her knees.

"Shit!" I hissed and held my breath. I narrowed my eyes and watched the top of her head. She sank her teeth into my briefs and pulled them down with her mouth. I never saw anything like that. My dick slapped her in the face, but she didn't take it in her mouth. Instead, she kissed my inner thighs. Her lips were hot and wet. She rubbed her face in my pubic hair. I was getting harder even though she hadn't even touched my dick yet. She was teasing me. I put my hand on her head and tried to guide her mouth to my dick. She put her hands on my thighs, stopping me. "Let's take our time baby," she mumbled. I nodded my head and enjoyed her kisses down there.

"Get in the tub," she ordered me and stood back up. I liked her aggressiveness, it was definitely a turn-on. I stepped into the hot water, sat down, and relaxed. She was right behind me. She straddled me and leaned in to kiss me.

"Do you want me?" She asked me between kisses.

"Yes! More than you fucking know!" I practically screamed at her. I was so horny, if she even touched my dick again, I was liable to cum right in her hands.

"Good." She lowered herself into the water.

"What the fuck?" She slid back and submerged herself in the water. The only part of her body not in the water was her ass. I was confused until I felt her mouth on my dick.

"NO YOU DIDN'T!" I screamed out in disbelief. Was she really sucking my dick underwater? Oh my god! My eyes flew to the ceiling, and I couldn't close my mouth. Pleasure filtered through my body and my vision got cloudy. The visual stimulation of seeing water running down her ass cheeks, added with her sucking my dick, sent me over the edge.

SAMARA

I took a deep breath and went under. I always wanted to do this, but I was too afraid to try it. But I felt free with Ryson, so I wasn't going to hold back. I tried my best to take all of him in my mouth, but with a lack of oxygen I didn't want to push it. I took as much as I could. I contracted my jaw muscles before releasing him from my mouth. I did this repeatedly, until Ryson's dick was so hard I felt like I was giving head to a steel rod. I couldn't hold my breath any longer, so I came above the water.

"Whew!" I wiped water from my eyes and face. I took a few deep breaths to control my breathing. Ryson was wide-eyed with his mouth open. I giggled at his expression. I guess he enjoyed it.

"That was fucking CRAZY!" He blew air out and gave me a half-smile. I straddled him and edged my wet body closer to his stomach, so I could give him the second part of my surprise.

"You're so fucking beautiful," he whispered and put his hands through my wet hair.

"Thank you baby. So are you. Really, you are." I put his thumb in my mouth and swirled my tongue around it. I couldn't wait any longer. I pushed myself up, then grabbed his dick. He put his head back and made a hissing sound. I then eased down onto his dick.

"AH!" I already knew what to expect when I saw his dick underwater, but the pleasure still shocked me. I was so wet, the water didn't have shit on me!

"Oh yeah!" Ryson panted and grabbed my hips. I started off with a slow grind, until I found my rhythm.

"Fuck, fuck, fuck!" Ryson reclined his head and closed his eyes. He was so hard, the head of his dick was massaging my G-spot. I could have cum just staring at the satisfaction on his face. I planted my palms on each of his shoulders, and plunged my pussy down as deep as I could onto his dick. It was almost too much for me to take. I had to squeeze my pussy muscles tight to prevent myself from cumming.

"OOOO RYSON!" Our eyes bulged at the same time at the force of my thrusts. I didn't stop.

"DAMN GIRL!" Ryson yelled at me and gripped my hips tighter. I jumped up and down on his dick, splashing water everywhere. My breasts bounced and jiggled.

"SHIT!" I screamed as I rocked on his dick harder and faster.

"OH! SLOW DOWN! SLOW DOWN!" Ryson grabbed the sides of the tub for dear life. I wasn't letting up. I wanted to cum on his dick.

"I CAN'T BABY!" I yelled and clenched my teeth. I arched my back and continued to ride his dick. It was steamy in the bathroom and the mirrors were fogged up. I didn't know if it was from the sex or from the bath. I slowed down and ground my hips in a circle on his dick, tickling my clit in the process. Ryson sprang up and gently bit my nipple. My cum spilled out of me nice and slow.

"AAAAHHHHHHHHHH!" I shouted over and over as Ryson moved his hips upwards and pumped his dick inside me. Water splashed over the tub and went splat on the floor.

"Keep cumming baby, keep cumming," Ryson's deep voice egged me on. I tried to grab the tub but my hand slipped. I closed my eyes and gave into the feeling. I felt his hot tongue on my neck. He kept pumping and I kept cumming.

RYSON

I felt her nails dig into my shoulders. She was in heaven and so was I. I couldn't believe she rode my dick like that. I tried to grab her to slow her down, because I didn't want to cum yet. I had the urge to, but I held it back. It surprised me that I was ready to cum, even though I didn't have her bent over. That was something new.

"Wow." She exhaled and lay breathless on my chest. I ran my hands through her wet wavy hair and listened to her breathe.

"How about we take this to dry land?" She laughed and sat up, misty eyed. She bit her lips and cradled my face in her hands. She loved me. I looked at her chocolate colored nipples that were dripping wet. She was so fucking sexy it was crazy. I was a lucky man. She bent down and I met her halfway for the kiss. Her tongue was so wet and thick. I put my hands in her hair and crushed her face to mine. I couldn't get enough of her. I put my hands in the water and grabbed her fat ass. She grabbed my dick and stroked it up and down. She broke the kiss and stepped out of the tub. Her naked body dripped with water. I analyzed her from head to toe and couldn't see one imperfection. I was blinded by love and lust, and in my eyes she was perfection.

"Come on baby," she cooed and walked out of the bathroom. I hoisted myself up out of the tub and made my way to her bedroom, dripping water everywhere. She scooted back onto the bed and sat with her back against the headboard. She brought her knees up to her chest and tilted her head. It was my turn to take over now. I crept into the bed and pulled on her ankles until she was lying flat on her back.

"Lay on your side." I instructed. I had a surprise of my own.

"Okay. I'll do whatever you want." She knew just what to say to get me going again. My dick was at attention once again. She got on her side and I did the same. But I lay so that her pussy was in my face and my dick was in hers. I always wanted to try a sideways sixty-nine. It took some adjusting. Samara was quite a bit shorter than me, but we found a good position. I lifted up her leg and put it on my shoulder, then spread the lips to her pink pussy and went to work. I slowly stuck my tongue inside of her. I heard her take a breath. I ran my tongue down to her clit and kissed it. She tried to move her leg but I put a firm hold on it. She wasn't getting away from me. Her mouth was on the head of my dick. She took her time and licked and sucked on the head, until I felt myself trying to get away from her. I tried to concentrate on her pussy, so I spread her lips wider and did a little sucking of my own. I bobbed my head up and down and sucked on her clit until it was swollen. She grabbed my leg and put it on her shoulder. With my mouth still on her clit, I glanced down at her and saw my dick going inside her mouth.

"SHIT!" I mumbled on her clit. She was trying to make me cum. Two could play that game. I put her clit in between my top lip and my tongue and sucked and squeezed. She screamed out in pleasure, then put my dick back in her mouth. She was so wet. I could see her juices pouring down her thigh and into the crack of her ass. I felt my dick hit the back of her throat. Her warm mouth was wrapped around my dick, driving me crazy. She tasted so sweet and savory, I wanted to keep my head buried between her legs forever. I slid and pumped two fingers inside of her as I swirled my tongue around her swollen clit. It was too much for her. She started to shake and tried to get her leg out of my grasp. I dug my fingers into her thigh and held on even tighter. She never took my dick out of her mouth as she came in mine. She moaned and whimpered as her nut spilled onto my fingers. Her body started to spasm. I replaced my fingers with my tongue and slid my tongue inside her again. My middle finger massaged her clit as I swallowed everything she had to offer. When the last of her orgasm left her body, she went deep on my dick again. I licked her juices off my lip and moved her leg. I lay on my back and closed my eyes. *Don't cum yet.* She took me whole at a steady pace. She went deeper and deeper until I heard her start to choke. The sound of her gagging on my dick made me hazy with desire. I had never felt so much enjoyment during sex. She took my dick out of her mouth. Thick white saliva oozed out of her mouth and down her neck.

"OH MY FUCKING GOD!" I couldn't hold on any longer. I felt my nut start to build up inside of me. She went deep on my dick again. I didn't think I should cum in her mouth, but she wouldn't let me go.

"LET ME GO BABY! LET ME GOOOOO!" It was too late. My nut burst out of me like a river. I came harder when I realized she was swallowing my nut. She grabbed the base of my dick while she sucked and jerked it, releasing more of my nut into her mouth.

SAMARA

My clit was tender. I was moist and sticky. My body seemed to vibrate from my orgasm. Ryson's tongue was like a weapon. I wiggled and tried to get away from him. He tasted and sucked on me, so soft and yet so firm. I couldn't handle the two sensations at once. My body jumped when I felt his fingers inside of me. I knew he was trying to make me cum, but I had something for him too. I wanted to taste his cum so bad. His dick was strangling me, but it turned me on to the point of no return. I choked and gagged and waited for him to bust. I knew he was fighting it, but I couldn't have that. Gripping his dick tightly in my hand, I jerked him up and down. He exploded so hard, my mouth was full of his nut. I struggled to swallow it all, even as more spilled into my mouth. Months' worth of cum were finally getting released. I was spent. I detangled myself from him and lay on my back. He crawled on top of me and spread my legs. He started covering every inch of my body with his lips. His wet warm lips touched and teased my breasts, my stomach, and my inner thighs.

"AH!" I screamed out. My body was on fire from his touches. With his lips trailing down my side, I grabbed the pillow and tried to elevate my breathing. His tongue was like hot lava on my clit. I rubbed the top of his head and let him taste me again. I didn't want to cum yet but he was making it so hard. His tongue was scorching hot on me. I moaned and let him have free range of my body. I came again on his tongue. My heart raced. I felt so overpowered by him.

"I want to see your face when we make love." Ryson slowly entered me. I didn't know why he said that, but I forgot about it as soon as he was inside me. I could feel the head of his dick on my G-spot again. I grabbed his muscular arms and braced myself. I held my breath as he started to grind and move his hips. He was so thick. He filled me completely. He was so gentle I wanted to cry. My hands glided down his arms, caressed his ribs, and landed on his hips. I looked up into his hazel eyes and begged him with my eyes to never stop. His dick was velvety smooth, sliding in and out of me with ease.

"OOOOOHHHHH RYSON!" I purred and kept my eyes locked on his. He stared at me intensely. His body glistened with sweat as he gave me more of him.

"OOOOH BABY!" I tried to catch my breath. He was hitting every spot. He induced every sexual frustration I had, then demolished them. He put his hand in my hair and brought my face up to his.

"Ryson." I whispered his name before he kissed me. I didn't want this to end. He gave me his tongue and a hard thrust.

"OH!" I cried out. His movements were rhythmic as he guided his dick in and out of my wetness. He wrapped his other hand around my waist and moved me backwards, pinning me against the headboard. I placed my hands on his lower back and grabbed his ass. His tongue plunged deeper in my mouth as he quickened his pace. I rocked my hips and matched his thrusts with my own.

"AHHHH! OOOOHHH! RYSON! BBBBAAAABBBY!" I screamed on his lips as he continued to kiss and stroke me. I knew I would be cumming soon. I felt faint. My clit felt so good rubbing up against his stomach. I didn't want to let him go.

"SAMARA!" Ryson choked out before growling in my ear. His lips were on my neck, kissing my spot. I opened my mouth in ecstasy and took all of the pleasure he was giving me. I was all his tonight. I surrendered to him.

RYSON

I couldn't imagine not seeing her beautiful face as we made love. I could never cum doing it missionary style, but I damn sure was going to try. My dick was so hard, it physically hurt. Her pussy was the only thing keeping me going. I didn't think I could stand the pain. Our bodies intertwined as she pumped her hips forward. I placed my hands on her cheeks, forcing her to look at me. Her eyes were burning with passion. Her body felt so hot in my arms. I wanted to tell her that I loved her, but I was afraid. I'd never been with anyone like Samara. I smelled her lavender scent and felt my dick start to tingle. Was it really happening? Was I about to cum? I didn't want to over think it. I lay my lips on hers and continued my slow grind inside of her. She was about to cum. I could see it all over her face. She wrinkled her brows and slowly licked her lips. I watched her intently, getting even more turned on by her tongue. I bent my head down and circled her tongue with mine. She sucked on mine and watched me watch her. My heart started to pound and that all too familiar feeling overcame me. I shoved a little harder into Samara. Her eyes got wider and she started to whimper. I grabbed her thighs and held her legs open. I repositioned myself so I could get deeper inside of her.

"YYYYYEEEEESSSSSS!" She screamed and pumped her hips forward matching my thrusts. I felt warm liquid on my dick and I knew she was cumming. Her pussy was gushing with her juices. I was right behind her.

"OH SHIT! OH SHIT! DDDDAAAAMMMMMNNNN! SAMARA!" Involuntarily, I screamed out in ecstasy and elation.

"OH GOD!" I felt my eyes tearing up and my mouth was dry. I stayed inside of her long enough to give her my nectar, then I pulled out. I lay on top of her in shock. I couldn't breathe. I closed my mouth and tried to breathe through my nose. My chest heaved in and out as I came down from the high of busting a nut. I felt her hands running down my head.

"Are you okay?" She whispered and kissed the top of my head. Her breathing was almost as labored as mine. I nodded my head yes and closed my eyes. She would never know or understand the significance of what just happened. I got comfortable on her body and snuggled up to her. Silence fell over the room, but it was a good quiet. A calm quiet. I let my hand glide up and down her soft body. She sighed and wrapped her arms around my back in an embrace. I sat up and looked down at her. God I loved this woman. It was going to kill me, but I had to find a way to tell her my secret. If I didn't, and she found out from someone else, it would all be over. I kissed her on the forehead and lay back down on her shoulder.

SAMARA

I was pleasantly surprised. I thought that the sex would be good, but I didn't think it would be as fantastic as it was. I felt so relaxed and loose after making love to Ryson. He made my whole body orgasm. From my head to my toes, I was satisfied in every way possible. He didn't have to do much. Just a touch from his hand or a gentle kiss sent me over the edge. That night I knew I loved Ryson. I didn't know how he felt about me, but I was head over heels in love with him. I needed him and I wanted him. Ryson fell asleep on me that night, and stayed with me the next day. He called out of work and catered to me that whole day. He made us breakfast in bed and then we made love. We went down to the park and had lunch under one of the big oak trees. Afterwards we sat in his Jeep talking and ended up making love again in the back seat. That night we ordered out for dinner and were making love before the food even hit the table. It wasn't rushed or hurried. Each time was tender and special. I wanted to punch myself for waiting so long to be with him. When he finally went home three days later to get more clothes, it was hard for the both of us to peel ourselves apart. I waved goodbye to Ryson and leaned against the door smiling. I couldn't help but reminisce on our lovemaking. I was excited about what we would get into tonight. It was Friday, so I knew Ryson would be tired after work and would need to wind down. I had just the remedy for that.

"Shit!" I slapped myself on the forehead. I had totally forgotten I promised Dwayne I would go out for a drink with him tonight. Damn. I couldn't cancel now. Or could I? No, that would be like going backwards. We had made too much progress for me to mess it up by cancelling on him. I said I would do it and I was keeping my word. I believed Dwayne was sincere, but I was no fool. With a flip of a switch the old Dwayne could resurface at any given time.

Ding dong!

My doorbell rang. Dwayne was here. I was upstairs trying to figure out what to wear. I didn't want to wear the wrong outfit and give Dwayne or Ryson the wrong impression. Ryson was watching ESPN downstairs when the doorbell rang. I was trying to keep the two of them from seeing each other tonight, but it was of no use. Ryson insisted on being here when Dwayne came. I didn't argue with him about it. I probably should have just met Dwayne where we were going, so he wouldn't come here at all. Too late for that now. I pulled out a black, silk button-up shirt, and slipped into a pair of light blue skinny jeans. I put on a pair of black strappy wedges and put my hair in a low ponytail. I looked like a college student. I didn't wear any jewelry except my charm bracelet. I made it a point not to spray on too much perfume as well. I was trying to give off friend vibes, plus I knew Ryson would be inspecting what I had on. I couldn't blame him for that though. I didn't want any trouble tonight. From either brother. I walked downstairs. Ryson and Dwayne were staring each other down. *Uh-oh*. The muscles in Ryson's arm flexed. Dwayne looked ready for anything. I cleared my throat.

"Hi Dwayne! Ready?" I asked him and stood in between the brothers. That was where I felt like I had been from the beginning. Stuck in between the two of them.

"More than ready." He finally looked down at me and smiled.

"Okay, I'll meet you at your car." I rubbed my hands together nervously. He nodded and left. I turned to Ryson, who was staring at the closed door.

"I don't like this shit," he muttered. I took a deep breath because I anticipated this happening. I put my hand on his arm and brought his attention back to me.

"I know. I'll be back in a little bit. You can text me the whole time if you want." I stood on my tiptoes and kissed him. He tried to just give me a little peck on the lips, but I grabbed his chin.

"Hey! Don't do that. Give me all of you." I pulled his face down and forced him to kiss me properly. I needed him to know that I only wanted him. He moaned on my lips and slipped me his tongue. My internal temperature rose a few degrees. His hand slid down to my ass. I broke the kiss before things got too hot, and tapped my fingers on his soft lips.

"We'll finish this later." I smiled at him and walked to the door. I looked back at him and saw the hurt on his face. I hoped he realized that he didn't have anything to worry about. I didn't think I was sexually attracted to Dwayne anymore. Especially after the ordeal we went through earlier this week. I walked out to find Dwayne sitting in a Ford Escort. It looked vaguely familiar, but I didn't know why. I opened the passenger side door and climbed in. I smelled his cologne all over the car. It was the same cologne he wore the first time we met.

I fastened my seatbelt and threw a smile his way. It was kind of awkward sitting right next to him after everything that happened.

"So… what's up?" he asked me cheerfully. I looked over at him and noticed that he'd let his facial hair grow. It looked good on him. I did a quick scan of his body. I had forgotten what good shape he was in. He was dressed simply in a white t-shirt, blue jeans, and black hiking boots.

"Nothing much. Everything is pretty much the same, except for the obvious." I commented, pointing towards my house referring to Ryson. He nodded and looked straight ahead. The lines around his eyes came together. He didn't want to talk about Ryson. I decided to change the subject and try to lighten the mood. We went through enough deep shit this week to last a lifetime.

"How is work?" That was always a safe subject. His eyes brightened again.

"Work is good! I'm actually up for a promotion." He smiled at me and I found myself blushing. What the hell? I looked out the window and closed my eyes. Why was I so nervous around him now? I feared and kind of hated him a few days ago, now this? I probably still had some residual feelings for him. The last time we were together intimately flashed in my mind. I felt my stomach start to tingle. Our arrangement had ended so abruptly. I could see how there would still be sexual feelings lingering. Then I thought about the night of the party, and those tingles quickly evaporated. I calmed my nerves and focused my attention straight ahead.

"That's great! By the way, thanks again for fixing my alarm. I haven't had any problems with it so far."

"That's good. I rewired your whole system so you shouldn't have any more mishaps with it." We were quiet for a minute. I needed a drink. Not an iced tea.

DWAYNE

I stood on her doorstep literally shaking in my boots. I longed to see her up close again. The last time we were together was so intense. I had been watching her from across the street, waiting for the right time to come over. It was making me antsy. Her elderly neighbor Ms. Rosie's bedroom window faced hers. So I did what I had to do. I picked Ms. Rosie's locks so I could watch Samara anytime I wanted. Ms. Rosie stayed downstairs knitting in her living room for the bulk of the day. Never even knew I was in her house. She was probably senile or losing her hearing I guessed. I didn't care either way. Daily, I sat on Ms. Rosie's windowsill with my binoculars, and watched Samara go about her day. I almost ran across the street the night I saw her and Ryson fucking. I gripped Ms. Rosie's dresser so hard it started to tip over. I caught it just before it hit the floor. Wigs, earrings, and all types of dumb ass trinkets, fell to the floor. I ran my hand up and down my face trying to calm down. I would let him have her this one time. I'd had Samara almost six times, so I guess I could give him one go round.

My eyes would burn from lack of sleep and my stomach would growl like I hadn't eaten in weeks. I didn't care though, I had to see her. Ryson didn't have shit on me. I watched him eat her pussy and knew she wasn't enjoying that shit. When he finally got around to giving her the dick, he didn't even pump that shit right. Samara was the type of girl you fucked, hard. I could tell she wasn't feeling that shit by the look on her face when she came. I knew what she liked and how to give it to her. Soon, I would be giving her what she wanted again. I smiled when the door opened, only to come face to face with Ryson. I hid my disgust and put on my best face. If Ryson knew that I was trying to get Samara back, he would shut this whole night down. I was so close, I couldn't fuck up now. So I bit down all of the resentment I had towards him, and put my hand out.

"What's up bro?" I shook his extended hand and stepped into the living room. His eyes studied me with suspicion.

"Where are you taking my girl tonight?" He had a slight grin on his face. He thought he was hurting my feelings by calling Samara his girl? He would never say that shit out in public. Ryson was funny that way. Samara would learn about the real Ryson soon enough. There was a reason why women didn't stay with him long. That shit didn't faze me.

"Just over to the café. Nothing fancy. I just want her to know how sorry I am. You know, clear the air." I tried to sound sincere. He nodded his head in agreement but looked me up and down. He didn't trust me, and he shouldn't. If only he knew the thoughts running through my mind right now.

"Yeah that's what I heard. FYI this is the one and *only* time you will ever take Samara anywhere." His voice was low and serious. His hazel eyes darkened and the muscles in his arm flexed. He was ready to make a move. I was ready too. Ryson thought his shit didn't stink. He thought because he was older he was able to tell me what the fuck to do. Fuck him! He wasn't better than me! I wanted him to start some shit, just so I could prove how superior I was to him. That night I attacked Samara, the beating he gave me was justified. But that was then, and this was now. If he started some shit, I wasn't backing down. I heard footsteps coming and my dick got hard. I would handle Ryson at another time.

"Hi Dwayne! You ready?" Samara skipped down the steps with a huge smile on her face. The silk shirt molded to her breasts perfectly. Her ass looked extra rotund in her tight jeans. I was going to have fun tonight. I told her I was ready and she told me to meet her at the car. I walked out and got in my truck. I cracked my neck and my knuckles. *Be cool.*

"I know, I know." I saw her walking towards the truck. She was so fucking sexy. Her hips switched from side to side and her curly ponytail bounced behind her. I sat up straighter so she couldn't see my hard dick. It was so hard, it could have ripped through my jeans. She hopped in the truck and buckled up. The tension was unmistakable. She was nervous and so was I. She tried to make small talk with me, but I could tell she was unsure of whether or not this was a good idea. I smiled at her and I could have sworn she blushed. She looked away just as her cheeks began to flush. Maybe it wouldn't be as hard as I thought to get her to come around.

We got a table in the back of the café and ordered drinks.

"Iced tea right?" I asked her. She smiled at me and nodded her head yes. There was soft music playing from the speakers. The mood in the café was very relaxed. I could tell a lot of people were on dates. She sipped her drink nervously. She was tense.

"Samara?" I called her name softly. She looked at me and swallowed what was in her mouth. I watched her throat as the liquid went down.

"Yes?" she asked me, trying to sound relaxed. She was anything but. I knew that unless we addressed the issue again, the night would drag by with both of us walking on eggshells. Even though we had hashed it out already, the effects of that night seemed to still linger.

"You know that I'm sorry for what I did to you right?" I slid my chair closer to hers. She didn't seem to mind. She put her head down and nodded.

"I know Dwayne. It's just… strange sitting next to you like this right now. I keep seeing how you looked at me that night. I was terrified of you and I don't scare easily." She laughed uneasily. Her plump lips moved but I barely listened. I cleared my throat.

"Look at me now. What do you see?" I searched her eyes and she did the same to mines. I felt a flutter in my stomach and felt my dick thumping in my jeans. I wanted to fuck her so bad, it was killing me not to. I wanted to say fuck it to my plan and just drag her ass into the bathroom and hit it from the back. I tried to control my breathing. I felt my skin getting hot.

"I see the Dwayne I met here five months ago. This tall, handsome, buff guy with clean fingernails," she giggled. I felt myself blushing then. She continued to giggle as she sipped her tea. Maybe I was imagining it, but I would swear she was loosening up to me.

"That night I took mercy on you. I could have kicked your ass, or at least caused more damage if I wanted to. I only held back because part of the blame was on me too. Ignoring you was pretty messed up. I could have kicked your ass though. But I didn't want to hurt you too bad." Her face was dead serious. I laughed anyway. She was so cute.

"I don't know about that Samara. I got a hundred plus pounds on you." I sipped my lemonade and saw a twinkle in her eyes. This felt good.

"Don't let my size fool you. I'm stronger than I look." She rolled up her shirt sleeve and put her elbow on the table. I thought about the punches she'd rained down on me the other day and believed her.

"Wrestle me!" she challenged me.

"What?" I laughed because I knew she was serious. I didn't want to wrestle her, but I loved this playful banter between us. I was willing to do anything she wanted.

"Okay, but I'm not holding back because you're a girl." I warned her and put my arm on the table.

"I wouldn't want you too." She licked her bottom lip involuntarily and grabbed my hand tight. Her palm was soft and warm. I had to concentrate. I was touching her. And she was letting me!

"On the count of three. One, two, three!" I figured I would give her the illusion of winning before I slammed her hand down on the table. But she was strong as shit, and was giving me a little run for my money. Fuck! This shit was turning me on. She put her other hand on her knee for leverage, and pulled my hand closer and closer to the table. If I didn't concentrate, I could possibly lose. She bit her bottom lip and pushed as hard as she could. In the end I let my knuckle hit the table. I let my baby win.

"WHOOP WHOOP!" She jumped up from her seat and put her hands over her head in celebration. She did the cabbage patch and started laughing. How the fuck did she give me any competition in arm wrestling? I watched her dance. Her shirt rose a few centimeters and I saw her belly button. I grabbed my drink and took a long chug. I stood up in front of her.

"Okay, okay. You won fair and square." She smiled up at me then flexed her muscles.

"What's my prize?" She slanted her head and smiled hard. I was so confused. Was she flirting with me or was she trying to show me she could get past the incident? I chose to believe she was flirting.

"How about a dance?" I offered and put my hand out. Her smile faltered a bit as she looked down at my hand. I could see the wheels in her head spinning. Should I or shouldn't I? She made her decision and put her hand in mine. Mayer Hawthorne's 'Get to Know You', flowed through the speakers, as we walked to an open space in the café. Technically, there wasn't a dance floor, but we moved our table closer to another table to make room.

'I really wanna get to know you, I wanna learn you inside out'

She didn't look at me at first. She stepped closer to me and put her hands on my shoulders.

'I really wanna get to know you, we can have some fun right now'

I was afraid. I didn't want to move too fast too soon. But I really wanted to put my hands on her ass.

'I really wanna get to know you, I wanna make you feel alright'

I laid my hands on her hips and slowly moved her closer to me.

'I really wanna get to know you, we can get it on tonight'

I saw her bite her lip. Then she looked up at me and pre-nut oozed out of my dick.

'On tonight'

I closed my eyes and held my breath. She hooked her hands around my neck and kept her eyes on me. Our bodies weren't touching, but I could feel heat emitting from her body. Her scent was in my nostrils.

SAMARA

He put his hands on my hips. I didn't feel anything. I was relieved. If any sparks flew between us, I knew I would be in trouble. How would I handle being sexually attracted to both Ryson and Dwayne again? Good thing that wasn't the case. I could see in Dwayne's eyes what was on his mind. I could see it when his eyes lit up as I came downstairs. But I knew I had to make sure to make it clear I just wanted to be friends. I knew men and I knew Dwayne. If I gave him the slightest hint that I was still interested, he would pounce on it and be all over me. I stared into his eyes, wondering what he was thinking. I was having a good time with him tonight and wished that we could have done this before jumping into bed together. That was the downside of having a fuck buddy. You never got to know them as a person before crossing that line. He pulled me closer to him, but I backed up a little. The song ended and I walked back to the table.

"I'm thirsty. I'm gonna order another drink!" I said enthusiastically. He nodded, but his smile was gone. I guess he could tell I wouldn't be buying what he was selling.

"We should do this more often," he said out of nowhere. I stared down at my nails unsure of how to handle this.

"That would be nice. I would like it if we could be *friends*." I put emphasis on that last word. He chuckled a little and shook his head. I knew I put a damper on his plans tonight. He asked me out as an apology, but deep down I suspected he might try to make a move. Of course I didn't tell Ryson that. I made it clear that it wasn't going down like that.

"Yeah. Friends. That's cool I guess." He looked up at me and winked. I winked back and called the waitress over.

We were heading back to my house. The rest of the night had sailed past smoothly. We ordered some fries and talked. I learned some things about Dwayne that I didn't know, like his obsession with exercising, and his fascination with science.

"When I fixate on something, I just can't get it out of my system." He'd said, turning on my block. It turned out he was also a very good listener. I told him about running into Devon and him making fun of me for not having a tablet. Somehow we got on the subject of my alarm system.

"It could have been a bunch of little things. Like the rain or a mouse chewing on the cord. Those wires could have been faulty." He explained it to me and it made sense. "Well, thank you for replacing it. The night it shorted out my ear drums almost burst. It made this loud blaring noise. It was so damn annoying I wanted to yank it off the wall, ha-ha." He laughed with me and pulled up in front of my house. I looked over at my house, then at Dwayne. This was the part of the night I was dreading. The goodbye. I wasn't sure if I should give him a handshake or a hug.

"I had a really good time," I said meaning it. He turned off the ignition and turned towards me.

"Me too." We sat in silence for a few minutes. I didn't know what else to say.

"Well... uh... I guess I will be seeing you then." I went to open the door when he called my name.

"Samara? You still have my number right?" He sat up straighter.

"Yeah I do," I told him, my hands a little shaky. I didn't know why I said yes. I did still have his number unbeknownst to Ryson, but maybe I shouldn't have told him that.

"Use it some time," he said softly and lifted my hand up to his lips. I let him kiss my hand. Again, no sparks flew. I nodded and got out of the truck. I turned back when I got to my door and waved at him. He beeped the horn twice and pulled off. That was... something.

RYSON

The door closed behind Samara. Her house suddenly felt like a shack. My head started to pound violently. I couldn't deal with this shit! It was a bad fucking idea to let her go. What the fuck was I thinking? I let my girlfriend go on a fucking date with my brother, her ex fuck buddy. I was a fucking idiot! No, no, calm down. I tried to stop freaking out. Samara wouldn't do anything to endanger our relationship. Would she? No she wouldn't. She had every opportunity to and she didn't. Samara was a sexy, smart, independent woman, who probably had men drooling after her all the time. I heard a few of my boys tried to get at her at my party that night and she totally ignored them. Samara wasn't like that. I tried to convince myself of that over and over. She was feeling me and only me. She spent all of her time with me. Even when we weren't together, we were on the phone with each other.

I noticed the whole left side of Dwayne's face was pink and swollen. He probably said something stupid to a female and got his ass slapped in the face for it. I knew Dwayne would try to make a move on her tonight. It was up to her to take the bait. The first time we met she took it, but things were different now, weren't they? I was stressing myself out just thinking about this shit.

I got up and walked around the house to keep busy. I ran downstairs to the basement and cleaned out the half bath. I checked the filter in her heating system. I went up to her second floor and straightened out her linen closet. I was working up a sweat, but it was working. Focusing on cleaning took my mind off of Samara and who she was with. I went into her bedroom and changed her sheets. I then organized all of her shoes. I put them in order by color, then got up and looked around for something else to do. I went downstairs and got the broom and a few rags. I swept her hallway upstairs and in her bedroom. I could have vacuumed, but I needed to expel this amped up tension. When I moved the bed, there was a box underneath it. It was a black shoe box. I sat on the floor and picked it up. I knew going through her personal stuff was a no-no, but I needed to take my mind off of who she was with at the moment. I took the lid off of the box and stared down at a bunch of photos. In the first few, I recognized her father instantly. Speaking at rallies and holding protests. I remembered that as a kid. The next set of photos were of Samara and who I assumed was her brother Julio, holding up campaign signs. Both were missing teeth, and Samara's curly hair was even crazier back then. Neither of them could have been over eight years old. In spite of how I felt, I couldn't help but smile down at the pictures. I leafed through the images capturing Samara and her family from birth through her teenage years. I couldn't be mad at Samara. She was trustworthy and never showed me any inclination that she would betray me. I was tripping over nothing. I put the photos back in the box and moved the bed back.

"You look so sexy cleaning up." I jumped and turned around. Samara was standing at her bedroom door. She had a big grin on her face.

"How sexy do I look?" I asked her and put my doubts about her on the back burner. I sauntered over to her and pulled her to me. I looked down at her and saw the love she had for me in her eyes.

"You look sexy enough to eat!" Her eyes lit up and she pulled my face down to hers.

"I missed you," she whispered and kissed me. Hearing her say that squashed the little birdie in my ear. I loved this woman and she loved me. I was having a hard time adjusting to that.

"I missed you too," I mumbled between kisses. She pushed me gently and I fell onto the bed. She unbuttoned her shirt and stood in between my legs. I put my palm on her stomach to feel her warm skin. She shuddered and closed her eyes. My tongue circled her navel while I squeezed her ass. She moaned and rubbed my head. Why the hell did I think she would want anyone else but me?

SHAR

"Where is this shit going down at?" the voice on the other end of the line asked me. How the fuck was I supposed to know? That's what I was paying *them* for!

"Wherever you want it to happen. I don't know!" What the hell! I gave them the fucking money weeks ago and they were *just* calling me to go over the details.

"Where does she work? What's her address?" he asked me impatiently.

"I DON'T FUCKING KNOW!" I yelled irritably.

"How the fuck are we supposed to do this shit if we don't know where the bitch lives?" the voice yelled at me. I bit my tongue so hard it bled. These motherfuckers were getting on my nerves already.

"I'll find out and text you!" I spat and hung up. FUCK! I threw my cell phone across the room in frustration. I looked down at my finger, now in a splint. That bitch was really going to fucking pay for doing that shit! I hated her now more than ever. I could get her address from Dwayne. He was so dimwitted, he wouldn't even notice me trying to get the shit out of him. I picked up my phone, which now had a cracked screen. SHIT!

"What Shar?" Dwayne answered, annoyed. Damn, what did I do? This bitch was really turning Dwayne and Ryson against me.

"Well damn! That's how you greet somebody on the phone? Anyway, I need to ask you something." I couldn't believe Dwayne, of all people, was acting like this. He was the one brother I thought I had on my side. Even though Samara had him wrapped around her finger, he still came to my house and chilled with me sometimes. I guess that shit was going to stop now too.

"It better not be for money. Because I'm still a little iffy on what you did with the money I gave you the last time," he said with an attitude.

"Dwayne, I used that money to pay my rent and buy shit for my apartment. You want to see the damn receipts?" Why was he so suspicious now?

"Yeah I do. I can come over right now," he said seriously. Fuck.

"Come on now Dwayne, stop playing! I need to know Samara's address," I said, knowing bringing up Samara would switch the subject.

"Why?" His tone was low and suspicious. What did it matter why?

"Because I need to apologize for acting like a bitch towards her. I want to send her a gift." Even saying her name was making me sick. I wasn't sorry for anything I did to that whore. She deserved everything.

"Get the fuck out of here! You're lying your ass off! What's the real reason Shar?" Dwayne screamed through the phone. He was starting to sound like Ryson. They were so protective of that half breed. It was sickening.

"So you can apologize, but I can't?" My voice shrieked in annoyance.

"Shar, if you're lying, I swear man..." He threatened me. For real though?

"I'm not! Damn!" This shit was crazy. Where did she live, at the Pentagon? There was a long pause and then he gave me her address. I took a deep breath and sent out the text while I was still on the phone with him.

"Thank you. What's up with you anyway?" I hadn't talked to him in a few days.

"I'm cool Shar. That's all you wanted?" He was rushing me off the phone. The nerve of him! I couldn't wait for this shit to go down. Then both of them would be banging on my fucking door begging for forgiveness.

"Yeah that's it. I miss you," I told him hoping he would come over. He didn't say anything back.

"Did you hear what I just said Dwayne?" I heard the dial tone. That motherfucker!

DWAYNE

"AAAAAHHHHHH!" I finished my last rep of push-ups. I usually did five reps of fifty, but recently I was trying to amp it up. I had to look good for Samara. When we finally reunited, I had to be in tip-top shape so I could fuck the shit out of her. I picked up my towel and wiped sweat from my forehead, then I ran up the basement steps and locked the door. I didn't need Ryson walking in on me. I ran back down the stairs. I turned on my iPod to the song we danced to at the café. Our song. I settled onto my workout bench and pulled my dick out of my sweats. I had the black shirt I took from Samara's room in one hand, and her lip gloss in the other hand. I smeared the lip gloss on my upper lip under my nose. I breathed it in and my dick instantly became hard like it always did.

"Ah, Samara..." I whispered her name and spit on my hand. I grabbed my dick and started to jerk it slowly. I put her shirt up to my nose. It still smelled like her, even though there were over fifty cum stains on it. After I broke into Samara's house, Ryson started hanging around more. I couldn't go back as often as I'd liked. I even had to stop watching her sleep once they started fucking. I had to settle for fantasizing about her and watching her from Ms. Rosie's bedroom window. I thought about the first time I broke in. Her round plump ass just sitting in the air waiting for my dick to run up in it. I jerked my dick faster. I was sweating more now than I was after my workout. I licked my lips and tasted her lip gloss. I stuffed her shirt in my mouth and pulled hard on my dick until I was sure it would come out its socket.

"MMMMMMMM!" My screams were muffled as my nut poured out of my dick. I took the shirt out of my mouth and cleaned myself up with it.

"SHIT!" It was getting harder and harder to pretend. I wanted the real thing. I jumped in the shower and got dressed. I needed to make a stop at Ms. Rosie's house. After Ryson started going over Samara's house on a daily basis, I started parking a block away and walking to Ms. Rosie's house. I didn't want to push my luck. Ms. Rosie wasn't home. I heard her talking to somebody on the phone about visiting her grandkids for the week, so I was in the clear. I let myself into her house with my newly made key. I grabbed a bottle of water from her refrigerator and my binoculars I had hidden them in one of her cabinets. I made my way upstairs. It was almost eight o'clock at night, so I knew Samara would be in her room getting ready for her time with Ryson. It irked me that she went out of her way to primp just for him. She saw his ass almost every day. They barely even left the house! What was the fucking point? She came into view and I brought the binoculars to my eyes.

"Yeah! Take that shit off." She was undressing. She had on a pair of white shorts and a yellow tank top. She pulled the shirt over her head and unhooked her bra.

"Turn towards the window!" She turned slightly towards the window then stopped. She looked down at something on the floor and bent down to pick it up. I couldn't make out what it was before she walked out of the frame of the binoculars.

"Shit!" I felt my hand ball into a fist. It was like she was teasing me. I should just go over there before Ryson showed up. She was already undressed. If I ran over there now, I probably had about ten minutes before Ryson's Jeep pulled up. I remembered how her mouth dropped when she saw how big my dick was. I needed to remind her of what she was missing. I felt my dick hardening, poking against the windowsill, and stretching my jeans. I licked my lips and prepared myself to make a run for it. She came back into view, but she was wearing a robe. Ryson was trailing behind her like a fucking dog.

"FUCK!" There went my window of opportunity! I didn't even see his Jeep pull up. I watched Ryson open her robe, pick her up, and sit her on her dresser. My head was starting to throb. I closed my eyes and hoped what I saw was a mirage. It wasn't. I put the binoculars down when Ryson got on his knees and put his face in between her legs. I never felt so much hate towards my own brother in my whole life. What was Samara doing to me? Why was I tripping over her like this? I didn't love her did I?

Yes, you love Samara.

It had to be love, what else could it be? I walked away from the window and sat on the floor to watch the full moon shine through the window. I pulled out my picture of Samara and put it up to the light.

"My baby." I wanted her so bad. Why did I have to go and attack her? More than likely I fucked up any chance I had of getting her back after that. I kept trying to convince myself that after she forgave me I could get her back. But I had to face the facts. Samara was with Ryson now. I had to accept that.

No! Fuck that!

The voice was right! I had her first, so she was technically mines! Ryson was a backstabber for going after her. That wasn't part of the fucking game. He was supposed to fuck and forget. Instead he caught feelings for my girl, and now he was trying to keep her from me. I had to fight for Samara. She was worth it. I ran my tongue across the picture and put it down my pants. I grabbed my dick with the picture in my hand and started to jerk. The edges of the picture cut into my skin, but I didn't care. I kept going until I couldn't take it anymore.

"Ouch! OUCH!" I pulled the picture out of my pants. It was dripping with blood and nut. I got on my knees and picked my binoculars back up. I looked across the street and saw curtains. Ryson must have pulled them closed. Samara never closed her curtains. Even when she was naked in her room, her curtains were always wide open. I wasn't worried. I would see her in the flesh soon. Very soon.

SAMARA

"You talk a lot of shit I see." Ryson's voice echoed around the track. I stretched my legs and laughed at him.

"I don't talk shit, I talk the truth. And I *will* beat you around this track," I challenged him. We were stretching out on the local high school track. It was a warm afternoon so I decided to go for a run. Ryson showed up just as I was leaving out and invited himself along. He had his workout clothes in the trunk of his car. He was so humorous. I don't know who he was trying to fool, but I knew what was going on. He was falling for me and I was falling for him. The difference was, I wasn't afraid to tell Ryson how I felt. I wasn't going to tell him first of course, because he was being too dodgy about his feelings. I didn't see what was so hard about telling someone that you cared about them. I loved being with Ryson, more than I thought I would. When we made love it was like our bodies were meant for each other. When I was with him, I couldn't imagine myself being with anyone else. But I wasn't stupid. I knew that Ryson had left a trail of broken hearts around town. Ryson slept with those women and got bored. He would be on the prowl soon after for something new. But he didn't do that with me, which solidified what I knew he felt for me. He seemed genuinely interested in the things I said and he would open up to me about his life as well. I felt extremely close to him. I just wished he would stop being so stubborn and tell me how he felt for me.

"I don't know Samara. All that junk might slow you down," he joked, reaching over to smack my ass.

"That's real funny. We'll see. On your mark." We got into position.

"Get set. Go!" We both took off running like bats out of hell. I willed my legs to keep pushing harder and to go faster. The warm air whizzed by me as I ran as fast as I could. Ryson was fast, but not fast enough. I was a good distance in front of him, when I heard him yell out in pain.

"DAMMIT!" I stopped and looked back. Ryson was sitting on the track holding his ankle, his face twisted in pain. I rushed over to him, my heart beating fast.

"What's wrong? What happened?" I asked, looking at his ankle.

"I don't know. I was running then all of a sudden I..." He didn't finish his sentence.

"All of a sudden what?" I asked frantically. I didn't know if he'd sprained his ankle or something worse. He grabbed my arms and pulled me down onto the track.

"Boy! What are you doing? What about your ankle?" I asked when he climbed on top of me. What the hell was he up to?

"Don't worry about that." He leaned down and kissed me. I lay on the track, sweaty and out of breath. I felt his tongue in my mouth. I realized we were outside on a public track. If Ryson didn't care, neither did I.

"Sucker!" He abruptly stopped kissing me and took off running.

"What? You little...!" He played me. I scrambled to my feet and ran off after him. Of course, he beat me to the finish line.

"You cheated you jerk!" I glared at him. He bent over and put his hands on his knees to catch his breath.

"You need to keep your guard up." He laughed.

"Oh really?" I ran over to him. I jumped on his back, almost making us both topple over. He grabbed my thighs and righted himself. I put my arms around his neck and caught my breath.

"You want to race again?" he had the nerve to ask me.

"Hell no!" He started to crack up laughing. He walked with me on his back around the track.

"You're fast." Ryson commented, squeezing my thighs.

"I ran track in high school."

"Oh yeah? That's cool. I was more into contact sports like football and basketball."

"Were you any good?"

"I had a full scholarship to play basketball. But I got injured my sophomore year. After that, I just focused on my studies. I got my bachelor's degree in accounting, and here I am." There was no bitterness in his voice. He seemed satisfied with the way his life had turned out.

"So if you didn't get injured, you would have been a famous athlete huh?"

"Probably. But I was so arrogant back then, I wouldn't have made it in any league for long."

"Arrogant back *then*?" I joked.

"Very funny, yes back then. Trust me. I'm nothing like I was in college." He got quiet.

"You can put me down if I'm getting heavy you know," I told him. He was on lap two and he was still supporting my weight on his back.

"You're not heavy, plus I can feel your goodies on my back." I plucked him in the ear.

"You pervert! Ha-ha." I swung my feet and we walked in silence for a while. This was the part of our relationship that I enjoyed the most. When we could just take pleasure in each other's company without having to say anything. It was as if we had an unspoken bond. I kissed him in the crook of his neck. Things couldn't get any better. We stopped suddenly.

"As a matter of fact, you are getting kind of heavy." Ryson's words were rushed as he arched his back, forcing me to get down. What had changed in the last thirty seconds?

"Alright." I was confused. I got down and straightened my clothes.

"Yo! Ryson!" Devon was jogging towards us. I looked at Ryson. He refused to look at me. Oh really?

"What's up man?" Ryson folded his arms and took a step to the right. He was distancing himself from me like I was the plague. What the fuck? I was instantly insulted, but I remained calm and reserved.

"Nothing, just came out here to run off some donuts I ate earlier, ha-ha," Devon joked then turned to me. I smiled politely, even though inside I was heating up like a hot plate.

"What's up Samara?" He smiled at me. He leaned in and we hugged. I took a deep breath and decided to be cordial, even though I wasn't in a friendly mood.

"Hey Devon." Ryson was fronting on me. But why? I couldn't just stand here like an idiot. It was time for me to go.

"I have to go. It was nice to see you again Devon." I turned to Ryson and stood on my tiptoes in an attempt to get a kiss. He kept his eyes on Devon the whole time. I couldn't believe he was really playing me like this! My insides instantly started to burn. I literally had my lips poked out and everything! I patted him on the arm and walked off. What an asshole! How could I be so fucking stupid? Of course he could act lovey-dovey with me in private. There was no one around to see it. But when he got in front of his friends, he was the same old Ryson. The player. He dissed me like he didn't even know me. I was furious! I walked with my head held high off the track. As I was walking, I felt my phone vibrate in the pocket of my hoodie. It was Ryson. I pressed ignore and continued down the street. I wasn't into games. I liked Ryson, I really did, but I'll be damned if I let him disrespect me. At least I found out who he really was before I fell for him. I was lying to myself, I already fell in love with his ass. How could he play me like that? I refused to let a tear fall. Ryson drove us over to the track, so I didn't have my car. My house wasn't that far, but it was a good distance away. I trekked it home, half running, half speed walking. I walked into my house and felt my phone vibrate once again. I looked at my phone and saw that I had more missed calls from Ryson and a voicemail. I put in my pass code and listened.

RYSON

Shit! I saw Devon jogging towards me and Samara. I hadn't told anybody that I was still hanging with Samara, and I didn't want to answer any questions. I hated to do this to her, but I didn't have a choice.

"As a matter of fact, you are getting kind of heavy." I let her legs go so she could get down.

"Alright." I heard her say. I felt her eyes scorch a hole in the side of my face. I couldn't look at her. I folded my arms and took a step to the right, just as Devon ran up on us. He looked at Samara and then back at me. I could only imagine the gossip he was going to spread after seeing us together. I had to do something.

"I have to go, it was nice to see you again Devon." Samara said goodbye and turned towards me. She wanted a kiss but I couldn't do it. If I kissed her, Devon would go back and tell everybody. I didn't care about what other people thought, but I didn't want any rumors getting started. Samara and I were getting closer, but that wasn't anybody's business but ours. I would explain everything to her later. She patted me on the arm and walked off. Damn, I knew I was going to have to kiss ass hard tonight.

"You didn't have to do her like that Ryson, that was cold, ha-ha." Devon laughed and playfully punched me in the arm after Samara was out of earshot. I shrugged like it was nothing major.

"She'll be okay. I'm not with that PDA shit." I said trying to play it off. What I did was fucked up, I knew that.

"But that's your lady man."

"She's not my lady, we're just... hanging out that's all. I don't date and I don't have girlfriends. You should know that by now, ha-ha. I don't let no female put a leash on me."

"I know that's right!" We slapped palms.

"Well, let me get my fat ass around this track before I change my mind. I'll see you." Devon took off running again. I pulled out my phone to call Samara and realized that I had called her already. Her voicemail was recording me. I had my phone in my hoodie side pocket, so when I folded my arms my phone must have called the last number I dialed. It went directly to her voicemail, but the whole exchange between me and Devon had been recorded. Fuck! I tried to call six more times with no answer. I ran over to my Jeep and got in. She was walking home. I could catch her and talk to her about what just happened. I was deeply in love with Samara, but I couldn't let that shit be known. Made no sense, I know. I couldn't even tell Samara, how could I tell my boys? Not only was this whole love thing new to me, but I knew deep down that once I crossed that threshold there was no turning back. Once I admitted to people and to her that she was my girl, I would have to expose myself. I would have to tell her my secret. It would be over after that. I was trying to prolong that from happening. Maybe I shouldn't have played her like that, but I didn't have any other choice. It was either front or have my feelings and everything else put on Front Street. I decided to look out for myself. Samara would be okay. I hoped. I wouldn't forgive myself if she stopped fucking with me because of this. I couldn't blame her though. What I did was childish and hurtful. She must have run home, because I didn't see her the whole drive back to her house. She really was fast. I parked, ran up her steps, and rang her doorbell. She opened the door immediately and stepped aside to let me in. She didn't look mad. She actually looked pretty normal. That wasn't a good sign.

"I got your message," she said and closed the door. I was hoping she hadn't listened to it.

"Look Samara, I didn't mean any of that shit. I was just... you know, talking shit. That's what men do." I knew it was a crock of shit. She nodded her head in agreement, but I knew she didn't agree with me.

"I'm not trying to hear that shit Ryson. I don't want you to feel like I'm putting a *leash* on you, so you're free to go. You can leave right now. No hard feelings." She shrugged and opened the door again. She stared at me expectantly. Damn, she was done with me? I couldn't let that shit happen.

"I'm sorry for saying that. You know I don't think that about you. I was just trying to save face. I didn't want Devon all in our business. You know how I feel about you!" I pleaded with her.

"Why would you care if Devon knew about us or not? And I don't know how you feel about me because you've never told me." She arched her eyebrow and looked at the open door.

"I'm here. That should tell you everything," I told her, using the same words she said to me that day on her couch against her. I still couldn't bring myself to say it. She knew how I felt, so why was she trying so hard to get me to say it?

"I don't like subliminal messages Ryson. I'd rather hear the actual words. If you can't tell me how you feel about me, then you might as well forget that you have feelings for me at all." Samara opened the door wider and waited for me to leave. I was stuck. I opened my mouth to say something but nothing came out. She was right. If I couldn't tell her how I felt, what was the point of being there?

"Then you played the *shit* out of me in front of your boy! That was fucked up and embarrassing! I have never, and will never, stand for that shit! How dare you treat me like that after everything that's happened between us! You really don't give a fuck about me." She shook her head at me in disgust.

"I'm so stupid," she said to herself and swallowed. I walked to the door and looked at her. She turned away from me like I had done to her. Her face was devoid of emotion. I walked in the doorway ready to leave. Fuck that shit! I grabbed the doorknob from her hand and slammed the door closed, shocking Samara. She stood there looking at me like I was crazy. I wasn't leaving that easy. I hoped I didn't regret this shit.

"I'm giving you your freedom Ryson, just take the shit!" she shouted. Now she was mad. Good, at least that meant she still cared.

"No," I said calmly. I was mentally preparing myself for what I had to say. If I didn't say it now I would explode.

"Why? You don't date and you don't have girlfriends remember? Why are you here? You're so disrespectful! Just leave me alone!" Her face was flushed. Her eyes glistened and blazed with fire. She never looked more beautiful.

"I can't leave Samara," I reached for her but she pulled away.

"Why? Why can't you leave? Don't touch me!" She swatted my hands away.

"Because I... I..." I stuttered on the words. I took a breath and tried to start again.

"Because you what?" She threw her hands up in frustration.

"Because... I..." My voice trailed off.

"You know what? Just get the fuck out!" She reached for the doorknob again. I had to be a damn man and just let this shit out. It was tearing me up inside. I put my hand over hers on the doorknob.

"Ryson, just go. Please!" She whimpered and her chest heaved in and out. I knew at any minute she would start crying. Was trying to save face and keep a secret worth seeing her in pain like this?

"I can't leave Samara," I said gently. She shook her head violently, trying to shake the tears away.

"Yes you can Ryson, just walk through the damn door and---"

"I love you." I said it. Damn. I let out a breath I didn't know I was holding. I was afraid to look at her, but I did. She didn't say anything at first. She just stood there watching me. I guess she was trying to see if I was lying or not.

"Say it again," she whispered as a tear fell from her eye. I smiled because I knew I had her.

"I love you." It wasn't as hard the second time around. She sobbed and put her face in her hands.

"I love you, I love you, I love you, I love you." I said it over and over until it came naturally. I pulled her to me and held her while she cried in my arms.

"I'm sorry," I said and kissed the top of her head. She looked up at me with her tear soaked face.

"Was that so hard?" She laughed through her tears and wrapped her arms around me.

"If only you knew." I laughed with her.

"Don't ever disrespect me like that again Ryson, or I'm gone." Her tear soaked face was set in stone. I gulped. She was serious. If I did that again I had no doubt she would leave me, whether she loved me or not. She definitely wasn't into bullshit. Another reason why I loved her. I shook my head up and down acknowledging what she said. I held her closer to me. That was the hardest thing I'd ever had to do. With that said, I didn't know how I was going to break this secret to her.

SAMARA

He loved me. Wow. I was blown away. I thought maybe he cared about me, but I never imagined that he loved me. Now what was I going to do about it? I didn't know. I felt like I was walking on air. I loved Ryson too, but I didn't want to tell him first. He seemed to have a hard time expressing his feelings for me. I was waiting for him to come around before I put my cards on the table. Ryson already knew how I felt about him anyway, but it was almost magical knowing that he felt the same way. Ryson was flawed, but he was my diamond in the rough. I knew our relationship would have its ups and downs from the beginning. But we both stuck in there, and now we were in love. It was so worth it! I had to tell somebody. I called up my girlfriend Sandra and asked her to come over to my house.

"I thought you dropped off the face of the planet. I haven't heard from you in a month of Sundays!" Sandra's southern accent was so funny. I couldn't help but laugh at it.

"I'm sorry girl. I've been busy. I met somebody." I played with my hair, waiting for the scream I knew would come.

"Aaaaahhhhh! Really? Who is he? What's his name?" She threw questions at me. I laughed and told her I would tell her everything the next time I saw her.

"I'm free now. Let me call Anna and Tatyana. They miss your big booty too." We both laughed and I said okay. I hung up and went into the kitchen to find some wine and appetizers. I pulled out a few glasses and cut up some fruit. I put crackers, cheese, and some chocolates on a tray and set all of it on the coffee table in the living room. I already talked to

Ryson, so I knew he was working overtime tonight. I wouldn't see him until tomorrow, so tonight it was just me and my girls. My bell rang an hour later.

"Wow! Anna look at you!" I pulled Anna in for a hug. Anna was the brains of our clique. She was tall as hell and lighter than me. Her hair was cut short and she was showing off her recent weight loss with a skintight purple mini dress.

"Yeah I know I look good right? Ha-ha." She walked past me and went straight for the wine.

"What about me?" Tatyana stepped up. She put her hands on her hips and pouted. She was the beauty of the group. People often mistook her for Naomi Campbell. She wasn't as tall and her cheekbones weren't as defined, but there definitely was a resemblance. She had on a leopard print romper with sky high red heels. Her make-up was on point as usual. Her long, straight, light brown hair weave was immaculate.

"Girl, you know you always look good. You don't need me to tell you that." We hugged and rocked from side to side. And last but not least, Sandra stepped in. She was the sweetheart. If it wasn't obvious enough yet, I was the smartass of the group. Sandra with her glasses and chubby face was the baby. She was only twenty-five, but she was one of my best friends. Her southern upbringing also made her the sweetest. She stepped in wearing a pair of blue jean shorts and a pink tank top. She had flip-flops on her feet.

"Hello darlin'," she said and kissed me on the cheek, before pulling me to her for a hug.

"Come in, come in! Oh my goodness I missed you heifers like crazy!" I plopped down on my couch in the middle of Anna and Sandra. Tatyana sat on the coffee table and nibbled on the chocolates.

"So Sandra told us you're fucking some actor type dude," Anna said and picked up her wine glass. Everyone started cracking up. Sandra probably did tell her some craziness like that too.

"What! I did not tell you that. I didn't tell you anything girl." I shook my head at the craziness.

"Well tell us then! My life is so boring! I need something juicy to get me through the day," Tatyana said and crossed her legs. Tatyana had sworn off men last year and was having a hard time getting used to a no dick diet.

"Well, he's an accountant," I started.

"Oooh, so he has a J-O-B?" Sandra chimed in.

"But does he have a big D-I-C-K?" Anna slurred. She was already tipsy.

"Wow! I'm not answering that question! Fuck it, yes he does!" We all squealed in delight and high fived each other. I missed my girls. There was something about talking and laughing with a room full of your girlfriends. It was one of the best feelings in the world, besides having an orgasm.

"What's his name?" Tatyana asked. That was the part I really didn't want to divulge. I didn't know if any of them had slept with Ryson. I wasn't calling him a man whore, but he obviously got around. It was a small damn town. It was amazing I never ran into him before that day. I chanced it and told them anyway.

"Ryson Turner." They all exchanged uncomfortable glances at each other. They knew him. Damn.

"Don't tell me one of you fucked him?" I asked, hoping it wasn't true. It would be so weird knowing one of my girlfriends had screwed my boyfriend. Sandra averted her eyes. Dead giveaway.

"I'm not going to get mad Sandra. We just started dating like six months ago. I don't have a right to be mad about anything before that. It wasn't after that, right?" She shook her head no fast and hard.

"Okay, well just tell me then." I wanted to know badly. I couldn't imagine Ryson with another woman. I scratched behind my ear to keep my hands busy. I looked at Sandra and saw how Ryson could be attracted to her. She had a sweet, innocent face and plump lips. She was short and thick, which I knew was Ryson's type. She was soft-spoken, and her glasses made her seem even more innocent. I was jealous. It was ridiculous, but I couldn't control it. Ryson had slept with one of my best friends. Now I understood how he felt about me being with Dwayne.

"Well, technically we didn't 'sleep' together. After it was over he nicely kicked me out," she said embarrassed. The Ryson I knew would never do that.

"Really? Damn that's fucked up!" Anna said and burped. We all looked over at her drunk ass and shook our heads.

"Tell me about it?" I asked her, referring to the sex. I could see it made her uncomfortable to talk about it, but I had to know.

"Um... we met him and his brother at a bar."

"We?" I asked out of curiosity.

"Yeah, me and Anna." Oh great! Now two of my friends have slept with the same men as me. This town was too fucking small.

"Oh yeah, we did. I forgot all about that night," Anna said and giggled.

"Oh okay, go ahead." I didn't really want to know now, but I was too far in to stop.

"They started flirting really hard with us. Anna was already tipsy, so Dwayne didn't have to do much to convince her to go home with him. But I didn't want to seem easy, so I tried to play it off like I wasn't interested. But Ryson was so good looking and charming. I gave in. We went back to their house. I went in Ryson's room and Anna went in Dwayne's room." Sandra stopped talking and looked at me for approval to continue. I nodded eagerly.

"We started touching and then one thing led to another. Then we were having sex." She shrugged as if to say, 'that's it'. I needed to know more.

"How was it?" I asked, not blinking. I didn't know why I wanted to know.

"The sex? It was good, really good. I mean there wasn't really any foreplay, but I got off, so I didn't care that much. Both times we had sex it was... doggy style." She blushed.

"He didn't want to do it missionary. That bothered me a little bit, but other than that it was pretty good. Afterwards, he told me he had work early the next morning. I got the hint. He walked me downstairs, gave me a hug, and off I went. Anna didn't call me until like two hours later, screaming in my ear about how Dwayne kicked her out afterwards too. It wasn't really memorable for the sex. I mostly remember feeling used. I mean he did pick me up in a bar, so what could I expect right? Sorry." She apologized and looked at me sadly. I felt embarrassed too. I felt all of their eyes on me. How could Ryson do that? The man of my dreams. How could he treat her like a piece of meat? He was so different now, I couldn't imagine him being such an ass. I expected that from Dwayne, but not him. But sadly, Sandra's story could have been my story. I met Ryson and Dwayne in a similar way.

"You don't have to be sorry. That was a shitty thing for them to do. But he's not like that anymore. I'm not just saying that because he's my man. You know I am the first person to call out a dog when I see one." They all nodded in agreement.

"I'm over it anyway," Sandra said and picked up her glass for the first time.

"If Samara is dating him, he must be a changed man, because she doesn't take shit from anybody," Tatyana said. We all clinked glasses to that. It was true. I had zero tolerance for a dog or a player.

"In that case, all is forgiven," Sandra joked. I smiled, glad that all of that was settled. I didn't want them to have the wrong perception of my Ryson.

"Speaking of men. This guy I know is throwing a birthday party for one of his boys in a couple weeks. We're all going, you in?" Tatyana turned her attention on me.

"Uh... I don't know. I have to see if Ryson has plans for us or not. I'll let you know. But what's up with you guys. I know you have the scoop on all the dirt and drama going on in town." I picked up my glass, and for the next few hours we reminisced and dished dirt. I really needed this. I was spending so much time with Ryson, I forgot I had a life and friends too. They left around eleven that night. I tried to push it out of my head, but I couldn't. Ryson had slept with Sandra. Dwayne had slept with Anna. It was so hard to grasp. First I found out about Shar, and now Sandra. I had my share of partners, but I always left them in my past. It seemed like Ryson's exes were showing up everywhere. I didn't think I could handle any more surprises from his past.

RYSON

"I know you're coming to my birthday party." Devon was sitting in my living room watching ESPN. It had been two weeks since I told Samara that I loved her. The only thing that was on my mind right now was Samara. I couldn't concentrate on the TV or what Devon was saying. I actually told a female that I loved her. What was I thinking? I knew that owning up to my feelings was part of being a man, but I was regretting it. Don't get me wrong, I was madly in love with Samara. But now that she knew, she would expect certain things to change. Like us going out together in public. Or both of us hanging out around my friends. I thought admitting my feelings were hard, but that would be much harder. I wasn't ready for the backlash I would get from my homies about Samara. Everybody knew that I was a player. Since high school, I'd had that reputation. I took pride in it. Kind of. I knew that I was too old for that shit now, but it still felt good to have that title. My boys looked up to me and Dwayne. We always had the baddest chicks on our arms and in our beds. Now I was the average Joe with a steady girlfriend. I didn't want to lose that adulation.

No, let me tell the truth and stop bullshitting myself. It wasn't my boys I was worried about. It was myself. I never had a relationship that lasted as long as this one. I had never been in love before, and I had definitely never enjoyed being with a woman as much as I enjoyed being with Samara. My punk ass was afraid of all these new feelings. I wasn't used to feeling this way about someone. It was scary as shit. I didn't want to fuck it up. Samara deserved a man who could hold her down and take care of business, in and out of the bedroom. I didn't think I was capable of being that man. She was so sure of herself and everything, but I wasn't. I secretly felt that all of this shit was a dream. That I would wake up one morning next to a random girl I had just fucked. Fear of losing Samara was eating away at me. She was too good for me and I knew it.

"Yeah. I might stop through. I don't know," I replied absently. Devon chuckled and turned towards me.

"What's on your mind man? You've been quiet as a mouse since I got here. What's up?" I shook my head. I really didn't want to talk about it. But knowing Devon, he wouldn't let it go that easily.

"It's Samara, right?" My eyes flew to his face in surprise. How the fuck did he know? He smirked and shook his head at me.

"No, it's not about her. Not really," I half lied.

"Yes it is man. Why do you keep trying to convince yourself that she's not your girl? I saw y'all remember? Twice. She's funny, pretty, and sexy as fuck man. And the body? Damn! Everybody, including me to be honest, was at your party taking a peek, wanting to get at her. What's the problem?" Devon asked me confused. It irked me to hear him saying those things about Samara. I didn't want him, or anyone else, looking at her and thinking she was sexy. Dammit! Was this how a jealous boyfriend was? Was I turning into one? He asked me what the problem was, like it was that fucking simple. People didn't understand the dynamics of my relationship with Samara. They never would. It was more complicated than anyone would ever know.

"I'm not saying she's my girl but she's... she's somebody that's in my life. And it's not a problem. I just have a lot of shit on my mind that's all. Let's talk about something else like... this party." I switched subjects quick. I still wasn't ready to tell Devon Samara was my girl. I know it was messed up to play house in private, but deny her in public. It would bite me in the ass once again but I just... I didn't know what was wrong with me.

"I'm turning the big three-five on Saturday. I rented out a place for a few hours. It's BYOB, free food, karaoke, and lots of ladies coming through." Devon's eyes shined just thinking about his party. Maybe I needed to go to his party. I could clear my head and have some fun. I was so stressed out lately worrying about what to do about Samara, I needed a reprieve.

"I'll be there man."

"Good. Now how are your picks looking in Fantasy football?" I was glad for the subject change. I needed to get my shit together before I lost Samara all together.

It was Saturday. Samara straddled me on her couch.

"I thought you couldn't go another round," she said, running her tongue along my lips. I was exhausted. We made love three times in the last two and a half hours. I grabbed her ass and buried my face in her breasts.

"I was wrong obviously, but I definitely can't go again." Her lavender scent tickled my nose. She wrapped her hands around my head and kissed me lightly on the lips.

"Okay, you can make it up to me later on tonight." She smiled and got up. She stood naked in front of me and stretched. My dick got hard again. I put one of her throw pillows over it to hide it. If she saw it, she would never let me leave. I wanted nothing more than to be inside her again, but I couldn't tonight. I had to get to Devon's party.

"Uh… I have plans tonight babe," I started slowly. I hadn't told her anything about the party yet, mainly because I wasn't planning on taking her with me.

"Really? What?" She picked up my shirt and put it on. I don't know how it was possible that she looked better in my clothes than in her own.

"One of my boys is having a birthday party. I told him I would come through for a little bit." I watched her face. She crinkled her eyebrows and looked at me funny. Here it comes.

"Is it just going to be your boys or is it an actual party?" I knew that question was coming.

"It's an actual party." I swallowed hard because I knew the next question she was going to ask me.

"Hmmm… okay." She bobbed her head up and down. That was it? I wasn't expecting that. She smirked and walked into the kitchen. Was it really going to be that easy? Oh well, I wasn't going to look a gift horse in the mouth. I ran upstairs and jumped in the shower. I was a little taken aback by Samara. She didn't ask me why she couldn't go with me. Maybe she wasn't worried about it. Samara was cool like that. Or maybe she saw right through me and knew I wasn't trying to bring her around my friends. Samara didn't play that shit, so if she suspected that, why didn't she say anything? Now I was worried. I went in Samara's closet to my side of it, and picked out something to wear. I dressed comfortably in a pair of dark denim jeans and a light blue t-shirt. I put on my black boots and one of my watches. I slipped on my leather jacket and brushed my hair. I walked cautiously down the steps and into the kitchen. She was at the sink cleaning the dishes. She didn't look back at me, although she had to have heard me come down the steps. I took a breath and walked over to her.

"I'm leaving now baby. I'll call you later." I kissed her on the cheek. She didn't respond at first, which made me even more paranoid.

"Have fun." She kept her eyes on the dirty dishes. I wanted to ask her what was wrong, but I already knew. I decided to leave while the getting was good.

The venue was packed and jumping with activity. They had the tables scattered around the edges of the room, leaving open space for dancing. There wasn't an official bar. They had set up a table where people could leave whatever liquor they brought. They had two waiters standing by the table ready to serve the liquor, and take food orders. I stepped in and instantly spotted Devon, my other childhood friend Rob, and a few other guys I knew. Everyone, except Devon, had a girl with them.

"Yo! What's up man! We were just talking about your ass!" Rob yelled over the music. It wasn't a huge space, so when it was crowded, it was shoulder to shoulder. And tonight, it was shoulder to shoulder. The music was blaring from the speakers. Drinks were being tossed back and the ladies were out in packs. It felt like old times, except I wasn't interested in any of the females in here. I decided to leave all thoughts of Samara back where I left her, so I could have fun and clear my head. I needed it. I walked up and slapped palms with everybody.

"Talking about what?" I looked over at Devon, hoping he hadn't opened up his big mouth about Samara. He gulped down a shot of vodka and looked away from me.

"Nobody has seen or heard from you but Devon. We thought you were dead!" Jim, one of Devon's cousins, chimed in. He was almost as tall as Devon, but was thin as a rail. We all thought he was on that shit, but we kept it to ourselves. They all laughed at that and started making jokes that I was hibernating.

"Ryson was probably knee deep in some pussy. You know he always got a dime piece stashed somewhere." Rob joked making everyone laughed. Except me and Devon. Some of their girlfriends gave me the side eye. I was glad I didn't recognize any of them. I wasn't trying to get into any of that shit tonight. I just wanted to relax and not think about women at all. It didn't look like that was going to happen.

"It's my job man. For the last few months we've been doing audits and shit. I've been doing a lot of overtime. That's all. Just trying to make this money," I said hoping they would leave it at that. They nodded in agreement and changed the subject. Everyone started bringing me up to speed with what was going on in their lives. I started to actually relax. I smelled Buffalo wings and felt my stomach growling.

"What are they serving Devon?" I yelled across the table at him.

"Wings and the usual bar food shit. Just order it, all the food is included with the party." He took another shot. He was going to be fucked up tomorrow. I got up from the table and walked over to where the makeshift bar was. I got three orders of wings, some fries, and a pitcher of beer. I waited, then took it all back to the table. I was walking back to the bar to get some napkins, when I spotted four females walking in. Two of them looked vaguely familiar, but I instantly recognized one. It was Samara!

"Shit!" I tried to scamper back over to my table, but she caught me. Our eyes locked for a good five seconds before she looked away. Her face registered recognition, then shock, then rage. I was going to hear this shit tonight. Fuck! I speed walked back over to the table sweating bullets, my heart beating out of my chest. I was scared as shit. I looked over my shoulder to see if she was making her way over to where I was, but she continued walking towards the makeshift bar. She didn't look my way. If I knew Samara, she was going to act like everything was cool until we were alone. I had a sinking feeling. I picked up a wing and shoved it in my mouth. The burning of the sauce didn't compare to the burning in my chest. She would leave me for sure after this. I put her through too much shit already. Between my insecurities and my resistance to let her know how I felt about her, enough was enough.

"What's wrong with you?" I heard Rob asked me. I felt like something sour was in my mouth and I wanted to cry. I felt fucked up inside. It was just my luck that she would come to the same fucking party I did. This small ass fucking town! So much for trying to relax, I was tenser than ever.

"Nothing, these wings are hot as shit." I put another one in my mouth and poured myself a cup of beer.

SAMARA

Ryson grabbed my ass and kissed my breasts. His lips sent a shiver down my back. I straddled him and kissed him on the lips. Round three was done and I was ready for round four. I couldn't get enough of Ryson. It seemed like he knew my body better than I did.

"Uh… I have plans tonight babe," he said a little hesitant. He hadn't told me about any plans. Ryson was hiding something. I knew him too well not to notice the subtle changes in his tone and demeanor.

"Really? What?" I picked up his shirt and put it on. He had already established we were done for the night. I looked over at him waiting for his answer. He looked nervous. He was definitely trying to hide something. This was the side of Ryson I didn't like. The Ryson that hid things from me. He was either going somewhere he had no business going, or somewhere he didn't want to take me. He thought that I didn't notice we never went anywhere besides my house and the park. I knew Ryson still didn't want his friends to know about me. I accepted it for now because I knew I shouldn't push him. I could only imagine how hard it was for him to admit he loved me. I couldn't expect him to suddenly introduce me to all of his friends yet. I was being patient, but he was making it very hard.

"One of my boys is having a birthday party. I told him I would come through for a little bit." I crinkled my eyebrows. So he was going to a party? Hmmm.

"Is it just going to be your boys or is it an actual party?" I asked, a little confused at his behavior. I didn't see what the secrecy was about.

"It's an actual party." Wow. I guess I wasn't on the guest list! As his woman, he should be inviting me instead of excluding me! I felt like the incident at the track had taught him nothing. I wasn't going to let my emotions get the best of me.

"Hmmm... okay." I said, acting nonchalant. I walked into the kitchen over to the sink. I turned the water on and began to fill the sink to wash the dishes. I was sweltering on the inside. I aggressively scrubbed dinner off the plates. How fucking dare he not invite me to this party! Why was he still acting like telling people would be the end of the world? Was loving me that bad? His problem was he didn't want his friends to clown him for having a girlfriend, I wasn't a fool. Ryson was a player, and had probably been one since he lost his virginity. That's all his friends saw him as. If he suddenly showed up with me on his arm, eyebrows would raise and assumptions would be made. Ryson was so caught up in appearances, he failed to see what was right in front of him. I did not like bullshit, nor did I tolerate it. If Ryson didn't get his shit together, I would have to do what I didn't want to do. I would give him tonight to reflect on what he did, but tomorrow, I would have a serious talk with him. I loved him, but I loved myself more. There were plenty of men out there who would love to claim me as theirs. Why was it that the only man I loved found it so hard to do that? I heard him come down the steps and into the kitchen.

"I'm leaving now baby. I'll call you later." He kissed me on the cheek. If he didn't man up, that just might be our last kiss. I decided not to ruin his night. Like I said, tomorrow I would talk to him about his behavior.

"Have fun." I kept my eyes on the dishes. If I looked at him there was no doubt I would want to curse him out. But that wasn't my style. So I let him leave. Now I was home alone washing fucking dishes. I finished and sat on the couch thinking about what to do. What if talking didn't get through to him? Was I really ready to just leave him over this? No, I had to admit I wasn't. But I also wasn't willing to hide in the shadows forever. I needed to do something to get my mind off of Ryson. I texted Sandra to see what she was doing.

What's on the agenda 2nite?

She texted me back instantly.

Birthday party remember? U R coming no ifs ands or buts, b ready in 30!

I had totally forgotten about the party they invited me to. I wasn't in the party mood, but I couldn't just sit in the house either. If Ryson could go out without me and have fun, then I could do the same to him. I ran upstairs and looked through my closet for something to wear. I felt like wearing something flashy and sexy. Ryson didn't know what he had. I could have any man I chose eating out of the palm of my hand. Why was I trying so hard with him? Because I loved him, I reasoned. Love fucking sucked! I saw a dress in the back of the closet that I only wore in case of emergencies. I called it my Honey dress, because it attracted men like honey attracted bees. I only wore it when I was extremely horny. I usually ended up with every man's attention wherever I went in that dress. The dress was hot pink, with spaghetti straps, and a low cut neckline. But the part that brought the men to my feet, was the back of the dress. The dress was crossed like an X. It exposed my back all the way down to just above the crack of my ass. It gave the illusion that I wasn't wearing any panties. Having an ass like mine didn't hurt either. I slipped my feet into a pair of five inch nude stiletto heels, and blew my hair out some. I heard a horn beep outside and ran to my bedroom window.

"Hurry up skeez!" Anna yelled out the driver's side window of her red Ford Focus. I laughed and shook my head.

"I'm coming hooker!" I yelled back and closed my window. I put on my charm bracelet and checked myself in the mirror. I came out to hoots and hollers from the girls.

"Shut up and drive!" I joked and got in the back seat with Tatyana. The car smelled like citrus. I tried to put on a brave face but I was feeling so hurt. Why couldn't Ryson get over his self-doubts and stop hiding? I shook my head and vowed to only think about partying tonight.

"What's up chica? You ready to party tonight?" Tatyana asked me, fixing her make-up.

"More than ready." I put my seat belt on. She had on a short red mini dress with spiked black heels. I didn't know how she walked around with those things on.

"Where's your man tonight?" Anna asked me at the light. Ugh.

"He's out with his boys," I said hoping that would suffice. I could see Anna really loved her new shape. She had on a pair of skintight jeans and a halter top. With her double D's almost spilling out, she was sure to grab almost as much attention as me. Sandra sat quietly in the front, sporting a spandex dress. It was cream colored and long-sleeved. It came to her knees. It was form-fitting and blended with her complexion beautifully. I had come to terms with the fact that she slept with Ryson. I was over it. It happened and it was over. She was still my friend and Ryson was still my man, at least for now. We pulled up to a venue I'd never been to before. There was a line to get in, which was unusual. The party must have been jumping. They were blasting a Jay-Z and Kanye West track, and bodies were everywhere. The placed smelled of sweat and food. I already knew it would be hard to get a table. There were so many people here.

"Damn! Devon sure knows how to throw a party!" Tatyana screamed over the music. My ears went on alert. We made our way into the venue, bumping into people the whole way.

"Did you say Devon?" I couldn't have heard her right. This was Devon's party? Of course there was more than one Devon in this town, but what were the odds this was the Devon I knew?

"Yeah, you know him?" she asked, scanning the room.

"Maybe." No sooner had that comment left my mouth, then my eyes landed on Ryson. At first, I was shocked to see him there. When that passed, I was irate. I was beyond angry. He looked caught and guilty. I wasn't going to be played like a fool again, especially in front of my girls. I turned my attention to the center of the room, where they had a makeshift bar set up. Hopefully none of them recognized Ryson and pointed out the fact he was here without me. I felt my hands shaking. Inside I wanted to cry. It was déjà vu all over again. This time I wouldn't be the bigger person and accept some 'I love you' bullshit and let it go. This time I was done. I considered myself single from that point on.

"Can I get an apple martini?" I yelled over the music to the waitress. There was a mountain of liquor on the table, and I knew they could wrestle me up anything I ordered. The girls and I stood at the make-shift bar, sipping our drinks, looking over the party. I made it a point not to look over in Ryson's direction. It wasn't long before the men started flocking towards us.

"Damn! You ladies are looking good! Can I interest you in a dance?" A sleazy looking guy walked up to us. He kept licking his lips. I didn't pay him any mind, but Sandra and Anna started chatting him up. I kept sipping my drink, hoping it would calm my nerves. Back to back, men came at us and offered to dance with us. None of them were my type. Ryson was my type. Fuck this shit! I didn't take bullshit like this sitting down. I was handling this shit now! I looked over at Devon's table and Ryson was watching me like I knew he would be. I shot a look his way and then excused myself. I pushed through the crowd of people, as I tried to make my way to where the bathrooms were. We were going to hash this shit out now! As soon as I hit the hallway leading to the bathroom, I could smell Ryson's cologne. I turned on him and stopped. His face was apologetic, but I wasn't in the forgiving mood. I wasn't in the mood for any of this shit.

"What the fuck is wrong with you? You're doing this shit to me again, really?" I decided not to pussy foot around my anger. I crossed my arms and narrowed my eyes. He shifted his weight to his other foot and looked down at the ground like a scolded child. That was exactly what he was acting like, a child.

"Babe, just let me explain alright." He looked at me. His eyes were watering. He looked so sad I felt my anger slipping away from me. I shook my head and brought that anger right back.

"Explain what? That you're here at Devon's party? A party you didn't invite me to. Even though I'm your girl and we both know Devon? Oh, and looks like your friends brought *their* girls with them. Please Ryson, explain to me how that shit is okay." I felt my cheeks getting hot and I knew my face was pink. I've never been so full of fury. I wanted to kick his ass!

"Tonight was just supposed to be about me chilling with my boys. I didn't know it was going to be this big of a party or that they were bringing dates." His lame excuse went in one ear and out the other.

"Who do you think you're talking to? I'm not one of these dumb ass tricks in here that you're used to lying to! Stop trying to play me like I'm dumb! You didn't want me to come to this fucking party, because you didn't want your boys to know you were fucking with me!" I wanted nothing more than to kick him in the nuts for thinking I was stupid enough to believe that excuse. He rolled his eyes like he was annoyed, but he didn't say anything. I was tired of being the angry one. For what? Where was it getting me? People pushed past us trying to get to the bathrooms.

"You're tripping. I'm not even worried about that shit." He shifted his gaze. He was so fucking guilty I could smell it.

"You're a bad liar Ryson. Since you're not concerned about that, introduce me to your friends right now!" I demanded through clenched teeth. I was so heated I could have boiled an egg on my forehead. His head snapped back in shock. He opened his mouth to say something, but got stuck.

"They're all chilling over there. Why are you trying to bring drama to the table Samara? This is none of their business. Let's go outside and talk baby, okay?" His lips moved, but I wasn't listening to what he had to say. I felt like a complete dunce.

"So your answer to me asking you to introduce me to your friends is, no it's none of their business? So it makes perfect sense to you to never introduce the woman you supposedly 'love' to your friends? Is that what you're trying to say Ryson?" I chuckled a little bit to myself, even though none of this shit was funny. He had a stupid look on his face. He knew his answer was bullshit. It was the most idiotic thing I ever heard coming out of an educated person's mouth. How the fuck did he justify that way of thinking? Once again, I was trying to convince him to let me in, and once again he was shutting me out. Fuck it! I gave up. I ran my fingers through my hair.

"You know what Ryson? I don't care anymore. Go back to the table with your boys, and I will go back over there with my girls. Tomorrow, you can come get your shit from my house. Then I want you to leave me alone altogether! You have too much shit with you. Every time I turn around it's another damn problem. You just fucked up the only real relationship you've ever had, and no one's to blame but you! I'm done!" I pushed him out of my way and started for the bar. I felt him grab my arm, but I yanked it away. I wasn't trying to hear anything else from his ass. I was halfway to the bar when I felt him grab me again, but this time his grip was firm. I turned around and faced him. We were smack dab in the middle of a crowd of people dancing to a Nicki Minaj track. He kept my arm in his grasp. I looked up at him and for the first time felt like he would never change. He would never be a man and own up to his feelings, or tell his friends about our relationship. I was ready to move on. It would hurt, it would probably shatter everything within me, but I would move on. His eyes penetrated mines, as he tried to make me understand him without speaking. I couldn't anymore. I was done trying to comprehend him. He looked reluctant to do so, but he let me go. I turned away from him and walked back to the bar. I touched the corner of my eye and wiped away the tear before it could fall, before he could see it. Only Anna was still there sipping on a Long Island iced tea.

"Those bitches on the dance floor left me up here by myself. Was that Ryson I saw you talking to?" Anna's speech was slurred, so I knew she was drunk. I ignored her and took a deep breath. I ordered another drink. I spotted Sandra and Tatyana dancing with one of the guys who had asked earlier. They looked happy and carefree. Maybe being single was the way to be. My head started to throb. I just wanted to go home.

"Anybody have any well wishes for the birthday boy?" A tall thin man asked the crowd over the microphone. He was standing on a table unsteady, his body tilting to one side. I heard somebody yell, "Sit your drunk ass down Jim!"

"Happy birthday Devon, with your fat ass!" Everyone, including Devon, laughed at Jim. Then Devon got up and helped him down off the table. Next a petite, dark-skinned woman got on the table and wished Devon a happy birthday. It went on like that for another five minutes or so. My head was pounding so badly now, I could barely see straight. The three martinis' that I'd had probably didn't help either.

"I'm going to call a cab. I'm out babe." I kissed Anna on the cheek and told her to say bye to the girls for me. She nodded, and I started to make my way through the crowd. I had to stop every couple of seconds to get my bearings. I was really feeling the effects of the liquor.

"Happy Birthday Devon. I hope you get everything you wish for." I heard Ryson's voice on the microphone. I turned towards him and shook my head at what could have been. I continued on stumbling and bumping into people, as I tried to reach the exit.

"Hey! Cut the music real quick. Sorry for spoiling the party mood, but I have to say this. I had everything I wished for, but I fucked it up. I didn't want to admit that somebody finally tamed my wild ass. Somebody finally made me feel something. That somebody took my player's card and ripped that shit up, ha-ha." The crowd erupted into laughter. I stopped just short of the exit door. It could have been the liquor, but it seemed like Ryson was about to do what he seemed to be incapable of doing. I tried to clear my head. I looked towards him.

"Everybody, I would like to introduce… my GIRLFRIEND! Samara Laida Cipriano. She's that sexy ass woman in hot pink standing by the exit. She's ready to leave my dumb ass. I don't care what anybody fucking thinks anymore. I love you Samara! I'm going to be that man you need me to be! I'm going to stop playing these childish games, and admit my feelings for you in front of anybody that will fucking listen! You got me up here pouring my soul out and shit. It's hot as shit up here too, ha-ha." The crowd laughed again. I didn't. I held my breath. "But all jokes aside, I was scared baby. I have never met anyone like you. One day I woke up and I was in love with you and it took me completely by surprise. I've never been in love before and I didn't know how to cope with it. Instead of trying to deal with it, I pushed you away. I'm sorry. Don't leave me baby please, I'm begging you. I'm putting my pride aside and my so called reputation. I need you and I don't want to lose you. Please forgive me." All eyes were on me. The room fell silent. Seconds ticked by like an eternity. The ball was in my court now. Shit. This time I didn't wipe the tears away. I stood frozen where I was, unsure of how to respond. He had just done the only thing I ever wanted him to do. And he did it in front of all of his friends and mines. My heart exploded with love for him. I bit my bottom lip to keep it from trembling, but I couldn't move. He got down from the table and made his way through the crowd to me. Everyone parted to let him through. It was dead silent as everyone watched us. My heart raced at the sight of him approaching me. He stood before me with regret written all over his face. I looked up at him, my mascara running down my face.

"I love you Samara," he whispered to me. I closed my eyes to savor this moment. I felt his warm lips on mine. I opened my mouth and slipped my tongue inside of his. The party went crazy after that. People were yelling, "Get a room!" and others were yelling, "That's so sweet!" I heard Devon yell out, "THAT'S RIGHT MAN! GET YOUR GIRL!" We stood there kissing. After a while, the music came back on and the party resumed. We were still kissing when the party shut down an hour later.

SHAR

"I thought you said Ryson was your man." Deidre had been blowing up my phone with calls and texts for the last hour. She worked at the same restaurant as me. We recently started hanging out, but I was starting to regret that shit now. I was waiting for those motherfuckers to call me back. I didn't know what the fucking hold up was. I gave them that bitch's address weeks ago, what the fuck? I was already jittery over this shit, now Deidre was on my phone making my headache worse.

"He is my man. What the fuck are you talking about?" I didn't have time for her right now. If I got a text or my other line rang, I was hanging up.

"Well, he was at Devon's party Saturday, professing his love for some chick named Sanana or some shit like that."

"SAMARA?" I yelled into the phone.

"YEAH! That was it. She had on this cute pink dress that had the back cut out. Oh, and her shoes---"

"Deidre! I don't care about what that bitch had on! What was he saying?" I couldn't breathe. It couldn't be true. Ryson would never tell a female he loved her, not even to get some pussy. He never even told *me* he loved me. Deidre must have heard that shit wrong.

"Well, he said a lot of shit. But what I remember the most was, when he said he woke up one day and realized he was in love with her. It was so sweet. Everybody went wild when they started kissing too. It was so romantic," she rambled on. I squeezed my cell phone so hard, the back cover came off and the battery fell out.

"THAT BITCH!" I screamed and scrambled to pick up the pieces to my phone. How could Ryson do that to me? I deserved more than getting fucked and tossed aside, like I was one of those desperate ass women he was used to fucking. I loved him and he loved me. At least I thought he did. I knew that he and Samara were getting closer, but love? I felt so betrayed.

He never professed his love for me and I had been there for him for more than four years. He just met Samara like six months ago and she was getting all of him? I closed my eyes and told myself not to cry. That wouldn't get me anywhere. I sat on the couch and thought of a solution to this new problem. I put my head in my hands and prayed for an answer. As if on cue, an idea popped into my head.

"No. I can't." What I had in mind would change the game completely. If I did this, Ryson would never respect me again. I would have him to myself, but he would hate me in the process and so would Dwayne. Samara was forcing me to sink to a new low. I will be fucking damned if she got a fucking happy ending, while I sat alone in my small shitty ass apartment forever! Fuck it. I was following through with it. First I needed to know what was going on with these fucking guys. Now I felt like I was getting taken for a ride. How long did it take to do one simple thing? As soon as my battery was back inside my phone, it vibrated.

FRIDAY

That's all the text said. I knew exactly what it meant. So I had until then to get Ryson back. That left me with four days. I had work to do.

DWAYNE

I watched Samara. She had tried on at least four outfits in the last ten minutes. She kept posing in the mirror, checking herself out, then shaking her head and changing. It was Monday morning and I was late for work. I had three house calls that day before eleven, but I couldn't leave without my morning fix of Samara. I saw her talking on her cell phone excitedly. When the call ended, she jumped up in joy and ran into her room. Ms. Rosie was still out of town. I sat perched on the windowsill watching her change clothes. She was wearing a purple thong and nothing else. I knew Ryson wouldn't be over until after he got off work, so I could go over there right now and have uninterrupted access to Samara. I heard about Ryson's little publicity stunt at Devon's party. That shit was all a front. Ryson didn't love Samara. Ryson didn't love anybody but himself. Samara fell for it like I knew she would. That was okay though, because I still had a few tricks up my sleeve. I would have gone to Devon's party too, but I couldn't trust myself not to punch Devon in the face. I didn't like how familiar he was acting with Samara. I was watching from my truck across the street, as his fat ass laughed and joked with her at the library a few weeks ago. I looked on from behind the bleachers, as he just so happened to show up at the track when she was out for a run with Ryson. Both times he put his dirty fucking arms around her for a hug. It took all my strength not to ram him with my truck. He was treading on thin ice. I put my binoculars down and made my way across the street. It took her five minutes to answer the door.

"Hey! What are you doing here?" She smiled cheerfully, happy to see me. My heart melted. She had on a pink robe and her hair was pinned up. She looked fresh faced and ready to be fucked.

"Is it my alarm?" Her expression changed from happiness to worry.

"Oh no! Nothing like that. I just came by to say hi. I had a couple of calls in the neighborhood." She nodded. I stood on her doorstep rocking back on my heels.

"Oh! I'm sorry, come in." She laughed and slapped herself on the forehead. We both laughed and I stepped inside her living room.

"So what's up? What you been up to Samara?" I sat down on her couch like I lived there. She sat on the coffee table facing me and crossed her bare legs. I snuck a peek at her calves.

"Actually, I just got a call from a job I applied for. I have an interview Friday at four-thirty." She smiled happily.

"That's good to hear. That's kind of late in the day though." I shifted my weight, so I was sitting on the edge of the couch. I was sitting there like I had nowhere else to be. She pulled on her ear and wrinkled her nose. She was so cute.

"Yeah I know, but it's the only time they had open so I took it. I don't know what to wear. I was just upstairs trying on everything I own, trying to decide ha-ha." *I know.*

"I'm scared." She rubbed her hands together nervously and giggled. My hands itched to touch her.

"Don't be. You have a great personality. That's all they're looking for nowadays anyway. You could have all of the experience in the world, but if your personality sucks, you're not getting the job," I said, trying to boost her confidence. And hopefully make her let her guard down.

"Thank you Dwayne. That was nice of you to say. You sound like you're in a good mood." She tilted her head and examined me. I smiled shyly and looked away. My phone vibrated in my pocket. I looked at the screen and recognized my boss's number. Shit.

"I have to go. Duty calls." She laughed at me and walked me to the door. At the door I chanced it. I bent down and kissed her on the cheek before she could react. She took a breath in surprise, but she didn't stop me.

"I'll see you later." I waved goodbye and left. My smile was so wide my cheeks hurt. I was getting through to her. It was only a matter of time before she let me back in her bed, and back into her life.

RYSON

I was making my way to Shar's apartment. She texted me that something happened and she needed my help. Usually I ignored her texts, but today I was feeling charitable. Ever since I told Samara I loved her at the party, I felt like a big weight had been lifted off of my shoulders. I was so fucking happy! That night I had a decision to make. It was either let her walk out of my life, or stop being a little bitch and tell her how I felt. I chose Samara. It was the best decision I ever made. After we left the party that night, we went to her place and made love until I was sore. She was my everything. I was over the moon in love with her. So when Shar texted me, instead of feeling the contempt I normally felt, I decided to help her out. This was more than likely the last time I would see her anyway. After I straightened everything out with Samara once and for all, I was distancing myself away from Shar. Possibly Dwayne too. I wasn't sure about him yet. I rang her bell and took the steps two at a time. I felt light on my feet, so I didn't take the elevator. Shar opened the door with a huge smile.

"Hi Ryson! I wasn't sure you would come." She moved to the side to let me in. It didn't seem like anything was wrong. Knowing Shar, that was just a ruse to get me here. I was in a good mood, so I wasn't mad at her.

"You said you needed help, so I came. What's wrong?" I plopped down on her couch and looked around her apartment. It smelled musty. Her curtains and carpet looked dusty. It looked like they hadn't been cleaned since the last time I was here probably. That was a long time ago. She walked over to me and sat down. She was wearing the yellow dress I used to love. She was trying to seduce me. It was actually comical. I turned towards Shar, so I could hear her spit her game at me. This would be funny.

"I miss you Ryson. I know we're in a weird place right now, but I wanted to know if you would give me another chance? We were good together once, don't you remember?" She licked her lips and slid closer to me. I burst into laughter. I couldn't hold it any longer. Tears were coming to my eyes.

"Are you serious? Oh my god you are?" I laughed harder. She never stopped smiling.

"Yes, I'm serious. I have a proposal for you that I think you should listen to." She put her hand on my knee. I pushed her hand away and stopped laughing. If Shar had a proposal, that meant she was plotting a scheme.

"What is it Shar?" It was a bad idea to come. The only thing Shar was good at, was causing trouble. I tried to give her the benefit of the doubt, but she always proved me right. It didn't matter. She couldn't kill my high no matter what she said. I had Samara and I had love, nothing could bring me down.

"There's no pretty way to say it, so I'm just going to give it to you straight. You're going to break-up with Samara today and then come back here and spend the night with me." She put her hand back on my knee. I watched her for a second to see if she was crazy. She had to be to think any of that shit was happening.

"Hold up, let me get this straight. You're not asking me, you're *telling* me to break-up with Samara, right?" She nodded her head yes.

"And on top of that, you want me to come back here afterwards and fuck you? I'm just trying to make sure I understood you right."

"Exactly." She ran her hand up my thigh. My parade was officially rained on. I was trying so hard to keep my cool with Shar, but she fucked it up. The rage inside of me built up so quick it almost scared me.

"First off Shar, I would NEVER, and I mean NEVER, put my dick anywhere near your body again! Second, what the fuck are you smoking? You think I'm going to break-up with Samara? For you? You're fucking tripping! I don't know what shit you're on, but you need help. I'm leaving before I say or do something I regret." This bitch was crazy. I didn't like to use that word to describe a female, but Shar was a bitch. I shook my head in loathing and got up to leave. This was the last time I was going to deal with Shar on any level.

"If you don't, I'll tell Samara everything," she said in a sing song voice. I stopped dead in my tracks. She wouldn't. I turned slowly towards Shar. I was going to tell Samara in my own time, but if she heard it from Shar, it would be over between us.

"Shar, I told you about that the last time you tried to pull this shit on me. Don't fucking threaten me!" I was more afraid than angry. I was finally in Samara's good graces. This would send her over the edge. It was a crushing secret. I would rather her hear it from me than Shar. I wasn't ready to tell her yet. Shar was desperate enough to do it. She laughed and stood up. She walked over to me and narrowed her eyes. She was serious. For the first time in my life, I was afraid of Shar.

"It's not a threat Ryson. You think Samara will still want to be with you when I tell her how we met? I don't think so, and neither do you. So I suggest you meet me back here at… let's say eight-thirty-ish? If you don't break-up with her by then, I will tell her everything. Every little freaky detail." She got in my face and kissed me. I was too terrified to stop her. I could see in her eyes how serious she was. Shar was willing to ruin my life without blinking an eye. I stood frozen while she wrapped her arms around me. My eyes burned and I wanted to cry. She was playing so fucking dirty. I instantly hated her. I wanted to kill her. I closed my eyes and took a breath. I had to be smart about this. I had to try to keep a clear head. Okay think. The worst that would happen was that Samara would look at me differently and never speak to me again. I would lose the only person I've ever loved. Or I could do what Shar wanted and still lose the love of my life. The only difference was Samara wouldn't look at me differently. She wouldn't think I was a monster. Both choices were dismal. I grabbed Shar's arms and pulled her off me. I couldn't stand to let her touch me. She repulsed me.

"I'll fucking do it!" I turned around and left, slamming the door behind me. Her smug fucking face would be forever imprinted into my brain. I didn't allow myself to cry until I was back in my Jeep.

SHAR

Things were starting to look up! About fucking time! I had waited for so long, I didn't know what to do with myself. I was ahead of schedule. I didn't think everything would fall into place until at least Thursday, but here it was, Wednesday afternoon, and I had my man back. I didn't see what the big fucking deal was anyway. Ryson and Dwayne were so fucking paranoid about everything. After the first time we fucked, we all agreed to keep that shit between us. But I didn't see why. We were all consenting adults and we should have been able to do whatever the fuck we wanted, no matter what anybody else thought. They just wanted to have their cake and eat it too. They wanted to fuck me, but not have to make a commitment. I wasn't fucking stupid. Oh well, that was all over now. Come Friday, Samara would get hers, and by eight-thirty tonight I would have mines. My pussy throbbed in anticipation of Ryson's dick. I missed him so much. Blackmail was my only recourse. I loved Ryson so much, I couldn't bear to see him with anyone else a second longer. He would hate me after this, I knew that for sure. It was a price I was willing to pay. He could hate me all he wanted. As long as he was mines I didn't care. Samara didn't deserve Ryson. I did. Next, I had to find a way to get the stars out of Dwayne's eyes. But for now, I was content with having Ryson back. I skipped back into my room to prepare for tonight.

RYSON

How was I going to do this shit? I couldn't go in there and look at her beautiful face, and hurt her yet *again*. It was bad enough I had to do this shit in the first place, and now I had a fucking time limit. I hated Shar so fucking much. I hated that conniving, desperate, miserable bitch! How could she force me to do this? She was so fucking selfish, it surprised me that I put up with her this long.

"What the fuck!" I punched the steering wheel and laid my head on it. I couldn't do it. Fuck Shar. I wasn't doing it. But if I didn't, she would tell Samara everything. All of this shit was happening because I couldn't keep my dick in my fucking pants! I had no choice. I had to break up with Samara. The only woman I had ever loved. This was karma for me dogging out all those women in my past. I knew one day that shit would catch up to me. Now I was feeling the hurt and pain they felt. It served me right I guess, but it still hurt like a motherfucker. I knew I couldn't just walk in her house and tell her it was over. It wouldn't be that easy. As soon as I saw her gorgeous face, I would have second thoughts and chicken out. I couldn't do that. If I was going to do this, I had to be angry about it. I had no shortage of anger coursing through my veins thanks to Shar. I just had to use that to my advantage. If I came at her angry enough, she would break up with me, and I would be off the hook. This shit was going to hurt so much. I choked back my tears. I was about to lose everything. *Be strong man, be strong*. I got out of my Jeep and walked up her steps. I took my key out and put it in the lock. Samara gave me this key two days after Devon's party, and this was the first time I was using it. I wiped the tears from my face and let my anger take over.

SAMARA

My wrist and arms were sore as hell. I was trying to surprise Ryson by straightening my hair. It was a good idea at first, until I realized that I was doing the straightening. It took me two and a half hours to do my whole head. I never wore my hair straight because it was too much maintenance. But I wanted to switch it up for Ryson. I slid the comb through it and put some hair oil on the ends. I heard the door opening downstairs and knew it was Ryson using his key. He had officially been granted a key after Devon's party. I put on my robe and ran down the stairs. I was naked underneath and ready for whatever. He stepped in and threw his keys across the room angrily.

"What's wrong baby?" He looked like he was ready to kill somebody. I walked over to him and hugged him to me. He stiffened up under my touch. Something definitely was not right. I looked up at his face. He looked stone cold. His gaze rested on the wall behind my head.

"Ryson are you okay? Did something happen?" I asked softly. There was obviously something eating at him, so I had to tread lightly.

"No," he said in a flat voice.

"So why do you look like that?" I asked, confused. I didn't know how to react. This was so unlike Ryson, it scared me. I hoped it wasn't more drama. I had enough of that from him already. I straightened up and let go of him.

"Talk to me babe. What's up?" I moved to the side so that I was in his line of vision. He moved his eyes away from me. What the hell? I had a bad feeling in my gut.

"I'm getting bored being with you," he said and finally looked at me. His hazel eyes were pink. He looked like he had been crying. He looked so sad.

"Baby what happened?" I reached for him but he grabbed my wrists.

"Didn't you just hear me? I said I'm fucking bored with you!" He screamed at me and pushed my hands away. I opened my mouth in shock then closed it. I looked at him sideways, trying to figure out what was going on. He was bored with me? Where was this coming from? I didn't believe that. I tucked away my hurt feelings so I could get to the bottom of what was really going on.

"I don't know why you just said that, but I'm not mad at you. Something obviously happened. You were crying weren't you? Whatever it is, just tell me. I promise I won't judge." I gave him an olive branch. I grabbed his hand and kissed his knuckle.

"I love you baby. You can tell me," I whispered to him. His gaze softened for a split second, then his eyes went completely blank. It was as if he was going to let me in, but decided against it at the last second. He was fighting against himself. He yanked his hand from me violently. I stood watching him, unsure. He looked angry all of a sudden. He stepped in my face and looked down at me. Why was he so angry?

"I am bored Samara. I'm tired of fucking the same person every fucking night! I'm not a one woman man! I'm not used to this shit and it's getting old. I don't want to be with you anymore." I slapped him hard across the face before I could stop myself. I couldn't believe he was saying these things to me! The most hurtful thing you could tell your woman was that you were bored with her. He was basically telling me he wanted to fuck other women! This was not my Ryson. Someone had to have put him up to this. Nonetheless, I refused to be talked to like this. After all of the shit I put up with to be with him, he was going to show me the respect I deserved! He touched his face where I'd hit him. He ground his teeth and his eyes nearly popped out his head.

"I don't know what the fuck is going on with you, but you are NOT going to talk to me like that. I'm not some fucking hooker you just met on the street! I deserve more respect than that. Why are you saying those hurtful things to me? You're trying awfully hard to make me mad, which I don't understand."

What was wrong with him? Who was this man in front of me? This was not how the night was supposed to end. I was scared and confused.

"Okay, fuck it! I was trying to spare your feelings, but oh well. Ever since you fucked my brother, I never thought you were girlfriend material. Anybody who would fuck somebody after knowing them for twenty minutes, is a hoe in my book. So after you started flirting with me, I decided to try to fuck you too. But you wanted to play house and shit and make me wait. Now that I got the pussy, I'm not impressed. It's no need to stick around. Every time I see you, all I can think about are those nights you let Dwayne fuck you like a whore! It makes me sick to my fucking stomach! I'm done with you! It's over! Finished! Is that clear enough for your ass now?" Pain exploded in my head and a dull ache appeared in my chest. I stood there listening to Ryson disrespect me and belittle the shit out of me. I stood there and swallowed every ounce of pride I had. I let the tears fall down my cheek and stain my satin robe. When Ryson was finished with his tirade, I breathed for the first time. I was too far gone to respond. If I opened my mouth, I was liable to break down into tears. No one had ever spoken to me with so much disgust and hate before. I felt ashamed of myself. I felt foolish and stupid. I blinked and let fresh tears fall. Ryson's face never changed. All I could see in his eyes were blocks of ice. Where was my Ryson? I gathered up all of the strength I had left, and decided to speak. I was hurt, embarrassed, and angry. There was no coming back from this. This had hit me out of nowhere. I couldn't make sense of how this had happened. I wiped my face and looked towards the door. My body was shaking. There was no use in defending myself. That would make matters worse and more hurtful things might get said. Usually I had a smart ass comeback, but all I wanted to do right now was crawl under a rock and disappear.

"If you want to leave, I won't stop you. I'm tired of trying to convince you to love me and to stay with me anyway. There's too much drama with you. Maybe it's best this way, because you're obviously not ready to be in a mature relationship." I looked down at my nails. My skin was getting hot, and the room seemed to be spinning. My hands were shaking uncontrollably. My eyes twitched. I was so dizzy. How had this all happened? How did I go from being blindly in love, to being utterly alone in the span of twenty-four hours?

"Good. I was tired of this domestic shit anyway." Ryson's snide remark was the last straw. If he wanted to leave, then he should just go. Why try to rub it in and hurt me even deeper?

"You don't have to be so mean about this Ryson! It's bad enough that you're acting like none of this shit matters to you. But at least have the decency to be civil about it!" His attitude was making me angrier and angrier. I was holding it in for as long as I could, but he was really testing me.

"How the fuck else am I supposed to act? You want me to send you a fucking fruit basket? WOULD THAT MAKE YOU FEEL BETTER?" He screamed at the top of his lungs. His veins bulged out of his neck from the strain.

"I can't believe you just fucking said that to me! I'm standing here trying not to let you see how much this shit is killing me inside, and you're just being an asshole! I still don't understand why you're doing this to me, but it's your decision! But don't stand here in my fucking face and try to degrade me and talk to me any kind of way. Don't act like what we had was all in my head! You felt it too!" My chest hurt. He was going to make me hit him again. I unclenched my fists and stepped back. He was taking me out of my character.

"You know what Ryson? GET THE FUCK OUT!" I pushed past him and yanked opened the door.

"Gladly," he spat out and walked out the door. I slammed the door behind him and slid down to the floor. I heard myself sobbing and crying. I was numb. What the fuck just happened? Mucus and tears dripped down my face. My heart ached. I slowly pulled myself off the floor. I dragged my feet to the stairway. I needed to lie down. My chest was killing me. If this headache didn't go away, I was going to rip the hair out of my head. How could he do this to me? To us? I knew Ryson loved me and something or someone had to have made him do this. I didn't make believe what we had was real, did I? I could feel it in my soul. When Ryson touched me I was in paradise. When his eyes looked into mines I was mesmerized. I knew the feeling was mutual. I could see how much he adored me. Why else would he declare his love for me in front of all his friends like that? There had to be another explanation. I was too weak to think about it. I made it up three steps before I collapsed and completely broke down. "What just happened?" I muttered through my tears.

DWAYNE

I couldn't tell exactly what happened, but Ryson left angry as shit. I was watching Samara from Ms. Rosie's house, when I saw Ryson's Jeep pull up. He sat in it for a few minutes before getting out. He was inside all of five minutes, before he came rushing back out, mad as shit. This was just the opening I needed. I couldn't see Samara through the window anymore, so I assumed she was making her way upstairs.

Ring! Ring! Ring!

Shit! I reached inside my jeans and pulled out my phone. It scared the shit out of me. I looked down at the number. I blinked over and over, trying to make sure what I was seeing was real. It was Samara! I took a deep breath and tried not to smile too hard.

"Hey Samara!" I answered happily. I couldn't believe she was calling me! I knew she had my number, but I never actually thought she would use it. I tried not to squeal with happiness into the phone. I pulled myself together.

"I need you Dwayne." Her voice was low and muffled.

"What? I can't hear you." She couldn't have said what I thought I'd heard.

"Ryson broke up with me. Can you come over please?" She was crying. What happened over there?

"Um... I'll be there in a few minutes. I'm... right down the street okay?" I heard her sniff and start crying again. She was in need and she called me. My baby finally came around! I waited for five minutes, then walked slowly down the steps, and out of Ms. Rosie's house. I didn't want to get there too fast. I walked like someone walking through the hood with a winning lottery ticket in their pocket. Scared and on the lookout. I didn't need Ryson coming back, and I didn't need her changing her mind. I rang her bell and waited. The door opened slowly. She had on a pink satin robe and she was bare foot. But what caught my attention was her hair. It was straightened and fell down to her stomach. I gulped. She never looked sexier. I looked at her pink face and smiled at her.

"It's okay. I'm here." I closed the door behind me and pulled her to me for a hug. My eyes popped open. She was naked underneath her robe. There was no way I could stop myself from getting hard. I put my hands in her soft hair and rubbed her back.

"Sshhhhh. It's okay Samara. Do you want to talk about it?" I didn't really care to hear the sordid details. All I cared about was that she was single now. Fuck Ryson. He didn't know what he had. His mistake would be my gain. She shook her head no and started to hiccup. I pulled myself off her and looked her over. Her eyes were puffy and her nose was red. Tears streamed down her face freely. She was breathing like an asthmatic.

"Do you want some tea?" I asked softly. She shook her head again saying no, and closed her eyes. She looked like she was physically hurting. Ryson was a fucking jerk. He went through that whole grandstand of telling everybody how much he loved her, just to dump her. He was an asshole who'd just fucked up. Now that Samara let me back in, I wasn't going anywhere. No matter what.

"You want to go upstairs and lie down?" I hoped her answer would be yes. I know she was hurting at the moment, but Samara loved sex. She was ready to go all the time. Once I got her upstairs, it would be on. She would cry a little longer, then I would make my move. There was no doubt in my mind she would let me hit tonight. She nodded her head yes. She reached behind me and punched in her alarm code. I took her hand and walked with her up the stairs. She wiped her face and let more tears fall. I didn't feel any sympathy for her. If she had stayed with me, none of this would have happened. Now she was feeling the effects of her bad decisions. Hopefully she would learn her lesson and see the light. We walked into her room in silence. She got into bed and curled up into a ball. I got in behind her.

"Everything is going to be fine. I'm here for you," I said into her ear. I kissed her earlobe and put my arm around her middle. I pulled her closer to me. My dick was hard as a rock against her ass, and I wasn't hiding it. She didn't protest. After about ten minutes, her breathing became shallow. I sat up and looked at her face, and realized she was asleep. I wasn't mad though. She had expelled so much energy crying, it was inevitable. At least I could still have my fun. I unhooked her robe and pulled it open, exposing some of her body. She shivered and turned around, facing me. I lay stiff, staring at her sleeping face. I wasn't expecting her to turn towards me, but that was even better. I waited until her breathing was heavy again to make my next move. I wanted to go straight to the pussy, but I paced myself. I glided my hand down her chest onto her stomach. I put my thumb inside her navel. Her hand came up quickly and grabbed my wrist. My heart stopped. I stopped breathing and waited in fear. Instead of pushing me away, she took my hand and moved it down her stomach. She led my hand down over her pubic hair and placed my index finger inside her pussy lips.

"Oh my god!" I choked out. She wasn't asleep! She was guiding me to her pussy! I knew she wanted me! I didn't need any further instruction. I plunged my finger inside her pussy and got on top of her. My lips were on her lips before she could protest. I was finally going to fuck Samara! I couldn't believe it. All of those nights masturbating and longing for her were coming to an end. She opened her legs wide and grabbed my face. She kissed me rough and fast on the lips and forced her tongue in my mouth. This was the Samara I remembered! Fuck yes! I started to unbuckle my pants with my free hand. Her pussy was soaking wet. Damn, she was ready for me. She wanted me as much as I wanted her. I took my finger out of her pussy and pulled my shirt over my head. I looked down at her. She had her eyes closed and was breathing hard. I got off the bed and took off the remainder of my clothes. I wanted to be inside her so fucking bad. I'd been fantasizing about this night for months, and I knew exactly how I wanted to fuck her. I got back onto the bed and flipped her over onto her stomach, pulling her up to her knees. I pushed her against the headboard and grabbed a fistful of her hair. She panted and put her hands on the headboard, grabbing onto it. I pulled her head back and sucked on her neck. Her ass was on my dick. She moaned, then reached out and put her hand on my hips. She was letting me know she was ready for my dick. I pushed her all the way up against the headboard, and drove my dick hard and quick into her pussy.

"AAAAAHHHHHHHH!" She screamed out in pleasure.

"You missed that didn't you?" I asked her through clenched teeth. Her pussy was even tighter than I remembered. I had to concentrate so I didn't cum too quickly. She was so wet. Our juices made a squishing noise every time I pumped my dick inside her pussy. I fucked her as hard as I could. She screamed out at the top of her lungs, giving me fuel to fuck harder. Oh god I missed her so much. I wanted to be in her pussy eternally. I took my dick out of her pussy and turned her around to face me. Her eyes were still closed, but I could tell she was about to cum. I knew her cum face better than anyone. All she needed was a few good strokes and she would be there. I picked her up and put her on my lap. She straddled my dick. I pushed my hips up and plunged my dick inside her wet pussy, hard. I continued to fuck her harder.

"RIDE THIS DICK! RIDE THIS DICK!" I screamed at her. Her hips swirled and bounced up and down on my dick. I was about to cum. Her pussy was so good. I still couldn't believe I was inside of her and she was riding my dick. Her breasts bounced in my face. I bit her nipples. She put her hands on my stomach and tried to make me slow down. Not tonight. I was going to fuck her so hard her pussy would remember me. I wanted her to say my name. I wanted her to know that I was the only man who could fuck her like this. I put both of my hands in her hair and pulled hard. I forced her to open her eyes.

"LOOK AT ME!" I was fucking her so hard the bed rocked and creaked. She looked down at me and screamed out in pain. I knew I was hurting her, but I didn't care. She needed to admit she wanted me and that my dick was the only dick for her.

"SAY MY NAME!" I screamed at her again. She tried to take my hands out of her hair. When I wouldn't let go she started crying.

"SAY…MY…FUCKING…NAME!" I started to cum. I was about to push her off me, then I stopped. She looked at me in a panic. She didn't want me to cum in her. She tried to get up but I wrapped my arms around her back and gripped her into a bear hug. I pushed my hips up and pumped faster. She was getting this entire nut inside her pussy, whether she wanted it or not.

"FFFFFUUUUUUCCCCCKKKKKK YYYYYYYEEEEEAAAAHHHHHH!" I screamed until my throat hurt. That was the best nut I'd ever bust. Samara's pussy was like no other. I wasn't about to let it go.

"We shouldn't have done that," she said tearfully and jumped off me. I lay on my back, trying to catch my breath. She was having regrets already? Damn. Oh well, we fucked and there was no turning back.

"Yes we should have. You wanted it and so did I. There's nothing wrong with it. Come here." I reached for her but she moved away. She got off the bed and put her robe back on. Oh hell no!

"What the fuck Samara?" I was pissed off. She was still worrying about Ryson after he fucking dumped her ass? I just gave her some of the best skills I had, and she was thinking about him? I wanted to fucking snap!

"Dwayne, you know that was wrong! I just broke up with Ryson less than an hour ago! I'm really vulnerable right now. I... I needed some comfort and you were here for me. I didn't mean to use you but... what we just did doesn't change anything. I still only want to be friends. Me and Ryson might get back together who knows?" I was seeing red. *Get up and break her fucking neck!*

"If he finds out we did this..." Her voice trailed off and she started crying again. I closed my eyes and calmed myself down. Like she said, she was vulnerable, which meant her mind was all over the place. She was in a fragile state. I could take advantage of that. The last time we were together, my anger got the best of me and drove her away from me. This time, I would keep a cool head about this. I sighed and sat up.

"You're right. We shouldn't have done that. I won't tell Ryson, okay? I just want you to be okay. Come lay back down. I promise I won't try anything." I put my hand out to her. She looked at my hand and took it. I pulled her to my naked body and sat her down next to me. She laid her head on my shoulder and cried some more. I squeezed her shoulder and let her vent for the rest of the night.

RYSON

"I can't get it up Shar! What the fuck do you want me to do?" She huffed in annoyance and closed her robe. She stalked out of the room, slamming the door behind her. I started to pull my pants back up. I don't know why the fuck she thought I would get hard after everything that happened today anyway. I was at my breaking point. I didn't have much time to cry over my loss of Samara before I had to get back over here. When I stepped into Shar's apartment, she fucking ambushed me. We ended up in the bedroom with her on her knees trying to get me hard. I cringed when she put her mouth on my dick. This was Samara's dick and nobody else's. I felt so powerless. Shar came back into the room naked. Her body repulsed me. She tried to walk sexy, but she just managed to look desperate and unappealing.

"Here. Take this." She put a small blue pill in my hand. I looked down at the pill, then up at Shar. Was she out of her fucking mind?

"I'm not taking a FUCKING Viagra Shar! This shit is not meant for men my age. You don't know what side effects this shit might have on me!" I put the pill back in her hand and finished putting my pants back on. This bitch was crazy. She was trying anything to get me to fuck her. I didn't want my dick anywhere near her.

"Okay then." She walked over to the dresser and picked up her cell phone. I stood up and walked over to her.

"What are you doing Shar?" I didn't trust this bitch one bit. She shrugged as if to say, 'nothing'.

"I'm calling Samara. You're not keeping up your end of the bargain, so I'm not keeping up mines." She smiled and flipped through her contacts. I saw Samara's number saved as *whore* in her phone. SHIT!

"Give me the fucking pill Shar!" She laughed as I snatched the pill from her hand. This was all a fucking game to her. I swallowed the Viagra and sat back down on the bed. I put my head in my hands. The musty smell of her apartment filled my nose. My heart was beating rapidly. I wanted to cry so badly. Whenever this pill kicked in, there was nothing I could do. I looked up at Shar and saw no compassion on her face.

"Why are you doing this to me Shar?" I heard my voice crack. Was she that coldblooded, that she would destroy everything I had because of jealousy?

"Boy please! I'm not doing anything to you! Stop being so dramatic. We both know Samara wasn't good enough for you anyway. She was just some hoe you tried to turn into a housewife." Shar was so blinded by hate and jealousy, she didn't realize how crazy she sounded.

"I love her Shar." My voice was low and miserable. I missed my baby already. I could only imagine what she was going through. I said some really hurtful things to her that weren't necessary.

"Ryson, you don't love that bitch! Please stop acting like you're the victim in all of this. You fucked me then just dumped me! How do you think I felt? I loved you! And you just got what you wanted from me and moved on. But I forgive you, because I know your dick was doing all of the thinking and not your heart. I know you love me." I watched her talk. I came to the conclusion that she was out of her fucking mind. There was no other reason she would be so delusional. She got on her knees in front of me and slid my zipper down. I bit back what I wanted to say and closed my eyes. The pill had kicked in already, but I was trying to stall.

"Look at that! All of this dick for little ole me?" Shar said and took my hard dick into her mouth. I turned my attention to the window. Shar sucked and slurped on my dick for damn near an hour. She was trying to make me cum. That was something that I couldn't take a pill for. I didn't have any desire to be with Shar, and it was revolting to sit there and let her molest me like this. With every flick of her tongue, I wanted to throw up. I have never felt as disgusted in my life, as I did sitting there. She got up and bent over the bed.

"Now hit it like you used to baby," she purred and spread her ass cheeks.

"Please don't make me do this Shar!" I begged her sadly. I knew that I sounded like a little bitch, but I didn't care. I never thought Shar would try to force herself on me. I hated her more than words could describe. Taking my jeans off, I slid my briefs down. I got behind Shar and took a breath. I looked down at her open pussy and sobbed. Then I swallowed and put my dick inside of her.

"Ah! Baby I missed you so much," Shar moaned and pushed back on my dick. I just had to get through tonight. I closed my eyes and thought of my baby. I thought about the first time we were together. I remembered how she gave me head underwater. In my mind, I saw her wet body dripping with bubbles as she rode my dick. I pumped harder into Shar.

"Oh yea FUCK ME!" she screamed out.

"SHUT UP!" I tuned her out and went back to thoughts of Samara. I fantasized about the way she looked when she opened her door to me tonight. She had straightened her hair for me. She was the most beautiful woman in the world in my eyes. I was about to cum. I pulled out of Shar.

"I want you to cum inside me baby," she cooed and grabbed my dick.

"NO SHAR!" I yelled out in anger. She was taking this shit too far now. It would be just my luck that she would end up pregnant. That was the last thing I wanted to happen. I pushed her hand away and moved back from the bed.

"4576." Shar recited the last four digits of Samara's phone number. My heart sank.

"YOU BITCH!" Angrily, I plunged my dick back inside her and pumped until I couldn't pump anymore. I felt myself cumming. I kept my dick in her pussy and she got her wish.

"FUCK!" I screamed out in frustration. That was the most disgusting, unsatisfying nut I'd ever bust. I pushed Shar away from me and put my pants back on. She turned over onto her back and smiled up at the ceiling.

"That was perfect," she breathed and sighed.

"That was rape Shar!" I spat at her and sat on the floor. Everything was spiraling out of control. How was I going to fix this? If Samara ever found out about this, I didn't know what I would do. Shar sat up and opened her legs.

"Ready for round two?" She looked down at my dick, which was still erect. I balled my hands into fists and pushed them into my eyes. Please let this be a nightmare. I let a sob escape my lips.

SAMARA

I didn't want to go to this stupid fucking interview now. I had totally forgotten it was Friday. I let the water rain down on me in the shower, as I contemplated whether I should go or not. I wasn't in the right frame of mind. I might burst into tears at any moment. I was so tired and miserable. I still couldn't believe Ryson had dumped me like that. He was so malicious and hurtful towards me, it made the sting even worse. I only called Dwayne because I needed someone to comfort me. I couldn't call my girlfriends because all they would say is, *"I told you so."* I never expected to sleep with Dwayne. But when he touched me, I was thinking about Ryson and I didn't want him to stop. I kept my eyes closed and pretended I was with Ryson and not Dwayne. But Ryson would never be so rough with me, so it got harder and harder to pretend. I wanted to stop halfway through, but I knew Dwayne wouldn't let me. When he told me to say his name, Ryson's name was on the tip of my tongue. I started to cry because I wanted Ryson. I wanted Ryson to come in and see me with Dwayne and realize the mistake he had made. That didn't happen. The only thing that happened was I managed to lead Dwayne on. I felt so cheap. I felt like the whore Ryson thought that I was. I couldn't cry anymore. I spent all of that night, most of the next day, and the next night crying on Dwayne's shoulder. He had to leave to go to work Friday morning, so I was all alone. He promised me he would be back later to make sure I was okay. I nodded and let him leave. He bent down and kissed me on the lips and I let him. It felt good to get some type of affection. Even if it wasn't from the man I loved.

I turned off the shower and walked into my bedroom. I would go to this damn interview. I wasn't going to let Ryson control my life. I wasn't the type of girl to sulk and eat a bucket of ice cream over a guy. I was going to continue on and live my life. That was what I did before I met him, and that was what I was going to do now. I pulled out a gray blazer and a pair of black slacks. I paired that with a white blouse and a pair of black low heeled pumps. I pinned my hair up into a bun and put on some stud earrings. I looked professional enough. I looked in the mirror and saw the bags underneath my eyes. I couldn't hide them, no matter how much concealer I caked on. I picked up my purse and went downstairs. The doorbell rang just as I was pouring myself a glass of orange juice. I was in no mood for company. I hoped whoever it was would go away, but they kept ringing the bell annoying the shit out of me. I stomped over to the door and peeked out. Two men I didn't recognize stood behind the door.

"How can I help you?" I asked through the door.

"Ms. Cipriano?" One of them called through the door.

"Yes?" Who the hell were these two weirdos and how did they know my name?

"There's a power shortage in the neighborhood. We're going around trying to figure out where it came from. We think it may have something to do with the alarm systems in this neighborhood. Can we come in and inspect your system?" I looked through the peephole again. They both had on navy blue jumpsuits and had clipboards in their hands. I couldn't really see their faces because they had their heads lowered. I wasn't having any electrical problems. But then again, I hadn't really used anything today, so what did I know? I unlocked the door, but didn't disable the alarm. Neither of them could have been a day over twenty. The one on the right had a black tear drop tattoo under his eye. The other one looked like he was high and stoned out of his mind. This didn't feel right. I opened the door a little and put myself in the doorframe.

"What company did you say you worked for?" Either they were playing a practical joke, or they were fresh out of prison. They looked a little rough around the edges to be electricians. Come to think of it, if they were electricians, their company logo would be on their uniforms wouldn't it? Dwayne would have called me if the problem was coming from my house. I looked at their nametags. Rico and Pedro. There was no way they were Hispanic.

"We didn't say." The one on the left said with an attitude. Okay?

"Uh... look I don't know what game you're playing or what you're selling, but I'm not in the damn mood! Have a good day." I went to close the door and one of those bastards put his foot on the threshold.

"What the fuck do you think you're doing?" Today was not the day to fuck with me! I was liable to kill somebody.

"We can do this the easy way or the hard way Samara, you pick." What the hell?

"How do you know my name?" I asked in surprise. He pushed the door with so much force, I fell backwards on my ass in shock. I watched them come into my house and close the door. What the hell was going on? I wasn't scared by any means. I was angry as hell. They picked the wrong day to mess with me. They didn't know what they were in for. If they were trying to rob me, they came to the wrong house.

"We have a message for you from Shar," the one with the tattoo on his face said. I stood up and took my shoes off. Shar? That bitch was *still* trying to fuck with me? She was due for another fucking visit it seemed.

"What's the message?" I took off my blazer, already preparing for what was about to go down. My energy surged and adrenaline coursed through my body.

"She wants you to stay the fuck away from Rashawn and Dwight," the stoned looking one said and locked my door. My alarm started sending out low steady beeps letting me know my door had been opened and the alarm hadn't been disabled. In a few minutes it was going to be blaring, and a signal was going to get sent out to the alarm company. They would immediately call my cell phone, which I had left upstairs. After that, I expected a police officer to come by to see if everything was okay. So I had about fifteen minutes, give or take, to either get them out of my house or have them arrested.

"Who the fuck are Rashawn and Dwight?" I asked, totally confused. They snuck glances at each other in confusion too.

"Ryson and Dwayne," the one with the tattoo corrected, after pulling out a piece of paper from his pocket.

"Idiots! And if I don't?" I challenged. I was in no mood for games today. I needed to take my anger out on somebody, they were perfect for the job. I knew I could take them. I was little, but I was strong and fast. I was so amped up with emotion and anger I could probably lift a car right now.

"That's why we're here to make sure you do." They advanced in on me, one standing to my left and one to my right. The one with the tattoo tried his luck first and swung on me, trying to punch me.

Here we go.

I pivoted my head to the left and punched him in the stomach swift and hard.

Whoosh!

The punch knocked the air out of him and he fell to his knees. His eyes went wide and he grabbed his middle. I backed up a few inches, ready for the next attack. The stoned one watched the whole exchange in surprise, but snapped out of it as soon as his partner hit the floor. He ran towards me with his hands out, bent on choking me. I let him grab me by the throat. He slammed me up against the wall.

"Aaaaahhhhh!" I gagged a little. I'd hit my head hard on a hanging picture. He pressed his thumb into my throat. My throat contracted as I tried to swallow. I wrapped my hands around his wrists and hoisted myself up. Veins bulged in his neck as he tried to choke the life out of me. I put my bare feet on his thighs and caught his attention. I couldn't breathe, but I wasn't concerned about that. He looked down at my feet in horror as I drove the heel of my right foot into his nut sack.

"OOOOOOOO!" His eyes rolled to the back of his head. He let me go and collapsed in front of me. I fell to the floor too, but quickly regained my balance. He squirmed on the floor and squealed in pain. I looked over at his friend, still gasping for air on the floor. I caught my breath. Now was a good time for me to get out of the house and wait for the police. But I wasn't done with them yet. They came here with the intent of hurting me, and now they were going to get their just desserts. My chest heaved in and out with my anger. I had them right where I wanted them. I walked over to tattoo boy and stood behind him. I saw him put his open palm on the floor and push himself up to his feet. He coughed and blew out an exasperated sigh.

"That was real fucking cute," he said and spit on the floor. He took in big gulps of air and righted himself. I stood with my legs apart and put my hands up, ready for some hand to hand combat. Smiling devilishly at him, I gave him the finger.

"You won't be smiling like that when I'm done with you bitch!" He made the mistake of trying to swing a punch at me again. This time I decided to play with him a little. I was kind of having fun. I ducked his hit and quickly ran behind him, forcing him to swivel around. I heard his partner trying to get up behind me. I knew he would try to sneak me. That was what I was counting on. Tattoo boy swung on me once again, but I grabbed his arm in midair. He grunted and went to hit me with his other arm, but I caught that one too. We struggled for dominance as my grip tightened on his forearms. He was at my mercy. Sweat ran down his forehead and formed on his upper lip. His eyes were like an inferno. I twisted his forearms so that his wrists were facing up and shoved my knee into his pelvic bone twice. He made a choking sound and his legs buckled. When he fell to his knees, I kicked him in the chest with the heel of my foot, and let him fall to the floor backwards. The back of his head made a cracking sound as it hit the floor. I turned around in time to elbow his partner in the gut. He was standing behind me, trying to catch me off guard.

"AAARRRGGGGHHHH!" He went down on one knee and took in a breath. I stood over him, trying to decide what to do. Fuck it. I pulled my arm back and punched him dead in the face. I heard a crack and knew his nose was broken. He flew to the side, hitting his head on the side of my coffee table, and screamed out in agony. Blood spewed from his nose and splattered on the floor. I was sweating now. SHIT! My knuckles ached. Blood rushed to my head at the high I was getting. I watched as they both writhed in pain on the floor. My shirt was sticking to me. My bun had come undone. Who the fuck did they think they were, trying to threaten me? I bent down and straddled tattoo boy.

SCCCCRRRRRRREEEEEECCCCCCCCHHHHHHH!

My alarm started blaring.

"How much did Shar pay you to get your ass kicked?" I yelled over the alarm. I was taunting him, but I really wanted to know. How did she convince these two thugs to take a huge risk and try to attack me? In broad daylight? In my own home? He coughed up blood and spit it in my face. I closed my eyes as his blood dripped down my cheek and onto my white shirt. The alarm sound was earsplitting, but I tuned it out. The only thing on my mind was kicking their asses.

"Wrong answer." I grabbed his forearm with my right hand and pressed the palm of my left hand onto his shoulder. I pressed down on the bone as hard as I could and pulled his arm towards me with as much force as I could muster, dislocating his shoulder. *Snap!*

"FFFUUUUCCCCKKKK! BITCH!" I dropped his dislocated arm. He tried to hit me with his other arm. I gripped his arm and bent his wrist back.

"AAAAAAHHHHHHH SHHHHIIIIITTTT!" I dropped his arms and slapped him savagely across the face.

"HOW MUCH DID SHAR PAY YOU?" I was getting impatient. I glanced back at his partner and saw him grab the coffee table, trying to get up.

"FIVE G'S BITCH!" he screamed out in pain. Five thousand dollars? What the fuck! I stood back up and looked over at the door. The police would be here any minute. Shar must have felt like I was a major threat to drop that much money and go this far. She was fucking nuts. I picked up one of my heels and walked over to the coffee table.

"Come on now!" the stoned one whined and put his hand up to defend himself. The other hand was unsuccessfully trying to contain the blood gushing out of the back of his head.

"What's your name?" I yelled, giving him a chance to redeem himself. His partner started laughing maniacally. I shook my head at these two pathetic losers.

"I'm not telling you SHIT!" He put his hand over his face. I sighed and hit him in the back of the head with my shoe, leaving another gash in the middle of his head.

"OOOOUUCCCCHHHHH DDAAAAMMMMNNN!" He felt his head and looked at his bloody hand.

"THIS IS THE POLICE! OPEN THE DOOR OR I'M COMING IN!" I ran to the door and pulled it open. A young white cop stood on my doorstep with his hand on his gun.

"These two men forced their way into my house! They tried to attack me so I defended myself." His name tag said 'Rodgers'. He was short and stocky but looked competent enough. He had a buzz cut and brown freckles covering his nose. He looked a little green. He inspected my face.

"Are you okay ma'am? Do you need emergency services?" he screamed over the noise. He was looking at the blood tattoo boy had spit in my face. I reached over and disabled the alarm.

"No, it's not my blood. I'm okay. I just want these motherfuckers out of my—"

Something hot and fast whizzed by my ear.

"WHOA!" The bullet hit the doorframe missing my face by inches. My shocked eyes went to the splinters falling from the door. Fear seized me as I grasped the fact that one of them had just shot at me.

"PUT THE WEAPON DOWN NOW!" I heard Officer Rodgers yell. He pushed me against the wall next to the door as another bullet whizzed past me, this time nicking me on the thigh. A burning sensation exploded into my leg and I fell to the floor on my ass.

"AAAAAHHHHHH!" I screamed out in surprise. The next thing I knew, Officer Rodgers opened fire and bullets started flying everywhere. I crawled to my staircase in a frenzy and scurried up the steps.

"OH MY GOD! AAAHHH!" My heart just about flew out of my chest. I saw one of them run towards my kitchen, then I heard the back door open. I cradled my arms around myself and prayed that I wouldn't get shot. My nerves were fucked up. I felt like I was having an asthma attack. Bullets flew and objects broke. It seemed like it lasted an hour when it was probably closer to three minutes. The house became dead quiet.

"MA'AM ARE YOU OKAY?" I shook uncontrollably. I heard the officer calling the incident in over his radio. I looked up from the ball I had curled myself into. I couldn't speak. I just nodded my head absently. Those bastards just tried to kill me! It frightened me to know that all along they had guns, and could have just shot me in the face when I opened the door. I looked at my shot up furniture and started to cry. I was in shock. The officer told me he was calling an ambulance and asked me was there anyone he could call for me. Instinctively Ryson came to mind. I was reminded of everything that happened between us and cried harder. I gave him Dwayne's number instead. Then I remembered out of nowhere that I had a job interview. This had been the worst fucking week ever.

DWAYNE

"They told you that Shar paid them five thousand dollars?" My blood pressure had to be through the roof. First I got a call from the cops saying Samara was attacked. Then I got to the hospital and she told me that they shot at her. Then I got the fucking shock of my life when Samara told me those two motherfuckers said Shar paid them five-thousand dollars. I thought back to the day Shar asked me for money to pay for her back rent. I was such a fucking dummy! I would handle Shar. Right now I had to focus on my baby. We were back home, that had a nice ring to it. She was lying in bed in a spaghetti strap black shirt and black boy shorts. I was cleaning her wound and putting new bandages on it. She hadn't said much since the hospital, only absently answering her phone a few times to assure her girlfriends that she was in fact alive and well. She looked scared as shit. She sat there biting her nails and playing with her hair. Not much changed when we pulled up to the house.

"Are you hungry?" I asked her, trying to get her to come back to reality. I hated to downplay the situation, but I was glad it happened. Not because I almost lost my baby, but because she called me. She could have given in and called Ryson or one of her girlfriends, but she called me. I knew we were getting closer. When she let me kiss her goodbye that morning, I knew I had her. Ryson would blow a gasket when he found out we were together now. It wasn't the first time I stole a girl from him, so he shouldn't be that surprised. I rubbed her legs and licked my lips. I wanted to fuck. I told her I wouldn't try anything but come on now, have you seen her? My hand slid up her leg and kept going up past her thighs.

"Dwayne don't," she whispered, still staring blankly at her bedroom door. I held my temper in check.

"Just let me taste you. It will make you feel better," I tried to persuade her. If she let me eat her pussy, I knew she would let me fuck. She shook her head no. I fumed inside, but I didn't stop. I sat up and leaned over towards her. She glanced at me and shook her head no again.

Damn! She didn't even know what the fuck I was about to do! I ignored her and kissed her on the neck. She moved her head away and put her hand on my chest, stopping me.

"Dwayne, please I can't. I'm fucked up right now! That's the last thing on my mind." She rolled her eyes and started to rock back and forth. She was making it difficult for me to sustain the mood I was in. I wanted some pussy and she owed it to me. All of this time waiting in the wings for her to come around had to count for something. Not to mention the fact that I'd been here for her twice in the last week. She'd better readjust her attitude. I ignored her again. I put my tongue into her ear. This time she didn't push me away. That was one of her spots.

"Dwayne don't do that," she whispered and closed her eyes. I rubbed on her pussy and licked her neck. She moaned and put her hand over mines, and moved it in a circle. My dick shot up. I inched closer to her.

"Mmmmm... Ryson," she moaned and tilted her neck. I abruptly stopped. She opened her eyes in surprise and covered her mouth. Her eyes went wide and she looked at me in fear.

"I... I... I'm sorry Dwayne it just slipped out," she said in a small voice. She closed her eyes and started crying. I was tired of this crying shit! WHAT THE FUCK! How dare she fucking call out Ryson's name while I was in her bed! Did she have a fucking death wish? Was she thinking about him while I kissed her? Was she fantasizing about him when I was fucking her? She was trying my fucking patience! I was going to give her the benefit of the doubt. It was just a slip of the tongue. This time, when we fucked, she was going to keep her eyes the fuck open the whole time. She had about three more minutes to cry, then it was on.

"SAMARA!" She stopped crying and looked up at her door in shock. I couldn't have heard right.

"SAMARA? ARE YOU HERE?" Ryson opened her bedroom door. He looked at Samara, then at me. I smiled because now he would see us together and get the fucking picture.

"Ryson? What are you doing here? How did you get in?" Samara pushed herself off the bed and limped slowly towards him. Ryson's eyes were red, like he had been crying.

"I made a copy of your key before I gave it back to you. I just heard what happened. Are you okay baby?" He called her baby like they were still together. It was time for me to put him in his place, and let him see there was a new man in her life. I stood up and walked around to the side of the bed where Samara was. I passed Ryson and eyed him up and down.

"She's okay. I took care of her. What do you want?" I put my arm around her shoulder possessively. She looked at me like I was crazy. Ryson ignored me and kept his eyes on her.

"Can we talk?" Ryson took her hands in his. She looked down at their joined hands and whimpered. Oh fuck no! Shit wasn't going down like that tonight! They were acting like I wasn't even standing here!

"No! We're busy. Why don't you just text her later." I pulled her hands from his. She turned on me, her eyes flashing with rage. She didn't say anything, then her eyes softened.

"Dwayne... I need to talk to Ryson. Please don't make this situation any more awkward than it already is. I'll call you later, I promise okay?" She spoke softly to me like I was a child. If I left her here alone with Ryson, her weak ass would just take him back. I couldn't have that. I opened my mouth to tell her fuck no.

"Please?" she begged and smiled at me. That was the first time she'd smiled at me in days. I would play her little game. I said okay and bent down and kissed her on the lips. She didn't stop me and actually kissed me back. I gave Ryson a warning with my eyes not to fuck with me. He didn't pay me any mind. I had to attend to another matter anyway. I walked out to my truck and put it in drive. It was time for me to have a little face to face chat with Shar. But trust and believe, Ryson was not getting Samara back. Not tonight. Not ever.

SHAR

Why didn't they call me yet? I paced my living room back and forth, waiting for some kind of news. My cell phone rang. I snatched it up off the table so fast, it slipped out of my hand. Shit! I picked it up and saw a private number.

"You set us up bitch!" the voice on the other end of the phone screamed.

"What the fuck are you talking about? Nobody set y'all up! What happened?"

Why was he tripping and yelling in my fucking ear?

"You didn't tell us that bitch knew how to fucking fight! She kicked our asses then called the fucking cops! We barely made it out of there. My homey got shot in the arm!" OH MY FUCKING GOD! Was there no way to stop this bitch? Damn!

"So... what now? Am I getting my money back since y'all didn't do the fucking job?" All that fucking money down the damn drain! I knew I should have handled that shit myself. If you wanted something done right, you had to do it yourself. You never sent a man to do a woman's job.

"FUCK NO! You lucky we don't come after your ass for this shit!" He hung up on me. SHIT! Why was it so hard to get rid of this skank? Fuck it. I was giving up on that shit. I had Ryson, so that was all that really mattered. Now it was time to separate Dwayne's sprung ass from her coattails. Somebody buzzed my bell. I was afraid it was the guys I hired, then I remembered they didn't know my apartment number. I had met them outside the building when I gave them the money. It was probably Ryson. I let him go get us something to eat. I told his ass to report right back here, and had given him thirty minutes. He was on minute twenty-two. I hit the buzzer and let him up, then opened the door to let him in. He walked in with two bags of Chinese food, brooding as usual. I needed to get my mind off of that Samara disaster.

"Let's skip dinner and go straight to dessert." I stood behind him and grabbed his limp dick. He sighed and turned towards me. Ryson had fucked me at least eight times over the last two days and I loved it. He complained every time, but eventually gave in.

"I'm hungry Shar." His voice lacked emotion. His eyes were dead, and his shoulders were slumped. He looked depressed. That bitch Samara had my Ryson in a funk. My pussy would bring him out of it.

"I have something you can eat." I opened my robe and let it fall. He didn't even look at my body. I ignored his disinterest and told him to get on his knees. He closed his eyes and got down on his knees. I put my thigh on his shoulder and spread my lips. His hot tongue glided over my clit.

"Ah! Yeah Ryson. Lick it like I like it." I put my head back and started to grind my pussy on his mouth. I heard a vibration. I looked at the table and saw Ryson's phone ringing. He stopped and got up. He roughly wiped his mouth off. He turned his back to me and answered it.

"Yo what's up? I'm kind of busy right now, I can't talk." I stood there waiting for him to end his call. He had about thirty seconds before I snatched that shit from his hand. It was my time now and nobody was going to distract him!

"WHAT? No... I didn't talk to her today. GUNSHOTS? WHAT? WHEN? I... OH MY GOD! I-I have to call you back!" Somebody told him about Samara! Fuck! I put my robe back on and tried to think quickly. There was no way I was letting him run to that bitch's aid. He was my man now. Fuck her! She was still alive so what was the big fucking deal? He turned around, frantically looking for his keys.

"Uh... where do you think you're going? We're not done here!" I stood in front of the door blocking him from leaving. He cracked his neck and shot daggers at me.

"Move out the FUCKING way Shar! I don't have time for this shit right now!" he yelled out in frustration.

"If you walk out this door, I'll send Samara the video we made last night!" I yelled at him. On the video it showed me riding his dick frontwards and backwards. Then I had him eating my pussy and my ass. I made him fuck me every which way I told him to. Samara wouldn't know it was Viagra keeping his dick hard all night. He put his hands on his head in frustration.

"AAARRRRRGGGG!" He turned around and punched a hole in the wall behind him. His aggression turned me on. If I pushed enough buttons, I could get him to fuck the shit out of me right here. He turned to me with his fists balled. I moved closer to the door. I knew Ryson wouldn't hit me, but he wanted to. The fire in his eyes turned me on.

"I don't care what the fuck you do Shar. I'm leaving!" He grabbed me by the shoulders and threw me to the floor. I panicked.

"Samara will never understand Ryson. She's going to hate you!" I yelled at him, trying to keep him here with me. He was slipping away from me again.

"Not as much as I hate you! You pathetic, desperate, pitiful bitch! You will NEVER see me again! I hope you DIE SLOW!"

"RYSON WAIT!" I cried his name as he slammed my door. All at once my whole body trembled and broke down on me. Oh god, I lost him forever! My chest ached so bad I couldn't breathe. I cried out so hard my head hurt. "WWWWHHHHHHYYYYYYYY?" Why did bad things always have to happen to me?

RYSON

"The light is green motherfucker!" I beeped the horn at the white Escalade in front of me. I had to get to Samara. If I had to run every light and break every fucking traffic law, I was going to do it! When Devon called me and told me he saw a story about Samara on the news, my heart dropped. Here I was, eating Shar's nasty ass pussy just so she wouldn't tell Samara my secret. While the whole time my baby was in trouble. If I lost her, I would never forgive myself. I would never forgive myself for breaking up with her, and I would never forgive myself for being such a coward. If I had just told Samara the truth in the first place, I wouldn't be in this predicament. I reached into the overnight bag I had from Shar's apartment, and pulled out a small bottle of mouthwash. I gargled mouthfuls of Listerine over and over to get the stench of Shar out of my mouth and off my lips. If only I could Listerine my whole body, I would feel less disgusting.

"Please let her be okay." I sent a prayer up and wiped the tears from my face. I could barely see the road through the tears. They streamed down my face like a canal. How could I leave her? How could I treat her like that? She was my baby, my future, and I treated her like she was Shar. I didn't care anymore. I was telling her everything. I just hoped she would listen to me. I had made a copy of her key before I broke up with her. I couldn't bring myself to just give the key back. I opened her door and punched in the code. The living room furniture had bullet holes in it, and so did the walls. Her trophies were all over the floor. Feathers from the couch cushions were everywhere. There was blood on the walls, the floor, and the steps. Her living room looked like a crime scene from a horror movie.

"Oh god. SAMARA!" I yelled her name, hoping she was home. I made my way up the steps.

"SAMARA? ARE YOU HERE?" I opened her bedroom door. The first thing I noticed was the bandage on her thigh. Then I noticed she was crying. I looked over at Dwayne sitting on her bed with a smug expression on his face. I wasn't surprised to see him. I already knew once word got out I dumped Samara, he would come sniffing around. I was kind of grateful that she wasn't here alone. I couldn't judge anything or anybody right now after the last few days I'd had. I cheated on Samara with Shar at least eight times in the last two days, so I couldn't say shit about Dwayne being in her bedroom. Her sad eyes came to mines and my heart melted. I missed her so much. I wanted to kiss her a million times, but I knew now wasn't the time. I had to make sure she was okay and tell her the truth about the other day. Dwayne got up and put his arm around Samara. If he was trying to make me jealous, it wasn't working. Right now, the only thing on my mind was Samara. She asked him to leave to let us talk and he said okay. He kissed her on the lips and she kissed him back. That hurt a little, but the feeling subsided once I was alone with Samara.

"Are you okay? I came as soon as I heard. I am so sorry I wasn't here," I said, my voice breaking.

"I'm okay. Dwayne took care of me," she said pointedly and limped towards her bed. That stung, but again, I wasn't in any position to judge. She sat on the edge of her bed and looked at the floor. I didn't even know where to start. I took a deep breath and decided to just come right out and say it. Trying to hold it in all of this time was what got me into this situation in the first place.

"Shar is our... sister." I exhaled and looked at the ceiling. I couldn't possibly look at Samara yet. I was appalled and embarrassed at myself and Dwayne.

"WHAT?" Her voice broke as she grabbed hold of her bedside dresser. She struggled to stand up. She found her balance and limped over to stand in front of me. Her stunned eyes stared into mines in disbelief.

"Shar is your SISTER? WHAT?... I don't even know what to say right now. Oh my god!" She ran her hands through her hair and limped over to the window. I wanted to cry. I never thought I would be telling anyone the truth about Shar. But here I was, telling Samara that Dwayne and I fucked our own little sister.

"You fucked your sister? And Dwayne too? This shit is crazy!" She was talking to herself. She turned to me with a sour look on her face. She had already formulated her new opinion about me.

"Why?" Her eyebrows furrowed in confusion. I didn't have an answer that made sense. But dumb reason or not, I had to tell her.

I walked over to the window and faced her. I had to man up.

"There is no reason. About four years ago, I got a call from my mom. A detective in Detroit said they found my dad's body. The last time Dwayne and I saw our dad, we were like ten years old. He just stopped calling and coming around all of a sudden. We assumed he had abandoned us. So when I got the call, it hit me hard. Dwayne and I went down to identify the body and it was him. He looked really bad. He was almost fifty pounds lighter than he was the last time we saw him. His skin was ashen and his hair was all gray. They said they found his body in an alley and they assumed he was homeless. But when they searched him they found his I.D. A search through their database brought up his criminal history and my mom's name." I took her hand and asked her to look at me. She seemed hesitant and I couldn't blame her. Her eyes were sullen. She looked so frail. I did that to her. My sassy, bold Samara was broken down.

"Apparently he was on the run from the cops. Our dad killed one of the women he was messing around with back in the nineties. Shar's mother." Samara's eyes widened in astonishment.

"Oh my god," she whispered and wrapped her fingers around my hand.

"That's how we met Shar. She was at his gravesite the day of the burial. We didn't recognize her so we went over to introduce ourselves. When she told us that he was her father, it dawned on us that it was her mother our dad had killed. We already knew the woman had a daughter after the truth about our father came to light. That day we talked and decided Shar should come back to town with us, her family. After a few weeks of staying with us, Shar hit on me. I was grossed out at first. I turned her down immediately and told her she was crazy because I was her brother. I thought it was over after that. Then one night she came in my room while I was asleep and... performed oral sex on me. I was so caught up, I didn't stop her and ended up crossing the line with her that night. It sickened me at first. I cried afterwards. I knew it was wrong and immoral. But I kept going back for more and she let me.

But to be honest, even to this day, I've never felt a sibling bond with Shar. She always felt like a complete stranger to me, not a sister. Not that it excuses *anything* that happened between us. After a while, Dwayne caught on to what we were doing, and he started sleeping with Shar too. It was so fucked up! We all knew we were in the wrong, but we didn't care. We promised not to tell anyone who Shar really was. We had a strange arrangement, but it kind of worked for a while. Then one random day, Dwayne and I were with Shar and I saw her reflection in the mirror. I instantly thought of my dad. I got freaked out and ran out of there. I never looked at her or myself the same again after that. It took me years to come to my senses, but when I did it was too late. Shar was a totally different person and so was I. I hated myself for that. And in turn it made me hate Shar. Shar didn't want to break our arrangement. She loved the attention Dwayne and I gave her. She was sicker than all of us." I stopped to see how Samara was dealing with this bomb I had dropped on her. She just watched and listened. Her face didn't convey any emotion. That scared me.

"I know you probably think I'm a perverted monster now after telling you all of this. I wouldn't blame you." She looked away for a second. I watched her swallow. Her scent was everywhere. I just wanted to reach out and stroke her cheek. I didn't want her to hate me or look at me differently now.

"I don't think you're a monster Ryson. I just... I don't know. It's a lot to digest right now." I nodded. It was the only thing I could do not to kiss her. That brought me to the next topic. I had to tell her the truth behind our break-up.

"Um... I have something else to tell you." She smiled a little and shook her head.

"I don't know if I can handle anything else right now Ryson, to be honest with you." She let go of my hand. She put her hand on the small of her back and paced the room.

"It's about what happened the other day." She licked her lips and avoided eye contact. She was hurt, I could tell that.

"Shar threatened to tell you everything if I didn't break-up with you. And I knew if that information came from her and not me, it would be the end of us. I told myself if I just broke it off, you would never know the truth. Once again I was looking out for myself instead of being up front with you. I knew I couldn't just come in here with some fake ass excuse for breaking up with you. That's why I was so mean to you. I'm so sorry Samara. I would have *never* spoken to you that way if I thought you would just let me go. I didn't mean any of that shit I said Samara. It ate me up to say those disrespectful and hateful things to you. I was desperate to keep this secret a secret. Devon called me and told me what happened to you. I just kept thinking to myself if something happened to you, the last memory you would have of me would be from that night."

"Why didn't you just tell me? From the beginning?" she asked me desperately. She sat down on the bed.

"I was scared as shit that you would leave me! I didn't want to lose you like that."

"But you ended up breaking my heart!" She sobbed and put her hand to her mouth. She was right. I tried to protect my secret and keep Samara from getting hurt with the truth. I ended up hurting her more in the long run and making the situation even messier.

"I knew I had to get to you. I told Shar to go to hell and rushed over here. I figured if I told you, at least she wouldn't have anything to hold over my head. She couldn't force me to do shit anymore." My voice was trembling. I was terrified of her reaction. I couldn't be without her. I just couldn't.

"Is breaking up with me all Shar forced you to do?" She turned to me, and this time I saw compassion in her eyes. I couldn't talk about the hell Shar had put me through in the last few days. I dropped my head and shook my head no. I couldn't hold it in any longer. My shoulders rocked with my cries. I let it all out. I'd never cried like that in my life. I sat down next to her and felt her arms wrap around me. She was crying too.

"I'm so sorry baby. I never meant for all of this shit to happen. Please don't leave me!" I didn't recognize my own voice.

"You hurt me baby," she wept in my ear.

"I know baby. I'm sorry, I'm sorry, I'm so fucking sorry!" I cried even harder and held her tighter. I wasn't letting her go and I wasn't letting anything get in my way of loving her ever again. I didn't care who or what it was.

SAMARA

I felt sick to my stomach. A bitter taste was in my mouth. He fucked his sister. I couldn't get that image out of my head. They all knowingly committed incest and thought it was okay. Granted, they were half-siblings, but they shared the same blood line. I vaguely remembered reading something about that before. Something called genetic sexual attraction. It was what happened when sexual attraction developed between close blood relatives who first meet as adults. They didn't grow up together, so they never established that sibling or familial bond. It was like they were strangers attracted to another stranger. It made the situation less perverted, but the optics alone made my skin crawl. I couldn't look at Ryson right now. How could he have done something so despicable? So horrid and disgusting? I didn't know if I should have been upset or repulsed. But could I really judge him? Yes I could. He did it and it was wrong. But he had stopped when he realized the error of his ways. It was the most revolting thing I ever heard of. At least he was man enough to face the truth and put an end to it. Could we move forward from this? I loved Ryson so much, I couldn't live without him. So the only solution was either to forgive and forget, or hold it against him and let him go. I picked the former. Maybe it was senseless of me to just embrace him after hearing a bomb dropped like that, but I didn't care. At the end of the day, I was in love with this man and he was in love with me. What was a relationship without trials and tribulations? Albeit, this situation went beyond the normal problems couples faced. Our whole relationship seemed to be based on one crazy situation after another, but I just couldn't leave him.

When he told me about Shar blackmailing him, I felt a huge weight lift off of my heart. I knew Ryson loved me and would never hurt me like that. Not of his own free will at least. It still disturbed me that he felt he couldn't tell me. How would I have reacted? I didn't know. It was a huge thing to ask someone to overlook. It was wrong on so many levels. It did explain Shar and her fanatical obsession with Ryson and Dwayne. They were the only family she had left. In her mind, they were hers and nobody else's. She looked at me as someone trying to take everyone she loved away from her. I almost felt bad for her. Almost. As I lay on Ryson's shoulder, holding him while we cried, I made a decision. I would forgive him for maliciously breaking-up with me, and I wouldn't hold his secret past against him. He was hurting too. I could only imagine the sick things Shar forced him to do to her. If I were in his shoes, I would have felt so alone. I didn't by any means condone what he and Dwayne did, but I couldn't shun him for it. If he could get past me sleeping with his brother, I could get past him sleeping with his sister. Yuck! It would take time, but I would come to terms with it. I wouldn't hold his past indiscretions against him. He was only human and he was a different man now.

"I'm so fucking sorry!" Ryson's tears landed on my back.

"Sshhhhh." I rubbed his back and talked to him in a soothing voice. We both needed this.

"Don't worry baby. I won't leave you. I love you. I need you." I spoke softly into his ear.

"I need you too." He kissed me in the crook of my neck. I missed him so much. I ran my hand up and down his head and pulled his head back so he could look at me. His eyes were brimming with tears, as were mine.

"From now on, don't hold *anything* back from me. Just be honest okay?" I murmured before kissing him. He nodded and put his hands in my hair. We kissed like we hadn't seen each other in years. I could taste his salty tears on my lips. I motioned for him to let me stand up. He helped me up and wiped his face. I went to the dresser, got my phone, and sent Dwayne a text because I knew he would be calling me soon. He was going to be so upset, but it had to be done.

Hey Dwayne. We decided to work it out. I appreciate everything you did for me. Thank you for being there for me when I needed you the most. You're a great friend.

I hit send, and hoped Dwayne didn't hold all of this back and forth against me. Ryson walked over to me and pulled me close to him. I let his smell flow through my body. I thought I would never smell it again.

"I love you." He rubbed his nose onto mine and kissed me softly on the lips.

"I love you too." I put my phone down and put my hands behind his ears, holding him. I eagerly gave him my tongue. I needed to be with him right now. I never wanted to stop kissing him. I put all of the drama of the past week out of my head. I stopped thinking about Dwayne and Shar. I pushed the attack to the back of my memory. The only thing I wanted to think about was Ryson. I relaxed and held onto my man.

DWAYNE

How long did it take to fucking talk? It was going on twenty minutes and Samara had yet to call me and tell me to come back. My phone buzzed. I picked it up and saw a text message from her.

Hey Dwayne. We decided to work it out. I appreciate everything you did for me. Thank you for being there for me when I needed you the most. You're a great friend.

Are you FUCKING kidding me? That was it? A fucking thank you text? I hope she didn't think that meant shit to me. She was still my girl. I knew she would give the fuck in to Ryson. She needed to grow a backbone or I would pound one into her. I parked in front of Shar's apartment building. The women in my life were driving me the fuck crazy! After this, I was making my way back to Samara's house. We were finishing what we started, whether Ryson was still there or not. I rang Shar's bell and waited for her to buzz me in. I ran up the steps and banged on her door. She opened the door slowly and moved back.

"You know why I'm here right?" I asked her and cracked my knuckles. She looked scared out of her mind, as she should be. She had on a ratty bathrobe and her face was puffy from crying.

"Before you say anything, let me tell you my side," she said, quickly closing the door.

"I'm not interested in that shit. I just have one question for you Shar." I stepped into her face and forced her against the wall. She cowered and turned her head away.

"What?" She put her hands on my chest, trying to push me back. I grabbed her wrists and squeezed.

"Where the FUCK did you get the money?" I bit my bottom lip and squeezed tighter.

"OUCH! Dwayne that hurts! Please don't be mad at me!" She started to cry. I had just about enough with crying females today.

"Shut the fuck up and answer the question!" I let her go and moved back.

Her shoulders slumped and she started to whine. I was done with Shar. I didn't even know what I ever saw in her sorry ass.

"I got the money from you Dwayne. I just couldn't sit back and let Samara take you and Ryson away from me! I love you!" She tried to reach for me. I pushed her hands away.

"The only person you were thinking about was yourself, as usual. I don't even know what to do with you!" I cracked my neck. She fiddled nervously with the belt on her robe.

"You did all of this for me, right?" I asked her quickly.

"Well yes, but mostly for Ryson." I could see in her eyes she immediately regretted saying that out loud. It was always Ryson wasn't it?

"So you took MY fucking money and paid somebody to hurt Samara, so you could have Ryson to yourself?" I got back in her face. I felt my temper flaring up, but I didn't push it away. It seemed like Ryson was getting everything. He already had Samara on his dick and Shar's retarded ass was right behind her. What was wrong with me? When Ryson stopped fucking with Shar, I made sure to be there for her even more. When Ryson dumped Samara, I was right there on her doorstep ready to step in. All these bitches did was use me to get to Ryson. I understood now why Samara called me instead of Ryson. She knew Ryson would come back eventually. She just used me as a fill in for the time in between. Damn. I felt so fucking used. Samara threw her pussy at me and made me fall in love with her, just to jump in bed with my brother! I didn't like to be played with. My heart wasn't a fucking toy! I went to the bathroom and left Shar in the hallway. I grabbed the sides of the sink and looked at myself in the mirror. I was good looking, in great shape, with a successful career. I had a long tongue and a big dick. What else did Samara and Shar want? I was a good fucking catch! I had to do something to set this shit straight. This was the last time I was letting Ryson get his way. I knew what I had to do. I planned for this day and it was finally here. I was only supposed to do this in case of an emergency. What was more of an emergency then losing the woman I loved? Change of plans for tonight then. I would deal with Samara in due time. I splashed some water on my face. *It's the only option.*

"I know." I walked back into the living room to Shar rocking back and forth in the chair. She jumped up as soon as she saw me.

"I'm sorry Dwayne. I swear to GOD I will pay you back." I already knew she would try to cover her ass. Shar worked as a waitress making two dollars an hour plus tips. How the fuck was she going to pay me back three thousand dollars? I didn't care about that though. After tonight, she wouldn't have to worry about the money or anything else.

"Come here Shar," I said, surprising her with my change of attitude. She looked at me sideways, and timidly walked over to me. She stood before me and took a shaky breath. She didn't know what to expect from me. She definitely wasn't expecting what I did next. I grabbed her short hair and put my lips on hers. She moaned in surprise and then put her arms around me. I picked her up and took her to the bedroom. I kissed her sloppy and wet, just like she liked it. I threw her on the bed.

"Get the cuffs I left here," I commanded. She crawled to the drawer on the side of her bed and got them. I locked her wrists in place tight behind her back. I got on the bed and opened my legs. I put her head in my lap and unzipped my jeans.

"Put your big brother's big dick in your mouth," I ordered her. Shar was a freak, so she did as she was told. She took the head of my dick into her mouth, and slowly took more and more into her mouth. I saw my hand on the top of her head and watched as my hand started pushing her head down further onto my dick, forcing her to take more. I was losing control of my body again, just like the night I had attacked Samara. NO! I can do this! I don't need any help. *Do it then!*

I will. I felt the sensation come back into my hands. I held her head there on my dick until she started to squirm, then I let her go.

"I can't breathe when you make me deep throat it baby," she said coughing and gasping for air. Her eyes were watering.

"I know," I said brusquely and pushed her head back down on my dick. She started to cough and gag on my dick. She tried to bring her head back up. I held it down even harder. Her eyes came to mines in horror, as she realized what I was doing. I could see the terror in her eyes as she struggled to breathe. Her body started to shake, and saliva rolled out of her mouth and down my dick. She started gagging and throwing up, but I didn't stop. She tried to scream, so I pinched her nostrils together to hurry the process up. I saw tears coming down her cheek, and her face was turning purple. It wouldn't be long now. She started biting me, but I could tell she was getting weak. She kicked her legs and screamed on my dick. My dick was enjoying this. I came in her mouth just as her eyes started to close. Shar would die doing what she did best. Sucking dick.

SHAR

This shit could not be happening to me again! I lost everything. Oh god! Ryson was done with me forever. The pain in my heart was so intense. Soon he would know the truth about my involvement in what happened to Samara. Then he and Dwayne would come looking for me. It was just a matter of time. There was nothing I could do but wallow in self-pity and wait for the inevitable. I walked sluggishly to the bathroom and got into the shower. I remember a time when Ryson and Dwayne would get into fights over who would get their dicks sucked next by me. Now it seemed that they couldn't care less about me. My tears mingled with the water from the shower as they streamed down my face. As an orphaned child, I grew up feeling so alone and isolated. When I found out my father had other children, it filled me with so much happiness, I knew I had to find them. But they found me first. After getting a call from a detective about the man who killed my mother, I rushed to attend his burial. I hated my father with a fucking passion. He made my mother's life a living hell. He made me an orphan after brutally murdering her right in front of me. I only went to try to get some closure. I stared down at his headstone, contemplating whether to spit on it or not, when I heard leaves rustling behind me.

"Hi... do you know the deceased?" This tall brown-skinned man walked over to me. I stood there in shock for a few seconds before I answered.

"Um... yes, he was my father. Who are you?" I asked, wiping my eyes. I couldn't believe I was crying over that fucking bastard.

"I'm sorry to disturb you. My name is Ryson Turner and this is my brother Dwayne Turner. Did you say the deceased was your father?"

Turner? That was my father's last name! They were my brothers? I took a deep breath and looked behind Ryson at the man standing behind him. He was tall like Ryson, but they both had totally different features. For one thing, Ryson was slim whereas Dwayne was very muscular. Dwayne had a bald head and Ryson was sporting waves. Ryson had beautiful light hazel eyes and Dwayne had dark brown eyes with long eyelashes. Despite all of that, there was definitely a resemblance between them. And they were both fine as fuck. I shouldn't be noticing that should I?

"I'm sorry to drop this on you like this, but he was also our father," Ryson was saying. I was stuck on the realization that I had two brothers.

"I don't mean to stare, but I didn't know I had other siblings until recently," I explained when Ryson caught me staring at him.

"Half-siblings," Dwayne pointed out.

"We just found out we had a sister too," Ryson said, looking at me a little strangely. If he knew about me, he probably knew that the dead scum had murdered my mother. My emotions were all over the place. They told me they were staying at a hotel downtown, and invited me back to their room so we could talk. I said okay and followed them in my car. It was a revealing and emotional night. I learned all about the father I never really knew, and the two new additions to my life. It was hard to let myself go in front of them. I still couldn't believe I had two brothers. I wasn't alone in this world anymore.

"Where are you staying?" Ryson asked me after our talk when Dwayne was in the shower. I felt a little funny being alone around him. I kept getting this knot in the pit of my stomach. It kind of felt like attraction. But he was my brother for god's sake! I was probably suffering from emotional overload, that was why I was having those crazy feelings.

"I'm not staying at a hotel. I wasn't planning on staying in town overnight. I actually have to get back to work in the morning," I told him and moved a few paces back. He seemed to be moving closer to me without even moving. Or maybe it was my imagination. I shook my head clear.

"What do you do?" he asked me, cocking his head to the side.

"I'm a customer service rep for a pharmaceutical company."

"Can't you do that from anywhere?" Ryson asked expectantly. Was he flirting with me? Hell no! What the hell was wrong with me? It was just a simple question!

"I guess I could. I work from home."

"Why don't you come back with us? We just found you and it would be a shame to make it a one time meeting. We have a nice sized house with three bedrooms on a nice quiet street. I don't want to wait another three decades for us to see our little sister again." Then he smiled at me. His whole face lit up with that smile. I instantly got horny. Something was very wrong with that. I nodded my head in agreement, and told him I would go back with them. Over the next couple weeks, things seemed to go rather smoothly. Ryson arranged for my things to be shipped to his house. I was still able to work, and best of all I had a family for the first time in my life. My life was perfect. Or so it seemed. Slowly but surely, that feeling inside me kept creeping back about Ryson. Ryson was nothing but nice to me, but something came over me every time I was around him. When he hugged me, I wanted to hold him a little longer than I should. I felt that same crazy attraction to Dwayne, but with Ryson it was like it was something pulling me to him. I couldn't control it. I couldn't keep hiding it either. So, I decided to just confront Ryson about my thoughts, and waited until his day off to approach him. He was up in his bedroom. I knocked on the door, then poked my head in.

"Hey Shar! What's up?" Ryson smiled and got up from his place on the bed. He walked over to the door and pulled it open wider, motioning for me to enter. I walked past him and leaned against his dresser with my arms crossed. I didn't feel right being in his bedroom. It brought all types of nasty thoughts to my already confused head.

"I just wanted to talk to you about something. It's kind of awkward to talk about, so bear with me." He nodded and came to stand in front of me. Oh god, he smelled so good. Focus!

"What's on your mind?" He asked, looking concerned. He was so sweet. It made my attraction to him even stronger.

"Um... I don't know if you've noticed but there's a... how do I say this? There's... tension between us." I looked into his eyes and saw confusion.

"What kind of tension? Did me or Dwayne do something to make you feel uncomfortable? If so then..." He looked upset now, like he'd hurt me.

"No! Nothing like that. It's um... something else that I've been feeling. Towards you actually." Ryson put his finger under his chin and looked confused.

"I'm not following you Shar. Just tell me what's on your mind." His voice was so comforting and soothing. I looked into his beautiful eyes and couldn't control myself. I launched myself at him and kissed him on the lips. The kiss lasted about three seconds, before Ryson grabbed me and positioned me back against the dresser. He looked at me in shock and didn't say anything. The room was quiet as we stared each other down. Me looking at him in expectation, and him looking at me in shock.

"What... the... hell... was that Shar?" he asked and shook his head.

"I don't even know what to say," I said in a small voice. I was embarrassed. I didn't regret it though.

"I'm sexually attracted to you and Dwayne. To you especially though. I can't explain it. I can't control it," I said looking at the floor.

"Shar you're our *sister*! What do you mean you're attracted to us?" Ryson practically screamed at me.

"But I don't feel like I'm your sister! I don't feel any brother sister type feelings towards either of you! We're total strangers. I feel like I'm attracted to two very sexy ass men." I pushed off of the dresser and walked closer to him. He put his hands up and backed up towards the bed.

"Shar, you're right. We are total strangers. And I agree, I don't feel a sibling like bond with you *yet*. But I KNOW you're my sister, so that trumps anything else." He was adamant about that.

He was still backing up and I was still walking towards him. I felt a tingle deep in my belly. I was within an inch of his face. He shook his head no and gave me a stern look. I ignored him. I got on my tiptoes and kissed his chin. Then trailed kisses down from his chin to his neck. He put his hand in my hair.

"Shar stop." His voice was husky. I had him.

"Make me." I challenged and rubbed my hand over his dick. His erection was almost immediate.

"Shit." He grabbed my hand.

"No Shar! This is wrong. It's incest!" He gently pushed me off of him and walked away. I was left standing there in his bedroom with wet panties.

I stayed in my room the rest of that day. I had formulated a plan and decided to put it into action. I waited until around two in the morning, and snuck into Ryson's bedroom. He was asleep on his back. I was completely naked. His room smelled like him. It made me wetter and wetter. I gingerly climbed onto his bed. He didn't stir. I took a deep breath and slowly pulled the covers back. He had on briefs. His body was fucking beautiful.

"It's now or never." I gave myself a pep talk, as I moved the fabric of Ryson's underwear to the side. I gently took his sleeping dick out of his briefs. I looked up to make sure he was still asleep. He was. I took a deep breath and bent down, ran my tongue across my lips to lubricate them, then slowly put his dick inside my mouth. It took about fifteen seconds of gentle sucking to wake Ryson. By then, his dick was erect and I was doing my best work.

"What the fuck Shar!" He gasped and put his hand on my head to push me away.

"STOP!" He yelled out and tried to sit up. I grabbed his dick at the base and started sucking the head. His dick got even harder. He didn't try to stop me after that. I sucked and licked and slurped on his dick, until I felt him start to tremble. He was going to cum. I abruptly stopped and laid down onto the bed. I spread my legs wide for him. He turned me over onto my stomach. I spread my ass cheeks and waited. It seemed like an eternity. It was so quiet and still. And just like I predicted, I felt his big thick dick slide easily into my waiting wet pussy.

"AAAHHHH!" He was so big.

"Is this what you really want?" Ryson whispered close to my ears. Did I? Fuck yes!

"YES!" I screamed out. Ten seconds later I came hard all over his dick. Ryson made love to me for hours. Each time he bent me over was even more thrilling than the last time. Ryson and I made love at every chance, everywhere we could. It was like I couldn't get enough of him. One night when Dwayne was supposed to be working late, Ryson decided he wanted to take me in Dwayne's bed. It was so naughty, I couldn't turn him down. As I was nearing my third climax, Dwayne's door burst open. Ryson immediately stopped his pounding into me. The room fell silent. My heart raced. What was Dwayne thinking? Would he tell anyone? Little did I know, Dwayne was not the least bit shocked. Dwayne got naked in seconds and climbed onto the bed in front of me. I gladly took him into my mouth. Ryson slowly eased back into me, and we caught a rhythm. It was as if we were perfectly molded together. That was the first of many trains that my brothers ran on me. It was so crazy! I was having the best sex of my life!

We decided I should get my own place to keep people from finding out what we were doing. It was our business and no one had to know. I agreed, and got my own apartment.

They were over there so often, it was as if I never left. It was understood that people wouldn't know who I really was, or that I was involved with them. It was too complicated and messy to have to explain. So I tried to keep a low profile in front of their friends and mines. I never spent time with them in public. I limited the times I came over. And we never ever brought others into our arrangement. They fucked endless hoes of course, but they never put them above my time. My life became consumed with pleasing them. I messed up with work so much, I lost my job. The only thing I could find on short notice was a waitressing gig at a restaurant downtown. Still, life was good for about three years. Then one day in the middle of love making, Ryson suddenly stopped.

"I can't do this! This shit is wrong!" Wait what? Since when? He left abruptly. Deep down inside, I was beyond hurt. I loved Ryson and Dwayne so much. I couldn't handle it if one of them left me. I loved Ryson the most. That night I seduced him, I told myself he was in love with me. Why else would he let me seduce him? After that, he avoided me at all costs, even going as far as not talking to me. I felt like I had lost the love of my life. I went into a deep depression and stopped caring for myself and my home. Dwayne was always there to pick me up, but I wanted Ryson back. I just had to make him fall in love with me again. I started to use every available penny I had on expensive sexy clothes. I made it a point to be around him as much as possible. Ryson started bringing even more women than usual into his bed, turning the knife even deeper into my heart. I didn't give up though, I just tried harder. The night we went to the café, was the first time Ryson had agreed to be in the same room with me since our separation. I thought that night was going to be the start of a new beginning. Then Ryson saw Samara, and it was all over before it even got started. I knew I shouldn't have blackmailed him, but what else could I do? I missed him so much! I would do anything to get him back.

I got out of the shower and put on my robe. I couldn't stop crying. What had I done? I heard my bell ringing. Was it Ryson? I hit the buzzer and waited at the peephole. It was Dwayne! Oh god. He was here about Samara I bet. That bitch was getting a happy ending after all it seemed. How did one female turn my own brothers against me? She made me look like the fucking villain without even lifting a finger. I slowly pulled the door open. I was scared of what Dwayne would do. He had a bad temper. He'd never hit me, but he had gotten pretty rough with me many times before. He didn't know his own strength.

"You know why I'm here right?" He pushed his way into the apartment. I was in so much trouble. I tried to stay calm.

"Before you say anything, let me tell you my side." I tried to explain to him why I did what I did, but he wasn't having it.

"I'm not interested in that shit. I just have one question for you Shar." He stepped into my face, forcing me back against the wall.

"What?" I asked and put my hands against his chest. He violently grabbed my wrists.

"Where the FUCK did you get the money?" He screamed at me and squeezed my wrists tighter. He was furious. I couldn't lose him too!

"OUCH! Dwayne that hurts! Please don't be mad at me!" I broke down. I couldn't stand being alone again! What had I done to deserve this? I was loyal to both of them and they repaid me by tossing me to the side for some bitch they met at a café? He blew air out his nose in frustration. My tears meant nothing to him.

"Shut the fuck up and answer the question!" He let me go and stepped back.

"I got the money from you Dwayne. I just couldn't sit back and let Samara take you and Ryson away from me! I love you!" I reached out for him, but he pushed me away. Why did they torture me with their rejection?

"The only person you were thinking about was yourself, as usual. I don't even know what to do with you." He ran his hand over his bald head and shook his head. He cracked his neck and closed his eyes. Couldn't he understand my reasoning behind all of this? Everything I did was for them. For their love.

"So you did all of this for me, right?" he asked me.

"Well yes, but mostly for Ryson." Shit! I didn't mean to blurt that out! Now I knew it was all over.

"So you took MY fucking money and paid somebody to hurt Samara, so you could have Ryson to yourself?" He was back in my face again. I held my breath and hoped he wouldn't hit me. I hated it when he was mad at me. He stormed off into the bathroom and slammed the door. I walked over to the couch and slumped down into it. What did I have without them? Nothing. It couldn't be over that easily. Just like I tried to fight for Ryson, I had to do the same for Dwayne. I really did love him, just not as much as I loved Ryson. I hopped up from the couch when he came out of the bathroom.

"I'm sorry Dwayne. I swear to GOD I will pay you back." That was a promise I couldn't keep. There was no way I could pay that money back on my current salary. I was grasping at straws.

"Come here Shar," Dwayne said softly. My eyes widened in surprise. I slowly walked over to him, not sure what to think. I licked my lips and swallowed. I never knew what to expect from Dwayne. This could be a trick. I stood in front of him and took a breath. There was no use in being scared now. Whatever Dwayne did to me I deserved. I scammed him out of thousands of dollars and used him. I deserved to be punished. Dwayne grabbed me by the waist and pulled me to him. I looked in his eyes and smiled. He wasn't mad! He put his hands in my hair and kissed me with intensity. Oh yes! I hadn't lost Dwayne! He had always been here for me as my rock. Starting right now, I was going to show him how much I appreciated and needed him. He picked me up and took me into the bedroom. He handcuffed my hands behind my back and told me to lie on my stomach. I knew exactly what he wanted. He got on the bed in front of me and opened his legs.

He unzipped his pants and let his thick dick free.

"Put your big brother's big dick in your mouth." I did as I was told, and started to work my magic on his dick. I felt his hand on the top of my head pushing me farther down onto his dick. I tried to take as much as I could, but he was too big. I started to gag and squirm to let him know I couldn't really breathe. He let my head go.

"I can't breathe when you make me deep throat it baby." He already knew that, but I let it go. I had to focus on pleasing him. Dwayne was all I had left now. I would do anything for him.

"I know," he said harshly and pushed my head back down onto his dick. What the fuck! I just told him I couldn't breathe! I tried to pull my head up, but he was so strong. I tried to move, but my arms were trapped. I looked up at Dwayne as I struggled to breathe. My body was panicking. I could still take in a little air through my nose, but it wasn't enough. I tried to cry out. Dwayne's eyes were empty and cold. He smirked at me. *OH GOD! He's killing me! NO! NO! NO! Not you Dwayne! Not like this! Not my own flesh and blood! Not my big brother!* I started to get lightheaded. Maybe he was trying to teach me a lesson and would let me up at any second. My heart raced in my ears and I felt faint. I started throwing up. I attempted to cry out. Dwayne pinched my nostrils closed. Now I had no air supply at all! *GOD HELP ME! RYSON HELP ME!* I felt Dwayne's hot cum in my mouth. I looked up to the ceiling and saw my mom. She smiled down at me and motioned for me to come to her. I stopped struggling and reached out to her. I missed her so much. She placed her cool hand in mine and pulled me towards her.

"Hi mommy!" I smiled tenderly, and felt at peace for the first time in my life.

RYSON

I wiped tears from my eyes for what seemed like the hundredth time that day. After Samara took me back once *again*, I told her we needed a fresh start. My job had firms in three other cities. The longer I stayed here the more I wanted out. I asked her to leave with me so we could try to build a life without all of this drama over our heads. I was beyond ecstatic when she said yes. The feeling was comparable to her accepting my marriage proposal. I was boxing my things up in my room, just reflecting on the last week of my life. I still couldn't believe Samara was so understanding with the Shar situation. I really had to give her props for that. Not only did she tell me she wouldn't hold it against me, she convinced me that it was nothing to be ashamed of. People made mistakes and they learned from them. I definitely learned my lesson. I was never going to hold anything back from Samara, even if I thought it would hurt her. She was a mature woman and could handle anything life threw at her. She had so much of her father in her. I was just realizing that now. I heard the door open and close downstairs. It was Dwayne. He hadn't slept here or spoken to me since that night at Samara's. I didn't give two fucks about it though. Dwayne was part of the problem too. He and Shar had caused a lot of friction between Samara and me. It was time to put some distance between us and them. I hadn't heard from Shar since that night either. It was for the best I guess. I had yet to tell Dwayne that Samara and I were moving. I knew he wouldn't take the news lightly. As much as I loved my brother, it was time for him to grow up. Maybe living on his own, and not having me around to fix his messes, would give him the chance to do that. We had fucked around and acted like kids long enough. I taped the last box closed and went downstairs to talk to Dwayne. He was in the kitchen standing next to the refrigerator, staring blankly into space.

"I'm moving out of town." I decided to cut right to the chase. He smirked and turned towards me.

"You think so?" His eyes seemed different. His skin looked unusually pale. He had let the hair on his face grow out more. He looked a little rugged.

"I'm transferring to a new firm. Samara is coming with me. We need a change of surroundings. Uh... I put a little something in your bank account. It's to help out with the bills for the first few months, until your promotion kicks in." His head turned slightly to look at me. He just watched me, not taking anything in. I felt a knot in my stomach. Something was off with Dwayne.

"Samara is not going anywhere unless I *let* her." He stood straight up and I saw blood on his hands. I ignored his comment and looked down at his dripping bloody hand.

"What the hell happened to your hand?" I walked towards him. He opened the freezer door right at that moment and the handle slammed into my nose. I wasn't expecting the hit. Pain exploded throughout my face. It caught me so off guard. I stood there, dazed for a few seconds, holding my nose. I fell backwards. The kitchen shifted from side to side. I looked up at his deranged face, as warm blood pooled out of my nose. I couldn't comprehend what just happened. The pain in my nose intensified and my eyes started to burn. My nose felt heavy on my face. I felt lightheaded. I knew I shouldn't close my eyes, but it was difficult trying to keep them open. I looked up in confusion at Dwayne's blank face. His face became blurry and everything turned black.

DWAYNE

The muscles in my back ached. I'd been digging for almost forty-five minutes straight. The ditch wasn't deep enough yet. It wasn't wide enough either, but I would have to make do with that. When I pulled Shar's dead mouth off of my dick, I went out to scout a place for the burial. My obvious choice was the park, but I didn't think I would have enough privacy to dig and bury the bodies. Luckily for me, there was a secluded picnic grove. No one ventured over there. It was run down, overgrown, and sparsely lit. I needed to get out there late for added privacy. I rolled Shar's body inside a blanket and carried her out to my truck. I drove back home and put the blanket in my work truck. I left her there, while I figured out how I was going to get Ryson and Samara. That was three days ago, and the smell of her decomposing body was pungent in my truck. I dug around in the back making sure I had everything I needed. A shovel, gasoline, matches, and an axe, just in case I had to dismember somebody. I slid my hand up and down the blade of the axe to test its sharpness.

"Shit!" I watched as blood trickled down my hand from the cut I'd just made. I guess it was sharp enough. I made my way into the house, knowing Ryson was home. It had rained most of the day, so it was wet outside. I had been watching Samara's house since yesterday, so I knew he spent the night and then came here in the morning. It was going to be hard to do this to my big brother, but it had to be done. It was the only logical thing I could think of. I walked into the kitchen and leaned against the counter near the refrigerator. I waited. I heard Ryson coming down the stairs.

"I'm transferring to another firm out of town and Samara is coming with me. We need a change of surroundings." I laughed a little inside. He actually thought that he would get away with stealing Samara from me twice? I felt so betrayed by my own brother.

"Samara is not going anywhere unless I *let* her." I stood up and faced him. He looked down at my hand and got distracted by the blood. Big mistake. He walked towards me. *Now's the time, do it!*

I grabbed the freezer door and hit him hard in the nose with the handle. He stood confused and stunned. He coughed and fell to his knees, then onto his back. He made a gurgling noise as blood spouted from his nose like a fountain. His eyes twitched, then he was out like a light. I went upstairs and got a blanket, and rolled him into it. He was much heavier than Shar, and it was difficult to walk with him out to my truck. I tried to look natural carrying him in the blanket on slippery ground.

"Aaaaahhhhh!" I threw his body into the truck next to Shar's. I put my hands on my sides and caught my breath. I looked over at my house. This would be the last time I would see it. Samara had a choice to make. Either she chose me, or she could be with Ryson, forever.

SAMARA

The storm was over. Literally and figuratively. Ryson and I were moving and starting over. And the weather was clearing up too. It had rained cats and dogs for most of the day. Now there was a dewy look to the sky as the sun was setting. Ryson and I talked long and hard that night after he dropped that bomb on me. I told him what happened to me and about Shar's involvement. He was furious. We both agreed it would be in our best interests to get away and try to start over. We decided on Philadelphia. It wasn't that far of a drive. It still had that city life we were accustomed to, but there was also a suburb where we could live comfortably. It was a big step for us. I was leaving behind my mother, but on the plus side I would be closer to Julio and Sofia. Saying goodbye to my best friends was bittersweet. We were all crying and messing up our make-up. But in the end, they understood why I had to leave. Why I needed a fresh start with Ryson. I didn't tell them all the details, but they knew enough about the situation to agree with my decision. Moving together was also a big commitment for Ryson and me. He wanted to build a life with me and I couldn't see myself with anyone else. It made perfect sense. He was home packing. He told me he would come by later to help me finish packing my stuff. My phone vibrated. I went to my messaging screen and read the text from Ryson.

Meet me at the park at the picnic groves, it's important

Huh? That didn't make any sense. What was he doing at the park? Especially at the picnic groves. No one ever went to that part of the park. I called his cell phone four times back to back, but it kept going straight to voicemail. A foreboding feeling came over me, and I sensed that Ryson was in trouble. I grabbed a hoodie and ran out of the house in a flash. I forgot my umbrella and didn't even remember if I locked my door on the way out. There was still a little drizzle coming down. I didn't think to drive, I just ran all the way to the park in my flats. By the time I reached the entrance of the picnic grove, my black hoodie was sticking to my body and my hair was wet. I was slipping and sliding everywhere. My injured leg ached painfully.

"RYSON?" I called out to him. Nothing but crickets responded. The smell of skunk irritated my nose. I hated being in the park at night. I was instantly on alert and afraid. I didn't want to believe something bad had happened, but my gut told me something was terribly wrong. It was dark, almost pitch black. The lights in this section of the park were always broken. The moonlight was the only illumination tonight. "RYSON? BABY WHERE ARE YOU?" I called out louder this time and walked further into the groves. It was a chilly night and I was freezing and wet. The smell of poison ivy filled my nose. I kicked a bug off of my foot. To say the picnic grove wasn't the safest place, especially around this time of night, was an understatement. I slipped on wet leaves and stepped in mud.

"RYSON?" Where was he? My voice echoed as I called out to him over and over. There was no one out here. I walked deeper into the grove, where people usually didn't go. I kept checking my surroundings. I felt so unsafe. Still no Ryson in sight. I didn't want to, but I slowly walked deeper into the picnic grove. There was a shovel sticking out of the ground a few feet up ahead, next to a mound of dirt. "What is that?" I asked myself out loud.

"SAMARA!"

"AAAAHHH!" I shrieked in fright. I damn near had a heart attack. I jumped and turned my head to my right at Dwayne's voice. I shook my head clear, not sure what the fuck was going on. I was so scared.

"Dwayne? What are you doing here? Where's Ryson?" That sinking feeling came over me again. Dwayne stepped out into the moonlight. His jeans and boots were covered in mud and debris from the park. Blood was dripping from his hand and splattered on his shirt. The sight of the blood put me on alert. I prayed it wasn't Ryson's blood. His shoulders were erect and his focused gaze was on me. This deep into the park, I wasn't sure anyone could even hear if I screamed. I fidgeted with my bracelet. My body shivered from the cold. My lips started to tremble. Dwayne had done something to Ryson, I just knew it. The look in Dwayne's eyes told me he was no longer in there. His eyes were glassy and empty.

"Dwayne?... Where is Ryson?" I asked softly. I started experiencing sharp pains in my chest. I had to force myself not to cry. Where was my Ryson? Dwayne walked closer to me. I took a step back, submerging my foot into a muddy pile of leaves. I impatiently kicked both my flats off, leaving my feet bare. I wrapped my arms around myself for warmth and comfort.

"He's right over there." Dwayne's voice was low like a hiss. He pointed to the mound of dirt. My eyes went wide in horror. I rushed over to the mound of dirt, hoping he hadn't buried Ryson alive. When I got closer, I noticed there was a hole in the ground next to the mound of dug up dirt. It was maybe ten feet deep. I looked down with more fear then I had ever felt in my life.

"OH GGGGGGOOOOOOOODDDDDD! RRRRYYYYYYSSSSSOOOOONNNNN!" Ryson's body lay motionless at the bottom of the pit. His face was covered in blood. I saw a hand and half of someone's face sticking out from underneath him. I strained to see whose hand it was. It was Shar! What has he done? I got down on all fours, and put my leg over the opening of the hole. I couldn't hold back my cries. If I had to jump down there and pull Ryson out myself, I would.

"Get the fuck back!" I turned towards Dwayne's voice and came face to face with the barrel of a gun. I felt like I was in a nightmare. I closed my eyes and opened them again, just to come face to face with the gun again. It wasn't a dream, it was real. Dwayne had snapped just like his father. I stood up slowly and moved away from the ditch. I wiped my muddy hands on my hoodie and tried to calm myself down. I saw my breath coming out in short bursts due to the chill in the air. I snuck a glance down at Ryson and sobbed. I put my hands up in surrender. I didn't know how this situation would play out. *Try to stay calm. Try to talk some sense into him. Deep down, he still loves his brother.*

"What's going on Dwayne? Are you alright?" I tried to talk to him as gentle as I could. I needed him to think I was more concerned about him than I was about Ryson. This was a territorial fight. Brother against brother. If I showed more favor to Ryson, Dwayne would see it as a betrayal.

"Like you fucking care!" He yelled at me and walked closer. This time I didn't step back. I needed his trust. My hands shook slightly. My feet were getting numb, and my teeth started chattering.

"I do care Dwayne. Why else would I ask you? You're my friend and I care about you." I took one step closer to him. He shook his head violently, and scratched his head with the gun. I bit my lip and tried to think of a way to get that gun out of his hands.

"FRIEND? A FUCKING FRIEND? Don't you get it? I don't want to be your fucking friend, I want to be your MAN!" He screamed and pointed the gun at my head. Shit. My heart pounded in my chest. I could hear it in my ears, and feel my body vibrating from it. Tonight would be my last night on earth. I could feel it. There would be no happy ending for me and Ryson. At least I could try to save Ryson.

"I didn't know that you wanted to date me seriously Dwayne. I just thought you wanted me for sex like in the beginning. If I would have known that, then—"

"Then what?" He was in my face now. He put the gun to my cheek and pressed it into my skin. The cold metal pressed into my jaw. I closed my eyes tight and whimpered. My nerves were so raw.

"Then we could have made a go at it. You have been there for me when I needed you. I trust you more than everyone, even Ryson. I would have definitely been open to dating you. I didn't know you felt so deeply for me." I started to cry again. I didn't want to die. I wanted to move to Philadelphia. I wanted to see my brother. I wanted to be with Ryson. I wanted to get married and have a child of my own. Dwayne took the gun off my cheek.

"Samara? Don't insult my fucking intelligence! You're just saying this shit to save your ass and Ryson's. You don't want to fucking be with me! Ryson has been your target since day one. You used me when you wanted me, and tossed me aside as soon as Ryson came back into the picture!" Spittle ran down his chin as he talked. He was so distressed. I shook my head no as tears burned my eyes and slid down my cheek.

"I LOVE YOU! I have never felt this way about anyone in my life! I gave you my heart. You knew I wanted you and you used me! Why would you sleep with me? Why give me false hope, then text me you were working it out with Ryson? A text? A FUCKING TEXT? You treated me like an afterthought Samara." He started to cry. I was stunned silent. He was absolutely right. It was right in front of me this whole time. Him wanting to hold me after sex. His anger at me when he attacked me. Him running to my rescue when I called. Him trying to lay claim to me so I wouldn't go back to Ryson. How could I have been so blind? Dwayne was in love with me. And I played him and led him on this whole time, unbeknownst to me. This was all my fault. I forgot about the gun in his hands. I forgot about Ryson in that hole. I closed the distance between us, wrapped my arms around him, and held him while he cried.

"I'm so sorry Dwayne. You're absolutely right. I have treated you so bad. You didn't deserve that. I'm so sorry. Sshhhhh." I ran my hand up and down his back trying to calm him down. He put the gun behind him in the waistband of his jeans. He wrapped both arms around me tight and sobbed onto my shoulders. I held him tight. I felt like such a bitch for my part in all of this. His body was so warm while I was freezing.

"Please forgive me," I mumbled into his chest. I felt hot tears rolling down my face. I couldn't believe I had hurt him so much. My heart ached from his pain. I sniffed and laid my head on his chest.

"You can't treat people that way," he said between sobs.

"I know. I'm so sorry. I'll never hurt you again," I promised him.

"You have to learn your lesson. You need to be punished," he sniffed and put his hands in my hair. I stopped crying. We were still in each other's embrace, but something had changed. He slowly let me go and looked down into my eyes. His were clear and focused. No more crying. No sign of the sadness from a few seconds ago.

"Wha...What do you mean?" I asked and took a few baby steps backwards. Again, fear gripped me. He had gone from angry, to hurt, to sad, to normal, in the span of two minutes. I couldn't keep up with his quickly changing emotions. He sighed, like he was explaining something to a child.

"Samara, you did something bad. You need to be punished for that." He reached out and put his index finger under my chin. I flinched away from him.

"You hurt my heart. Do you know how that feels?" He shook his head at me. I was so confused. I felt guilty for hurting him, but I was starting to get the feeling that his crying had all been a show.

"It feels kind of like this." In the split second it took me to realize that something was terribly wrong, he brutally punched me in the chest. The force of the blow threw me backwards, until my back hit a tree. I landed on my ass on the wet grass. My vision blurred. I couldn't breathe. My body was in shock. I choked on the spit that was in my mouth. I felt like my airways were in a vice grip.

"That pain in your chest is only a *fraction* of the pain I feel every day because of the pain you've caused me," Dwayne said. He was right in front of me. I hadn't even seen him walking towards me. I was dazed and struggling to breathe. I tried to take normal breaths, then I started crying. It hurt like hell. My chest felt like there was an inferno raging inside it. I couldn't stop the tears. The aching pain intensified as I tried to get more air.

"Aww, you're okay. Come here baby." Dwayne pulled me to my feet like I weighed nothing, and turned me so I was facing the tree. He pushed my face into the tree bark.

"OWW!" I sobbed as the bark cut into my face. I felt his erection on me as he did a slow grind on my ass. He buried his face in my hair and inhaled deeply.

"You smell so fucking good! You're all mines. I'm going to make sure you never forget that." I didn't respond. I couldn't. Every breath felt like it was harder and more painful to take than the last. The pain was almost unbearable. I felt myself being dragged. All of a sudden, I was lying flat on my back on something solid, wet, and cold. It was a decrepit picnic table.

DWAYNE

She passed the test. All I wanted was a sincere apology. For her to recognize how badly she had treated me. I almost died from happiness when she hugged me and apologized again. I felt so much better. But I couldn't forgive her that easily. She had to atone for her mistakes. Then we could move on.

"You can't treat people that way," I told her. She held me tighter and promised not to hurt me again. Wasn't she sweet?

"You have to learn your lesson. You need to be punished." I didn't want to, but I had no choice. She couldn't get away with how she'd treated me. She was confused and started to move away from me. She didn't understand. I tried to explain to her as patiently as I could.

"Samara, you did something bad. You need to be punished for that." She shook her head like she couldn't wrap her head around that concept. Did she think she would come out of this situation unscathed? I reached down to tip her chin up towards me and she flinched away from me. I didn't appreciate that.

"You hurt my heart. Do you know how that feels?" I had to show her. How else would she ever understand? I balled my fist up and rammed it into her chest. My fist connected in the dead center. I didn't hold my strength back, and she flew at least four feet into the tree behind us. Her head jerked. I saw her eyes lose focus. Her hands quickly flew to her chest. I watched her face start to contort in pain. I heard her gasping and wheezing for air. She tried to cry, but it came out like whimpers. Like an injured puppy.

"That pain in your chest is a *fraction* of the pain I feel every day because of the pain you've caused me." I stood above her. I had no sympathy for her. She deserved this. I watched her for a few more minutes as she made choking noises and tried to catch her breath.

"Aww, you're okay. Come here baby." I grabbed her by the arms and stood her up. It was like picking up a limp doll. I turned her towards the tree so I could see that beautiful ass of hers. My dick was instantly hard. I pressed my body onto hers and did a slow grind on her ass.

"OWW!" she cried out and started sobbing. I buried my face in her hair and smelled that shampoo I loved so much.

"You smell so fucking good! You're all mines. I'm going to make sure you never forget that." She didn't say anything. She was taking her punishment like a champ. Only thing left to do was to let the world know she was mines. Once I was done with that, I would finish off Ryson. She hadn't even spared that hole he was in a second glance since she'd apologized. Maybe she did love me. I pulled her from the tree and dragged her over to the run down picnic tables. She put up no resistance. She was being so cooperative. I laid her on her back and climbed over her. I sat down on her chest, straddling her, pinning her arms to her sides. She winced in pain and gasped for air.

"My chest!" she choked out in pain. Her eyes bulged out of her head as I sat down deeper, putting almost all my weight onto her chest. I slid my knife out my back pocket. Her eyes went wild and she started screaming.

"NOOOOO! HELLLLPPPP!" Her screams came out raspy due to her lack of air. She started to squirm left and right. She wouldn't stop screaming. She wasn't taking her punishment graciously anymore. It was making me angry. I took my t-shirt off, and shoved as much of it into her mouth as would fit. She started to gag and choke, but she continued trying to scream. She was crying so hard now. Tears were just falling down the side of her face, one after the other. I heard her muffled voice screaming, 'please', or something sounding like that, I couldn't tell. I didn't care. I leaned down closer to her, and squeezed her face in my hand. Left or right cheek? I couldn't decide. I looked into her scared eyes. So much fear and pain. She struggled and continued to scream through the shirt. I'm hurting her. What am I doing? *The right thing!* She was lucky I didn't get rid of her like I did Shar. I still could. All it would take was a little pressure from the knife across her throat. *Do it!*

Shut the fuck up! That fucking voice was driving me crazy all of a sudden. All day, telling me to do this and do that. I was in control!

She played you! They all did. Kill her!

I shook it out of my head. I decided on the left cheek and went to work carving a 'D' into it. She started bucking like a bull and screaming even louder. The veins in her neck and forehead swelled from the force of her muffled screams. I grabbed her face even tighter to hold her still. I pushed her head into the table, so she couldn't move it from side to side. She was fucking up my handiwork. How was I supposed to get my name carved into her face if she was moving so fucking much? I finished the first letter and inspected my creation. It was bleeding of course, but the 'D' was distinguishable. I pressed the blade against her cheek again and started on the 'W'. She made more whimpering noises. I glanced at her and realized her eyes were fluttering. Her breathing was sounding labored and ragged. She was losing consciousness. I needed her fully awake while I did this. If she couldn't feel the pain, she wouldn't learn her lesson. Shit! I had to ease up a little or this would be over way too quick. I got off her and took the shirt out of her mouth. She started gasping for air and coughing. I wanted her more than I ever have. Even laying there bleeding and crying, she was fucking beautiful. I stood in front of the table in between her legs. Her thighs were so thick, the jeans barely contained them. I grabbed her arms to sit her up. She was breathing erratically and sobbing. She was feeling the pain from her bad decisions. She was learning not to hurt me again.

"I love you so much." Her disheveled hair was all over the place. I bent down and kissed her. She kissed me back. Good girl. I gripped her by the throat and put my tongue in her mouth. She opened her mouth wide for me. I knew how she liked it. Rough and hard. We kissed until I couldn't take it anymore.

I pressed the gun to her forehead.

"Look at me!" I commanded. Her scared eyes slowly met mine.

"Are you sorry?"

"Yes," she sobbed. She looked me square in the eyes, making my dick even harder.

"Open your mouth." She blinked and hesitated for a split second before slowly parting her lips.

"Good girl." I shoved the gun in her mouth, pushing it to the back of her throat. Her face scrunched up in pain. She coughed and started to gag.

"Suck it." More tears fell down her face.

"NOW!" I pushed the gun deeper into her mouth. She gagged again then grabbed for the gun.

"Put your fucking hands down and take it!" She sobbed with the gun in her mouth.

"I'm not repeating myself again," I warned her. She put her hands down and looked at me with such fear. I almost felt bad for how I was treating her. Then I thought of how she strung me along all this time, and I wanted to push the gun even farther down her throat.

"Get it nice and wet." I put my hands down my pants and grabbed my dick. Hearing her slurping on my gun was driving me crazy. I took the gun out of her mouth. She put her hands on her throat and took a deep breath.

"Now demonstrate that on me." I grabbed the back of her neck and pushed her down to her knees. She gave little resistance. She knew she had no choice, or maybe she was finally realizing how important I was to her. Her hands went down to my belt buckle. She took my hard dick out of my underwear. Oh yeah, she wanted me. Her warm mouth enveloped my dick.

"Goddamn!" My dick was in the back of her throat. I put my hand on the top of her head and fed her my dick. I looked down and watched her take me deep in her mouth. I put my head back and looked at the moon. This was exactly how things were supposed to be.

"AAAAAAAAAAAHHHHHHHHHHHH!" She fucking BIT me!

"OOOO GGGOOOOODDDD SSSSHHHHIIIIITTTTT!" She sank her teeth deeper into the sensitive flesh of my dick. I cried out in agony. She released me and knocked the gun out of my hand. I was too preoccupied with the pain in my dick to care.

"FFFFFUUUUCCCCKKKKK!" That fucking lying bitch! She wasn't sorry. She was as good as dead.

RYSON

Something wet was dripping onto my face. I turned my face to the side. I opened my eyes and tried to sit up. Where the fuck was I? How did I get here? My face felt sticky. I put my hand up to my face and winced in pain. I touched my nose. My nose... *I remembered!* Dwayne hit me in the face with the freezer door handle! He had snapped. I could hear voices above me. I looked up and realized I was down in some sort of pit. Like a grave. Fear seized me. Was he going to bury me alive? I put my hand on the dirt and tried to prop myself up. My hand landed on something hard and wet. I looked down and saw a human hand.

"What the fuck?" I yelped and pulled my hand back. I crawled to the other end of the pit. It was Shar!

"No!" I heard myself choke out. Her eyes were dead, wide open, staring up into the night. Horror paralyzed me. Dwayne had killed his only sister, our baby sister. The smell was awful! I almost gagged on it. Her body was decomposing, which meant she had been dead for some time, days even. There was no coming back from this. He had officially gone crazy. As much as I hated Shar for blackmailing me, I wouldn't have wished this fate on her. I brought my fist to my mouth and shook the tears away. I had to try and figure out a way to get out of this fucking ditch. There was nothing I could do for Shar now, but I had to save Samara. If she was even still alive. The thought shook me. Samara! I could hear her voice.

She was crying. She must have seen me and Shar in this pit and realized Dwayne had lost it. I dug my fingers into the dirt and tried to get a good grip on it. The rain had softened the dirt and it was more like putty. I jammed my foot into the mud and pulled myself up one inch at a time. I wasn't going to let Dwayne hurt Samara. He could kill me for all I cared, but I wouldn't let him hurt her. He obviously wouldn't hesitate. If he would kill his own sister and try to kill his own brother, Samara didn't stand a chance. I ignored the pain in my nose and kept pulling myself up. I heard anguished screams that shook my body. It was Dwayne. He yelled out again and then Samara was at the top of the pit. I had never been so happy to see her beautiful face. Her hair was all types of crazy and her face was bleeding. She put her finger up to her lips to signal me not to say anything. I nodded and continued to make my way up. She put her hand out to me. It was only a few inches out of my reach. I grabbed another chunk of mud and willed my arms to pull me up. My foot slipped and I slid down a few inches. Shit! She shook her fingers impatiently. She looked frantic. She knew we didn't have much time. She looked to her left and then covered her head.

"OOOOWWWWWW!" She screamed out in pain and fell backwards. I wanted to call out to her. I knew if Dwayne saw me climbing up, he would kill me. I pushed my concern out of my mind and kept going. Her second scream was deafening. What was he doing to her? Fuck this shit! I hoisted myself up and threw my arm over the top of the pit. I heard a gunshot and turned towards it. Dwayne had a gun! *God please let her be okay. Take me if you have to. Just don't take her please!*

I crawled over the top and watched in panic as Dwayne grabbed the gun from Samara's hand. There was a tree branch on the ground behind Dwayne. The storm must have blown it off one of the trees. I hastily picked it up and swung it full force at Dwayne's head. When the branch made contact, I knew he was out. It killed me inside to do that to my little brother, but he was going to kill Samara if I didn't do something. His body fell to the ground with a loud hard thud. Samara was crying and shaking. She was on the ground holding her leg. I bent down and picked her up. Her face and hoodie were splattered with dirt and blood.

"We need to call the cops." She wrapped her arms around my neck and passed out.

DWAYNE

Kill the bitch! Kill that traitor bitch! Shoot her right between the fucking eyes! No! I love her. I don't want to hurt her. I just want her to love me. *She has to die! She will NEVER love you. She loves Ryson. Everybody loves Ryson. Just get it over with and put the bullet in her head. She tricked you so she could save Ryson. She doesn't deserve to live! Trust me. DO IT!* Okay. I paid no attention to the pain coming from my dick. I zipped up my pants and picked up a fallen branch. She had run over to the grave I dug, to try to save Ryson. Once again, choosing him over me. I brought the branch down hard on her injured leg. It turned me on to hear her scream. I had to hear it again. She tried to crawl away from me, which only heightened my arousal. I followed her slowly. She had nowhere to go. She was crying and huffing in pain. I wanted to laugh. She thought I would let her just walk away from this? Once again she had played me, used me, and tortured my heart. She had to pay. I hit her again in the same spot even harder. Her eyes went glassy as her veins bulged in her neck. She screamed so loud my ears rang. That's what I liked to hear. I wanted to hear it again and again. I lifted my hands above my head ready to strike her even harder, maybe drawing blood this time. She had something shiny in her hands. My arms stalled. She had my gun! The bullet tore through my arm. I looked at the steady stream of blood running down my arm in surprise. I dropped the branch behind me. I couldn't feel any pain. I looked at her shaking and crying. The voice was right. She didn't love me. I couldn't let her live. She would only continue to break my heart. I couldn't let that happen. She pleaded with me to stop. I couldn't. I grabbed the gun from her hands. Goodbye Samara. Say hello to Shar for me.

SAMARA

He sat down on my chest, causing the sharpest pain I'd ever experienced in my life to course through my upper body. I winced and tried to breathe.

"My chest!" I choked out in pain. He completely ignored me and put more of his weight on my chest. I felt like my head would explode from the pressure building up inside of it. My vision was hazy. I watched as he slid a knife out from his back pocket. It hit the moonlight just right, glinting like a diamond. OH GOD! Fear gripped my entire body. I knew screaming would be excruciatingly painful, but I had to try. I screamed as loud as I could.

"NOOOOO! HELLLLPPPP!" I could barely breathe. I tried to squirm, but he was so heavy and I was so weak. I just kept painfully screaming. I knew he was getting angrier and angrier, but I had to do something. Someone had to hear me eventually, I hoped. He pulled his t-shirt over his head. He balled it up, then started shoving it into my mouth. He was so rough. I started to gag and choke, but I didn't stop trying to scream. I was terrified. He was beyond reason. He deliberately wanted to hurt me, to make me suffer. I pleaded through the shirt for him to stop. He leaned down closer to me, putting more pain and pressure on my chest. I could have passed out. It was so painful. He took my face in his hand and looked me in the eyes. His eyes were totally devoid of any emotion. That was the scariest thing of all.

He pressed the knife against my cheek, and to my horror, started carving into me. I panicked and started bucking wildly. He grabbed my face even tighter and firmly pushed my head into the table. The wooden planks of the picnic table were digging into my scalp. I couldn't move if I wanted to. I had to take the torture. The burning, searing pain was too much. He ignored my screams and my tears. I bit down hard on his shirt as I felt my flesh ripping apart under his blade. I felt warm liquid running down my legs as my bladder emptied. Hot blood seeped out of my cuts. It ran down the side of my face, filling up in my ear. He stopped for a second, then put the knife back on my cheek and started again. The agonizing pain caused a wave of nausea to pass over me. I felt my eyes closing against my will. I was so tired. My body wanted sleep. But I knew if I did, I might not wake up again. The ripping stopped suddenly. The pressure in my chest disappeared. I realized he wasn't on top of me anymore. The shirt came out of my mouth. I started coughing and trying to get as much air into my lungs as I could. My body was traumatized from pain and shock at what he'd just done. I couldn't believe he'd maimed me. He pulled me up to a sitting position and then kissed me. Instinct told me not to fight him. I was barely holding on, but I knew any resistance from me could send him further over the edge. His hand gripped my throat, but he didn't squeeze.

He pushed his tongue into my mouth and all I wanted to do was vomit. But I held it in and kissed him back. My body was numb with cold. The stench of blood and dirt assaulted my nostrils. My face burned like there was a hot iron on it. I felt cold air hitting the open skin. I don't know how long he held me in that position forcing his tongue in and out of my mouth. He suddenly stopped. I was exhausted. Half conscious, dizzy, tired, aching, face burning, and sharp pains coursing through my chest. I felt half dead.

He took the gun out and pressed it to my forehead. My stomach dropped. *He's going to kill me*, I kept repeating in my head.

"Look at me!" he commanded. I slowly looked at him. I struggled for every breath. His eyes were frightening.

"Are you sorry?" He asked me in such a sweet tone of voice, I almost forgot he was torturing me. I started to tremble in fear.

"Yes," I cried, looking him square in the eyes. He smiled cruelly.

"Open your mouth." What? I blinked and hesitated. His eyes darkened in rage. I slowly opened my mouth and waited.

"Good girl." My heart rate sped up when he shoved his gun into my mouth. I opened my eyes wide in shock. The cold metal gun felt like a knife in my throat. I started to gag. The metal clanged against my teeth, almost chipping one in the back.

"Suck it!" he ordered. I let more tears fall. I just wanted this to be over. What else could I do but comply?

"NOW!" He pushed it farther down my throat. I almost threw up. I grabbed the gun to try to stop him from pushing it farther into my mouth.

"Put your fucking hands down and take it!" I broke down and cried with the gun in my mouth. I couldn't take this abuse anymore.

"I'm not repeating myself again." His voice was deadly. I quickly stopped crying. I was so scared at that point.

"Get it nice and wet," he said huskily. He put his hands down his pants and began to feel on himself. I closed my eyes and did what he told me. He pulled the gun out of my mouth. I gasped for breath and rubbed my sore throat. I sniffed and tried to still my shaking hands. I just knew he wasn't done with me yet.

"Now demonstrate that on me." I looked at him in astonishment. Oh god, was he really going to sodomize me? He grabbed the back of my neck and pushed me down onto my knees. I didn't fight or resist. The longer he spent violating me, the better chance Ryson had. At least that was what I told myself as I reached down and undid his pants. I was willing to do anything to end this and save Ryson. The mud seeped into my already urine soaked jeans, and sent a chill over my already freezing body. I felt so degraded, but I focused on Ryson. That was the only way I could get through it.

"Goddamn." I heard him moaning. He pushed his dick further in my mouth. I wanted to die. My love for Ryson kept me going. I waited until he was nice and hard to go in for an attack. I sank my teeth down into his dick. His body froze and he shouted at the top of his lungs. I bit him again and jumped up. I felt a rush of adrenaline and I knew I couldn't waste it. I knocked the gun out of his hand. It flew out of his reach. He would never find it in the dark. My vision shifted. Everything looked like it was swaying sideways as I ran over to the hole and looked down into it. Ryson was crawling up! He opened his mouth, but I gestured for him to be quiet. If Dwayne knew he was making his way up, there was no doubt in my mind he would kill him. I didn't want to admit it, but I thought that Ryson was dead. It was a relief and a blessing to see him now, bloody face and all. I grasped the fact that I didn't hear Dwayne's screams anymore. I slowly turned my head. Dwayne was standing right behind me holding something over his head. It was a tree branch. I covered my head to brace for the hit, but he didn't have my head in mind. The branch came down hard on my thigh, where the bullet had grazed me.

"OOOOWWWWWW!" The pain took my breath away. I blinked back tears and rolled over onto my back and grabbed my leg. I looked up at Dwayne in terror. If looks could kill, I'd be dead. I turned on my stomach and tried to crawl away from him using my good leg. He was too close to the hole. I didn't want him to see Ryson. I almost made it to a tree. He was right behind me with the stick. I turned my body and tried to slide backwards to lean my back against the tree. He raised the stick above his head.

"NO! NO! PLEEEEAAAAASSSSSSEEEEEE!" I screamed and put my hands up in defense. He hit me in the same spot even harder. Colors flashed in front of my eyes from the intense pain. My scream echoed throughout the park. Through my tears, I saw him smiling. I tried to move closer to the tree, but I knew there was no escape. I screamed through clenched teeth and tried to breathe through my nose. He raised the branch to hit me again. I scooted back even closer to the tree and felt something cold and metal on the ground. *It was the gun!* I picked it up without thinking. I let off a shot. I looked at my shaking hand in surprise. I didn't mean to shoot him! I looked at Dwayne, who was looking at his arm. Blood was running down his bicep. His eyes turned on me. He ground his teeth and started towards me again.

"PLEASE DWAYNE STOP! Please don't make me do this!" I pleaded with him. I didn't want to kill him. Even after everything he'd put me through, I couldn't bring myself to shoot him again. He kept coming at me. I started crying again. He grabbed the gun from my shaking hand and turned it on me. I closed my eyes.

I love you Ryson.

There was a grunt and a loud thud. I opened my eyes and saw Ryson standing there. He was breathing heavy, heaving in and out. He dropped the branch Dwayne had attacked me with. Dwayne's body lay still on the ground as blood poured down the side of his head.

"I didn't want to shoot him, but he kept coming at me!" I cried when Ryson picked me up. I shook in his embrace.

"Sshhhhh. I know baby. It's okay. We need to call the cops." I wrapped my arms around him tight. I heard his cries with mine. Shar was dead and Dwayne was out cold. Ryson's family lay in front of us in shambles. I promptly passed out.

EPILOGUE

RYSON

We followed behind the coroner's van in the ambulance. Both vehicles going to the same hospital. Except Shar was going to the morgue. She and her mother had suffered the same unfortunate fate. Murdered by their lovers. I found out later that Shar died from asphyxiation. Dwayne had held his own sister down and watched as she struggled to breathe. Waited until her life poured out of her, and didn't have any remorse for it. Bones in Samara's leg were shattered, she had a chest contusion, and needed stitches in her face. It killed me to see how Dwayne had brutalized her. I had a fractured nose and Dwayne had suffered a concussion. The bullet wound wasn't serious. I couldn't ride with him when the police and ambulance came. They were taking him to the hospital, but they would be admitting him to a psychiatric facility. That's where he belonged. I still couldn't believe he had snapped like that. Committing murder, attacking me, and sexually assaulting and mutilating Samara. He was a sick fucking bastard! She'd lost consciousness and hadn't come to until a few hours later. Her face was permanently scarred with Dwayne's partial initials. She would never be able to look in the mirror again, and not relive the horror he'd put her through. She cried and trembled as she recounted to me and the Special Victims officer, what he'd done to her. I hated him. This time around she was definitely pressing charges.

Originally, we were going to wait until next week to leave. But after what just happened, there was no time like the present. You never knew when your last day on this planet was. I was living it to the fullest. And that meant getting the woman I loved the hell out of harm's way. I paid for Shar to be buried next to her mother. I was putting the house up for sale. I was done with Dwayne. I tried my best to raise him right, but I'd failed him. Now it was time for him to worry about himself. I thought about Samara, and how close I came to losing her yet again. It was time for us to get out now. I intended on asking Samara to marry me the moment we got settled. I wanted to start a new family. Somehow, the one I had, had taken a turn for the worse. I couldn't stop the tears that escaped me as I called and told my mother what happened. Dwayne and I had never told her we found our other sibling, so that was a shock to her in itself. I didn't tell her about the nature of our messed up relationship with Shar. I told her that Shar had been Dwayne's first victim. She wasn't surprised that Dwayne had gone off the deep end. She admitted that our father had beat and abused her. I was blown away. I'd never witnessed any abuse. She reminded me of the times she was hospitalized with what she told us was the flu every time my dad left. Things started making sense. She never wanted us to see her bruises, so she hid them and tried to shield us from the ugliness that was our father's behavior.

By the end of the call, we were both consoling each other. My family was completely ruined. The only person I had to help me pick up the pieces was Samara. I was excited and ready to start a new chapter in life with Samara. I had spent so many years running away from love. When I finally stopped running, Samara was at the finish line. I couldn't have felt more blessed. Now it was time to take advantage of my good fortune.

FOUR MONTHS LATER

SAMARA

I sat in the basement with my laptop on my lap, scared shitless looking at the screen. I looked at the calendar on my phone for the hundredth time. I double checked what my doctor said my conception date was, yet again. It wasn't like it had changed, but I thought maybe I had read it wrong. I was pregnant. Even though I was terrified of being a mother, that wasn't the problem. I didn't know who this little bundle belonged to. According to my doctor's estimation, I had conceived around seventeen weeks ago. The same week I had made love to Ryson, then days later had rebound sex with Dwayne. Neither of them had used a condom. I really was a whore.

I didn't want to get the amniocentesis for a DNA test. There was a risk of having a miscarriage. But I had to know for sure. I hadn't told Ryson about the possibility of Dwayne being the father. He was the happiest man on earth right now. In love for the first time in his life, with a baby on the way. How could I take that joy away from him? I was miserable. I convinced him we should get the amniocentesis to make sure there weren't any abnormalities with the baby. He'd agreed. His family history wasn't exactly normal. I had never lied to Ryson before, but I felt like I had no choice. I clicked the link to the results of the amniocentesis to see if there were any abnormalities. Breathe. Everything was normal with the baby. I took a deep breath and read the paternity percentage.

99% chance of paternity

I visibly shook. I couldn't control the tears of relief that rushed from me. I said a little prayer for small favors. I didn't even finish reading the email, I was so happy. I deleted the email and closed the laptop. Ryson would be home soon, and I couldn't wait to give him the results of the abnormality test. I can never tell him about the DNA test. With that burden off my chest, I could finally start to enjoy my pregnancy. My elation disappeared as a sad thought crossed my mind. Even though Dwayne wasn't the father of my child, he would never be gone from my life. I touched the 'D' and partial 'W' that was forever carved into my flesh. It would fade away in the upcoming years, maybe, but the memories would never go away. In the end Dwayne had been right. I was his. And just like he'd predicted, I would never forget that.

PEACHY

"All smiles again I see." Rita remarked watching Peachy as she breezed through the door. Peachy rolled her eyes and continued on down the hallway. She knew Rita, and every other female working there, was jealous of her new relationship. Yes, it was a little unconventional, but how many people did you know with perfectly normal relationships? Not many. She stopped in the employee bathroom first to make sure her make-up was right. She reapplied her lip gloss. It was a brand she'd never used before, but it just drove him crazy when she wore it. He'd mentioned he liked the scent in passing, so she made sure to run out and buy a few tubes of it as a surprise. You should have seen his eyes light up with desire when she had kissed him wearing it. She pushed her small, but perky breasts up, trying to give them a lift. She adjusted her uniform. His therapy session was over twenty minutes ago, but she had to wait until the director left for the night to visit her lover. She looked at her watch, then headed out and down the corridor where the inpatients were housed. She'd made a replica of the director's master key after her first night with her lover.

She cut her eyes to the left slightly so as to not to seem so obvious. The director's car was gone. She walked nervously to his room and knocked three times, before unlocking the door and stepping in. Every time she saw him, her pussy ached. He was the most beautiful creature she'd ever laid eyes on. She was beyond surprised the first time he had hit on her after one of his therapy sessions. She knew she was no prize. With small breasts, glasses, and a shy mousy personality, men rarely paid her any attention. One day he was walking down the hall with the therapist, and just as he was moving past her, she felt his finger run across the back of her hand. Her head jolted up in surprise. For the first time since he had arrived there, she looked into his eyes. All she saw was lust. Her juices could have run down her legs at that point. The next time they came into contact with each other in the hallway, he'd slipped a note into the pocket of her uniform.

8 o'clock tonight, get the keys, knock three times

Her heart beat rapidly at the invitation. She knew it would be no problem getting the keys. The director was very absentminded. She could get the keys and put them back before he would even know they were gone. So that night, with fingers trembling, she had unlocked the door. She knocked three times and walked into his room. She was so nervous, she just stood by the door looking at the floor. She had only been with one person before, and it was nothing to write home about. Just when she thought she couldn't stand it anymore, she felt him close the distance between them. He stood directly in front of her, and put his finger in her hair. She wore a long curly weave with brown highlights in it.

"I like your hair." His deep voice echoed throughout his small room. Before she could respond, he was on his knees pulling her thighs apart. She gasped and took in a sharp breath. His warm hands pulled her panties down her hips and down to the floor. She closed her eyes tightly.

"Oh god!" She whimpered when his hot tongue glided over her clit. Her body shook as he licked and sucked on her clit in rapid succession. She started to grind her hips to match his rhythm.

"Oh god, don't stop!" She was about to cum. He stopped all of a sudden, throwing her off for a second. He grabbed her hips and roughly spun her around, pressing her cheek up against the door. He separated her ass cheeks and slid his tongue over her sensitive hole.

"AHHH!" She had never been touched back there, let alone licked and sucked. Her arousal came back in full force! No man had ever made her feel this way. She wanted to prolong it but she couldn't. Her body wasn't used to having so much pleasure. She couldn't contain the orgasm when it burst out of her. She heard herself screaming, but didn't care who would hear. When she could no longer stand, she slid down to the floor to get her bearings.

"Same time next week. I like cherry lip gloss by MAC, by the way," was all he said before getting into his bed and turning away from her. Peachy wasn't even offended that he'd just dismissed her like that. Nor was she suspicious as to why he would recommend a lip gloss to her. All she could think of was her pulsating clit and ass hole. She realized that she'd never really had an orgasm until then. The only sensations she felt when she had sex with her ex, was a sense of urgency for him to finish. She slowly got up, fixed herself, and left the room with the biggest smile she'd ever had on her face. The next day she made a copy of the key. Week after week she returned, and he would always please her and then dismiss her. She was disappointed that they had yet to have actual intercourse. She wasn't complaining by any means, she just wished she could return the favor. She had to admit she was becoming obsessed with seeing him and getting pleased by him. She would do anything for him, and had started breaking even more rules in order to keep him happy. Every week after he completely satisfied her body, he would put a note in her pocket before dismissing her. His notes would plead for her to find and take various pictures of his baby sister for him.

It broke her heart to know that no one ever came to visit him. He gave her his sister's name. It was fairly easy to look up her address once she paid the subscription fee to a people locator website. She decided it wasn't too much of a burden to make a trip every Saturday out to Philadelphia. He'd told her that his sister's husband was a mean vindictive man, and wouldn't let his sister see him. Peachy knew she had to be discreet. She would sit in her car outside his sister's house and take pictures of her. To be thorough, she would follow her if she went on errands and take a few candid pictures. He was so happy each week when she showed him new pictures of his sister. There was so much love in his eyes for his sister. The last few weeks, Peachy noticed that his sister was developing a little baby bump. *He's going to be so excited to find out his little sister is pregnant!* It was their twentieth weekly visit. She showed him the pictures from her phone. She saw his face completely change when he got to the picture of his sister's baby bump. Peachy made sure to zoom in on her that day to highlight his sister's little round belly. "You're going to be an uncle!" Peachy squealed in delight. She couldn't contain her happiness for him. His eyes seemed to glaze over and he smiled a little. He looked down at the picture again and then up at her. He walked over to the bed and picked up something shiny. Metal handcuffs dangled from his index finger.

"Where did you get handcuffs?" She asked him, a little confused about how and why he had those. He never had any visitors, so it was unlikely someone brought them in here to him. Maybe someone on the inside had given them to him. The only three people he had contact with were her, the doctor, and Paul when he dished out the meds. Her thoughts were interrupted by his voice.

"Take off your clothes. Get on the bed with your ass up." She got so turned on by this, all thought and reason fled her mind and body. She did as she was told and got onto the bed. Her pussy throbbed just thinking about his tongue. He roughly grabbed her wrists, and just as roughly clamped the cuffs on her. He put them on really tight, cutting off her circulation. It hurt her. She didn't know how to feel about that. She held her tongue because she didn't want to disappoint him. He was so experienced. She didn't want him to think she was afraid to get kinky with him. Plus, she didn't want whatever it was they had to end. She heard shuffling noises behind her and looked back to see him naked. Her mouth physically dropped open in shock. His body was perfect. He was bigger than her ex, even though he wasn't fully aroused yet. All those weeks wishing she could feel him inside her could never have prepared her for how big and thick he was. Inside she was giddy with excitement, and outside she could already feel herself getting wet. He climbed in the bed and positioned himself behind her. Her arms were a little uncomfortable in the position they were in due to the handcuffs, but she didn't care. Nothing was going to stop her from enjoying this. He slid his thick dick down to her wet pussy and rubbed the head of it into her juices.

"Mmmmm." Just the feel of him on her was sending goose bumps up her back. He slid the head back into the wetness and then brought it up to her ass. Right onto the hole. Her eyes popped open and she tensed, instantly clenching her cheeks closed.

"Relax!" He growled at her. Even that turned her on. But she still couldn't relax.

"I never did it like... that before." Her voice was barely audible. She was so embarrassed. The one chance she got to show him that she could please him just like he pleased her, and she failed. Her mood was slipping. She wanted to crawl under a rock and die! He was silent for a few seconds. Then he spoke softly to her.

"Don't you love me Peachy?"

He had never spoken her name before. It rolled off his tongue so fluidly. She turned her head so she could look at him. His intense stare penetrated deep within her. Could she trust him? He was a patient at a mental institution, but she never knew why. He seemed more normal than some people she knew in her everyday life. He never once gave her any indication that he was dangerous. So she swallowed all her fear and insecurities. She unclenched herself. She returned his stare with one of her own and said,

"Yes Dwayne, I love you."

DWAYNE

"I really wanna get to know you, I wanna learn you inside out." I sang the lyrics to our song out loud in my room. 'Get to Know You' by Mayer Hawthorne, was on a constant loop in my head. I'd woken up in the hospital five months ago dazed, confused, and handcuffed to the bed. It didn't take me long to realize what had happened. Samara had abandoned me.

Just like your mom did.

With a clear head, I realized that killing Samara would have been the worst thing I could have done. I loved her so much it hurt. She deserved another chance to prove her love and loyalty to me. When I saw her again, I wouldn't even punish her for shooting me. Well, not that much anyway. She'd had no choice. I almost killed the love of my life. By shooting me she had done me a favor. She could have shot me in the head, but she gave me a warning shot to the arm. That had to be love. The first few weeks at the hospital weren't as bad as I thought they'd be. The food was decent. There was cable. I was allowed outside an hour a day to workout. What made my stay even more tolerable was Peachy and Paul. Peachy was a quiet, shy little twig, that I'd noticed watching me whenever we walked by each other. She was *nothing* compared to my Samara, but I knew with the right manipulation she had the potential to be exactly what I needed. I could tell by the way she walked that she'd never had good dick before. Her steps were clumsy and hurried all the time. I couldn't imagine getting a hard on for her, but if I played this right I would never have to. She looked so shocked the day I'd touched her hand as I walked by. She probably had an orgasm just from that little bit of contact. *Pathetic*. This was going to be easier than I thought. I slipped her a note and told her to get the keys to my room and meet me. It was a test. If she could manage to get the keys and slip into my room unnoticed, the first phase of my plan would be accomplished. The rest would be easy.

Peachy was so desperate for any type of affection, that all I had to do was put her clit in my mouth, and she was putty in my hands. I absolutely hated tasting and touching her. She didn't taste anything like Samara. I immediately and repeatedly rinsed with mouthwash afterwards whenever I had to put my mouth on her. The more orgasms I gave her, the more she went out of her way to please me. I made her find Samara and get me some pictures of her. I was starving for Samara. Peachy was good at taking direction. She found Samara just like I'd instructed, and took great pictures of her. She was so fucking beautiful. I almost bust a nut right there in front of Peachy looking at a picture of Samara with my initials on her face. The letters healed darker than her skin tone and really stuck out. She would always remember who she belonged to. Week after week Peachy gave me my fix of Samara, and I gave her five minutes of my tongue. It was worth it. One day I would be reunited with my baby, and she was going to be surprised at how well I kept up with her life. I couldn't care less about Ryson and made sure to tell Peachy I NEVER wanted to see a picture of him. *He's dead to us.*

He didn't exist anymore. Today for some reason, Peachy looked extra excited to see me. It definitely wasn't mutual, but I played along. I waited patiently for her to give me her phone so I could get my Samara fix. I slowly savored, and swiped, through all of the pictures of my baby. I paused on the last one. She was wearing a long white dress that accentuated her ass beautifully. She was glowing. Her face looked rounder. Her hair was even longer. My hands shook slightly. I zoomed in on the picture to make sure what I was seeing was real. I had been having fantasies about Samara that included this very thing so many times, I wanted to make sure I wasn't dreaming.

"You're going to be an uncle!" Peachy squealed in delight. Samara was pregnant? *With your baby.*

I had to see her. I needed to make sure she and my baby were alright. I felt drunk with love and happiness. It was time to leave this place. I looked down at the picture again and then I looked at Peachy. Her smile was so wide. She was brimming with happiness for me. I knew what had to be done next. I walked over to the bed and picked up the handcuffs. That's where Paul came into the picture. He was the orderly in charge of giving me my medication. Medicine I would hide under my tongue, then quickly flush down the drain as soon as he would leave of course. Paul was tall and rail thin. He had long, sandy brown hair that constantly fell into his nervous green eyes. He was probably younger than twenty. His pale skin would blush every time he came into my room. I had asked him to get the handcuffs and sneak them in to me a few days before. It was one of the many things I'd had Paul sneak in to me since I was admitted. I'd managed to get Paul to bring me small things like foods that weren't served at the hospital, to big things like toiletries and underwear I preferred, just to test him out. He had done it with no argument. I knew I could get him to bring me anything once I gave him some of what he was craving. Paul, just like Peachy, couldn't take his eyes off me the first time we met. He would lick his thin pink lips every time I walked up to him to receive my medicine. Once I noticed his weakness for me, I pounced on it. One day he came to deliver my meds, I told him to shut the door behind him. He didn't question it. Obedient, just like Peachy. Once the door was closed, I got completely naked in front of him. His eyes lit up at the sight of my perfect body.

"No lips and no ass. The rest is all yours," I said and got on the bed. There was no way I was doing anything sexual to Paul, but I had to make sacrifices so I could get back to my Samara. From that day on, twice a week, I would let Paul have control of my body. I would get naked and spread my legs open on my bed. He would lick on me and kiss me from neck to toe. I would close my eyes and think of Samara. My dick would instantly get hard. I imagined myself making hard passionate love to Samara in her and Ryson's bed. I stayed in that fantasy place until Paul was finished.

"You're so sexy." Paul would say breathlessly as he sucked on my nipples.

"Oh god, you taste so good!" He would moan as he licked and slurped on my clean shaven balls. The last time I surprised him. I grabbed the back of his head, and pushed his face down to my hard dick. He didn't hesitate to try to swallow me whole. I went back to my fantasy place. I thought about the morning Samara surprised me by waking me up. She had ordered me to stuff my dick down her throat. She was a fucking expert at pleasing me. The memory of her swallowing my cum made me cum in Paul's mouth almost instantly. After he swallowed every drop and licked me clean, I turned over onto my stomach and spread my ass cheeks.

"Cum in my ass crack," I commanded of him. I turned around to see him grab his small dick and jerk it frenziedly. I turned away and patiently waited until I felt his hot cum land on my ass cheeks. The warm sticky cum slid down into my ass crack. I kicked him out afterwards. I knew after that he would do anything for me. So when I told him I wanted some handcuffs, he didn't hesitate to get them for me. Probably thinking I would use them on him. If I thought too hard about what I was doing to myself, I might have been repulsed. But I focused all my thoughts on getting back to Samara. The molestation I was putting my body through was bearable. It was worth it.

"Where did you get handcuffs?" Peachy asked me. She seemed a little scared. I didn't need her worrying about that.

"Take off your clothes. Get on the bed with your ass up." I knew I couldn't look at her and get a hard on. But I also knew for what I needed next, I definitely had to give her some dick. I vowed to never put my dick in anyone's pussy besides Samara's, so Peachy was stuck with anal. I knew she'd never done this before, so the handcuffs were a must. I didn't need her squirming or trying to get away. She did as she was told and bent over. She had such a small, boney ass compared to Samara's. It was going to take a lot of concentration to get my dick even semi hard. I quickly got undressed and closed my eyes. I thought about how spectacular Samara looked in that pink dress the night she went to Devon's party. As I watched from Ms. Rosie's window, my lust for her grew even more. It was one of the sexiest things she'd ever worn. Like always, my dick got hard instantly. I rubbed the head of my dick into Peachy's juices. I didn't have any lube, so her juices would have to be enough. I didn't feel like putting in the effort to loosen her up either. She would have to do that on her own.

"Mmmmm." She moaned as I rubbed my dick on her clit. I saw goosebumps form on her back and go all the way up her spine. I had her right where I wanted her. I pushed the head of my dick on her ass hole. She clenched like I knew she would.

"Relax!" I growled at her. Even that turned her on. She got even wetter.

"I never did it like... that before," she said in a low voice. That wasn't a fucking shocker. I was sure she was as close to a virgin as someone could get, without actually being one. I had to tread lightly or what I needed from her I'd never get. I leaned down and spoke softly to her.

"Don't you love me Peachy?" It was clear as day that she did. How could she not? She looked like she had to think about it. What the fuck! My dick was starting to get soft. She looked at me and I saw a combination of lust and love in her eyes. I knew I had her then. I felt her relax beneath me.

"Yes Dwayne, I love you." I pushed the head of my dick slowly into her hole. It was so tight. I wanted to get this over with, but I knew I couldn't rush it. I eased my way into Peachy slow and easy.

"It's so big." I heard her whine. I ignored her and kept going until I was in enough to start stroking. She wasn't getting all of me. That was reserved for Samara. I halfheartedly pushed about half my dick in and out of Peachy until I heard her start moaning in pleasure. She was close to an orgasm when I sealed the deal.

"I love you Peachy." I said, pretending to be out of breath. She cried out in pleasure and started to cum. Once she was done, I took my dick out of her. She lay face down trying to catch her breath. I un-cuffed her as fast as I could. I couldn't make it to the bathroom fast enough to clean her off of me. *Yuck!* I looked at myself in the mirror. *Good job. Time for phase two.*

I cleaned myself quickly. I plastered on the biggest, fakest smile I could, and walked back out into my room. Peachy was still on the bed. She was laying on her back with the covers pulled up, covering her thin body. Good thing too, because I didn't want to ever see it again.

"Peachy. I can't go another day only being with you in here. I want us to be together outside of this place. Freely." She sat up slowly.

"Really? You... you want me?" She was so insecure. It was just too easy.

"I love you. I want to build a life with you. We can't do that from in here. You have to get me out of here Peachy so we can be together!" I said excitedly. She started crying. *Get rid of her!*

In due time.

"Oh my gosh! I want to be with you too. But I don't know how I can get you out of here." I held in my temper. Patience would get me through this. I sat down on the bed next to her. I was still naked. It distracted Peachy from seeing what was really going on.

"You already have a key to my room. The hardest part is done. All you have to do now is sneak me out during the shift change at ten tonight. Get a food cart from the cafeteria, then come to my room. I'll get in and hide in the cart. Then you can push me out to your car. That's it. Easy." She looked uncertain. This bitch wasn't going to ruin my chance of reuniting with Samara.

"I'm scared. What if we get caught? Wha... What if..."

"Marry me!" I blurted out, cutting her off. She gasped and opened her eyes wide. Her hands started trembling as she brought them up to cover her mouth.

"Tomorrow! Marry me tomorrow Peachy, and make me the happiest man on this earth!" I leaned forward and pretended she was Samara. I kissed her with everything I had. She looked dizzy when I let her go. She nodded her head up and down.

"Okay. I'll get you out tonight," she said and hugged me. I rolled my eyes above her head and hugged her back.

The food cart was smaller than I anticipated. I wasn't a small man by any means, so it was difficult to keep all my limbs hidden. She pushed me out towards the loading dock at the back of the building. I felt a cool breeze hit my face and knew we had made it outside. I told Peachy to drive her car around there earlier so I could slip into it unnoticed. I also told her to empty her bank accounts so we could go wedding shopping. I almost laughed in her face when she fell for that line. She checked us into a motel on the outskirts of town. I wasn't due for medication until nine the next morning. I had about ten to eleven hours to get to Samara before anyone knew I was missing. I wasn't going to waste any more time than I had to. Peachy grabbed me and pulled me into yet another hug once we got into the motel room. I smiled politely and kissed her on the forehead.

"I'm so happy Dwayne. I can't believe this is all happening," she gushed and squeezed me tighter.

"Me neither baby. Hey uh... how about you go take a shower. I want to lick you from head to toe," I said seductively and grabbed her small ass. She looked at me with pure desire and practically ran to the bathroom.

"Thank god." I said in irritation when the bathroom door closed. I looked around the room for the landline and saw it on the nightstand.

"I can't wait for you to meet my sister Peachy," I yelled out to her. I ripped the phone cord from the wall and detached it from the phone. I wrapped it around my palms and pulled on it. It was good and taunt.

"You and Shar are going to get along just great." I laughed at that. I tried to calculate how long it would take someone Peachy's size to suffocate. It hadn't taken Shar long. It would probably be even shorter for Peachy though. Once I had the cord around her neck, I would squeeze as hard as I could. I had shit to do. Hopefully her neck would just snap and I wouldn't have to wait for her to stop breathing. Things were going so smoothly. Samara would be so surprised to see me. I sat on the edge of the bed with the telephone cord in my hands. I was waiting for Peachy to finish her shower. "I really wanna get to know you, I wanna learn you inside out." I sang our song. I cracked my neck and smiled. I needed to get this over with. I had to go see my baby. Both my babies.

Made in the USA
Middletown, DE
07 March 2021